Toward Freedom

March - September 1873

Book # 20 in The Bregdan Chronicles

Sequel to Courage To Stand

Ginny Dye

Walking Toward Freedom

March - September 1873

Published by Bregdan Publishing
Bellingham, WA 98229

www.BregdanChronicles.net

www.GinnyDye.com

www.BregdanPublishing.com

ISBN# 9798388347497

Printed in the United States of America

A Note from the Author

My great hope is that *Walking Toward Freedom* will both entertain, challenge you, and give you hope to discover and walk into your own freedom – whatever that looks like for you.

I hope you will learn as much as I did during the months of research it took to write this book. Once again, I couldn't make it through an entire year, because there was just too much happening. As I move forward in the series, there is so much going on in so many arenas. I refuse to gloss over them. As a reader, you deserve to know all the things that created the world you live in now.

When I ended the Civil War in *The Last, Long Night,* I knew virtually nothing about Reconstruction. I have been shocked and mesmerized by all I have learned – not just about the North and the South – but also about the West.

The things I learned while writing *Walking Toward Freedom* blew my mind!

I grew up in the South and lived for eleven years in Richmond, VA. I spent countless hours exploring the plantations that still line the banks of the James River and became fascinated by the history.

But you know, it's not the events that fascinate me so much – it's the people. That's all history is you know. History is the story of people's lives. History reflects the consequences of their choices and actions – both good and bad. History is what has given you the world you live in today – both good and bad.

This truth is why I named this series The Bregdan Chronicles. Bregdan is a Gaelic term for weaving: Braiding. Every life that has been lived until today is a part of the woven braid of life. It takes every person's story to create history. Your life will help determine the course of history. You may think you don't have much of an impact. You do. Every action you take will reflect in someone else's life. Someone else's decisions. Someone else's future. Both good and bad. That is the ***Bregdan Principle***...

Every life that has been lived until today is a part of the woven braid of life.
It takes every person's story to create history.
Your life will help determine the course of history.
You may think you don't have much of an impact.
You do.
Every action you take will reflect in someone else's life.
Someone else's decisions.
Someone else's future.
Both good and bad.

My great hope as you read this book, and all that will follow, is that you will acknowledge the power you have, every day, to change the world around you by your decisions and actions. Then I will know the research and writing were all worthwhile.

Oh, and I hope you enjoy every moment of it and learn to love the characters as much as I do!

I'm constantly asked how many books will be in this series. I guess that depends on how long I live! My intention is to release two books a year – continuing to weave the lives of my characters into the times they lived. I hate to end a good book as much as anyone – always feeling so sad that I must leave the characters. You shouldn't have to be sad for a long time!

You are now reading the 20th book - # 21 will be released in late 2023. If you like what you read, you'll want to make sure you're on my mailing list at www.BregdanChronicles.net. I'll let you know each time a new one comes out so you can take advantage of my fun launch events, and you can enjoy my BLOG in between books!

Many more are coming!

Sincerely,
Ginny Dye

Chapter One

March 15, 1873

Carrie took a deep breath as she emerged from the barn, reveling in the fresh air that filled her lungs. She knew winter could very well deal out one last blast of frigid weather, but at the moment a soft, warm breeze rustled the new leaves emerging on the trees. She planned to soak up every ray of the glorious sun beaming down on her upturned face, not going into the house until it had dipped below the trees.

A splash of yellow caught her attention. She gasped with delight as she looked toward the house. Hundreds of daffodils, nothing but buds bursting at their seams this morning, had exploded into a riot of glorious color. She feasted her eyes on the first official harbingers of spring tucked around the boxwoods lining the circular drive.

"Welcome to 1873," she said softly. Tulips would follow, and then the fragrant lilacs would perfume the air as the trees continued to dress themselves for a new year. Each day would be a delight of new growth and beginnings.

Spring had returned to Cromwell Plantation. Carrie loved all the seasons, but spring was easily her favorite. There was nothing like watching life burst from the barren ground, and from the trees that had stood as silent gray sentinels through the long winter.

A soft nicker from the barn brought a happy smile to her face. Granite was thanking her for the bran mash she had poured into his bucket after grooming him. His iron gray winter fur remained thick and luxuriant, but the warm weather would prompt shedding very soon.

Carrie had left the medical clinic early, determined to make the most of this first warm day. Janie and Polly had assured her they could handle the patient load. No persuading had been needed.

She had saddled up No Regrets and ridden to the James River. Granite, with the exuberance she loved, had pranced and galloped around them. She could hardly wait until he was old enough to ride, but she was also patient enough to let him grow to maturity.

Carrie took another deep breath, inhaling the peace that flowed around her. The first months of the year had been blessedly uneventful. Winter cold and snow had created wonderful nights full of games and conversation in front of the fire, delicious meals, and singing around the piano.

Was it possible the uneventful peace would continue?

A loud voice broke into her reverie.

"You can't be serious, Thomas!"

Carrie tensed and frowned. The voice floating to her belonged to her stepmother, Abby Cromwell. Carrie couldn't remember the last time the calm, thoughtful woman had raised her voice. She looked toward the porch with its enormous pillars that bracketed the three-story, white plantation house. Through the shadows cast by the towering twin oak trees, she could make out two shapes.

"Thomas, please tell me you're not going to do this!"

Carrie caught her breath at the fear resonating in Abby's voice. She didn't make a habit of involving herself in conversations between her father and Abby, but unconsciously she began to move in that direction.

It wasn't until she got closer to the porch that she could hear the continued murmur of their conversation. One look at Abby's face confirmed the fear she had heard.

Her footsteps on the stairs caused them to fall silent and look in her direction. Carrie waited for them to say something, but neither spoke. A flash of irritation stirred in her. They must have known she had overheard them and would be concerned. The memory of the fear in Abby's voice, however, caused the irritation to dissipate as quickly as it had appeared.

"Is everything alright?" Carrie asked. She settled down into another of the rockers on the porch, a subtle signal that she wouldn't leave until she had an answer.

Silence continued to stretch between them.

While she waited, Carrie examined her parents. Thomas was aging, but his glorious silver hair framed a handsome and vigorous face. Abby, elegant as always--even in the riding breeches that revealed her plans for the afternoon--was a beautiful, vibrant woman. Soft, graying brown hair framed light blue eyes that were now dark with trouble.

The longer the silence stretched out, the more worried Carrie became. She forced herself to sit silently.

Her father was the first to speak. "We received another letter from Willie Calhoun."

Carrie racked her brain to remember who he was talking about. Her parents communicated on a regular basis with people all around the country. She thought back to the long conversations they'd had over the winter. "The planter from Louisiana?"

"Yes," Thomas confirmed. "He's also a Louisiana legislator now."

Carrie continued to pull up fragments of their past conversations, her memory growing clearer. "Willie Calhoun is the one who inherited his father's vast plantations, set his slaves free before the war ended, and gave them land so they could farm for themselves. He contacted you last year when he discovered what you and Moses are doing here on Cromwell."

"That's the one," Thomas agreed. He took a deep breath and cast a concerned look in his wife's direction. "Abby and I have been writing him regularly. He's asked me to come to Louisiana."

Carrie didn't miss the fear and angst that filled Abby's eyes as her father spoke. "Why?" She couldn't understand what was going on without more information, but she knew her stepmother didn't scare easily.

"Evidently, there's some trouble down there," Thomas said vaguely.

Abby's lips tightened, but she remained silent.

"What kind of trouble?" Carrie probed. Her father was a direct man. He only became vague when he didn't want to talk about the topic at hand. Her gut tightened even more.

"There are some people down in Louisiana that don't approve of what Willie has done on his plantation with his freed slaves."

"The same type of people that killed Robert?" Carrie asked bluntly. She was beginning to understand the source of Abby's fear. She fought to keep her breathing steady as the memories of her first husband's murder surged through her mind.

Thomas shifted uneasily but didn't look away. "Yes," he said reluctantly. "The Ku Klux Klan and the Knights of the White Camelia are active down there."

Carrie hated the flutters of fear that rose in her belly and threatened to strangle her. They had battled KKK members more than once on the plantation. The hatred they exuded never ceased to sicken her. "Why does Mr. Calhoun want you there?" she repeated.

Thomas shrugged. "Moral support?" He glanced at Abby again. "He feels rather alone with the forces arrayed against him."

"I see," Carrie murmured. In the end, her father would do what he thought best, but she couldn't ignore the alarm bells ringing in her heart and mind. "Is it dangerous?"

Thomas glanced away. "I don't believe he would invite me to come if he felt I would be in danger."

Carrie could see the emotion swirling in Abby's eyes. She knew it wouldn't be long before it erupted. Her usually calm mother had battled insurmountable odds to build factories in Philadelphia in a man's world after her first husband died. It had been necessary to reveal a toughness most women never imagined revealing. Abby's gentleness concealed a spine of steel.

The eruption came.

"Nonsense," Abby said. Her voice was quiet now, but somehow more intense with the suppressed anger and fear. "You are well aware of the danger, Thomas."

Thomas didn't dispute her words.

"What danger?" Carrie pressed. She could tell her father wanted to make the trip to Louisiana. Actually, *want* may have been too strong a word – she could tell he felt compelled to go.

Abby was the one to answer her question. "Louisiana may be the most violent state in the South right now. Klan activity has diminished in most states since President Grant created the Enforcement Acts to protect blacks, but the new laws seem to have done nothing but ignite even *more* violence in Louisiana. Multitudes of blacks have been beaten, tortured, and killed, but it hasn't stopped there." She paused for a steadying breath. "The white supremacists have no problem killing white Republicans as well. A few months ago, a mob attacked the home of a former Grant County sheriff and a former regional judge who were living together for safety. They set the house on fire, killed the sheriff when he tried to escape, and left the judge for dead. Remarkably, he survived, but no action is being taken to bring the identified killers to justice."

Carrie felt bile rise in her throat. "Father..."

"I agree it's bad," Thomas replied.

"Then why--?" Carrie began. She could hear the fear in her voice, but decided it was justified.

"Because Willie feels alone. He doesn't have the support we have here."

Carrie thought about his words. There wasn't a night that passed without a guard of men patrolling Cromwell. They had learned the hard way to never let their guard down. "Our support comes from within the plantation. What about all the freed slaves who are benefiting from Mr. Calhoun treating them like equal citizens? Won't they protect their homes?"

"Louisiana is a quagmire of racism and hatred," Abby said tightly. "It's a keg of dynamite that already has the fuse inserted. Tiny fires are burning everywhere. It will take but a single match to blow the whole thing up. The freedmen are fighting back, but they're woefully outnumbered and outgunned."

Thomas said nothing to protest her dire assessment.

Carrie realized he couldn't deny the obvious. "And you really believe you should go?" She thought back to the fall before when he, Anthony, and Matthew had gone out west to investigate the Diamond Hoax of 1872, which remained front and center in all the newspapers. "I thought you said you didn't want to leave the plantation again for a long time?"

"I did," Thomas muttered as he looked toward the horse pastures starting to turn the brilliant green that would support the new foals soon to be born.

Spring was his favorite time of the year. He loved to watch the new tobacco sprigs go into the rich, fertile soil. He spent hours in the barns and the pastures, rejoicing in each new birth. He spent the afternoons riding the fields and roads with his grandchildren. With Moses handling all the plantation operations, he was free to simply enjoy what he had spent his entire life building.

Carrie let the silence extend, gazing out at the fields as she fought to regain her earlier peace. It was a futile attempt.

"Willie Calhoun is a lonely man," Thomas finally said. "In a state where Republicans aren't popular, he is particularly hated."

"Like you are?" Carrie asked gently. She was trying to understand what was compelling her father to make this decision.

Thomas stared at her for a long moment. "Worse. Much worse." His voice was tight and hoarse. "I've made neighbors angry with what I've done with Cromwell, it's true." He paused again, obviously searching for the right words. "The people in Louisiana seem to have a depth of anger that isn't as obvious here."

Carrie, thinking of Robert dying in her arms, didn't see how that was possible.

"He's right about that," Abby conceded. "There have been sporadic bursts of anger and violence here, but Louisiana has sunk deep into killing and torture as the new normal for how to deal with the freed slaves."

Carrie felt bile rise in her throat again. She thought about the trip Matthew and Harold had taken to Alabama last year. "Are they imprisoning blacks in the mines like they are in Alabama?"

Thomas shrugged. "Willie and I have never discussed it. I don't know."

"I do." Matthew Justin climbed the steps, a scowl on his usually pleasant face. Thick red hair blew about his head as the breeze turned into a steady wind. "Why are you asking about Louisiana?"

Carrie breathed a silent sigh of relief. If anyone could talk sense into her father, it would be Matthew. "Because Father is planning a trip to Louisiana."

Thomas raised a hand in protest. "I'm *considering*. I haven't gotten to the planning stage yet."

Carrie could tell it was taking every ounce of Abby's restraint to remain silent. Her mother had no trouble speaking her mind, but she was also wise. If she pushed too hard, Thomas would make a rash decision out of sheer stubbornness. Carrie adored her father, but she had seen him do exactly that many times.

Carrie listened as Thomas responded to Matthew's probing questions. Though Matthew had left the world of journalism and become a bestselling author of books he co-wrote with his twin, Harold, he was diligent in keeping his finger on the pulse of national happenings.

"How does Willie Calhoun think you can help him?"

Thomas sighed. "I don't believe he thinks a visit from me would change anything. It's just that he wouldn't feel so alone in his battle."

Matthew nodded thoughtfully. "Willie Calhoun is a complicated man."

"You know him?" Carrie asked.

"Not personally," Matthew replied. "But the decision to free his slaves, marry a mulatto woman, and create a county for the freedmen so they would have political power, created more than a stir. Combine that with the fact that a childhood accident turned him into a severely disabled hunchback, and he is a man that draws attention. The tension has been building for years, even before the war ended. The political drama between the Radical Republicans and the Southern Democrats has reached a fever pitch. Combine that with a worsening economy for the planters, and you've got the recipe for something bad to happen."

Carrie didn't need an explanation for the bleak look in his eyes. Matthew, in his reporting days, had seen more tragedy and senseless killing than any one person should have to deal with. He had turned his back on all of it but kept getting pulled back into the fray because of his natural curiosity and determination for the truth to be told. Those qualities had taken both him and Harold to Alabama the year before, uncovering the truth behind enforced black labor in the mines. Slavery there had simply taken on a different name.

Matthew turned to Abby. He had known her far longer than any of them and held a great deal of respect for her. "How do you feel about this?"

Abby gazed at Thomas for a long moment, her eyes now full of compassion and understanding. "I love my husband for wanting to help a friend, especially one he has only met through correspondence, but I believe it would be nothing more than a futile attempt that could very well be extremely dangerous. I don't want to lose the man I love to Louisiana stupidity."

Matthew chuckled. "I can always trust you to be honest."

Abby nodded calmly. "You can." Her eyes glimmered with amusement for a moment before growing serious again. "What do you think, Matthew?"

Matthew locked eyes with her and then abruptly stood. He walked to the edge of the porch and looked out. Clint and Amber were taking the horses in for their evening feed. Soft nickers and whinnies blended with the symphony of birdsong celebrating spring, but even the tranquil peace of the golden afternoon couldn't hide the tension reverberating through the air.

Carrie watched, knowing Matthew was processing everything he'd heard, combining it with the knowledge he already had of the situation in the South.

When he spun around, he didn't answer Abby's question; instead, his eyes sought out Carrie. "You asked if Louisiana is arresting blacks as enforced labor for the mines. They aren't."

Carrie remained silent, knowing he wasn't done.

"The situation in Louisiana is far more sophisticated," Matthew said. "The entire South has started using the prison system to enslave blacks again. Louisiana was eager to follow the same path. Seven years ago, in 1868, they were appropriated three times more money than the previous year for their penitentiary."

"Why?" Thomas asked keenly.

"Because the system was being flooded with blacks. Supposedly, they were being arrested primarily for larceny, but it's likely most of them were innocent. It would follow the pattern in other states," Matthew said. "There were men in Louisiana eager to capitalize on the increased funding." He looked at Thomas. "Have you heard of Samuel L. James?"

Thomas shook his head, his expression revealing he was unsure how this fit in with his plans to visit Willie Calhoun.

"James paid one hundred thousand dollars for a twenty-one-year lease on all the Louisiana state prisoners."

Carrie and Abby gasped simultaneously.

"All of them?" Carrie demanded.

"All of them," Matthew confirmed. "I'm not sure the state could tell you exactly how many that was, but you can trust the number was high. James could do what he wanted with the prisoners, and all the profits would be his. He immediately purchased hundreds of thousands of dollars of machinery to turn the three-story prison into a factory."

"My God..." Abby murmured in a stricken voice.

Matthew's lips tightened. "I read about it a few years ago. The factory produced ten thousand yards of cotton cloth, three hundred fifty molasses barrels, and fifty thousand bricks per day. It also produced six thousand pairs of shoes per week. The factory was so large it stimulated Louisiana's economy by increasing demand for cotton, wool, lumber, and other raw materials."

Thomas raised a brow. "*Was*?"

"The penitentiary is virtually empty now," Matthew replied. "The state didn't even know. Last month, a joint committee of senators and representatives went to inspect it, and there were no prisoners."

Carrie's mind spun as she tried to absorb what she was hearing. How could this be happening?

"Almost as soon as the factory was running, James abandoned it," Matthew continued. "He found he could make a lot more money subcontracting his prisoners to labor camps. He's been doing it for years. The prisoners are now working on building levees and railroads. A convict costs about one-twentieth the labor of a regular worker. Needless to say, James is a very wealthy man."

Carrie listened with fascinated horror.

Matthew wasn't done. "James retains a percentage of the convicts to live on his plantation, called Angola." His expression grew grimmer. "A friend of mine talked with a few prisoners who somehow managed to escape last year. What they told my friend is sickening. James keeps about fifty men in an ill-ventilated, fifteen-by-twenty-foot shack to perform all the work on the plantation property.

Thomas' face was white. "They're slaves."

"They're slaves," Matthew agreed. "Except that most slaves were treated better than these poor men. There's a very high death rate. James doesn't care because he's paid very little for the convicts, and there's a steady supply of more to replace the ones that don't make it. There is no motivation to provide care."

"And Louisiana is alright with this?" Carrie cried.

Matthew met her eyes. "They haven't stopped it," he said simply.

Carrie hated the feeling of helplessness that engulfed her. Abolitionists had fought for decades to end slavery. The nation had endured four years of a brutal war to grant freedom to slaves. "The South has simply found a new way to enslave black people," she said angrily.

Matthew gazed at her with compassionate understanding before turning to Thomas. "This is the state you're talking about going to visit. It's not a place that cares about law and order. It's not a place that cares about justice. It's a powder keg." He paused. "One that is going to blow very soon."

Matthew held up a hand when Thomas opened his mouth to reply. "Instead of you going to Louisiana, I would like to go in your place."

Carrie stared at him, dumbstruck. From the expression on her father's face, Thomas felt the same way.

"No one should go!" Abby said passionately. "I don't want Thomas to go. I don't want you to go either, Matthew. It's too dangerous!"

Matthew didn't bother to deny what she said. "It's not on my list of how I planned to spend this spring, but it makes sense."

"How does it make sense?" Thomas demanded. "I may be willing to take the risks involved, but I'm certainly not asking you to."

"You didn't ask," Matthew said. "Look, I led you and Anthony on a wild-goose chase that almost ended up with you dying in a blizzard last fall."

"A wild-goose chase that I chose to take," Thomas reminded him.

"Yes," Matthew conceded, "but we thought we were going on a luxurious train ride to San Francisco. I was the one who set us up to go on a long trail ride through the Rocky Mountains in the dead of winter." He held up a hand when Thomas tried to interrupt him. "Regardless, that's not the only reason I'm offering to go. Willie Calhoun is a fascinating man. He has offered equal treatment to his freed slaves, despite grave danger to himself. While I'm sure he would benefit from your moral support, I suspect he would benefit more from articles written about him. The country needs to know what is happening. The people of Louisiana will think more carefully before they harm a man known throughout America." He glanced at Abby. "Despite the prevailing stupidity of the state, there are enough men with brains to not want more federal attention on their state."

Thomas stared at him. "I should come with you."

Matthew glanced away uneasily before leveling his gaze on Thomas. "You could, but I'm asking you not to. Quite honestly, I'll be able to achieve my objectives more easily if I'm alone."

Thomas smiled tightly. "There aren't blizzards in Louisiana, Matthew. I don't think I would be a detriment."

Carrie recognized the combination of hurt and anger in his eyes. Her father was loath to admit to getting older.

"Not a detriment," Matthew acknowledged, "but most certainly a distraction. If my trip to Louisiana is anything like my trip to Alabama, I already know I'm going to have to move fast to stay ahead of trouble." He hesitated. "I'm not trying to offend you, Thomas."

Carrie's breath caught as she thought of Janie. Her friend and partner at the clinic was going to be horrified to learn her husband was heading into danger once again.

She knew Matthew had planned on staying on the plantation for all of 1873 while he worked on a new book. He had promised Janie he was going to dedicate this year to their family. How would she take his reversal of plans?

Silence stretched out on the porch as the sun dipped toward the horizon, kissing the sky with a rosy, golden hue. The orb's yellow fingers reached for the clouds in celebration of spring. It was beautiful, but the peace Carrie had hoped for was long gone.

In the distance, the sound of excited voices announced the children were returning from their ride through the fields with Moses.

The sound shook Thomas from his thoughts. With a resigned sigh, he said, "As much as I don't want to admit it, you're probably right. I would rather not acknowledge that I'm getting older. The whole point of the trip is to help Willie. You're the one who can best give him what he needs. I need to be content with that."

"It's his friendship with you and Abby that is making this possible," Matthew replied. "You've both already played the most important role."

Carrie watched the battle between relief and worry play out on Abby's face.

"Do you really think you need to go down there, Matthew?" Abby asked. "Can't we let Louisiana figure out its own issues?"

Matthew raised a brow and looked at her for a long moment.

Abby managed a chuckle. "Thank you for not saying what you're thinking. You're right that Willie Calhoun needs support. You're right that national attention might offer him protection. I know you're the best person to do that." Her brow creased again. "Still, Matthew, how much are you supposed to take on your shoulders? You've already experienced too much." Her voice shook slightly. "I thought all this was behind you."

Matthew laughed dryly. "Every person on this porch knows we can't predict what will happen tomorrow, or even today," he said. "We can make all the plans we want, but life has a funny way of taking control of what we *think* we're in control of. When I write, people listen. As much as I might want to remain silent and enjoy the peace of the plantation, I could never live with myself if I didn't speak out when I have the opportunity."

"Will you ask Harold to join you?" Abby asked.

"Absolutely not," Matthew said firmly, and then hesitated. "I'm certain he'll offer, but Susan is pregnant again. They haven't told anyone yet because her last pregnancy ended in miscarriage."

In the midst of concern for Matthew, Carrie felt a surge of joy. "Susan is pregnant again? That's wonderful!"

"It is," Matthew agreed. I won't separate the two of them. I did that once and it ended badly. It won't happen again. I'll be fine," he said firmly. "I should only be gone a few weeks."

Carrie couldn't shake the feeling that he was very wrong.

Chapter Two

All conversation stopped when Moses and the children rode up to the house, yelling and calling out to them.

Carrie smiled, unable to make sense of anything they were saying. She walked to the edge of the porch and held up a hand for silence. When the cacophony stopped, she looked at Moses. “What in the world are they talking about?”

Moses laughed easily, his giant shoulders shaking with amusement. His deep voice rang through the late afternoon air. “Depends on who you’re listening to. Frances saw a new bird she’s been searching for. Russell helped one of the men in the barn fix a piece of equipment he couldn’t figure out.” He turned his eyes toward his own children. “Jed and John helped plant the first tobacco sprigs of the year. Hope jumped Patches over a log for the first time.” His dark eyes gazed at the children with pride. “It’s been quite the afternoon.”

Carrie smiled with delight. “I want to hear all about it, but I suspect your horses are hungry.”

“I’m hungry too!” Jed called.

Carrie grinned at the newest addition to the Samuels family. The tragedy of his parents being killed by the KKK in South Carolina had not destroyed his spirit. Being loved by Moses and Rose had turned him into a confident, happy child.

"Then you'd best hurry and take care of your horses," Carrie replied. She lifted her nose and sniffed. "There are some good smells coming from the house."

"Of course there are," Frances called, her blue eyes glowing with excitement. "Annie and Minnie are frying chicken for dinner."

"And making rhubarb cobbler with the first crop from the garden," Russell added. "I helped harvest it this morning before school. Minnie showed me the best stalks."

Carrie's stomach growled as she turned her attention to her son. Russell had grown at least four inches since they had rescued him from living under the Richmond bridge. Even though she had watched the transformation, it was hard to believe he was the same boy Anthony had caught stealing from River City Carriages almost a year ago. He and his sister Minnie, adopted after her family was killed in a Pennsylvania tenement fire, had become best friends. Russell loved Frances as well, but he and Minnie were the same age. There had been an instant connection.

"I bet it's delicious," Carrie said warmly, as she waved her hand in the direction of the barn. "Go take care of your horses. Dinner will be waiting when you get back."

At that moment, the front door opened. Annie's voice boomed out as she appeared. "You heard Miss Carrie," she called. "Get going. We all be wantin' to eat. Your lollygaggin' around ain't doin' nothin' but slowing things down and keepin' people hungry."

Laughing, Moses and the children wheeled their horses around and trotted toward the barn.

Annie watched them leave with a beam of approval. "That's a fine group of chillun," she said with satisfaction before she turned to gaze at the others. "I got some hot tea and cookies ready on a tray in the kitchen. Can you wait till dinner, or you want me to bring it on out?"

"Bring it out," Carrie said. "I don't know about anyone else, but if I don't put something in my stomach, I might start eating the porch wood."

Annie eyed her sternly. "You comparin' my cookies to porch wood, Miss Carrie?"

Carrie laughed. "Not a chance, Annie. I'm proud to say I'm a much smarter woman than that. It's merely a sign of my desperation." She thought back to earlier. "Did I smell oatmeal cookies when I came in to change?"

"You might have," Annie said. "What 'bout the rest of you?" As her gaze swept the porch, her smile faded. "What be goin' on here?" Her eyes latched on to Abby. "What's wrong?" she asked sharply.

"Nothing is wrong," Abby assured her. "The plantation, and everyone on it, are perfectly fine."

Annie considered Abby's answer. "Then the trouble be somewhere else," she stated decisively. "I know trouble when I feel it."

Carrie knew that was true. Moses' mother had uncanny perception.

When the door opened again, it was Rose who appeared. "I don't know anything about trouble, but there's a little girl who desperately wants to see her mama."

Carrie stepped forward to scoop Bridget out of her best friend's arms. "This mama desperately wants to see her little girl." She smiled into her daughter's glowing green eyes, noticing the tousled black curls and the heavy eyelids. "Did someone just wake up from a late nap?"

Abby chuckled. "I took her out earlier for a long walk. She ran around exploring everything she saw. When she got tired, I pulled her home in the wagon, but she could hardly hold her eyes open."

Bridget reached her arms up. "Mama..." she said sleepily.

Carrie's heart expanded with so much love she thought it would explode from her chest. She hoped she never took the miracle of her daughter for granted. Their closest guess was that she had been eight months old when they rescued the frail, sick baby from beneath the bridge along with Russell. That had been eleven months ago. The toddler was now healthy and full of life. "Hello, sweetheart," she crooned, lowering her head to nuzzle Bridget's neck.

Bridget shrieked with laughter.

Everyone on the porch laughed with her.

Knowing she had an audience, the little girl waved her arms and laughed harder.

Carrie shook her head. "I've never seen such a little actress. She knows how to turn everything into drama."

"She fits into this family perfectly," Thomas said, amusement dancing in his bright blue eyes. "You were exactly like her when you were her age. God knew the right mama for this little angel."

Tears filled Carrie's eyes as she thought of her first daughter, Bridget, who was stillborn just minutes after Robert died in her arms. Carrie had almost died as well and had been told it was too dangerous for her to ever give birth again. She and Anthony had filled their home with adopted children instead. She loved them all fiercely, but when eight-month-old Bridget was placed in her arms, it had felt like a second chance.

When Bridget snuggled close and laid her head against Carrie's shoulder, Carrie settled down into a rocking chair, content to watch the last of the day sink behind the trees.

For that moment, Carrie could forget the drama and potential danger waiting for Matthew in Louisiana.

"So, was Annie right about there being trouble?"

Carrie cocked a brow at Rose. "I'm surprised you waited so long to ask."

Rose smiled, but her eyes, illuminated by the lantern light on the porch, remained serious and probing. "I saw no reason to bring trouble to the dinner table. The children were too excited about their fun afternoon."

"I'm glad you waited," Carrie replied. "It was thrilling to hear their accounts of what they did. They certainly made the most of the first day of warm weather." She smiled as she remembered Frances' enthusiasm. In the last year, her oldest daughter had fallen in love with birdwatching and was rapidly becoming an expert on Virginia birds. She spent hours poring over the ornithology volumes in her grandfather's vast library. "Frances was thrilled to see her first red-winged blackbird, as well as an indigo bunting."

Moses chuckled. "She didn't want to come back to the house until it was too dark to see. I had to entice her by reminding her how hungry she was."

"Perhaps she'll decide to become an ornithologist instead of a doctor," Carrie replied.

"Would that bother you?" Rose asked.

Carrie was surprised at how easy it was to shake her head. Frances had declared she wanted to be a doctor. Carrie longed for the day when her daughter would graduate medical school and join her at the clinic, but her happiness was much more important. “No, I want Frances to do what she wants to do. Women are finally able to have more independence and freedom. I don’t want anyone’s expectations but her own to determine what she does in life.” She thought about how hard she had fought to become a doctor. Frances was certain she wanted to follow in her mother’s footsteps, but Carrie knew that could change.

Thinking about Frances turned her thoughts to Rose and Moses’ oldest child. “Felicia was very quiet at dinner tonight.”

Rose nodded. “She spent most of the day in the library, reading the books your father and Abby recommended to her about business. I know she’s processing what she learned.” She laughed. “When she gets that look on her face, she isn’t aware of anything going on around her. I’ve never seen anyone so gifted in shutting out distractions.”

“That girl is like a sponge when it comes to information,” Carrie answered. “She may have graduated from college a few months ago, but she’ll spend her entire life learning.”

Rose smiled. “As you and I do.”

Carrie shook her head. “I believe Felicia takes it to a different level. I’m determined to know everything I can about medicine. You’re determined to learn everything about educating.” She glanced at Moses. “You’re determined to know everything about tobacco growing, but Felicia seems determined to know everything about *everything.*”

"That's true," Rose agreed. "I've never known anyone with such a thirst for knowledge. More importantly, she's determined to use what she learns to make things better for all black Americans, but especially for women."

"Has she decided when she wants to go to San Francisco to visit Mary Ellen Pleasant?"

Felicia had met the very successful, wealthy black businesswoman after her graduation from Oberlin College in December. The fact that Felicia was a college graduate at seventeen spoke of her passion and determination. Mary Ellen Pleasant had been taken with her and extended an invitation to San Francisco so that she could mentor her. She had also offered to finance her in a business, but Felicia wanted to go into business with her daddy. Moses was thrilled to invest in a new venture and had offered to accompany her to San Francisco when she wanted to go.

Rose shook her head. "We talked a little about it today. She knows it's planting season, so she's thinking about leaving in May." She looked at Moses. "She told me y'all have talked about it."

"We have," Moses confirmed. "I told her I would go whenever she wanted, but if I could choose, it would be around May. I imagine we'll be gone at least two months. Everything will be planted, and even if it takes longer, we'll be back long before harvest. The men can handle everything while I'm gone."

Talking about being gone for two months seemed to make Moses eager to change the subject. He turned his attention to Carrie. "You're still avoiding the question."

Carrie squirmed. She wasn't avoiding the question; she simply wasn't eager to revisit the conversation that had stolen her earlier peace.

"So, there is trouble," Rose said calmly. "Go ahead and tell us what it is."

Carrie relayed the conversation from earlier as Moses and Rose listened intently. She wished Anthony was with them to hear the news, but her husband had ridden into Richmond the day before to handle business matters at River City Carriages. He planned on being home in two days.

"Matthew is going to Louisiana?" Rose asked. "I know Abby has to be relieved that Thomas decided to stay here, but does Matthew truly need to go?"

Carrie felt as uneasy about it as she had earlier. "He seems to believe so." She could only imagine the conversation Matthew was having with Janie tonight.

"Alone?" Moses demanded.

"Yes," Carrie answered. "Father offered to go, but Matthew said it would be better if he went alone." She sighed. "I know Harold would go, but Matthew won't take him away from Susan."

Rose looked at her sharply. "Is there something we should know?"

"Know and not repeat," Carrie answered. "Susan is pregnant again. After her miscarriage last time, they aren't ready for people to know. Matthew only told us in order to explain why he wouldn't ask Harold to join him."

Moses tightened his lips and looked away into the darkness.

Carrie exchanged a nervous look with Rose. When Moses got that look, he was thinking hard about something he wasn't ready to reveal.

A long silence stretched out on the porch. A hooting owl was the only thing to break the silence. It was too early in the spring for the orchestra of frogs and crickets that would come soon. What should have been a peaceful evening was full of taut emotion.

Moses stood and walked to the edge of the porch, the lantern casting light on his massive body, outlining it against the inky blackness of the moonless sky. A smattering of stars failed to pierce the darkness. He swung around suddenly. "I'm going with Matthew."

Rose gasped and covered her mouth with her hand.

Carrie saw the frantic look in her best friend's eyes. "Why?" she asked, fighting to keep her voice even.

"The blacks in Colfax are going to need help," Moses said. "They are woefully outnumbered. I wanted to go to Alabama last year but didn't. This is my chance."

"Your chance to be thrown into prison and placed on one of the labor gangs that Samuel James is sending convicts to," Rose said indignantly. "You may be big and strong, but enough white men with guns can arrest you and end your life. The children and I will most likely never see you again." Her indignation had morphed into fear.

Carrie watched Moses carefully. She completely agreed with Rose, but this was something for the two of them to decide.

Moses looked at his wife, his expression a mixture of compassion and determination. "We've talked about not letting fear stop us from doing the right thing."

"We have," Rose agreed, fighting to bring the emotion in her voice under control. "We've also talked about the difference between courage and wisdom. What do you really think you'll accomplish down there?"

"Moral support? Cromwell runs like their plantation does. There might be others, but I don't know of another one in the country. My presence will make them feel not so alone."

"Or will it just make *you* feel better?" Rose probed. Her voice was gentle, but her eyes blazed with passion. "I know you often feel guilty about how much we have, when most of our people are suffering, but Cromwell is a haven for the men who work here. What you and Thomas have created has given many men a new life." Her voice trembled "Why can't that be enough?"

Moses turned away, his body stiff with emotion "I know how desperate these men must be feeling right now, Rose."

"And nothing you can do will help them," Rose insisted. "Matthew bringing everything to light has the potential to create change. You'll simply be another black target for the white supremacists in Louisiana." She paused. "A very *large* target."

Moses' eyes flashed with anger.

Carrie knew she couldn't truly understand what Moses was feeling, but it was easy to put herself in Rose's shoes.

The passion faded from Rose's eyes, replaced by a deep sadness that settled over her beautiful face. "I'm afraid," she said softly.

Moses knelt in front of his wife, his face now soft with compassion, and took her hands into his. "I'm sorry, honey. I'll be careful."

If possible, Rose's eyes took on a deeper despair.

Like Rose, Carrie knew being careful would mean nothing. Louisiana blacks were nothing but a commodity to most whites. When they saw one as large and strong as Moses, they would view him as little more than an acquisition that must be obtained. It would be nothing but insanity for Moses to go there, but she didn't know the words to keep it from happening.

The door to the porch burst open suddenly.

Chapter Three

Felicia strode out onto the porch, her tall, slender figure emanating emotion. Felicia held her mother's gaze as she moved closer to where they were sitting.

Rose couldn't quite identify what she was trying to communicate, but the mute appeal in her daughter's eyes kept her silent.

"Daddy," Felicia began. "I've changed my mind."

Moses breathed deeply as he turned his eyes to his daughter, obviously trying to shift his attention from his decision to go to Louisiana.

"About what, honey?"

"I don't want to wait until May to go to San Francisco," Felicia stated in her soft, steady voice. "Did you mean it when you said we could go whenever I want?"

Moses stared at her, looking like he knew he was walking into a trap. "I always mean what I say."

Felicia smiled. "I want to leave next week."

Rose gasped. "Next week?" Her head spun as she listened to the pronouncement.

"Why?" Moses asked sharply.

Felicia met Rose's eyes for a moment before she turned to her father. In that instant, Rose realized Felicia had overheard the conversation about Louisiana.

Felicia shrugged. "I spent a lot of time in the library today reading business journals and magazines. I believe it will be wise for us to open our business sooner rather than later, and I don't want to miss the opportunity for Mrs. Pleasant to mentor me."

Moses gazed at her. "Why do you think it should happen sooner? Will two months truly make a difference?"

When Felicia answered, Rose realized the serendipity of what Felicia had learned through her research. Her decision was going to resolve the immediate problem of Moses' desire to go to Louisiana, but it was also what her daughter thought was best.

"Reconstruction is losing the support of the American people," Felicia answered. "I don't think it will disappear so long as President Grant is in office, but there is growing opposition to the money and effort being spent on the freed slaves. It will be to our benefit if we can start our business as soon as possible, because I will be able to become established before there is a major shift in the country."

Seventeen... Seventeen...

Rose had to constantly remind herself how young Felicia was. She spoke with the intelligence and wisdom of someone much older.

Moses looked thoughtful but didn't deny her analysis. "You've been having long conversations with Thomas and Abby."

"I have," Felicia agreed. "If I want to succeed, it's important to know about more than business. I also have to understand our country."

Rose felt her heartbeat slow and begin to steady. No matter how much Moses believed he should go to Louisiana, he wouldn't turn down his daughter's request.

"Next week?" Moses asked.

Felicia nodded, shooting a quick glance at Rose. Out of the corner of her eye, Rose saw Carrie watching the exchange with a relieved amusement on her face. Carrie knew exactly what Felicia was doing. Rose resisted jumping up to hug her daughter. That could come later.

"You told me we could leave whenever I want. This is what I want," Felicia said.

Moses acquiesced. "Then next week it is, honey. Can we agree on ten days from now? We'll have most of the tobacco crop planted by then."

"That sounds perfect," Felicia agreed sweetly.

It took all of Rose's control to not burst into laughter. Felicia seemed to have already mastered the art of negotiating. Her daughter was going to be a formidable businesswoman.

When Felicia disappeared back into the house, Moses turned to her. "How did you manage that?"

Rose smiled, hoping she matched Felicia's sweet demeanor of a few moments earlier. "I didn't manage anything, my dear. As far as I can tell, Felicia's change of mind was an act of God."

Moses stared at her, smiled, and shifted his eyes toward the door. "She heard us talking, didn't she?"

"I don't know," Rose answered honestly. She had her suspicions, but she didn't know for certain. "I can say, however, that if she did, she is exhibiting the wisdom we believe she has."

Moses sighed, his face a mixture of emotions. "I'm not going to Louisiana, but I still believe I should."

Rose decided to duplicate her daughter's wisdom and remained silent. Thanks to Felicia, Moses wasn't going to throw himself into the midst of danger in the deep South. There was no reason to debate his beliefs.

Janie finished tucking Robert and Annabelle into bed and headed straight for the living room of their cozy home. The charm of the crackling fire and the colorful quilts created by the Bregdan Women were lost on her tonight. The tension had been palpable throughout dinner. It had taken all of Janie's control not to demand answers then.

"What don't you want to tell me?" she asked as soon as she drew close to the flames. Ignoring the quilt, which would be welcome on the warm day that had turned chilly, she settled down in the wingback chair, fixed her eyes on Matthew, and waited. She hated the feeling of doom that had lurked in the house from the moment he had walked in with an unusually sober expression. She had pushed aside her dread in order to spend a fun evening with the children, but there was no more avoiding whatever he was hiding.

Matthew shifted uncomfortably.

Janie's heart pounded as she fixed her light blue eyes on him. "Please tell me, Matthew." She braced herself, knowing she was about to hear something that would upset her. Her normally direct husband was seldom evasive.

The silence lingered as she watched the emotions roam over his handsome face. She could tell he was searching for words but coming up short. An unwelcome suspicion began to form.

"You're leaving, aren't you?" As soon as Janie uttered the words, she knew they were true.

Matthew looked at her directly, obviously relieved she had been the one to give voice to what he didn't want to admit. "Yes."

Janie gritted her teeth but somehow managed to keep her voice calm. "Why? You promised you would stay here with us all year."

"I did," Matthew agreed uncomfortably. "Something has happened."

Janie wanted to scream that *something always happened* but remained quiet while he explained the situation he had walked into with Thomas and Abby. She reached for a quilt and pulled it over her lap – not for warmth, but to hide her clenched fists.

"I have to go," Matthew said when he finished the long recital.

"No, you don't," Janie corrected him. "You're *choosing* to go."

Matthew opened his mouth to protest but closed it before he uttered a word. He met her eyes and nodded. "I suppose I am."

"Why?" Janie repeated. "Surely, there was another way to keep Thomas from going?" Everything in her wanted to scream, but she also respected her husband. She had to hear him out.

"I'm not sure," Matthew said as he shifted his gaze toward the fire for a long moment. He finally turned and met her eyes full on. "I didn't want to offer to go. I wanted to let Thomas go visit his friend." His voice trailed off as he shook his head. "I'm not really going to keep Thomas from making the trip..."

Janie waited patiently as he struggled to explain. She had married a journalist. She had faced this situation many times in the past but had believed him when he said he would stay on the plantation for a year. She had let herself relax into the knowledge of an entire twelve months as a family – the first they would have shared in seven years of marriage.

"It's important," Matthew finally said, lifting and dropping his hands in frustration. "I can't tell you why it's important enough to break my promise..." He shook his head as his voice trailed off. "It just is." His eyes met hers. "I know that's a terrible explanation."

"It's not," Janie said softly as her heart settled into acceptance. "You seem to have forgotten how well I know you. I've watched you follow your heart and your instincts all over the country. I've supported you every time."

Matthew gazed at her tenderly. "Can you do it one more time?"

Janie considered her answer carefully. "I think the question is whether *you* can do it one more time. I've watched you almost shatter beneath what you've seen and experienced. I've watched you fight to come back to yourself, and to me." She paused. "Do you really believe you can do it again?"

Matthew stared into the fire again for a long moment before he spoke. "I believe it's important that I go, and I have no reason to believe there's going to be violence. I simply think Willie Calhoun's story deserves to be told. If it provides him extra protection, then it will be even better."

Janie stiffened, not willing to let her husband get away with half-truths. "You and I both know that anytime you rile up white supremacists there is a risk of danger. You told me Louisiana is a powder keg ready to explode. What if it explodes while you're there?"

Matthew looked up quickly. "You're alright with me going?"

"Would it matter if I wasn't?" As soon as she asked the question, she held up her hand. "Don't answer that. I knew who you were long before you fell in love and married me. Your commitment to truth and justice is one of the reasons I love you so much. I won't pretend I'm excited about you going, but I'll never ask you to be less than who you are, Matthew."

Matthew walked to Janie and pulled her into his arms. "Have I told you recently how much I love you?"

Janie managed a light laugh around the boulder sitting on her chest. "You have, but I never get tired of hearing it." She laid her hand on his whiskered cheek. "Go do what you must. The children and I will be waiting for you when you get back."

Matthew claimed her lips in a passionate kiss. "I'm the luckiest man in the world," he whispered.

"You might just be," Janie whispered in return.

Carrie relaxed into the cushioned rocking chair in their bedroom and pulled Bridget closer into her arms, positioning the quilt to fit snugly around them. The night had grown chilly, but she was loath to close the window and block out the fresh air that drifted through the light curtains.

"Mama."

Carrie knew she would never tire of hearing that word, no matter which of her children it came from, but to hear it flow in Bridget's sleepy voice was something she would always treasure. "Hi, little girl," she said softly.

Her daughter didn't have many words yet, but after being malnourished for her first eight months under the bridge, that was to be expected. The other children had done their best to care for her, but they'd had little to eat themselves. The fact that she had survived was a miracle Carrie and Anthony celebrated every day.

Bridget stared up at her, black lashes fringing the green eyes that were so much like Carrie's. The dark curls framing her face made the resemblance even more uncanny. She reached up and pulled at Carrie's hair, chortling when a strand of ebony hair came loose from the braid that hung down Carrie's back.

"You think that's funny, do you?" Carrie said with amusement. She tickled Bridget lightly, laughing with her as the chortle turned into giggles. She was doing nothing to help her daughter fall back to sleep, but she couldn't resist the time with her.

Bridget fixed her eyes on Carrie's face while she listened to her mama talk.

Carrie told her about the patients who had come to the clinic, about going for a ride on No Regrets while Granite played around them, about Moses wanting to go to Louisiana, and about Felicia saving the day. She knew Bridget didn't truly understand her, but it didn't matter; she was hearing her mama's voice and she was discovering new words.

Carrie smiled tenderly when Bridget yawned and rubbed her eyes. She stopped talking, replacing her words with gentle humming. Bridget snuggled closer, closed her eyes, and within moments was sound asleep. Carrie kissed her softly on her tousled head and continued to rock gently. With Anthony still in Richmond, there was no reason to go to bed. She loved the feeling of her daughter's tiny body in her arms.

As she rocked, she thought of Matthew's decision to go to Louisiana. Anthony would be home in two days. What if he decided he should go to Louisiana with his friend? Carrie didn't want Matthew to go alone, but she shivered at the thought of Anthony in the powder keg Matthew had described. There was no trip to San Francisco to keep him from heading South.

She felt a flicker of hope at the thought of Janie talking her husband out of the trip, but she pushed it aside almost as soon as she considered the idea. Janie would be unhappy with Matthew's decision, but she already knew she would support him.

Would she be able to do the same with Anthony?

She continued to rock, letting the cool breeze soothe her troubled thoughts. The warmth of Bridget's tiny body finally lulled her to sleep.

She had not moved from the rocker when a soft knock jolted her from sleep. A quick glance at the window told her it was still night, though she had no idea what time it was. It could only mean trouble had found the plantation again.

Fighting to keep her breathing steady, Carrie gently laid Bridget in the crib that had been her haven when she was a baby. She gave a sigh of relief when Bridget slept on and moved silently to the door.

Chapter Four

Moses stared at her with concern when Carrie opened the door and slipped out into the hallway. "Weren't you wearing that last night?"

Carrie relaxed slightly when he didn't immediately greet her with a warning of danger. "I fell asleep rocking Bridget." She took a deep breath. Why had Moses come to wake her? "What's wrong?"

"Nothing," Moses assured her. "Miles came over to tell you the first foal of 1873 is on the way."

Carrie grinned, her fatigue completely forgotten. "What time is it?"

"About five o'clock, I think. Miles knew I would be on the porch."

It was well known that Moses, no matter the weather, was usually outside by four o'clock in the morning. He used the early morning hours to plan his day and enjoy the only moments of silence he was likely to get.

She also knew Miles was sleeping downstairs in the barn right now. Foaling season was the only time he was willing to leave Annie upstairs alone in their apartment. Horses could have foals on their own, but if there was even a hint of trouble, he would want to be there to assist.

"I'm on my way in just a minute," Carrie said. She slipped back into her bedroom, pulled her hair back into a braid, washed her face, and brushed her teeth. Thankful she was fully dressed, Carrie checked to make sure

Bridget was sleeping peacefully before she made her way to the front door, grabbing a thick barn coat and gloves on her way out. Spring was on its way, but the mornings were still cold.

"Will you have Rose listen for Bridget if I'm not back before she wakes up?"

"Of course," Moses agreed.

As Carrie strode across the expanse toward the barn, she gazed up at stars blinking in the sky. The clouds from earlier had dissipated, leaving a crystal-clear canvas for the constellations above. She took a moment to identify the Big and Little Dipper, smiled at the North Star glimmering in the sky, and strode into the barn.

Miles stood next to a stall door, his lined and weathered face glowing with delight. He spoke softly when she drew close. "It's Felicity."

Carrie refrained from clapping her hands, not wanting to alarm any of the horses. Felicity was a Cleveland Bay mare that Miles had brought from Canada when he returned to the plantation six years earlier. Her first foal, Dancer, had sold for an impressive amount the year before. "That's wonderful!"

Carrie moved forward quietly so she could peer over the stall door. Granite snuffled a greeting from the other side of the barn. She smiled in his direction but didn't want to miss the birth.

"You made it just in time," Miles whispered.

Carrie watched in awe as Felicity laid back and groaned. Her sides were slick with sweat, but she didn't seem to be in distress.

Miles read her mind. "She's doing fine."

Moments later, a slick membrane appeared. Two front hooves broke free from Felicity first, followed quickly by the foal's nose. Felicity snorted and pushed harder. The foal slid out easily, landing in the thick straw that filled the stall.

Carrie and Miles were content to watch. Mares giving birth to foals was as old as time; they would only step in if it seemed she needed help.

Felicity continued to strain with contractions that would deliver the remainder of the placenta.

The foal lay quietly for several moments and then began to move within the translucent-gray and bluish amniotic sac.

Breaking free from the sac could take anywhere from several minutes to several hours. Carrie watched closely, listening to the sounds of the barn coming to life. Glancing toward the open door, she could see the glow of dawn casting aside the night.

"It's breaking free," Miles said, a wide grin splitting his face. He loved every horse on Cromwell, but the Cleveland Bays were special to him. He had escaped the plantation in 1860, heading north to Canada. His impressive horseman skills had found him a job at Carson Farms raising Cleveland Bays. When he decided to return to the plantation a few years after the war ended, he arrived with Felicity, hoping to start breeding them in Virginia. Eclipse had proven to be the perfect stud. The Thoroughbred and Cleveland Bay mix offspring were already in demand as carriage horses.

As the foal broke free from the sac, another huge smile appeared on Miles' face. "It's a colt," he said reverently. "My Felicity done had a little boy."

Carrie leaned her head on Miles' shoulder, knowing how much it meant to him. Even just minutes old, it was easy to see he was a beautiful colt. "He's magnificent. You can already see both Felicity and Eclipse in him."

Miles nodded. "Yep, I can see that huge Thoroughbred in him. He couldn't have a better daddy than Eclipse."

Carrie was grateful she was experiencing another foaling season with her old friend. He had been a part of her world for as long as she could remember. When he had escaped the plantation, she had been happy for him but brokenhearted for herself. She would never forget the day he arrived on the plantation again, hoping for a job. This would be their seventh foaling season as equals. "This is just the beginning."

As Cromwell Stables had grown, each foaling season had gotten bigger. If all went well, they would have seventy-five new foals in the next several weeks. It wouldn't be enough to meet the demand for Cromwell Stables' horses, but having a limited stock kept the demand and the prices high. As always, her mind went to Robert. This had been his dream. She knew he would be immeasurably proud of her, but she wished he could be here to experience it for himself.

"Mr. Anthony coming home tomorrow?"

"He is," Carrie confirmed. "He's only been gone to Richmond a few days, but I've missed him." She knew how fortunate she was to have another husband she loved with her whole heart.

"You think he's gonna head to Louisiana with Mr. Matthew?"

Carrie's mouth gaped open. "How do you know about that?" As soon as she asked the question, she knew the answer. "Annie." His wife didn't miss anything.

Miles smiled but his eyes were serious. "I don't reckon anybody ought to be headin' down there, Carrie Girl."

Carrie sighed. "I couldn't agree with you more, but the hardheaded men on this plantation are hard to convince otherwise."

"I'm real proud of my granddaughter for keeping her daddy out of there. I'm gonna miss Felicia when she heads to San Francisco, but she was gonna go anyway. Leavin' early keeps Moses from heading south." Miles' eyes gleamed with pride. "You know, Carrie Girl, it's those hardheaded men who done given a whole heap of other men the chance to do somethin' with their lives here on this plantation."

"I know," Carrie agreed. "I'm proud of everything the plantation has done, but I'm not eager to risk the lives of our men."

"Especially Anthony," Miles said quietly.

Carrie tightened her lips and turned away from the stall. She moved to the barn door to gaze outside at the sun coating the sky with streaks of yellow, mixed with the cobalt blue rapidly retreating before its advance. She wished the new day had done the same with her fear. "Especially Anthony." She wasn't ashamed of the crack in her voice. It didn't matter how much time had passed; she would never forget the horror of losing Robert.

"You figure he's gonna want to go with Matthew."

Carrie knew it wasn't a question. "Yes."

"What you gonna tell him?"

Carrie managed to chuckle. "*Tell* him? Anthony and I don't *tell* each other much of anything."

"'Cause if you did, there be a lot of things he would have kept you from doin'."

Carrie didn't deny the fact. She and Anthony had both put themselves in dangerous positions for what they believed was right. A beam of light burst free from the clouds and flashed across her eyes. "This is different."

"Why?"

"I don't know," she admitted. She couldn't explain the dread she felt; she simply knew she felt it. She was also certain Anthony would choose to join Matthew. Matthew and her first husband, Robert, had been best friends since they were college roommates. When Robert was murdered and Anthony had entered her life, Anthony had become fast friends with Matthew as well.

"You borrowin' trouble, Carrie Girl?" Miles asked.

"Maybe," Carrie conceded. "I prefer to think I've learned how to analyze situations in order to lower the risk of danger."

Miles threw back his head and laughed. "That right, Carrie Girl? Ain't you the woman who rode through a blizzard to help a Klan member's son a few months back? How careful you figure you analyzed that situation?"

Carrie chuckled weakly. "I didn't go alone," she protested. "Anthony, Moses, and Rose went with me."

Miles was silent for a few moments. "You didn't go alone," he said softly. He turned to face her. "Mr. Anthony ain't gonna want Mr. Matthew to go alone neither."

Carrie couldn't deny the logic of his words, but she knew in her gut that the situation in Louisiana was far more dangerous than going to the house of a Klan member who needed help for his wounded son. She stood, letting the rising sun warm her face. "Do you think it will ever stop, Miles?"

"All the danger?" Miles shook his head firmly. "I don't reckon it will. I done been on this earth for close to seventy years, Carrie Girl. There ain't been a year I ain't had to worry 'bout somethin'." He took Carrie's arm and turned her toward him. "There also ain't never been a time that the answer didn't show up somewhere. This plantation done been through a lot, but we still be here."

"Robert isn't," Carrie reminded him in a brittle voice. She had lost one husband to the KKK. She didn't want to lose another to the hatred sweeping through America.

"That be true enough," Miles said heavily. "No matter what, there be bad things that happen. I still be standin' here, but I known lots of people from the slave days that didn't make it through."

"Don't you wonder why? Don't you try to make sense of it?"

"Not no more, Carrie Girl. I used to think I couldn't live if I couldn't make sense of things. I spent all my time tryin' to find answers. Not no more."

Carrie stared at him. "Why?"

Miles took her hand and squeezed it gently. "'Cause there ain't no answers," he said. "There ain't no sense in your Robert being killed. Or your first little Bridget dying. Or all my friends who died tryin' to escape to freedom." He took a deep breath. "Or all them soldiers who died in the war. Or them men down in Alabama slaving away in mines after they believed they weren't gonna be slaves again." He shook his head sorrowfully. "No, there ain't no answers. There's only what is. That's all there ever gonna be, Carrie Girl. I always gonna help where I can. I always gonna love when I can. I always gonna do what I can to set things right, but I ain't gonna waste my time tryin' to figure everythin' out. That don't do nothin' but drive a person crazy."

Carrie considered his words. "That doesn't make me feel better."

"Don't 'magine it does," Miles acknowledged. "You be a woman who gotta have answers to everythin'."

"Do you think I'm wrong?"

"Nope, not wrong. Just tired." He squeezed her hands again. "It be real tirin' to try to find answers when there ain't none."

Carrie absorbed the compassion in his eyes and voice. "Doesn't it feel like you're giving up?"

"I ain't givin' up. I's always gonna do all I can."

Carrie turned and looked out over the plantation, listening as birds came to life. Their song was both a celebration of Felicity's new colt and a mockery of the angst she felt. "Is this what happens when you get old, Miles?"

He chuckled. "You callin' me old, Carrie Girl?"

"Well," Carrie said hastily, "at least older than me."

"That be true 'nuff," Miles replied. "When I was a young man, I didn't figure I would ever get old. I figured I was gonna die young. Then I just kept goin' on livin'. The longer I lived, the more I figured I ought to add some wisdom to how I see things." His words lingered in the morning air. "That's what I be tryin' to do." He paused again and gazed around. "I reckon the thing that matters most to me now is peace. I find peace here on Cromwell." He glanced upward. "I find peace with my Annie. And with all those grandchillun."

Behind them, they could hear horses snorting and pawing at the ground, demanding food.

Miles' eyes were warm with affection when he looked at Carrie. "I find lots of peace being here with you, Carrie Girl. You always been one of the best things in my life. I reckon you still are."

Carrie pushed aside thoughts of trouble and flung her arms around her old friend. "I love you, Miles."

"I love you too, Carrie Girl," Miles said hoarsely.

As Carrie pulled away, she could hear hoofbeats in the distance. "Amber and Clint are almost here."

"Yep. Clint let us know we was gonna have early mornings until all the foalin' be done. Course, there ain't nobody gonna be here before me."

Carrie smiled. Clint was the perfect stable manager. Amber, his younger sister, might well be the best horse trainer on the east coast. Word was spreading about the quality of the horses she finished off.

"You reckon there be another sixteen-year-old black girl in the country who makes as much money as our Amber?"

Carrie laughed, thinking of how Amber had negotiated a percentage of the profits from every horse she trained beyond the six-month stage. Most of the foals born in the next few weeks were already claimed. They would go to their new owners in October. Amber handpicked eight to ten horses she would finish off until they reached three or four years old. As far as Carrie could tell, people would pay whatever they asked for them. Amber consulted with Abby before she set the prices. No one had even bothered to negotiate for a lower amount – they were simply eager to have one of the horses she had trained.

Amber and Clint appeared on the horizon.

"Has Amber told you what she's going to do with the money she's making?" Carrie asked. She and Susan had asked her themselves, but Amber never gave a straight answer.

"No," Miles replied. "Smart as that girl is, I know she's got plans, but she don't talk 'bout things till she's good and ready."

Carrie knew that was true. "I hope she won't leave." She couldn't envision Cromwell Stables without the girl she loved as a daughter.

Miles snorted. "That girl ain't going nowhere for a good, long time I reckon. She loves this place like it be her own. Besides, she done told me she ain't goin' nowhere she can't feel Mr. Robert."

Carrie swallowed the lump in her throat. Robert and Amber had been especially close. He had given his life to protect Amber from a bullet meant for her. "I'm glad she feels that way," Carrie said. "I can't imagine Cromwell without her."

"Good morning!" Amber called as she pulled All My Heart to a stop. The dark bay filly with a perfect heart-shaped marking on her forehead pranced in place for a moment and then stood rock steady.

Clint waved a hand before he vaulted off his gelding, Pegasus.

Amber looked at Miles. "Any news?"

Carrie smiled when Miles tried to shrug nonchalantly.

"Only if you count Felicity having a fine colt 'bout thirty minutes ago." The smile he had tried to suppress spread across his face.

Amber laughed and swung off her mare. "That's fabulous news! I know you were hoping for a colt this time."

She led All My Heart into the barn, tied her quickly, and ran to look into the stall. "He's beautiful!" she called over her shoulder.

Carrie walked back over in time to see the colt struggle to stand.

He collapsed four times before he tucked his legs, pushed hard, and finally stood. He looked around with a comical expression as he swayed unsteadily. Moments later, he was sucking greedily on Felicity.

"That's it, little boy!" Amber cheered. "You're going to be just like your daddy!"

"He'll do Eclipse proud," Miles proclaimed. "I figure all the Cleveland Bay mares we brought in last fall will be in foal next spring."

They had hoped to have a larger number of Cleveland Bay/Thoroughbred-mix foals for this season, but the delay in shipping the mares from Canada because of the disastrous Equine Flu the spring before had killed those plans. She and Susan weren't concerned; the Cleveland Bay breeding program was only one part of their long-term plan.

"How many more today?" Amber asked.

"I figure we gonna have another seven or eight young'uns by the end of the day," Miles replied.

Carrie grinned as she pushed away from the stall door. "I've got a medical clinic to run. As much as I'd like to stay right here, I have patients who would not appreciate that decision. I'll be back at the end of the day to check in."

"And I'll handle things in the meantime."

Carrie whirled around when she heard Susan Justin's voice behind her. "Good morning, partner!" She tried not to be obvious as she examined her for signs of pregnancy. She could appreciate Susan's desire for privacy, but she yearned to share this experience with her friend.

Susan, her long, blond hair pulled back into a braid, swung down from her towering black mare, Silver Wings. "Good morning, everyone. I figure we have a new foal since all of you are clustered around Felicity's stall."

"You know," Miles said, "y'all is a much faster way to say that. 'All of you' is a mouthful."

Susan shook her head. "I'm afraid I have too much northern blood in me to ever say y'all.'"

Carrie chuckled. "That's alright. We love you despite it." She waved her hand toward the stall. "Felicity had Eclipse's colt just about a half hour ago. He's perfect."

Susan grinned. "Of course he's perfect. You couldn't possibly breed Felicity and Eclipse and come up with anything short of perfection."

Carrie couldn't have agreed more. She pulled her pocket watch from her breeches and gasped. "I have to get out of here."

Susan followed her out of the barn. When they were far enough from the door, she spoke. "You know, don't you?"

So much for not being obvious, Carrie thought wryly. "The exciting news of your being pregnant again? I do." She quickly explained why Matthew had told them.

Susan's eyes darkened. "I appreciate him not wanting Harold to go to Louisiana, but we're going to worry about him every single minute he's gone." She frowned. "It will be terrible for Harold not to join his twin."

Carrie took her hand. "It will be more terrible for Harold if something were to happen to you and the baby while he's gone. He's still burdened with the knowledge that he wasn't here when you lost your first child."

Susan's eyes glazed with sadness. "I know," she said. "I don't want Matthew to go alone, but I don't want Harold to go. I need him here with me."

"And he needs to be here," Carrie said. "You're not keeping him from something. Even if Matthew wanted him to go, I already know he would choose to stay here with you."

Susan smiled gratefully. "You're right."

Carrie asked the question she most wanted the answer to. "How far along are you?"

"I figure about four months."

"That's good," Carrie told her. "You're further along than last time. It's a good sign that you won't miscarry this time." She knew Susan's condition had been more precarious because of the terrible flu she had contracted, but four months was a good sign.

"I hope so," Susan said fervently as she waved her hand. "Now, get ready for work, Dr. Wallington. You're needed."

Janie rode up to the clinic at the same time Carrie appeared from the woods. "Good morning," she called.

Carrie waved as she drew closer.

Janie saw the questioning look on Carrie's face, and appreciated the compassion in her eyes, but she looked away. The knot in her throat made talking impossible.

Carrie stepped forward to envelope her in a warm embrace. "We might as well talk about it. I'm quite certain Anthony will insist on joining Matthew."

Janie hated the flicker of relief, but she couldn't deny she would feel better if Matthew wasn't alone. "So, my husband is going to lure yours into danger again?"

"Looks like it," Carrie said lightly.

Janie didn't miss the worried concern in her friend's eyes. "I'm sorry, Carrie."

Carrie managed a rueful smile. "It feels like a repeat of last fall."

Janie couldn't summon a returning smile. The weeks their husbands had disappeared, with no contact, seemed like nothing now. "I'd much rather they be riding in the middle of a snowstorm, looking for diamonds that don't exist." The weight in her chest took her breath away as she thought about the things Matthew had told her regarding Louisiana.

Carrie scowled. "When is he leaving?"

"Four days," Janie said.

Carrie gazed at her, trying to absorb the reality that Anthony may only be home for two days. "How are you really doing with this? Matthew promised to stay here for an entire year with you, Robert, and Annabelle."

Janie didn't have to pretend with Carrie. She might choose to play the supportive wife with everyone else, but with her friend and partner she could be honest. "I'm sick about it," she said candidly. "I was angry at first, but I do understand my husband. He doesn't want to go, but he feels he must. I reminded him he was *choosing* to go and leave us."

Carrie took Janie's hand. "What did he say?"

"What he always says," Janie replied as she clenched her fists tightly. "He doesn't want to go, and he can't understand why he feels compelled to do it, but he simply knows he must." This time she was able to manage a smile. “As much as I hate it, you and I both know how he feels.”

Carrie nodded soberly. “I guess we do,” she admitted. Silently, she pulled off No Regrets’ saddle and bridle, and then turned her into the small paddock behind the medical clinic.

“Is Anthony still coming home tomorrow?”

“As far as I know.” Carrie replied, turning to stare out into the woods.

Even without seeing her face, Janie could envision the bleak expression in her eyes. “Anthony might decide to stay here,” she said softly, hoping her voice didn’t betray how much she hoped he wouldn’t make that decision. She knew it was selfish, but it made her even more frantic to think of Matthew in Louisiana alone.

“He might,” Carrie answered, still gazing into the woods.

Janie knew she didn’t believe it. “So, we do what we’ve always done,” she said. “We support each other and believe in the best.”

Carrie nodded and turned to face her. “We’re Bregdan Women. We’ll face it together,” she agreed.

Janie smiled, but the expression in Carrie’s eyes caused the smile to fade as soon as it quivered to life on her lips. “What is it?”

Carrie remained silent.

“Carrie!” Janie said sharply. “Do you know something I don’t know?” Her breathing became shallow as she struggled to interpret what she was seeing. “Please tell me.”

“I don’t know anything you don’t know,” Carrie said. “It’s just a feeling, Janie. Matthew told us yesterday that Louisiana is a powder keg close to exploding. Everything in me says it's going to explode while they're there." She hesitated. "I'm afraid."

"Me too," Janie whispered.

A sound in the distance broke them out of their thoughts. Children were arriving for the day in the schoolhouse adjacent to the clinic. Patients would appear soon. There was work to be done.

Janie reached out for Carrie. The two women clasped hands, knowing there were no words to diminish what they were feeling.

They would live with fear until their husbands returned.

Chapter Five

Carrie leaned back against an oak tree and watched the children running around, their shrieks of laughter bringing a smile to her face. The only two not involved in the game of chase were Felicia and Frances. The two young women were huddled together under the limbs of a weeping willow tree with vibrant, new leaves bursting forth. By the expressions on their faces, Carrie could tell they were having an intense conversation.

Carrie ached for her oldest. She and Felicia had become close when Frances had arrived on the plantation. Frances had missed her friend dreadfully when she was away at Oberlin College. She hadn't shared Felicia's desire to go to college so young, but there had been a void the younger children couldn't fill. Frances and Minnie were close, but the age gap had become more of an issue as Frances grew up.

The two had been inseparable since Felicia had returned home, having conversations late into the night. She knew it was breaking her daughter's heart for her friend to leave again so soon.

"Do you think they're plotting something?"

Carrie smiled as she gazed at Anthony, her heart beating harder as she thought of saying good-bye to him the next day. She'd only had him home for two days. As she had expected, he'd chosen to accompany Matthew to Louisiana. They were riding into Richmond tomorrow, taking the train west the following morning, and then catching a steamboat down the Mississippi River that would deliver them within riding distance of Colfax.

"They're nearly always plotting something," Carrie replied. "Their minds seem to never stop." She felt a swell of pride. "Those two girls are really going to be something," she said. "They're able to do things at this age that I could hardly even dream about. Women still have a long way to go, but it's certainly easier for them now."

Frances leapt up and dashed toward them, her face alight with excitement.

"Uh oh," Anthony muttered. "I can feel an ambush coming."

Carrie watched her daughter run across the opening, her brown eyes gleaming beneath the chestnut hair flowing around her shoulders. She had turned into a beautiful girl. *Young woman*, she corrected herself. Frances would be seventeen soon.

Carrie relished an ambush. Anything that would keep her from thinking about Anthony leaving for the Louisiana powder keg.

Frances skidded to a stop. Her eager face faded into uncertainty as she dropped down cross-legged in front of them. "Mama? Daddy?"

"Go ahead, Frances," Anthony said. "What do you want to ask us?"

Frances clasped her hands tightly in front of her. "I want to go to San Francisco with Felicia and Moses," she blurted out.

Carrie sucked in her breath. She didn't know what she had expected, but it wasn't this. "San Francisco?"

Frances nodded as she leaned forward and gazed into Carrie's eyes. "Yes, Mama. I know school won't be out, but you know I'm way ahead of everyone else. You've always told me experience is the best teacher. I believe a train trip across the country, and time in San Francisco, would be a very educational experience," she said earnestly.

Anthony chuckled. "*Educational*, huh?"

"Yes," Frances said. "And great fun as well," she admitted with twinkling eyes. "If everything goes as planned, I'll start college in the fall, and then go to medical school. This seems like the perfect time to travel to California. I know I'm young, but we'll have Moses with us. No one will bother me with him around."

Carrie couldn't debate her logic. She also knew she would have jumped at an opportunity like this when she was seventeen. She would have jumped at *any* opportunity. Frances had already experienced more than she had at the same age, but traveling cross-country would be exciting. If she could, Carrie would probably beg to join her. She longed to see the vastness of the west for herself. Taking a train across the entire country would be a much different experience than her wagon train trip to Sante Fe years before.

The idea of Felicia leaving, though, made her breath catch, especially with Anthony also leaving. Could her heart handle worrying about them both? She could hear Abby's voice in her head as soon as she had the thought. *Worrying is a choice, Carrie. You can choose trust over worry.*

Frances met her eyes. "I'll be alright, Mama. I know this is a big thing, but it will certainly be safer than the wagon train to Santa Fe."

Carrie had vivid memories of the wagon train trip she had made to New Mexico to aid the Navajo Indians. She had met Frances on that trip.

"I believe I'm old enough to handle it," Frances said earnestly.

"I know you are, honey," Carrie said. She looked at Anthony but couldn't read the expression in his eyes. "Your father and I will have to talk about it."

"I know," Frances agreed, but laughter lurked in her eyes. "Since Daddy leaves in the morning, I know I won't have to wait long for an answer."

Carrie hoped her expression didn't reveal Frances' words were like a hard kick to her stomach. If they agreed she could go, Anthony would leave tomorrow, and Frances would leave five days later.

Had it been just a week earlier that Carrie believed life was finally going to be easy and peaceful? That notion had been completely shattered.

Frances jumped up again. "I'm going to tell Felicia you're thinking about it."

Carrie held up her hand, stopped by a sudden thought. "Does Moses know about this plan?"

"Not yet," Frances acknowledged sheepishly. "But you know he'll be fine with it if you say I can go. My going with them will make everything more fun." She turned and skipped off.

Carrie smiled and shook her head, remembering the frightened little girl she had rescued from the orphanage.

"She's something," Anthony muttered. "I can't believe it's only been four years since she came home with you."

"And six months later I married you," Carrie said quietly, assailed by the memories. She didn't want her fears to stop those she loved from doing what they were meant to do, but it was also impossible to not feel them.

Anthony took her hand. “I'll only be gone a few weeks, Carrie,” he said gently.

Carrie smiled briefly but didn't respond. He might believe it, but there was no way he could promise to return. She knew all too well how quickly you could lose someone you loved. “What do you think about Frances going?” she asked, more to take her mind off him leaving than anything else.

Anthony opened his mouth to answer but was interrupted when Annie stepped out onto the porch.

“Y'all get yourselves around back of this house,” Annie hollered. “I ain't been workin' myself to the bone all day just to have a feast go to waste.”

The children turned as one and began to race around to the back of the house. They had considered having their first spring picnic by the James River, but a strong breeze had picked up early in the afternoon. Air blowing off a river that hadn't warmed yet would feel frigid, while the house and the surrounding trees blocked the wind, creating a haven where the afternoon sun beat down on them.

“I'm first in line,” John hollered.

“Only if you get there first,” Jed yelled back.

“I'm going to beat you both!” Russell called.

Anthony laughed as he watched the boys race around the house. “John and Jed are fast, but they're no match for Russell's long legs. He'll be first in line at the table,” he said confidently.

Carrie chuckled. “Don't be too sure of that, my dear.” She nodded her head toward the edge of the woods.

Minnie was a blur of action as she raced after the boys, catching up to them and passing them as if it required no effort. Her red braid bounced on her back as her laughter rang through the afternoon air.

Anthony stared at his daughter with astonishment. "I had no idea Minnie could run like that."

"Me either," Carrie admitted. "More importantly, I don't believe she knew. She grew several inches this winter. Her legs are longer than the boys now. Russell asked if they could run together so he could practice and be fast enough to beat John and Jed. I'm sure he never imagined Minnie would be faster than him." She laughed loudly and jumped up. "We'll talk about Frances later. Right now, I'm starving. Let's eat!"

It wasn't until they were alone on the front porch, snuggled beneath a heavy quilt, that Carrie and Anthony were able to talk freely again.

"We have to decide about Frances," Carrie said reluctantly.

Anthony looked at her closely. "You don't want her to go?"

"Of course not," Carrie said. "But I also can't imagine stopping her. I simply wish she could have these wonderful experiences without ever leaving home."

Anthony chuckled. "I never thought the hardest part of being a parent would be watching them grow up and become independent."

"I completely agree," Carrie muttered, her mind spinning as she thought of letting Frances leave for several months. "We're going to let her go, aren't we?"

"Like you, I can't imagine stopping her," Anthony answered. "I'll be home long before she returns from San Francisco, so we'll be able to miss her together."

Carrie pulled back, not wanting to think about Louisiana.

Anthony reached around her shoulders and pulled her close. "I'll be home before you know it, honey."

Carrie flushed with sudden anger. "Please don't say that," she said sharply, regretting her tone as soon as she spoke the words. She didn't want their last interaction to be a fight. She took a deep breath. "You can't promise me you'll come home, Anthony. Louisiana is a dangerous place right now." A feeling of helplessness swept over her. "No one can promise Frances will come home. I suspect a train ride to San Francisco is safer, but things happen."

"They do," Anthony said. He turned her face so he could look at her. "Now you know how your father felt through the years. How Robert felt. How I have felt at times." His voice was tender but direct.

Carrie wanted to resent his observation, but she was too honest to deny the obvious. She sighed heavily. "I suppose it's much easier to be the person taking the risk," she admitted. "You're caught up in the excitement of the experience, not waiting at home to see if your loved one will return." As she spoke the words, she recognized their truth. It didn't necessarily make her feel better, but she realized maturity required her to release the hold on those she loved.

"So, Frances is going to San Francisco," Carrie said. "And you leave for Louisiana in the morning." Despite her determination to let go, she couldn't control the crack in her voice.

Anthony pulled her against him again. "I know I can't make promises to return, my love, but I *can* promise to be as careful as possible and come home as soon as I can."

Carrie knew that would have to be enough. She also knew she didn't want her husband to leave under a blanket of fear. "I suppose that means I'll have to promise to not do anything reckless while you're gone," she said, forcing amusement into her voice.

Anthony smiled, his eyes communicating that he appreciated her effort. "I think it's better if you don't make a promise you're not capable of keeping," he said playfully. "I do know my wife."

Carrie snuggled against him, wanting to imprint the memory of his lean, strong body.

A quarter of a waning moon hung above the tree line. The first lilacs had burst into bloom that afternoon. Their sweet perfume wafted over them. They could hear the shrill whinny of the twenty new foals that had joined them in the last few days, along with the quiet snorts of their mothers.

Anthony sighed. "I love the plantation in the spring. I'm going to miss this." He stroked her head. "I'm going to miss *you*."

In that moment, Carrie recognized the sacrifice her husband was making for his friend. He wasn't thoughtlessly going into danger; he was doing what he believed was best for Matthew. He couldn't stand the reality of Matthew going into possible danger alone. She lifted her face and kissed him. "You're a good man, Anthony Wallington. I'm proud of you."

Anthony gazed down at her tenderly. "Thank you," he whispered.

Carrie reached up to stroke his cheek. "Are you afraid?" She'd been so focused on her own fear that she'd forgotten to consider his.

Anthony started to shake his head but stopped. His voice was low as he answered. "Honestly? Yes." He took a deep breath. "Matthew told me more about the situation down there. I suggested he get what he needed from correspondence with Calhoun, but he insists the only way to be able to write a truly powerful story is to actually spend time with the man. Still, I think any sane man would be worried about walking into the middle of it."

Carrie bit her lip so hard she could taste blood. She wanted to scream her protest. She wanted to remind him that he and Matthew weren't acting like sane men. None of that would help, so she swallowed the words dancing on her tongue. "You'll go down, meet Willie Calhoun, get what Matthew needs to write the articles, and then come home," she said calmly, amazing herself with how steady her voice was.

Anthony grinned. "That was quite impressive, honey."

Carrie, despite the emotions swirling through her, laughed. "It was, wasn't it? Perhaps I'll grow up eventually."

"You've grown up beautifully," Anthony assured her.

Carrie smiled but kept her focus on what he'd said. "There's nothing wrong with being afraid. It will help make you more aware of danger, and hopefully you'll be more careful." She gripped his hand tightly. "The children and I will be waiting for you to come home. Keep remembering that, and you'll find your way through every challenge."

Anthony took a deep breath as he squeezed her hand. She could feel him gazing out into the darkness.

"You're not going to miss much of the spring, Anthony. You'll be home before you know it. A month, if you're gone that long, is a lengthy time, but it will still be spring when you return." Even as Carrie spoke the words, she knew she had no confidence in what she was saying. What's more, she was certain Anthony knew that too.

"Wasn't it Old Sarah that told you 'eber day got more than 'nuff trouble? You ain't got to think 'bout nothin' more den the day you be livin'?"

Carrie laughed as Anthony did a passable job of imitating Old Sarah. "She did." Even laughing, Carrie could feel the wisdom and the power of Rose's mama. "I reckon we just gonna have to live the days we got in front of us. Ain't nobody kin do more than dat."

"How'd my mama get out here on this porch?" Rose demanded as she stepped outside.

Carrie waved a hand. "Your mama's wisdom is always needed."

"Especially tonight?" Rose asked. She pulled a quilt tightly around her shoulders and settled into a rocker. She leaned her head against the wood and closed her eyes. She didn't wait for an answer she already knew. "It's been a long day."

"That it has," Carrie agreed.

"Are you letting Frances join Moses and Felicia on the trip?"

"We are," Carrie replied. "How do you feel, though, about her missing the rest of the school year?"

Rose chuckled. "That girl could be teaching. She knows everything she can learn from us. She keeps learning because she spends almost as much time in the library as Felicia. San Francisco will be good for her," she added.

"You're not nervous about Felicia going?"

"Of course I am," Rose responded. "If I could keep my husband and children from ever leaving Cromwell Plantation, I would. Since I can't, you and I will have to worry together."

"We'll have Janie for company," Carrie assured her. "Anthony told me it was only fair that I should have to worry after everything I've put others through."

"I don't think I phrased it in those words," Anthony protested.

Carrie eyed him. "Perhaps not, but it's exactly what you meant."

Anthony grinned. "That could be true."

Rose lifted a brow. "I don't think I'm fond of growing up. It's tiring when you have to act like an adult all the time." She looked up at the window with the glowing light. "Felicia and Frances are awake. Are you going up to give Frances the news, or are you going to let her suffer in suspense until morning?"

Anthony rapped lightly on the solid oak door to the bedroom the girls shared.

"Come in," Frances called.

Carrie walked in behind her husband. The three girls were huddled together on one narrow bed, their legs tangled together. "Is there more plotting going on up here?"

"No plotting," Minnie informed her.

Frances and Felicia remained quiet, their expressions tense and questioning.

Minnie looked at them, waited for a moment, and then shook her head. "Are you going to let Frances go to San Francisco? She's too afraid to ask you because you might say no."

Carrie chuckled. Minnie was definitely the most precocious of her children. Instead of answering the question, though, she asked another one. "Did you beat all the boys in the race to the picnic table tonight? I didn't get back there in time to see who won."

Minnie grinned and nodded. "They didn't like getting beaten by a girl." Her eyes flashed with pride. "I didn't know I was so fast."

"You're very fast, honey," Anthony told her. "I was quite impressed."

Minnie's eyes shone brightly. "Thanks, Daddy! I bet I'll be even faster when you get back from Louisiana." A shadow spread over her face, devouring her smile and the light in her bright blue eyes. "Do you really have to go to Louisiana?"

Carrie listened to the exchange. Minnie was the first of the children to ask. The others hadn't been happy, but they hadn't questioned it.

Anthony sank down onto the bed next to the girls. "No."

Carrie's eyes widened with surprise.

"Then why are you going?" Minnie demanded. "I don't want you to. Neither does Russell." She glanced at her sister. "Frances doesn't want you to go either, but if she's going to San Francisco, she won't really care."

Anthony held her gaze. "I don't *have* to go to Louisiana, honey. No one is making me. In fact, I wish I could stay right here on the plantation."

Minnie's eyes grew wide. "You do?"

Anthony nodded. "I wish I never had to leave your mama or my children."

"Then why are you?" This time it was Frances who demanded an answer.

"Because someone I love is going into a dangerous situation. Because he's my friend, I don't want him to be alone. If something were to happen, and I wasn't there to help him, I don't know if I could ever forgive myself." Anthony's deep voice filled the room.

A long silence followed his words. Only the clattering of limbs in the breeze broke the quiet.

"But Daddy," Minnie asked, "what if something bad happens here?"

Carrie continued to listen quietly, appreciating her husband's honesty.

"I hope it doesn't," Anthony replied. "But if it does, you'll have everyone here on the plantation to take care of you. Just like when I have to go to Richmond for business. Don't you always feel safe here?"

Minnie nodded slowly. "But I'm going to miss you."

"I'm going to miss you too," Anthony said soberly. "More than you can know. I'll be home as soon as I can."

"When will that be?" Minnie demanded.

Anthony shook his head, looking away from her penetrating gaze for the first time. "I don't know, honey. Matthew and I don't think we'll be gone a long time, but we don't know for sure. We have to get there before we can understand what's going on."

Another long silence filled the room. Carrie knew her daughters were processing what Anthony had said.

"Alright," Minnie finally said. "I'm glad Mr. Matthew doesn't have to go by himself." She shook her head. "You still didn't answer my first question though, Daddy."

"I didn't," Anthony agreed. He glanced up at Carrie and then looked at Frances. "Have you and Felicia talked about what you're taking to wear on the trip to California?"

Frances' hazel eyes widened. "I can go?" She jumped up to sit on her knees, bouncing slightly on the mattress. "I can really go to California?" She looked at Carrie for confirmation.

"You can go," Carrie assured her. Now that the decision was made, she was excited for her daughter. "We agree that it's a wonderful opportunity."

"You have to do exactly what Moses tells you," Anthony said sternly. "Don't come up with some wild scheme that will make his life miserable."

Frances grinned slightly. "Like Mama would have at my age?"

Anthony snorted. "Not just at your age. Your mama has been coming up with wild schemes her whole life."

"At least I come by it honestly," Frances retorted. "I suppose that I could blame it on her if something happens."

"Don't even think it," Carrie warned, biting back the laugh that wanted to erupt.

"Don't worry, Carrie," Felicia said. "I'll keep her out of trouble."

Carrie was comforted by Felicia's promise. The young lady was more serious and focused than she could ever dream of being. "I'm going to hold you to that, Felicia."

Carrie blinked back tears as she snuggled into Anthony, thankful for the quilt that covered their bed. It wasn't cold enough for a fire, but the warm quilts were welcomed. "I'm going to miss you." She always hated the night before a trip. She wanted to savor every moment, but the knowledge that it would end made it difficult.

"I'm going to miss you too," Anthony murmured. He pulled her close and kissed her warmly. "I wish I never had to climb out of this bed with you."

Carrie was struck by the passion in his voice. She thought of his earlier fear and fought to conquer her own. She refused to consider the possibility that he wouldn't return.

Old Sarah's voice rose in her mind again. *Ain't nobody know when they gonna leave this ole earth. Best yous can do is live each day the best you can. Love the best you can.*

Carrie stroked her husband's cheek and deepened the kiss. Whatever the future might bring, she was going to make sure this was a night to remember.

Chapter Six

Moses, Felicia, and Frances stepped into the Pullman sleeping car.

Felicia stared around with wide-eyed disbelief. "Wow! Are we really riding across the country in this car, Daddy?"

In truth, Moses was as impressed as she was. Thomas, Anthony, and Matthew had told him how spectacular the cars were, but even he wasn't expecting so much opulence. "Black walnut woodwork with inlay," he murmured as he gazed around. "Framed mirrors between the windows, plush upholstery, polished brass fixtures."

He thought about what else he knew. "Matthew wrote an article about the Pullman sleeper cars. There are good beds, ample linens, and deep pile carpeting on the floors. All the cars are somewhat influenced by the furnishings of the saloons and cabins of river steamboats." He pointed upward with a grin. "The upper berths are folded into the ceiling during the day. Our porter will fold them down for tonight. They've already been made up with clean sheets. The heat comes from a hot-air furnace under the floor that will be lit with candles at night. It's ventilated through the deck windows."

Frances was equally awestruck. "I've only been on a train once, when Mama brought me from the orphanage in Illinois. It was nothing like this." She walked over to stare out the window that overlooked the Broad Street

Station. Richmond was glorious with beds of tulips and vibrant azaleas lining almost every yard. She turned around with a grin. "I sure am glad Mama and Daddy decided I could come with you!"

"I thought we would be sitting up the entire trip, like I did traveling back and forth to college," Felicia said, her eyes scanning the car. "The coach cars are nothing like this. Are we the only three in here?"

"We are," Moses assured her. He wasn't going to tell the girls how much it had cost. He and Rose had decided it was worth the expense to surprise them. They spent little of the money they made from the plantation. Never having had much, he was happy to let it accumulate. He was certain, however, that there would not be many cross-country train trips, so he intended to enjoy every minute of it.

A noise at the door drew his attention. Moses looked up as a porter, dressed immaculately in his uniform, stopped at the door to their car. He smiled at the man's dumbstruck expression. Moses interpreted the look glimmering in his eyes. "Don't have many black passengers in the Pullman sleeping cars?"

The short, slender black man blinked, cleared his throat, and then stood taller. "No sir," he admitted in a gravelly voice. "You be my first."

Moses chuckled. "What's your name?"

"George, sir."

Moses shook his head, remembering what Anthony had told him. "What's your real name?"

The porter blinked again and shuffled his feet. "Sir?"

Moses smiled, hoping he could put the man at ease. He knew Felicia and Frances were listening closely to the conversation. "Your real name," he repeated. "I know

George Pullman tells every one of his porters to call themselves George. We'd prefer to know your real name." He paused. "The way I understand it, you're going to be the one taking care of us all the way across the country."

"Yes sir," the porter repeated.

"We'd like to know your real name."

The porter hesitated, looked over his shoulder, and stepped a little closer. "My name is Reggie." He cleared his throat. "Yes, sir, my name is Reggie." His eyes lit with pride.

"It's nice to meet you, Reggie," Moses said, holding out his hand.

Reggie stared at him hard and then shook his hand firmly. "It's gonna be a pleasure being your porter, sir."

"My name is Moses Samuels." Moses turned to the girls. "This is my daughter, Felicia, and our dear family friend, Frances."

The girls smiled, their expressions warm and open.

"It's nice to meet you," they said in unison.

Reggie nodded his appreciation.

"I know you're busy getting everyone settled," Moses said. "When we're underway, we'd love to hear your story."

Reggie sucked in his breath. "My story, sir?"

Moses grinned. "Everybody has a story, Reggie. I was a slave until I was almost twenty. I escaped a plantation outside Richmond, went to Philadelphia, and served in the Union Army until the end of the war. Now, I co-own the plantation."

Reggie's eyes, already wide, nearly bulged from his face. "You own the plantation where you be a slave once?"

"I do," Moses said. He wanted Reggie to know his current situation didn't have to dictate his future.

Reggie looked thoughtful. "Then that be the Cromwell Plantation I done heard about?"

Moses cocked his head. "You've heard of the plantation?"

Reggie nodded again. "You bet. I know some of the fellas who went there looking for a job after the war."

"Is that right?" Moses felt pride swell in his chest. He still felt badly about not going to Louisiana with Matthew, but he knew it was true that the plantation was making a difference for a lot of men. "Who are they?"

Reggie opened his mouth to answer but was interrupted by a whistle blast. He backed out of the room hurriedly. "I got work to do, Mr. Samuels. I'll check on y'all later. We can talk more then."

"Daddy," Felicia said softly, "people are looking at us like we shouldn't be here."

Moses had noticed as soon as they entered the dining car. "This country has to get used to black people being where white people are. The law passed two years ago says we can ride this train. That's what we're doing." He looked down at the plate of roast beef, mashed potatoes, and green beans, taking a deep breath to control his frustration. "Ignore them and enjoy your meal. I intend to."

Felicia looked uncomfortable but picked up her fork.

"You've done a lot of train travel," Frances said. "Aren't you used to this?"

Felicia shook her head. "No. I always rode in one of the coach cars, and I was always accompanied by a teacher. We brought our food with us and tried not to garner too much attention." She looked around again. "I know the law says we can be here, but that doesn't mean we're welcome."

Moses scowled. He hated that his beautiful, brilliant daughter was being made to feel like she was inferior in any way.

Felicia read the expression on his face. "I know I'm not inferior, Daddy," she said softly. "I merely have to decide what battles I'm willing to fight."

"I'll fight this one for you," Moses vowed. He thought back to the little girl who had watched her parents be brutally murdered during the Memphis Riot seven years earlier. "You don't have to worry."

Felicia grinned. "I know, which is why I'm going to enjoy my meal!"

When the food was gone, Felicia looked at Frances. "Have you ever heard of Elizabeth Jennings?"

Frances placed her folded napkin on the table and shook her head. "No. Who is she?"

"A big reason why we're riding on this train today," Felicia answered. "I met her when Sojourner Truth and I were speaking in New York. She's the reason blacks are riding streetcars and steamboats in New York City."

Moses eyed her, his curiosity piqued. "I've never heard of her either."

"Mrs. Jennings is a fascinating woman," Felicia began. "She's a schoolteacher in New York City, committed to educating black children. Anyway, almost twenty years ago, back in 1854, she was on her way to church. She was late, so she decided to ride a whites-only streetcar in Manhattan. The conductor told her they weren't accepting black passengers, but she got on anyway."

"Oh my..." Frances murmured.

Felicia's eyes flashed. "The conductor threw her off onto the ground."

"Onto the ground?" Frances gasped.

Felicia nodded. "She stood up, dusted off her clothes, and got back on."

Moses listened with fascination. "What happened next?"

"A policeman came along and threw her off again."

Moses flushed with anger but kept his features impassive. "And then?"

"The policeman drove her off like she was a dog," Felicia said with a scowl. A moment later, the scowl was replaced by a grin. "So, she sued the city of New York," she said triumphantly.

"And won?" Frances' eyes widened with excitement.

"And won," Felicia confirmed. "Her attorney, Chester Arthur, had only been admitted to the bar a couple of months earlier, but he took her case. Evidently, there was a recently enacted state law that made the streetcar company liable for the acts of their agents and employees." She paused and took a sip of the hot tea that had been brought to their table. "She won her court case one year later. The judge awarded her two hundred and fifty dollars and ruled that state statutes allowed blacks to ride on any public conveyance. The very next day, the line she was thrown off was desegregated. By 1865, the entire city was desegrated."

"Hurrah for Elizabeth!" Frances said excitedly. She reached over and grasped Felicia's hand. "You and I are going to make things like that happen, too."

Moses listened to the girls. He knew they were right, but he couldn't help wondering what price they would have to pay. He thought about Felicia's reason for deciding to go to San Francisco early. How much was the country moving away from the values of Reconstruction? He considered what was drawing Matthew and Anthony to Louisiana, and the atrocities happening all through the South. What did it mean to the country? What did it mean to the strides made since the end of the war?

The day passed rapidly, with the girls glued to the large windows in their Pullman car. They didn't want to miss any of the countryside they were passing through.

Frances turned to gaze at Moses. "It's fascinating to see America like this!" she said. "It was almost fully spring on the plantation, but now that we're moving into the mountains, there aren't as many flowers and trees."

"The elevation plays a big role," Moses told her. "It's definitely not as warm here. I grew up on a plantation in the mountains. Spring didn't come as early, and fall arrived sooner."

Felicia stared at him. "You know, Daddy, sometimes I forget you were ever a slave." She paused. "I bet you don't forget."

"That's true," Moses acknowledged. No matter how wonderful his life was now, he would never forget his torturous years as a slave. If nothing else, the mudflat of scars on his back from whippings in the field would remind him. He forced the thoughts from his mind so he could focus on the girls. "We're going to see a lot of the country."

Frances turned to stare back out the window. "We're really going to be on the train for a week?"

"A whole week," Moses confirmed. He couldn't quite wrap his mind around it either. He'd never been confined in one place for that long. Still, it was much better than the options that had been available earlier. "The Transcontinental Railroad was completed four years ago. It used to take months to cross the country. Instead of this luxurious car, we could be on a wagon train for months on end, through all kinds of weather."

"I know all about that," Frances said somberly. "I met Mama on a wagon train to Santa Fe. There was a horrible blizzard during the trip, and my sister and I almost died." Her voice cracked. "My brother did die." She shook her head. "You would have never talked me into a wagon train, no matter how much I want to visit San Francisco. Once was enough." She glanced around the comfortable car. "I never dreamed of traveling like this."

Felicia jumped up and opened a large drawer. "Look, Daddy, there are a lot of games for us to play. Frances and I found them."

Moses grinned when she pulled out backgammon, chess, checkers, and cards. The week on the train already seemed less daunting.

"And there is a shelf full of books," Frances proclaimed. "I even saw a room on our way to the dining hall that looks like a library."

Moses' grin grew broader. He had often dreamed of having time to relax and read without the demands of the plantation pulling at him every second. "Looks like we have everything we could want, girls."

"Daddy, come look!" Felicia cried. "There's a huge waterfall!"

Moses joined them at the window, admiring the frothy plume of water gushing down the mountainside. He watched as the water exploded on the rocks below the tracks, spiraling beneath the bridge they were crossing. The crystal-clear water danced in the air, throwing glorious rainbows toward them. He could see new ferns unfurling on the hillside, clinging to the rocks forming the waterfall.

"Just imagine everything we're going to see!" Frances cried, clapping her hands with delight.

Moses could feel Felicia watching him. He didn't have to wait long to know what she was thinking.

"You've never had a time when you weren't working, have you, Daddy?"

Moses had already considered that. "No, I guess I haven't, honey. I always worked hard as a slave. When your mama and I escaped the plantation, I worked in Philadelphia before I joined the Union Army." He thought back. "I suppose the time I was healing from having a musket ball lodged in my chest would count as not working, but I can't say it was enjoyable."

Frances looked at him sympathetically. "Mama told me about finding you in the wagon after Richmond burned at the end of the war. She didn't think you would live."

Moses grimaced. "No one did. The infection had set in badly."

"But Mama saved your life," Frances said proudly.

"She did indeed," Moses told her. He had barely any memory of the weeks that had passed before he came out of the infection stupor he had languished in. When he came to, he was no longer on the battlefield. Instead, he was in a comfortable bed in Thomas' Richmond home. "If it weren't for your mama, I wouldn't be here today."

"Neither would I," Felicia said. "You wouldn't have been in Memphis to save my life."

"That would have been a great tragedy," Moses responded. The conversation made him realize how much time he would be able to spend with the girls during their trip. The thought warmed and delighted him and made it easier to push his feelings about Louisiana to the back of his mind.

It was evening before Reggie knocked on their door.

Moses opened it and beckoned the porter inside. "Please come in, Reggie."

"Do you need anything, sir?"

"Please call me Moses."

"That ain't allowed, sir."

Moses glanced at the girls. "Are you two going to tell anyone?" When they shook their heads, he turned back to the anxious porter. "I won't tell anyone either," he promised. He waved a hand toward the empty chair next to their small table. "Have a seat."

Reggie's eyes widened as he shook his head.

Moses smiled. "Reggie, you're going to be taking care of us for seven days. I can accept that you're doing your job, but that doesn't mean we can't know each other as men."

Reggie eyed him skeptically. "I'm a porter. You own a plantation, sir."

Moses shrugged. "I was lucky. That doesn't make me special."

"Not what I hear, sir. Cromwell Plantation sounds like a special place."

"Oh, the plantation is special," Moses agreed. He decided further explanation was necessary. "Turns out my wife, Rose, who was a slave on Cromwell until she escaped with me, is also Thomas Cromwell's half-sister. His father raped Rose's mama. She was born a twin, but her brother came out white, so they sold him away from the plantation to hide what had been done. It wasn't until the war that everyone discovered the truth, and Rose was reunited with her twin. Thomas Cromwell changed his thinking about slavery and blacks during the war. One of the results was him offering me half-ownership in the plantation."

Reggie's mouth hung open while he listened. "I see..." he managed. "That's quite a story."

"It is," Moses agreed. "So you see, I could just as easily be struggling to figure out how to live as a freedman. I'm probably too big to fit into any of the porter uniforms, so I couldn't have even had this job."

"You have a point there, s--," Reggie cleared his throat. "Moses."

Moses grinned. "Thank you." He remembered their earlier conversation. "You told me you have some friends who work at Cromwell. Who are they?"

Reggie shrugged. "You probably don't know 'em."

Moses smiled. "I know every man who works on the plantation, Reggie. I also know their wives and their children. My wife, Rose, teaches all of them."

Reggie's eyes widened. "For real?"

Moses nodded. "Tell me who they are."

"Gerald Fisher and Martin Kingston."

"Fine men," Moses replied. "They came looking for jobs the year after the war. They've been at Cromwell ever since. Between the two of them they have five children. Except for Danny, the youngest boy, my wife has all of them in school."

Reggie laughed. "It makes me real happy to hear that!"

Felicia jumped in. "My mama also has a school for all the white children, too. We used to be students together; until the Virginia State Board of Education decided blacks and whites couldn't be in the same school," she said angrily. "Anyway, every fall we have a huge harvest festival. All the plantation families and all the white families in the area come together for a day of fun and celebration."

Reggie was silent for a long moment. "That don't happen nowhere else in this country," he said flatly.

"Actually, that's not true," Moses informed him. "There's a plantation down in Louisiana that runs the same way. It's a place called…" He stopped talking when he saw terror come to life in Reggie's eyes. "What's wrong?"

Reggie shook his head and narrowed his lips. He stood abruptly. "I got work to do, sir."

Moses held up a hand. "You're safe here, Reggie." His suspicions that the porter had a story worth telling swelled into a deep knowing. "I take it you come from Louisiana?" Reggie didn't answer, but the look on his face was all the confirmation Moses needed. "Talking about it might help."

Reggie scowled. "Talking don't change nothin', Moses."

"I agree," Moses said. "I didn't say it would change things. Nothing can change what happened to you." He thought back to the first time he had told Old Sarah and Rose about his early life before he ended up at Cromwell. "Sometimes saying it to someone can help lighten the load, though."

Reggie sank back down in the chair and glanced at the girls with apprehension.

"We know about hard things," Felicia said, walking over to put a hand on his shoulder. "I watched my parents be murdered in the Memphis Riot seven years ago." Her voice faltered. "I will never forget watching the blood pool under their bodies. Moses is my daddy now. He saved me that day and brought me to the plantation."

Moses would never feel anything but horror when his daughter talked about that day. He could recall every minute of it as clearly as she could.

Frances spoke next. "I know I'm white, but I know hard things too. My whole family died from the flu four years ago and I ended up in an orphanage. I figured I'd be there until I was old enough to leave, but my mama adopted me and gave me a new life."

Reggie's eyes had softened with sympathy as he listened to the girls. He spoke to Felicia first. "I'm real sorry 'bout your parents, Felicia." He turned to Frances next. "Who's your mama?"

Frances smiled. "Dr. Carrie Wallington. That's her name now. She's the only daughter of Thomas Cromwell, who owns the other half of the plantation. Her first husband, Robert Borden, was murdered by the KKK when he was trying to save Amber's life."

"Amber is black," Moses told him. "She trains horses at Cromwell Stables. She and Robert were very close. When the KKK attacked the plantation one night, Robert dove in front of a bullet meant for her."

Reggie was obviously trying to absorb what he was hearing. "I guess everybody goes through hard times," he muttered.

"We all have our stories," Moses agreed. It was up to Reggie whether he wanted to reveal what put such terror in his eyes.

Silence fell on the car. The only sounds were the clacking of the wheels against the tracks and the sizzle of the candlelit lanterns.

"I come…from…Louisiana," Reggie said in a halting voice. "From a place called Angola Plantation."

Moses stiffened, remembering what Matthew had told him.

"Before that, I was a slave on another plantation," Reggie continued. "I ran away the first year of the war and went north. I ended up in the army and fought until the end." His voice trailed away.

Moses knew he was remembering all the death and suffering he'd seen. There wasn't a day that went by when the memories didn't haunt his thoughts. His early mornings on the porch helped him deal with them.

No one spoke.

Reggie finally cleared his throat and continued. "I wanted to go back to Louisiana after the war. I never wanted to be cold again, and I figured things would be better since the war was over. I wanted some of the land they talked about giving to black men. I was gonna find me a wife and start a new life." His voice grew bitter. "There was no new life waitin'. I weren't home more than a month or so when I got thrown in jail."

"For what?" Moses asked.

"Standin' on a corner for too long," Reggie growled. "I was waitin' for a friend who wanted me to work for him. I reckon I was there for 'bout five minutes. The next thing I knew, I was in jail. I didn't have no money to pay bail and the fines, so they shipped me off to prison."

"The Louisiana State Penitentiary?" Moses asked.

Reggie nodded, his glazed eyes lost in his memories. "Weren't there for more than a handful of days though.

Next thing I knew, I been thrown in a wagon and taken to Angola Plantation to work in the fields."

Moses tightened with anger. "I heard no one leaves that place."

"Most don't," Reggie agreed. "Course, most just die there. I thought bein' a slave on my first plantation was bad, but this was worse. I can't remember a day when I didn't get the lash. I watched men beat to death out in the fields. I watched them die from hunger and thirst on real hot days."

"That's terrible!" Felicia cried, her features twisted with anguish.

Reggie looked at her, almost as if he was surprised she was there.

"How did you get away?" Moses asked, his hands tightened into fists.

"I'm not sure," Reggie admitted. "One day we were out workin' in the fields until it was dark. The man beside me was sick. He tried to work, but it weren't good enough for them. The prison guard rode up and... shot him. He told us it was an example so we would work harder." Reggie choked back tears. "I guess I snapped. I took off runnin' into the woods. I figured they would shoot me while I ran, but I didn't care anymore. Being shot was better than how I be livin'." He shrugged. "I heard some guns go off, but none of them got me."

Tears streaked down Frances' cheeks. "I'm so sorry," she whispered.

Reggie descended again into his memories. "I don't know how long I ran," he whispered. "I just ran. I kinda remember sloshing through bogs. I could feel snakes whipping up against me, but nothin' bit me. The mosquitoes ate me up pretty good, but I didn't know it till later. I just ran. Ain't nobody ever got away from Angola, so I knew I was gonna die, but at least I was runnin'." He paused. "Every time I done thought about stoppin', I thought about Gil. He was the man next to me that got shot." His voice faltered again. "He was my friend."

"How long did you run?" Felicia asked.

Reggie grimaced. "Until I ran into the Mississippi River. I don't remember nothin' about it, but I reckon I jumped into that water. I don't know how long I swam. I kinda remember grabbin' on to somethin'. The next thing I knew, I was bumpin' up against the shore, holdin' onto a big log. I got out and kept runnin'."

"How was that even possible?" Frances asked breathlessly. "How could you keep running?"

"Don't really know. Fear be a powerful thing. Freedom, too. I knew I weren't going back to that place. I ran till I passed out. When I woke up the next day, I was lying beside a rotten old log in a pool of water. Couldn't hardly open my eyes 'cause of all the mosquito bites. My body were cut up pretty bad, but I didn't have no bullets in me." He took a deep breath. "Since I weren't dead yet, I kept goin'. Found some fresh water that I dunked my head in till my eyes opened up enough to see. I didn't have no idea where I was, or where I was goin', so I just kept heading north. I mostly traveled at night, till I figured I be far enough from Angola that they couldn't catch me."

"How long was that?" Moses asked, sickened by what he was hearing.

"Couple weeks," Reggie said. "I figured they got a long reach down there. One night, when I be followin' some train tracks, I heard somebody talkin' about being in Arkansas. That's why I started traveling some during the day, but I kept walkin' at night too. I done figured the whole South weren't no place for any black man to be. I reckon I walked eighteen hours a day. I stayed away from towns 'cause I figured they be lookin' for more black men to put in jail. I weren't stoppin' until I got to Chicago."

"How long did that take you?" Frances asked.

"'Bout four weeks," Reggie stated.

Moses stared at him. "You walked from Louisiana to Chicago in *four weeks*?"

"Didn't figure I be safe until I got to Chicago," Reggie replied. "I been told it was about nine hundred miles. You can cover a lot of miles in eighteen hours a day. All I wanted was to get out of the South. I have family in Chicago. They'd told me I was crazy to go back to Louisiana. They were right."

"When was this?" Moses asked.

"I been livin' in Chicago for five years." Reggie looked around him. "Well, I'm not really livin' there anymore. I pretty much live on one of the trains since I started workin' for the railroads."

"Do you like it?" Felicia asked.

Reggie considered the question. "It's better than prison," he replied. "It ain't all bad, but I got to admit it sometimes feels like bein' a slave again. Ain't many days I don't work. I got a little cubicle I sleep in at night for about six hours, and then I get up and keep workin'. I don't get paid much, and I don't like being called George, but things could be a lot worse. Ain't nobody beatin' me. I got food and a place to sleep." He stared at his reflection in the window for several minutes. "I know most black men be jealous of what I do. I admit I like seein' the country, but I done seen it a lot in the last few years. I'd kinda like to stay home for a while, but I know I shouldn't complain."

"What would make it better for you?" Felicia asked.

Reggie stared at her. "Make what better?"

"This job."

Reggie glanced at Moses with a question in his eyes, but Felicia saw it.

"I'm going to be a businesswoman, Reggie. I'm going to own many businesses. I want to employ our people and give them an opportunity. I have to make money, but I want to be fair, and I want them to enjoy working for me."

Reggie's eyes widened again. "I see..."

"Believe her," Moses advised him. "This young lady is going to do things you and I could never have dreamed when we were her age."

Reggie licked his lips and answered her question. "I'd like to be treated like a human being, Felicia. I'd like to be seen as a man, not just a way to make money. I'd like to be told I'm doin' a good job, and I want to earn more money," he added firmly. "I work hard. I know how much money the railroads make. All the porters should make more money."

Felicia listened intently. "What else?"

Reggie cocked his head. "I shouldn't have to work so many hours a day. I'd like to have some time to be in Chicago. Don't have to be much, but everybody needs rest. Black men ain't no different. And I want my name. Ain't none of the porters really be named George. We ought to have our names."

"I agree," Felicia said. "Thank you."

Moses had listened to Reggie's story with a sick feeling. "Do you know what it's like in Louisiana now?"

Reggie's face settled into rigid lines. "Ain't no black man oughta step foot in that state. It be just about as dangerous for any white man who don't think the way the

KKK does. They may have lost the war, but they still believe they got the right to run their state any way they want to. That includes puttin' as many black men as they can back into slavery, even if they don't call it that." He took a closer look at Moses. "Why you askin'?"

Moses took a deep breath. "I have friends headed there now to try to make things better in Colfax. They should be getting there soon."

Reggie shook his head. "That ain't good, Moses. I been hearin' some things 'bout what be goin' on down there. Your friends could be walkin' into a real mess."

Moses was quite certain he was right.

Chapter Seven

April 2, 1873

Matthew and Anthony stepped down from the steamboat onto the gangplank that led to the landing snugged against the shoreline. The morning sun was high in the sky, illuminating a dark band of clouds on the horizon. A flock of pelicans skimmed the whitecaps on the Mississippi River in search of food. A bald eagle perched on a rotten branch of a nearby tree, its sharp eyes scanning the waters below.

Matthew breathed in the humid air, already missing the plantation. During the trip across the country, he had wished he could turn around and go back to Cromwell. His belief that Willie Calhoun needed his help kept him moving forward.

"It's got to be eighty degrees," Anthony said, wiping his forehead with a handkerchief. He glanced around as they walked onto the landing, their luggage in hand.

"At least," Matthew agreed. "If you're hot now, you don't want to be here in the summer. The heat is intense, but the humidity makes you feel like you're breathing underwater." When Anthony looked at him with a questioning expression, Matthew realized he hadn't hidden the distaste in his voice.

Anthony frowned. "When was your last time here?"

"During the New Orleans riot, seven years ago." Matthew said, trying to block the images swarming his mind. He hadn't known Anthony then but was sure Carrie had told him about the massacre.

"Carrie said it was bad," Anthony said carefully.

Bad was not the word Matthew would use. *Horrifying. Sickening. Wrong.* "Close to a hundred and fifty peaceful black protestors were murdered." He pressed his lips closed again. Saying the words turned the images into a full onslaught to his mind. He could hear the screams. See the blood. Feel the fear that had almost swallowed him.

"You were lucky to get out alive."

Matthew nodded, blinking his eyes against the memories. When he left Louisiana seven years ago, he vowed to never return. It took all he had not to turn around and climb back onto the steamboat. "Can we change the subject?" he asked abruptly.

"Of course," Anthony replied, sympathy shining in his eyes. "Where are we going first?"

Matthew was glad to have something else to think about. "Willie Calhoun's plantation, although I'm not sure he's even there. There wasn't time to get a letter to him, even if I knew for certain where to send it. We may have to go downriver to New Orleans. Since he's a legislator, he may be in the city, but since we're passing this area I think we should check to see if he's home."

As they strode to the top of the landing, Anthony took in the lush greenery surrounding them. "The plantation is beautiful, but I'm not sure I've ever seen anything quite like this."

A thick forest, as far as they could see, spread along the bank of the river. Towering cottonwoods, hackberry, pecan, elm, and willow created a wall of greenery that pulsed with life. The groundcover was virtually impenetrable, but you could feel the eyes of

animals peeking out to identify the intrusion.

"The almost tropical climate here creates a different reality," Matthew agreed. He could remember the admiration he had felt for the state when he first arrived; before his feelings had morphed into disgust and fear. He could acknowledge the beauty, but admiration had dissolved into horror. At some level, he knew it wasn't fair to the good people that inhabited the state, but his emotions made little room for reason.

Matthew looked back at the Mississippi River, its brown waters proof of the spring rains that had filled it with runoff. He turned away, vivid memories threatening to overwhelm him once more. He had spent years trying to forget the horrifying night he had spent in the river after the Sultana exploded into flames, days after the end of the war.

Matthew had thought the worst of the danger was over when the war ended, but what he had experienced that night was far worse than what he'd seen during the war. The steamboat Sultana had sunk into the frigid waters, killing more than eleven hundred people, most of them Union soldiers eager to return home to family and loved ones. They had never made it.

The young man he had tried to save had died in his arms as he clung to a floating log, swept along by a rapid current.

Matthew ground his teeth.

What was he doing in Louisiana? What was he doing on the Mississippi River?

"How do we get to the plantation?"

Matthew was again glad when Anthony offered him a distraction. He could also admit how thankful he was that Anthony had joined him. He felt guilty about Anthony leaving Carrie and the children, but until he'd gotten here, he hadn't realized exactly how much being back in Louisiana would impact him. Having Anthony at his side gave him the courage to do what he'd come to do.

"Horseback. It's not easy to get to Colfax from the river, but it's our only option."

"How far is it?"

"About eighty-five miles."

Anthony stared at him. "Eighty-five miles?" he asked. "I thought the plantation was along the river?"

"The Red River," Matthew corrected. "Not the Mississippi. Grant Parish is close to the center of the state. You can reach New Orleans on the Red River but coming by train made things more complicated. The Mississippi was our only choice."

Anthony stared off into the distance and shrugged. "It's not like we're on a timetable. We're here until we've done what we came to do. How long will it take to get there?"

"Should take two long days, but if it rains it's going to slow things down," Matthew admitted. "It's been eight years since the end of the war, but Louisiana was hit hard by Union battles and occupation. There's a lot of poverty, and they're struggling to rebuild their infrastructure."

Anthony nodded thoughtfully. "Which makes the whole political situation more dangerous. People are desperate."

"Both of those things are true," Matthew agreed. They stepped out into the small area surrounding the Concord landing. "Let's find some horses." It was already late morning, but he was eager to get to Colfax and accomplish what they had come for. He wanted to go home.

Two days later, late in the afternoon, they rode into the area of Grant Parish known as Colfax. Matthew frowned as they entered a clearing around the old stables that had been converted into the Parish courthouse. He thought about what he'd learned from the letters Willie Calhoun had sent Thomas and Abby.

Willie had given a large part of his plantation to the freed slaves who had worked for him before the war. He went one step further and allowed the men to have a political voice by forming a new parish. The freedmen had named it Grant Parish, in honor of President Ulysses S. Grant, and they had named the town Colfax, in honor of Vice President Schuyler M. Colfax.

Thomas had endured massive amounts of resentment from what he had done with Cromwell, but the growth of white supremacy in Louisiana had taken the hatred to new levels. Combined with the explosive nature of Louisiana politics, and the things that had already happened in Colfax, it was a dangerous place.

Matthew wasn't prepared for what he saw when they arrived at the courthouse. The old stables sat on the edge of one of the plantation fields. Cotton plants were sending out fresh, green shoots, with long rows stretching out until the field reached a thick bank of trees in the distance.

Dozens of black people were gathered around the courthouse. Judging by the smell of cooking meat and the smoke of campfires, they were evidently living there.

"They're mostly women and children," Anthony observed.

Matthew rode closer, wondering what their presence would provoke.

Two men noticed them, sprang into saddles, and rode forward, their bodies rigid and defiant, their hands resting on the pistols strapped to their waists.

Not wanting to appear threatening, Matthew and Anthony pulled their horses to a stop.

"Good afternoon," Matthew said when the strangers approached. One man was tall, with a narrow face, and hard dark eyes. The other was shorter and rounder, but with the same hard, suspicious eyes.

"What you want?" the taller man said.

"We're looking for Willie Calhoun," Matthew said pleasantly.

Neither man looked impressed. Their faces remained blank as they stared at the intruders.

"Why?" the shorter man barked.

Matthew decided the absolute truth was his best course of action. "My name is Matthew Justin. I'm from Richmond, Virginia. Mr. Calhoun has been writing to Thomas Cromwell, the owner of the plantation I live on. Mr. Calhoun said you're having some trouble down here and asked Mr. Cromwell if he would visit. We decided I would be the one to come." He waved a hand toward Anthony. "This is Anthony Wallington. Mr. Cromwell's son-in-law. He decided to join me."

"Why?" the shorter man asked again, his eyes intense and probing, almost as if he could see into their minds.

"Because we've heard there's been a lot of trouble," Matthew responded. "I didn't want to come alone."

The tall man cocked his head. "What you figure you can do down here, Mr. Justin?"

Matthew met his eyes evenly. "I'm a newspaper reporter and a writer. I thought it might help Mr. Calhoun, and the rest of you, if the entire country became more aware of your situation. I want to tell the story of what's happening here."

The shorter man seemed to know only one word. "Why?"

It was a fair question. These men had every reason to be suspicious. "Because I know what it's like down here," Matthew replied. "I was in New Orleans in 1866, when so many of your people were killed in the massacre. I almost died too. I made sure the country knew the truth of what happened."

The shorter man found more words. "Maybe so, but it didn't make a difference. They still out to kill us all."

Matthew knew that was probably true. "We've had KKK attacks at Cromwell Plantation too. The whites in the area don't appreciate that the black workers on the plantation are treated fairly. They especially hate that Mr. Cromwell gave a large portion of the plantation to a group of freed slaves who came to work after the war ended. They hated it even more when he gave half the plantation to a man who was once his slave. Just last year, members of the Klan burned down the barn at Cromwell Stables. Now, the men guard the plantation every night."

The shorter man eyed him for a long moment before his rigid shoulders relaxed. "My name is Alford." He pointed to the other man. "This tall drink of water be Ronnie."

"It's a pleasure to meet you," Matthew said.

"Same here," Anthony added. "Why is everyone camping around the courthouse?"

Alford scowled. "It's our best chance of keeping the women and children safe. The Klan and the other whites intent on getting rid of us be on a killing spree. Just yesterday, a friend of mine named Jesse was working out in his front yard. His wife and son were with him. A group of white men rode up and shot him in the head. They laughed and rode off." His eyes glittered with anger and fear. "They be raping our women and terrorizing our children. Ain't a man around here who don't figure he gonna die soon."

Matthew flinched. He could well imagine the horror they were feeling. "What's being done to help you?" he demanded. "President Grant passed laws to keep this from happening."

Ronnie shrugged, his shoulders slumped with fatigue. "There be people tryin', but the Klan be killin' them too. The state don't seem to care too much about that. You heard about the sheriff and the judge that got shot here in the parish?"

Matthew's gut tightened. "I don't know much. Calhoun mentioned it in one of his letters."

"The Klan set their house on fire back about eighteen months ago. The judge is a good man. Sheriff White was too, but the folks down in New Orleans took his office away 'cause the white folks around here didn't like what he was doin'. The Klan managed to get him out of office just for wanting to treat us fairly. Both of them got their share of death threats. They was livin' together 'cause they thought it be safer," Ronnie explained.

"Put them in one place to be killed," Alford said wearily.

"They both died?" Anthony asked.

"No," Ronnie replied. "A couple of the men around here were hidin' in the woods so they could watch. They saw a group of 'bout fifty men set the house on fire and aim their rifles at the windows so no one could escape. They intended for them to cook inside that house," he said angrily. "Sheriff White ran out the front door to escape the fire..."

Alford took over the recitation when Ronnie's voice faltered. "When Sheriff White opened the door, he done came face-to-face with Deputy Sheriff Nash. That man be real bad news. Nash shot him with both barrels of his gun," he said bitterly. "White didn't stand a chance."

Matthew gritted his teeth. He wished he could end this conversation, but he'd come looking for the truth. He couldn't tell the story without knowing it. "And the judge?"

"A bunch of that mob started shootin'," Alford replied. "The judge got shot up pretty bad. My friends thought he died too, 'cause he fell down and didn't move again. After the attack, my friends went deeper into the woods so they ain't got caught, so they didn't see him get up."

"Turns out the judge weren't dead," Ronnie said. "He just pretended to be so they would leave. He managed to crawl through the house. He climbed out a back window right before the roof collapsed. He was all shot up, but he got through them woods somehow. Some friends bandaged him up and took him in. When he could, the judge took a boat down to New Orleans. When he got there he done took out warrants against a bunch of the men in that mob. He'd seen 'em and knew who they was."

Matthew didn't want to ask the next question because he was certain he wouldn't like the answer. "What happened to the murderers?"

"Things got real complicated," Alford said. "The government people down in New Orleans didn't want to come up here and arrest 'em 'cause they figured it gonna make things worse here in the parish. Instead, they sent Ward a whole bunch of new rifles but told him not to do anything till they said so." His expression revealed his opinion of the politician's actions. "New rifles ain't gonna do no good unless you can use 'em."

Matthew thought of what he'd read. "William Ward is the head of the county militia, isn't he?"

Ronnie's eyes glistened with helpless fury. "He is...not that it means nothin'," he said bitterly. "Them folks down in New Orleans don't figure a bunch of black men arrestin' the white men around here gonna help calm things down."

"Surely they did something." Anthony protested.

Matthew listened closely. The judge and sheriff were both white. Was the government allowing murder as long as the victim was a Republican of *any* color?

"Ward did somethin'," Ronnie said. "He weren't gonna sit around until Governor Warmouth gave him permission. He went right ahead and arrested them eight men. He put 'em under guard and told a federal marshal to come take 'em on down to New Orleans."

Matthew listened with fascination. Ward was an incredibly courageous man. "What happened?"

Alford sighed. "It's a long story, Mr. Justin. Ward did his best, but there ain't a court in Louisiana that was gonna punish them murderers. The governor ended the militia and told Ward he ain't' got no power anymore. He also took back the guns."

Matthew stared at him. "The murderers got off?"

"And Nash is still our sheriff," Ronnie growled. "Some jury down in New Orleans decided there weren't enough evidence to bring charges, so they let him come on back up here. Don't seem to matter none that he's a murderer."

Anthony shook his head with disbelief. "They really made him sheriff again?"

Both men nodded, their faces twisted with disgust.

"Ain't nothin' but a losin' battle 'round here," Ronnie said.

Matthew's mind was whirling. "I'm hoping what I write will improve things for you." Even as he said the words, he didn't truly believe them.

Ronnie sighed. "We appreciate that, Mr. Justin, but I figure it be too late."

Matthew's gut tightened at the expression on Ronnie's face. "Why?"

"Things ain't been good all along," Ronnie explained.

"But they be gettin' worse," Alford added. "What did Mr. Calhoun tell you folks 'bout what be happenin' down here?"

Matthew considered his answer. Once he'd decided to come, he'd done his research. "I know Louisiana is a hotbed of political nonsense," he said. "I know the election in 1868 was rife with violence and fraud, but the one last year was even worse."

Anthony had done his research too. "There was a lot of dispute over who your governor was going to be last year. It seems the voters elected the Democrat, John McEnery, to office. That is, until the voting board divided and decided that because of the obvious fraud, William Kellogg actually won the election. A Republican judge down in New Orleans ruled that the Republican legislature should be seated, so Governor Kellogg is in office."

"That's the truth," Alford stated. "But it means nothin' to the Democrats. They hate anyone that voted Republican even more than they did already." Alford looked around him. "I used to be a slave right here. Willie Calhoun's daddy weren't nothing like him. He didn't have no problem using the whip. He treated us slaves real poorly. He got tired of the way things be goin' in the country right before the war, so he took off for Europe and done gave everything to Mr. Calhoun. Willie Calhoun be a good man," he said firmly. "He be tryin' to make things right for us, but he be losin'."

"He did a real fine thing four years ago," Ronnie added. "He led a big group of us to the votin' place. First time black men got to vote. The ballot box was at a store owned by Mr. Hooe." His eyes narrowed. "Mr. Hooe already told us that if we voted Republican, he was gonna make sure we got whipped by the Klan and the Knights." Ronnie's face twisted. "We knew it was true, so Mr. Calhoun got that ballot box moved to another store that be owned by a Republican. We went right in and voted. Mr. Calhoun even brought in a hundred fifty votes from men on the plantation who couldn't get to the store. When them votes be counted, the Republicans had over three hundred votes. The Democrats ain't had but thirty-nine."

"Not that it mattered," Alford scoffed.

"What happened?" Matthew asked.

"When Sheriff Taylor carried it here to the courthouse, a group of whites grabbed the ballot box. They threw it right into the Red River," Ronnie told them. "Then they arrested Mr. Calhoun and charged him with election fraud. Without no ballot box, they said the Republicans ain't won nothin'. Them Democrats claimed they won and took office."

Matthew scowled. This was a part of the story he didn't know. "What happened to Mr. Calhoun?"

"They decided down in New Orleans that he might be guilty and told him he had to have a trial," Alford replied. "He thought they was gonna kill him, but they didn't. He paid a thousand-dollar fine and got to come home. A bunch of us kept watch on his house for a long while. I reckon that thousand dollars saved him."

Matthew could tell by the look on his face that Alford couldn't imagine being able to pay one thousand dollars for his freedom. Any black man who was arrested would be incarcerated in the Louisiana prison system, working as a slave somewhere in the state because they couldn't pay the fines.

"It's what he did next that's got white folks 'round here so riled up," Ronnie said. "He decided that the only way our votes gonna count is if we had our own parish. So, he up and created one on his plantation." He looked around. "We standin' in it right now."

"Calhoun was already a member of the Louisiana House of Representatives?" Anthony asked keenly.

Ronnie smiled tightly. "Yep. Worked right well for him, too. When he formed Grant Parish, they had to move the election fraud case over to our courthouse. Weren't too long 'fore it got dismissed." He waved his hand toward the sturdy brick building behind him. "His daddy's slaves built this here stables. Now it's our courthouse," he said proudly. His pride dimmed as quickly as it had appeared. "At least for today."

Matthew looked over Ronnie's shoulder at the people huddled around cooking fires. Without exception, every eye was trained on them. The whitewashed, one-story brick courthouse was about seventy-five feet long by twenty-five feet wide. He knew from what he'd read that the bricks had been made from the soil of the Red River, by the same slaves that had constructed the building. The roof consisted of overlapping cypress shingles. The short side of the building faced the levee that separated the land from the river. A grassy field that eventually joined the cotton fields surrounded the building.

The fear in the air was as palpable as the smoke spiraling upward into the late afternoon sky.

"Why is everyone here, Ronnie?" Matthew wanted to understand why these people believed the courthouse was their refuge.

Ronnie glanced over his shoulder before he turned back, a grave expression etching lines in his narrow face. "Only place they feel safe," he said. He looked at Matthew with narrowed eyes. "You picked a real dangerous time to come here, Mr. Justin. The Democrats tried to steal the last election 'round here. We won, but they went right on and installed their officers right here in our courthouse. Last week, we broke into the courthouse and took everythin' back. The Republicans we rightly elected came in and took oaths of office." He spat onto the dusty ground. "The Democrats ain't real happy about it."

Alford chuckled. "You shoulda seen the look on their faces that mornin' when they rode up and saw us guardin' the courthouse."

Matthew tightened, wondering exactly what he and Anthony had ridden into the middle of. "Just how unhappy are they?" he asked carefully.

Alford gave the answer. "They done sent men to take it back, but we was ready for 'em. We called in everyone we could. They wasn't gonna leave their families behind, so their wives and children came with 'em. When them white fellas arrived a few mornings ago to take things back, they realized real quick that they be outnumbered." He smiled briefly. "They turned and rode away."

Matthew knew they would be back.

Ronnie confirmed it. "It's just a matter of time 'fore they get serious 'bout things," he said. "There done been a few small fights, but we got word Sheriff Nash is puttin' together enough men to come take control."

"When?" Matthew asked.

Ronnie shrugged. "Don't rightly know. We figure it gonna be real soon. We ain't gonna leave the courthouse until we know we beat them back."

Anthony's face was growing more concerned. "Do you have the arms and ammunition to do that?"

Ronnie looked defiant for a moment, but his eyes dropped. "Not enough," he admitted. "When the governor got rid of the militia, he took back the good guns we had. Most of our men got some kind of gun, but there ain't that many bullets."

Matthew sucked in his breath. From the look on Ronnie's face, he was sure the man expected an attack very soon. Matthew was also certain the men Nash was gathering would mostly be Confederate veterans. They were well-trained, and would have much better weapons.

"They was here yesterday," Alford said.

"Who was here?" Matthew demanded. It made him sick to realize he'd put Anthony into yet another dangerous situation. He'd known there was risk involved in their trip, but he hadn't anticipated this.

"The one who showed up was Charles Smith. He be a white Republican parish official. A group of them Democrats sent a proposal to us and had him bring it."

"What did it say?" Matthew was trying to slow his heartbeat. He could feel Anthony glancing over his shoulder periodically, watching for Nash's threatened posse to attack from the woods.

Alford curled his lip with disdain. "Oh, they gave us a promise of peace." His tone of voice clearly revealed how he felt about the supposed oath. "They said the armed forces in Grant Parish, both black and white, would disband. Anybody who done got driven from their homes would be able to return without worryin' 'bout what might happen." His disdain deepened. "They said that in the future, everybody just won't talk 'bout politics no more."

"And everybody gonna be more friendly from now on," Ronnie finished sarcastically.

Matthew understood their skepticism, but also knew there was more to the story. "In exchange for what?"

Ronnie barked out a hoarse laugh. "In exchange for the surrender and decapitation of the Republican Party," he said carefully. "That's how they said it."

Matthew tried to process what he was hearing. The Democrats couldn't possibly believe their offer would be accepted.

"That ain't all," Alford continued. "Mr. Rutland be one of the Klan 'round here. When we got into the courthouse last week, we found out there be some books missin', so one of the fellas took some deputies and went to Mr. Rutland's house to get 'em back."

"Rutland be a lawyer fella," Ronnie clarified. "He helped try to steal the election."

"What happened when they went to get the books?" Anthony asked.

Matthew could easily imagine many scenarios that wouldn't have gone well.

"Rutland and his family were gone," Alford said. "We heard they took off and hid in the woods when they found out we was comin'. They got in a boat and went upriver.

Our fellas tore up the house pretty good lookin' for the books," he said defiantly. "Rutland had it comin'."

Matthew couldn't say he blamed them, but he knew it was going to make the reprisal worse.

"Anyway," Alford continued. "Rutland, being a lawyer, put out an arrest warrant for the men who came into his house."

"He didn't stop there though," Ronnie said. "He went ahead and added Ward, a couple of other fellas, and Willie Calhoun."

"Was Calhoun there?" Matthew asked.

"Course not," Alford answered. "None of those four were anywhere near that house. Didn't stop Rutland from trying to get them thrown in jail, though. Anyway, when they brung their offer

yesterday, the promise of peace was only good if the men on the arrest warrant were turned over to them."

"Which wasn't going to happen," Anthony said.

"Nope," Ronnie agreed. "Everyone on that warrant, 'cept Mr. Calhoun, was right here. Our fellas wrote another letter right away, statin' they weren't gonna do nothin' like give those men up, but they promised peace if we would be left alone."

"Which didn't go over well?" Matthew guessed.

Ronnie's eyes glittered with rage. "It might've, but just when they was talkin' about it, we found out some of those men murdered Jesse in his front yard." His voice cracked with pain. "We known right away that their coming here weren't nothing but some kind of setup." He glanced behind him again. "You can't see everybody who be here. When word about Jesse got out last night, people started pourin' in. They figure they be safer here."

"How many?" Matthew asked.

"I reckon about four hundred be here right now," Alford offered.

Matthew examined the courthouse area again. In the waning daylight, the courthouse resembled a fort. Ward and his men held a strong, defensible position, but Matthew didn't know what kind of chance they had without adequate guns and ammunition. The courthouse could easily become a trap.

Ronnie took a glance at the sky and straightened in his saddle. "You're not safe here," he said roughly. It don't matter that you be white. They'll shoot you as quick as they'll shoot us. You came lookin' for Mr. Calhoun. I'm takin' you to his house." He turned his horse around. "Follow me."

Matthew exchanged a look with Anthony. They both knew staying at the courthouse wasn't safe. He doubted there was anywhere in Grant Parish that was actually safe, but leaving the courthouse should at least improve their odds.

Moments later, they were cantering down the road next to Ronnie.

Matthew could feel the darkness closing in around them. The sun was barely below the horizon, but the threat and fear floating in the air seemed to suck the light from the day. Even the birds had gone silent. The trees seemed to stretch out their branches to block their progress. On one side of the road, the dark, brackish water of a slow-flowing creek seemed to stand still. It was as if every living thing was afraid of drawing attention.

"How long before we reach Mr. Calhoun's?" Anthony called over the loud hoofbeats that shouted their presence.

Matthew knew they would be more concealed if they slowed to a stealthy walk, but everything in him screamed to get out of the open. He had no intention of slowing down.

"It won't be too long," Ronnie promised, but his voice was tense. "Keep your eyes open. They already be comin'. I don't reckon none of us gonna be able to leave the courthouse after tonight."

Matthew heard stark terror in the man's voice. He realized Ronnie was taking a grave risk to bring them to Willie Calhoun's. "Can you stay at the house with us tonight?"

Ronnie shook his head. "Ain't leavin' my family without me to take care of 'em. My wife and four children be back there."

Matthew said no more. All he could do was hope they would each reach their destination safely.

Chapter Eight

"Mama! Come look!" Russell cried. "There are two more foals!"

Carrie hurried into the barn. It was her favorite time of the year. There wasn't a day that went by when three or four foals weren't being born. She was glad they had fenced in more pastureland over the winter. As the foals were born, they were turned out into the pastures with their dams. The fields were lush with new growth, but they would continue supplementing with hay that had been stored through the winter. It wouldn't be long before it wasn't needed.

Spring had arrived.

Carrie put an arm over Russell's narrow shoulders as she peered over the stall door. "Twins!" she exclaimed with surprise. Sassy Lady, a tall bay mare, looked at her calmly as she licked one of her babies.

Carrie glanced around for Miles or Susan.

Susan appeared moments later, her eyes lined with fatigue. "Surprise!" she said lightly.

As far as Carrie knew, there had never been twins born on the plantation. They were extremely rare. When they were born, it was even rarer for both foals to survive. She looked closely at Susan's face. "Tough birth?"

"Actually no. Sassy Lady went into labor right after you left for the clinic. Miles and I were both here. The first one came fairly easily. When she started pushing again, we figured she was expelling the placenta. We were both shocked when we saw another hoof."

"Did you have to help her?" Carrie demanded.

Susan shook her head. "We thought we would, but it only took a few minutes for the second one to slip out." She didn't add that she assumed the second one would be dead. The awe on her face spoke volumes. "He was standing within about thirty minutes."

Carrie, understanding the dazed disbelief in Susan's voice, turned back to look at the foals. The bay colt and filly were small but seemed to be doing well. Their perfect confirmation was what she would have expected from Eclipse and Sassy Lady.

She opened the stall door and slipped inside. Sassy Lady gazed at her without alarm as Carrie eased up to the foals.

"Are they going to be alright, Mama?" Russell asked softly.

Carrie examined them. "Their eyes are clear, and their breathing is fine. Neither of them seems to be in distress." In the rare instance of twin horses, usually one of them would die within two weeks. In this case, she saw absolutely no reason for alarm.

"How come they're not out in the pasture with the other foals?" Russell asked in a worried voice.

Susan slipped her arm around him. "Twins are a very special thing, Russell. We're going to keep them here in the stall for a while, until we know they're healthy."

Russell appraised them for a moment. "They're not as big as the other foals."

"Sassy Lady couldn't carry two babies that were regular size," Carrie replied, stroking the mare's neck. She glanced at the feed bucket and saw the mare had eaten most of her thick bran mash. It would take a lot of feed to make certain Sassy Lady could nurse two foals.

Miles appeared at the stall door. "What you think of them miracle babies?"

"Are they miracles?" Russell asked breathlessly.

Miles shrugged. "I been working with horses my whole life, Russell. Ain't never seen twins born. I read somewhere one time that twins happen 'bout once in every ten thousand births."

"Wow!" Russell exclaimed. He leaned farther over the stall door. "They're really alright?"

"Yes," Carrie assured him. Someone would check on the foals every hour for the first couple weeks. If they indicated any kind of distress, Carrie had homeopathic treatments to help them. She hated what had happened with the epizootic the year before, but the homeopathic veterinary medicine book Janie had brought back from New York was a godsend. Carrie had pored over it during the winter months and was now much better prepared to care for every Cromwell horse.

Carrie stroked the foals for a moment before she slipped out of the stall. Unless there was trouble, the best thing was to leave the foals alone with their mama. She glanced at Russell. "Didn't you say this morning that you have something to show me?"

Russell's eyes glittered with excitement. "Yes. It's in my workshop!"

Miles appeared, leading No Regrets and Russell's gelding, Bridger. "When you was late gettin' home from the clinic, I went ahead and got them ready for you."

"Thank you," Carrie said warmly. "Jethro broke his arm today. I had to set and cast it."

Russell spun around. "Jethro? What happened? He was fine when I left to come home."

Jethro was Russell's best friend at school. The two twelve-year-olds, both of whom had lived under the Richmond bridge until they had found homes, were inseparable.

"He's going to be fine," Carrie assured him. "He was playing chase out on the school playground before he went home. Evidently, he missed seeing a big root. He landed on his arm and broke it, but it's a clean break. He'll have to be careful, but the cast will come off in about eight weeks. Even with the cast on, he'll be able to use his hand soon."

Russell frowned. "He was going to help me with my project."

"What project? Jethro can probably still help you, honey." She walked to Granite's stall, let him out, led No Regrets outside the barn, and mounted. She wanted to take Russell's mind off his friend. "Let's go see what you're doing."

Russell smiled, leapt onto his black gelding, and broke into an easy trot beside her. "I

want you to see it, Mama, but I sure wish Daddy was here to see it too." A frown dimmed his eyes.

"Me too," Carrie said brightly, pushing down the worry that threatened to overwhelm her every time she thought of her husband. She knew Frances was safe on a train making her way across the country. She had no idea what Anthony and Matthew were dealing with. He and Matthew should have arrived in Louisiana by now, but not knowing what was happening each moment was difficult. "He'll be excited to see it when he gets home."

Russell sighed. "We just don't know when that will be."

"No," Carrie agreed. She managed to grin. "On the other hand, I don't usually get to be the one who sees things first." She nudged No Regrets into a canter, laughing as Granite surged ahead, tossing his head with joy. "I'm going to take full advantage of it!"

Russell laughed and cantered up beside her. "I think Bridget will love it!"

Carrie turned to stare at him. "Your little sister will love it? What in the world have you made?"

"You'll see." Russell snapped his mouth closed and urged Bridger into a gallop.

Carrie laughed as No Regrets leapt forward to catch him.

Russell's workshop was attached to the tobacco-drying barn and snugged next to the sprawling greenhouse that produced food for the plantation and its neighbors year-round. Knowing their son's engineering ability, Anthony had helped him create the workshop. If Russell wasn't riding Bridger, he could be found right here.

Carrie stared at the contraption on the bench for several minutes before she cocked her head and circled it carefully. There were two-foot-long rectangular pieces of wood standing on end about fourteen inches apart. Russell had drilled holes in both boards and stuck a wooden dowel through them. Hanging on the wooden dowel between the boards was a round piece of wood that looked to be eight inches in diameter. Wire had been twisted to form circles about two inches wide, and then stuck at regular intervals into holes he had drilled on the round circle.

Try as she might, Carrie could not ascertain its purpose. She finally shook her head in defeat. "What is it?"

"I'll show you," Russell said eagerly. He stepped over to the bench, picked up a bar of soap, and shaved it carefully into a bowl of water. He added glycerin and alcohol and stirred it carefully, his face intense with concentration. He looked like a scientist in his laboratory.

Carrie watched with delight, imagining the wonderful things her son would do as he grew up.

Finally, Russell stepped over to his workbench, poured the soap solution into a metal pan, and placed it between the blocks of wood beneath the wheel.

Carrie regarded the process with fascination. She hadn't yet figured out what he was doing, but she loved the passion shining in Russell's eyes.

"Watch!" Russell commanded. He stepped behind the contraption and began to spin the wheel slowly, using the dowel to turn it. The metal rings dipped through the soapy liquid. As the first one returned to where he was waiting, he began to blow air toward the ring.

Carrie gasped as big bubbles floated from the rings. *One. Two. Three. Four.* As they hovered in the air, catching the glint of the sun from the window, she clapped with delight. "It's a bubble machine!"

Russell grinned broadly. "Yes!"

Carrie gazed at her son with admiration. "I'm truly impressed, Russell. Where did you come up with the idea?"

"Grandpa's library." Russell's eyes shone. "Grandpa already has books with lots of ideas, but Daddy subscribed to a magazine for engineers. I get lots of ideas from it. I read about the bubble machine in the last magazine." He rolled the wheel again, creating a new cascade of bubbles as he blew toward the wire rings. "Do you think Bridget will like it?" He paused. "I want to be a good big brother."

Carrie laughed. "You're the perfect big brother. Bridget will love it, but she won't be the only one. I predict everyone will want to make bubbles as soon as they see your machine!"

Russell laughed with delight. "I'll have Franklin bring it over to the house tonight in the wagon. It's not big, but it would be awkward to carry on a horse."

"I know what we'll be doing tonight," Carrie replied, imagining the fun everyone would have.

"Do you want to go ride some more, Mama?" Russell asked.

"Certainly," she replied as she stepped behind the machine he had created. "But not until I've blown some bubbles. I'm quite sure I won't get near it once everyone else sees it!"

After there were dozens of bubbles bobbing around the workshop, she remembered what her son had said earlier. "You said you wanted Jethro to help you with your project, but isn't it finished?"

"This one is," Russell agreed. "Jethro was going to help me cut more pieces of wood—especially the circles. I figure everyone at school will want one. I talked to Rose about it. She said I could teach everyone how to make them, so they can take them home to their families." His eyes shone.

"What a wonderful plan," Carrie cried. "Jethro will need a few days for the swelling in his arm to go down. After that, there's no reason he can't help you."

"You sure about this, Miss Rose?"

Rose didn't have to consider the question for long. "No."

Jeb, her driver and personal protector at the school, cocked his head, his dark eyes studying her. "Then why are we doing it?"

Rose knew it was a fair question. As the carriage rattled down the road, she pushed aside strands of dark hair and lifted her caramel-colored face to the warm sun. She had left the schoolhouse right after the last student. What she had really wanted to do was go home and be with her children on a beautiful spring afternoon.

What was compelling her to do what she was doing?

When she didn't answer, Jeb pushed a little harder. "I reckon it's a good thing Moses ain't here. If he knew what I was doing, he would never trust me to take care of you again. The thing is, I figure he would be right." His face twisted with worry. "We ain't there yet. We can still turn around and go right back home."

Rose, despite the fact that he was probably right, shook her head firmly. "No, we're going."

"Why?" Jeb persisted. "Rose, me and you been together for a long time. You know you can be honest with me."

"I know," Rose assured him quickly. "I don't know why we're doing it, Jeb," she admitted. That was as honest as she knew how to be.

Jeb shook his head. "You don't know why two black people be driving to the home of a Ku Klux Klan member?" His lips tightened. "Let me be the one to tell you it ain't a good idea. How do you know there ain't a whole bunch of the Klan waiting for us right now? It sure would go over good if the Klan killed the wife of the black man who owns half of Cromwell Plantation." His voice grew more tense. "If you're lucky, they won't do more before they kill you."

Rose felt the air leave her lungs. She wished she could refute what Jeb was saying, but she knew he might be speaking the truth. She thought of Moses, and then she thought of her four children.

What was she doing?

She made up her mind. They were going home.

"Jeb..." Her words trailed away as she fought to form them. As quickly as she had decided to go home, she had changed it.

"Yes, ma'am?" Jeb asked eagerly. He gathered up the reins so he could stop the horses and turn the carriage around.

"It's going to be alright," Rose finally managed. She didn't understand the compulsion that was driving her forward, but life had taught her to follow it when she felt it so strongly. "I can't tell you why we're going," she said softly. "I can only say I truly believe we're meant to."

Jeb sighed heavily. "I hate it when you say that, Rose. Ain't nothing I can do other than go along with it." He released the reins again, urging the horses into a faster trot. "We got to get there before we get to head home," he said resignedly.

Rose settled back in her seat, staring up at the oak and maple trees arching over the road. What had been green shadows a few weeks earlier were now brilliantly colored leaves fluttering in the breeze. Virginia bluebells and toadshade trilliums peeked out from the dense undergrowth. Not a single cloud appeared in the brilliantly blue sky.

She had been more than surprised when Rodney Rawlings had come to her after school with a message that his daddy would appreciate her coming to their house when she was done for the day. Rodney didn't know why she was being asked, but he didn't seem worried. Of course, he probably had no idea of his daddy's intentions. She didn't know how much he, or his younger brother Jimmy, knew about Rawlings' KKK activities.

Everything in her had wanted to say no, but instead she had agreed to go. She'd offered him a ride, but he'd made plans to go home with a friend. It was hard not to think he was being kept away to protect him from what might happen at his house.

Now, it was just she and Jeb traveling down a road that seemed suspiciously empty of other vehicles or horses. When they could see Rawlings' small house in the distance, Jeb looked back once more.

"It ain't too late to change your mind."

Rose shook her head firmly. She had come this far. She was going to see it through to the end. As they traveled the last quarter mile, she thought about what had happened on Christmas Eve a few months earlier. Moses and Anthony had ridden with her and Carrie when Carrie had been forced to provide medical care for Rawlings' youngest son, who had accidentally been shot by his big brother. Rose had helped as her assistant.

At the end of the awkward visit, Rawlings had surprised them by asking if Rodney could come to the school. While the black and white students could no longer be taught together, none of the area Klan members allowed their children to attend the school.

Nevertheless, Rose had agreed, and now Rodney was a student. His accomplishments proved his mother, Kathy, had done a good job teaching him at home. He was eager to learn and always did more than he was asked.

Her thoughts were interrupted when the carriage rolled to a stop in front of the wooden gate. The small white house looked worn and tired, much different in broad daylight than it had that fateful night.

Kathy Rawlings stepped out onto the porch the moment the carriage stopped. Her warm, welcoming smile did much to put Rose at ease. She wouldn't look so friendly if she knew her husband was going to kill her, would she?

"Your driver can pull the carriage around back," Kathy called. "There's a chair under the big oak tree. I put some tea and a fresh loaf of bread out there for him."

"Thank you," Rose responded. She wished she could haul Jeb into the house with her, but if she was going to believe she was meant to be here, she wouldn't need his protection. She pushed aside the suspicion about having the carriage pulled into the backyard so that no one would see what happened. She forced herself to smile into Jeb's protesting eyes. "It's alright. I will be fine." She hoped they both would be.

"You've had some foolish ideas," Jeb muttered, his eyes blazing with worry. "I figure one be at the top of the list of them ideas."

In spite of Rose's own fears, she laughed. "Go enjoy the tea and bread. We can't stay very long if we're going to be home before dark."

Rose climbed down from the carriage and opened the gate. "Hello, Mrs. Rawlings."

Kathy held the door open for her. "Thank you for coming, Mrs. Samuels. I'm certain you're wondering why you're here."

Rose saw no reason to not be honest. "I was surprised when I got the invitation. Is everything alright?"

"Yes," Kathy assured her. "Conrad will be here soon."

That solved one mystery for Rose. She'd never heard the man called anything but Rawlings. Knowing his first name somehow made him more human. Until she remembered he was a Klan member...

The clump of boots on the steps confirmed Kathy's statement. Rose fought to keep her breathing steady. Kathy's warm welcome could well be a cover for a sinister KKK plan. Or perhaps the woman had no knowledge of what her husband was involved in.

Only time would tell if she had made a very foolish decision.

Just as Carrie predicted, the bubble machine was a huge hit.

Russell set it up on the porch and watched proudly as everyone took a turn. Laughter and cries of delight rang through the air.

Annie pushed through the front door, her face a mixture of curiosity and puzzlement. "How does that thing work?" she demanded.

Russell explained it to her, demonstrating as he talked. "Do you want to try it?"

Annie moved forward eagerly.

"Just roll the wire rings through the soapy water," Russell instructed. "Then blow."

Annie lowered her stout frame enough to put her mouth close to the rings. "My Miles done tell me I got lots of hot air. I reckon that be enough to blow some bubbles."

Russell giggled but stopped quickly when Annie shot a warning glare his way. "Yes, ma'am," he said solemnly.

Annie took a deep breath and blew through the first ring. Her eyes widened with disbelief when a stream of small bubbles flowed into the air. "Would you look at that!"

Russell clapped his hands. "You've got it! Now with the next one, blow slowly. The slower you blow, the bigger the bubble will be."

Annie shot him a skeptical look but followed his directions. Three large bubbles flowed from the ring at the same moment the sun shot a beam of light beneath the porch overhang. The bubbles resembled golden orbs as they floated off the porch and into the yard. When they floated further into the yard, the sun turned them into a rainbow. "Well, I'll be corn-smacked," Annie muttered.

For the next ten minutes, no one else could get near the bubble machine, not that any of the children seemed to mind. They quickly formed a new game of seeing who could pop the most bubbles, keeping count in loud voices.

When Annie had finally gotten her fill of the bubble machine, she straightened. A look of wonder remained on her face. "I reckon y'all done earned yourself some cookies!" She turned and swept into the house.

Carrie sank back into a rocker, luxuriating in the warm breeze. Now that it was the first week of April, she was confident the balmy weather was here to stay. The daffodils and lilacs were in full bloom, their heady aroma hanging in the air like bubbles from the machine. She watched as the bubbles floated off the porch and made their way over the boxwoods, bursting as soon as they touched anything.

Bridget was off the porch, running after every bubble she could see, her tiny hands shooting out to grab them. She squealed joyfully every time she caught one, only to pout when they burst in her hands. "More!" she demanded, facing the porch with her fists on her hips.

"She is clearly your daughter," Thomas said with amusement. "She looks just like you at that age."

"Surely, I wasn't so demanding," Carrie protested.

Thomas stared at her for a moment and then burst into laughter. "Oh, honey, you were far more demanding. Your mother despaired of ever turning you into a compliant daughter."

Carrie joined in his laughter. "She had every right to despair. I never became that compliant daughter she longed for."

Thomas gazed at her, his eyes softening. "No, but you became something much better. You became the strongminded woman that kept her alive longer than she would have been if you hadn't known how to help her when she got sick."

Carrie shook her head. "I merely followed Old Sarah's directions. I didn't have a clue what I was doing."

"Yet, still you did it," Abby said gently. "Your mother didn't live long enough to see you become a doctor, but I know she would have been proud of you."

Carrie started to shake her head but stopped. Abby was right. It had taken a long time for her mother to accept who Carrie was, but shortly before she died, she'd told her how proud she was. It was a memory Carrie held closely in her heart.

"More!" Bridget's voice sounded into the early evening air again. "More!" She waved her hands impatiently, dancing in place as she kept her eyes on the bubble machine.

Carrie smiled. "I hope she's always exactly like this. I want her to expect more from life than society deems she should. I want her to demand more and then do what it takes to get it."

"She will," Abby said confidently. "She is growing up watching her mama do that every day. I predict she'll never settle for less than what she believes she should have."

Minnie walked over and perched on Carrie's knee. "Just like me, Mama. I'm going to make fire laws safer throughout the country. People's homes will stop burning down." She continued in a serious voice. "And cities will stop burning down."

"I believe you will," Carrie said tenderly, reaching up to stroke the red braid that hung down Minnie's back. She knew her daughter would never forget watching her family perish in a Philadelphia boarding-house blaze. She was also confident Minnie would never lose her passion to make a difference.

Minnie leaned back and rested her head on Carrie's shoulder. "Because you've taught me girls and women can do anything, Mama." She smiled brightly. "But until I grow up, I'm going to keep cooking with Annie."

"I hope you do," Carrie told her. "I would be so sad if you stopped making treats for us." Her stomach growled slightly. "Speaking of treats...I was in the barn looking after the new twin foals during dinner. Are there any treats coming from the kitchen tonight?" she asked hopefully.

Minnie laughed and leapt up. "How about some chocolate puffs?"

Carrie cocked her head. "What are chocolate puffs? Is it a new recipe?"

Minnie giggled. "I don't know why they're called that. They're just cookies." She looked toward Abby. "Grandma got me a new cookbook called *The New Art of Cookery*. It came today when a load was delivered from Richmond. The chocolate puffs are the first thing I've tried."

"Are they good?" Thomas asked.

Minnie cocked her brow. "Good, Grandpa? I say they are delectable!"

The porch erupted with laughter.

"Was that a new word in the cookbook?" Abby asked when she caught her breath.

Minnie nodded. "You need the right words to describe what you create," she said primly.

"Well," Carrie said, swallowing her mirth enough to make her tone match the gravity of her daughter's. "I believe I need to be the one to determine that for myself."

At that moment, the front door swung open. Annie strode out with a large tray. "Who wants tea and cookies?" she called cheerfully. "My Minnie Girl done outdid herself with these new cookies."

Within moments everyone was gathered around the tray, eager hands reaching forward.

Annie snatched the tray out of reach. "You think we be raisin' a bunch of animals 'round here?" she asked sternly. "You chillun be as filthy as pigs. Y'all run in and wash them dirty hands before you have some of these fine chocolate puffs."

When the porch was empty, she turned with a smile. "Y'all weren't gonna get none of these here cookies if those chillun got to 'em first." She held out the tray.

Carrie reached for a cup of tea and added three small cookies to her plate. She smiled when she took the first bite. "These are delicious!" she exclaimed. She ate the first one slowly. "I don't know quite how to describe them. They taste like a combination between a cookie...and candy."

"They do," Annie agreed. "The recipe don't call for nothin' but sugar, cocoa, and egg white. When I first saw it, I didn't think it would be too good." She shook her head. "I reckon for once in my life, I be wrong."

Carrie smiled. "Only once, Annie?"

Annie eyed her and pulled the tray out of reach. "I ain't admittin' to more than once, Miss Carrie. You got a problem with that?"

Carrie shook her head quickly. "Not as long as you keep bringing me cookies like these. You can go on being right about everything."

"That's what I figured," Annie muttered, her lips quirked upward.

The children streamed out the door and gathered around the cookie tray.

Carrie sank back in her chair, relishing the last two cookies as she turned her gaze to the pastures full of mares and foals. "We're lucky," she said quietly.

"Luckier than we'll ever truly understand," Thomas agreed. His voice changed as his eyes turned serious. "Honey, how upset are you with me?"

Carrie didn't pretend to not know what he was talking about. "I'm not," she said, glad the children had grabbed their cookies and run down to play chase in the yard during the last rays of light. It would be dark and time for bedtime rituals soon.

Thomas shook his head. "Anthony is in Louisiana because of me."

There were moments when Carrie felt that way, but she knew it wasn't true. "He and Matthew are in Louisiana because they made the choice to go, Father. You didn't ask them to, and you didn't make them. It was their choice." She wanted to scream that she wished neither one of them had made that choice, but it wouldn't do any good.

Carrie reached out to take her father's hand. "I don't blame you, Father. If there's anything I've learned, it's that life doesn't always go the way you think it will." Her lips twisted. "It doesn't *usually* go the way you think it will."

"And yet we have so much to be grateful for," Abby reminded her.

"We absolutely do," Carrie said. "In the midst of the hard, there's always good."

She looked down at the yard. Minnie, her face split with a grin, was running away from the boys as they futilely chased her. Russell, his earlier triumph with the bubble machine shining in his eyes, raced after her. Bridget giggled as she toddled across the yard, her arms spread wide as if she was embracing life. John, Jed, and Hope laughed as they raced around and dashed behind trees to keep from getting caught.

"There is so much good," Carrie murmured. A sudden burst of worry for Anthony pushed past her gratitude.

"Carrie?" Abby asked softly.

Carrie was certain the two men were facing grave danger in Louisiana. It was as if she could feel it across the miles. To admit to her fear would make her father feel even guiltier. All she could do was pray and hope they would come home.

Carrie shook her head and looked around as she licked the last cookie crumbs from her fingers. "Where's Rose?" She thought back quickly. She hadn't seen her best friend since early that morning.

Abby hesitated and glanced at Thomas.

Carrie's heartbeat, already fast, sped up even more. "Abby? What aren't you telling me?" she asked sharply, aware her fear for Anthony and Matthew was being reflected in her voice.

"She'll be home any minute," Abby replied evasively.

"Where is she?" Carrie demanded. She should have already realized Rose wasn't here, though she could have been one of many places around the plantation.

Abby hesitated again but looked at Carrie directly. "She is at the Rawlings' house."

Carrie stared, certain she wasn't hearing correctly. When Abby didn't look away, it was as if the air had been sucked from her lungs. "The Rawlings? As in the Klan member who had our barn burned down?" Just because she had chosen to forgive him and had treated his son when he was accidentally shot on Christmas Eve, that didn't mean she thought he could be trusted.

"Yes," Thomas replied uneasily.

"Why?" Carrie demanded. She jumped up and moved to the edge of the porch, peering into the encroaching darkness. The empty hollowness threatened to swallow her. Suddenly, she didn't care about the reason why Rose had gone to Rawlings' house. There was only one thing she cared about now. "Why isn't she back?"

Carrie was already worried about Anthony and Matthew. The additional concern for Rose was more than she could stomach. It was almost dark. If Rose wasn't back, something must be wrong.

Her mind whirled as Carrie created a plan to rescue her best friend.

If it wasn't too late.

Chapter Nine

Carrie had turned around to start delivering orders when she heard a sound in the distance. She spun back to gaze into the darkness, knowing she wouldn't be able to identify who was coming until they were almost to the house.

It could be Rose.

It could be another KKK attack.

She hated the terror that gripped her heart and stole her breath.

Her father appeared at her side, taking hold of her arm firmly. "If it were anyone but Rose, the men guarding the plantation would have already raised an alarm." His voice was calm and steady.

The truth of his words enabled Carrie to catch her breath. "You're right," she murmured. She managed to wait until the wagon drew close enough to identify Jeb and Rose before she dashed off the porch and ran to the carriage. "Where have you been?" she cried. She wasn't aware she was sobbing until she felt the wind cool the wetness on her cheeks.

"I'm alright," Rose said soothingly, stepping down from the carriage and enveloping her in a hug. "I'm sorry you worried. I thought I would be home long before now."

"You should have been!" Carrie said, aware her voice was trembling as she gulped back her tears. "What were you thinking?" She knew she was probably overreacting, but the days of worry about Anthony and Matthew had stretched her to her breaking point. She pulled back to look at her friend's face. "Were you really at Rawlings' place?"

"I was," Rose replied, a hint of wonder in her voice. "In fact, he rode to the gate with us to make sure we were safe."

"Not that he could have done much if a whole bunch of them Klan members had got it into their minds to stop us," Jeb muttered.

Carrie held Rose more tightly. "Will you ever stop doing foolish things?"

Rose pushed her away and laughed until she bent over, gasping for air. "Will *I* stop doing foolish things?" She took several deep breaths. "I tell you what, Mrs. Carrie Cromwell Borden Wallington. I'll stop doing foolish things as soon as you agree to do the same."

Chuckles came from the porch.

Carrie cast a glare at her parents, but knew Rose was right. The laughter, more than anything else could have, dispelled her fear. She finally managed a rueful chuckle. "I suppose you have a point." She turned away, knowing she couldn't agree to never do another foolish thing. "Are you at least going to tell us what happened?"

"I will," Rose agreed, "but not until I've seen my children. Did they have a good evening?"

Carrie laughed. "A bubble machine, chocolate puff cookies, and endless games of chase. I predict our children will sleep well tonight."

Annie and Miles joined them on the porch with a tray of hot tea to stave off the cooler night air once the children were settled in bed.

Rose sank into one of the rockers, reached for a drink, and grabbed a few of the cookies. "John told me these are the best cookies Minnie has made yet."

"They be real fine eatin'," Annie agreed. "That girl gonna be as good a cook as me in time."

Rose took a bite and closed her eyes. "These are delicious," she said.

Annie eyed her sternly. "You done had anything to eat for dinner, Rose?"

"Kathy Rawlings gave Jeb and me a bowl of soup and some bread." Rose didn't need to see the others on the porch to know they wore expressions of surprise.

Carrie took a deep breath. "Please tell us what happened."

Rose swallowed her cookie before she filled them in on the events of the afternoon. "At the end of school, Rodney Rawlings told me his father asked me to come by their house if possible."

"He said if possible?" Thomas asked keenly. "Or was it more of an order to appear?"

"He said *if possible.*" Rose confirmed. "I wouldn't have gone if it seemed like an order. Rodney has been doing so well in school. He's happy and making new friends. He didn't seem to think it odd that his father was asking me to come."

"How did Jeb feel about it?" Carrie asked.

Rose chuckled wryly. "He thought I might be losing my mind," she admitted. "In the end, though, he agreed I'd done the right thing." She thought back as she told the story. "Kathy Rawlings greeted me warmly. She even had tea and bread out back for Jeb." She didn't see any reason to add that, at first, she had considered they might be hiding Jeb away in the back so no one would suspect anything. Everyone on the porch was already thinking it. "Mr. Rawlings came in shortly after I arrived."

"Were you afraid?" Annie blurted.

Rose saw no reason to not be honest. "I was nervous," she clarified.

Annie shook her head. "If my Moses done knew you were over there at Rawlings' house, he'd have gone after you." She glared at Rose. "Jeb was right. I kinda think maybe you be losin' your mind."

Rose smiled. She could always trust Annie to be bluntly honest. "Mr. Rawlings asked me to come so he could apologize."

"Apologize?" Miles demanded. "For real?"

Rose nodded, before realizing they couldn't see her in the dark. No one had lit the lanterns yet. "He started out by telling me he had to rethink everything about his life and beliefs after Christmas Eve. He knew how hard it was for me and Moses to come with Carrie and Anthony. The fact that we did, and the fact that I could help Carrie save Jimmy, made him realize what he'd learned about black people wasn't true. When he listened to us speak, and when he learned I was a teacher at the school, his beliefs were challenged even more."

Rose paused, thinking about how she had felt as he talked. It made her realize so much of the hatred flowing through people was based on nothing but lies and fear. "He told me he's never seen his son so happy. Rodney comes home and teaches Jimmy everything he learns at school. When Jimmy comes to school next year, he'll already be reading and doing math." Once again, she felt the wonder that had washed through her when she learned what the older boy was doing.

"It was more than that," Rose continued. "When we were done talking about the children, I decided to be bold and ask him why he was a KKK member."

"That was *very* bold," Abby commented "What did he say?"

"Well, he started by telling me that it's a fact that blacks are inferior to whites. He explained he was taught that blacks have much smaller brains than whites, and that they aren't capable of taking care of themselves without whites to handle them." Rose thought about how difficult it had been to listen calmly.

"I used to believe that myself," Thomas said sadly. "It makes me sick to hear you speak those words, because that's something I would have said."

"You changed," Rose said gently. "Mr. Rawlings went on to say the reason it was so easy to believe that is because he was afraid and angry. Before the war, he never thought that much about blacks. He knew he would never have enough money to own slaves himself, so his energy went to creating a life for his wife and son. Jimmy didn't come along until after the war."

"The war changed him," Abby observed.

Rose shook her head. "The *reason* for the war changed him. All of a sudden, he was being sent off to fight battles to protect slavery – something he could never take part in. He was watching men die because the rich people of the South wanted to keep their slaves." She paused, thinking through everything he'd said. "He changed even more when the slaves were freed and given the right to vote. He realized black men could control his life because there are more black men in the South than there are white men. He felt powerless."

"And the KKK gave him a way to feel powerful again," Thomas said.

"Yes," Rose agreed. "He was afraid of losing the little he had created. The KKK told him the only way to resolve the problem was to kill and terrorize black people. They told him it was his duty to make sure white people in the South wouldn't support anything that helped the freed slaves." Her lips tightened. "He lost his brother when the Klan attacked the plantation on Christmas Eve a few years ago."

"Ain't nobody's fault but his own," Miles growled.

"He knows," Rose replied.

"But it's another reason why he hates me so much," Thomas said.

"He *used* to hate you," Rose corrected. "He feels terrible about the barn burning down."

"He didn't do that," Carrie protested. "Abe burned the barn in retaliation for us taking Charlotte and the children away instead of letting him beat them."

"We knew someone probably told Abe to do it. Rawlings was the one who went to his house and gave him the plan for burning the barn." Rose paused, wondering if she should say the next part, but these weren't people she kept secrets from. She saw no reason to start now.

"Rawlings killed Abe."

A shocked silence fell on the porch. "He told you that?" Thomas demanded. "Why?"

Rose shrugged. She had wondered the same thing. "I think he needed to confess to everything and get it off his chest."

"For what purpose?" Thomas sounded genuinely confused. "We could have him arrested and thrown in jail."

"He knows," Rose answered. "He said leaving the Klan made him realize how much being in it had changed him." She thought about the conversation. "Kathy told me her husband is a good man who got caught up in a real bad thing." She understood the vibrations of disbelief all around her.

"Did he really leave the Klan?" Miles demanded.

"He has," Rose confirmed.

"Then they gonna be comin' for him," Miles said flatly. "A man don't just walk away."

"He knows," Rose agreed. She took a deep breath. "That was the other reason he asked me to come over. He asked if we could..."

"He wants us to protect him?" Carrie demanded. "After what he did? I agreed to treat his son because Abby convinced me that you can't fight hate with hate, but that doesn't mean I think we should protect the man who almost destroyed Cromwell Stables." Her voice shook. "I still think about what could have happened. Father... the horses..."

Rose understood. She'd had the entire return trip to think about what Rawlings had told her.

"He doesn't want us to protect him. He figures he deserves whatever is coming." She could recall with vivid clarity the look on his face when he had said that. It was a stark, hopeless type of knowing that left no room for discussion. Kathy had burst into tears when he said it. Rose, despite everything, had felt a surge of sympathy for the man who had made very bad choices and decisions.

"What does he want?" Abby asked.

"He asked us to keep the boys in school and help his wife. He loves his family," she said softly.

"That don't undo everythin' he done," Miles stated.

"He knows." The conversation had made Rose think deeply about the ongoing repercussions of bad decisions. Just because you felt bad about doing something, it didn't mean you wouldn't have to pay the consequences. Saying sorry didn't wipe away the pain of your actions.

"He fully expects to die," Rose repeated. "He's surprised they haven't already come for him. He wasn't just a part of the Klan; he was one of their leaders. Miles is right. Evidently, it's not something you can just walk away from."

"They control by fear," Thomas said starkly. "Anger and fear will persuade a man to do almost anything. You feed the anger and fear, and then give them a way to fight back against it, and you develop a loyal following." He shook his head. "When men join the Klan, they stay in because they know they'll be punished for trying to leave."

A deep fatigue gripped Rose. The numbers in the Klan were growing daily. Other white supremacy groups were springing up across the country, but especially in the South. Once again, she was grateful Moses was on a train west, instead of risking his freedom and life in Louisiana.

Carrie reached over and took her hand. Rose gripped it tightly, glad to know her friend could feel her emotional turmoil.

"What did you tell him?" Carrie asked gently.

"I promised him I would keep the children at school, and that I would make sure the Bregdan Women took care of Kathy," Rose replied. "What else could I do?" She blinked her eyes rapidly, pushing back the emotion that threatened to overwhelm her.

"You wouldn't have been the Rose I love if you hadn't done that," Carrie replied, squeezing her hand more tightly. Her voice grew more direct. "Do you really believe we can protect them? The Klan will no doubt come after them too. Wouldn't it be best if we sent them somewhere else?"

"Like you did with Charlotte and the children?" Rose asked. An unexpected burst of hope swept through her.

"Yes. They're safe and happy with family in Philadelphia. Sometimes the only way to protect people is to send them far away."

"Like with Hobbs six years ago?" Rose asked. She thought of the young man who had saved Robert's life during the war. Hobbs would have done anything for his lieutenant. He had risked his life for Carrie, and then risked it again when he took Matthew into the KKK convention so the inner workings could be exposed. Matthew had placed him on a train the next morning and sent him out to Missouri, so he could catch a wagon train going to Oregon. From the little communication they had received, he was doing well in his new life.

"Exactly like that," Carrie replied.

"They don't have family anywhere," Rose said. "They don't have anywhere to go." The possibility had never crossed her mind.

"That doesn't mean we can't help," Abby said. "We can send the family to Philadelphia." She paused. "The whole family."

"What?" Rose asked in surprise. "What do you mean?"

Abby answered slowly, reaching for her husband's hand. "It takes a tremendous amount of courage to leave the KKK. I don't see why we should wait around for Rawlings to be killed, and then try to figure out how to help his family. We know the Klan is coming for him. Let's get the entire family out of here now."

Thomas sucked in his breath sharply. "That's doing an awful lot for someone who had the barn burned down."

Rose knew he was also remembering the painful burns he had endured from the flaming embers that had dropped on him while he was rescuing horses.

"It is," Abby agreed. "I don't believe it's enough to choose to not fight hate with hate. Sometimes you have to be the one to reach out with compassion and grace. When it is so completely undeserved, it usually has the most powerful impact."

A long silence fell on the porch.

"You married a good woman," Miles finally muttered.

"Better than me," Annie grumbled. "Rose ain't the only one who seems to have lost her mind."

"And much better than me," Thomas said hoarsely. He stood and walked to the edge of the porch, staring out into the night barely illuminated by a quarter moon hovering in the sky. "Abby's right though." Thomas didn't turn as he spoke. "If Carrie hadn't reached out to me with compassion and grace, I don't know that I would have ever changed my views about slavery and black people. She gave me room to change by treating me with love, not anger." His voice strengthened as he swung around to look at them. "I agree with my beautiful wife. We should get Rawlings and his family out of here."

"When?" Rose asked, shocked by the sudden turn of events. At the same time, she knew they were completely right. The sole way to protect the family was to move them to a new location so they could start over. Perhaps doing so was the single way to affect any meaningful change.

"Will he agree to go?" Carrie asked.

Rose considered the question. "I believe so," she finally said. "He's preparing to die, but I know he doesn't want to leave his family. He doesn't believe he has other options."

"We'll go see him in the morning," Thomas said. "I don't imagine there's any time to waste."

"What are you planning?" Carrie demanded.

Rose knew what she was feeling. With Anthony, Moses, and Matthew gone, Thomas wouldn't have the support he was used to. "You can't take the family by yourself," she said.

A plan was taking shape in her mind.

Chapter Ten

April 8, 1873

Anthony leaned back in his chair beneath the sprawling live oak tree. Tendrils of Spanish moss danced and swayed in the breeze above him. A thicket of jasmine tucked next to the porch covered him with its sweet perfume. A string of clear whistles burst from the undergrowth. Without looking, he knew a flock of robins was scrounging for their morning worms.

Cheerily…cheer up…cheer up…cheerily…cheer up.

Anthony knew his family back in Virginia was hearing the same spring robin chorus. That thought caused his heart to seize with longing. He thought of Carrie waking up in an empty bed but forced himself instead to imagine her in the barn with her beloved horses. He wondered what Russell was creating in his workshop, what Minnie would create in the kitchen, whether Frances would discover new birds, and what new words Bridget would learn. He didn't regret his decision to join Matthew, but he yearned to be with his family on the plantation. It was his favorite place on earth and grew more beloved with each passing day. Sitting in solitude gave him the perfect opportunity to remember everything that had led him to this point in life. He was well aware how fortunate he was.

Anthony reached for the coffee sitting on the table next to him. Winnie, Calhoun's cook, a wonderful woman who had once been the man's slave, had fixed him a platter of ham biscuits and fresh fruit. The afternoon would be warm and humid, but the cool morning air embraced him. Cardinals and blue jays darted through the trees surrounding Willie Calhoun's brick plantation home.

Calhoun had welcomed them warmly once he realized Thomas had been responsible for their appearance. He had arrived home the day before they arrived, after hiding out in the woods for several days. The area supremacists were blatant about their desire to murder him. He had agreed to let Matthew interview him, though he was candid about admitting it was most likely too late to protect him. His hope now was that somehow the freedmen in the area would find a way to survive what was coming.

When William Ward, the black militia leader, had arrived at the house the night before and asked Calhoun to hand deliver a letter to Governor Kellogg asking for U.S. troops to help in what they knew was a dire situation, Calhoun had agreed. He asked Matthew to join him. They had left earlier that morning.

Anthony sighed. Under different circumstances, Calhoun's plantation would be the perfect picture of peace. Unfortunately, he knew the danger and death lurking in the air around him. Two days had passed since they arrived in Colfax, but the menace had thickened like the early morning fog that hung over the Red River.

Nevertheless, he was certain he was safer than Matthew.

He scowled up at the sun beams filtering down through the lush foliage. He would have preferred to travel with

Matthew and Calhoun to New Orleans to meet with Governor Kellogg but had been convinced to stay behind to act as a communication portal until they returned home.

At the sound of hoofbeats in the distance, Anthony leapt up and moved into the shadows next to the porch. He edged closer to the secret door that led to a safe haven under the porch, where a crawl space would allow him to hide under the house if there was danger.

He suppressed a shudder at the idea of confining himself in a shallow depression that was most certainly home to spiders and snakes. He thought longingly of the tunnel that provided protection on Cromwell.

Anthony knew an ambush could happen at any moment. While everyone thought the courthouse would be the primary target, it was highly likely that Calhoun would also be attacked. To say the area whites blamed him for the chaos in Grant Parish would be putting it mildly. Willie had been candid about his constant expectation of death.

Anthony kept his eyes on the drive, remaining motionless until he identified the visitor. He relaxed when Ward rode into view. Stepping out from the shadows, he walked to the front of the porch and waited silently. For Ward to arrive so early in the morning, after being at the house until late last evening, was not a good sign.

As Ward drew closer, Anthony's gut tightened even more. The look on the man's face didn't portend good news.

Ward drew to a stop, his tall figure erect in the saddle. The Union veteran was almost six feet tall. His dark, chocolate face was creased by a deep, three-inch-long scar he had picked up from a barroom brawl that had ended with someone smashing him in the head with a brick. It served to make him more imposing to everyone who knew him. Despite his imposing figure, however, tuberculosis had almost taken his life seven years earlier. He had survived, but his illness would often flare up, making him incapable of getting out of bed.

"What's wrong?"

Ward scowled. "I just got some news."

Matthew stood on the deck of the steamboat *LaBelle* as it plied its way down the Red River. He was fascinated by the brick red color of the water, created by the iron-rich bedrock the river flowed through farther west. It didn't have the same appeal as the clear waters of the James River, but it intrigued him.

"Matthew!"

Matthew looked up sharply. Willie Calhoun, his short, hunchbacked figure silhouetted against the dissipating fog, waved him forward.

"We got trouble," Calhoun announced. He nodded his head toward the upcoming landing.

Matthew peered through the fog. His perusal of the map earlier told him they were approaching the twin towns of Alexandria and Pineville. He stiffened when he saw a large group of armed men on the Pineville side. There was no doubt who they were waiting for. "Who told them you were on the boat?" he demanded.

Calhoun shrugged, a resigned look making his face haggard. "It hardly matters, does it?"

Matthew thought quickly. "Come with me. We've got to hide you."

Calhoun looked dubious but followed him.

Matthew headed straight for a cargo hold he had spotted earlier. It wasn't ideal, but he couldn't think of a better solution. He held the door open for Calhoun, watching as the man stuffed the precious letter into his boot and climbed laboriously down the narrow ladder into the hold. "I'll do what I can to keep them away from you," he said, though in reality they both knew he had no influence over anything. He gritted his teeth as he closed the cargo door and latched it securely. He wished for a lock but had no idea where to look for one. Asking a crewmember would simply alert them to Calhoun's hiding place.

Matthew moved back to the deck, forcing himself to push aside his previous experiences in the state he had learned to hate. He couldn't allow his mind to be fogged with memories. He had to stay in the present moment and think quickly.

As soon as the boat docked, the group of armed men shoved their way onboard, hollering for Calhoun.

Matthew stepped out from beneath an overhang. "Who is this Calhoun fellow you're looking for?"

The man who seemed to be in charge scowled at him. "What's it to you?"

Matthew decided to use his position as a reporter to attempt to gain control of the situation. "My name is Matthew Justin. I'm a reporter for the *Philadelphia Inquirer.*" He saw no reason to point out that his position with them was in the past. "I'm down here to report on Louisiana's political situation. Who are you gentlemen?" It was almost impossible to force the word *gentlemen* out of his mouth, but his best idea was to attempt to diffuse the situation, not anger them further by saying how he actually perceived them.

The leader gazed at him for a moment. "Another Yankee carpetbagger down here trying to involve yourself in our business," he snarled. "It doesn't matter who we are. We're here to find Willie Calhoun. Get out of our way. We have a warrant for his arrest."

Matthew knew that wasn't true, but revealing his connection to Calhoun would put the man in more danger. He stepped aside, praying they wouldn't locate the hold.

For the next twenty minutes, the boat rang with the sound of men's boots and opening doors as they searched for their prey.

"I found him!"

Matthew's eyes closed in despair as the call rang out.

"He's hiding down in a cargo hold!"

Matthew stayed where he was as the posse pressed further into the boat.

"Search him," a deep voice ordered.

Several minutes of silence ensued.

Matthew held his breath.

"Look what I found," a man called out triumphantly. "Calhoun hid a letter in his boot!"

"Read it," the leader demanded.

The man who had discovered the letter read it. "It's from Ward. He's asking the governor to send troops to protect the niggers." He chortled suddenly. "Seems Ward knows those fellas protecting the courthouse don't stand a chance against us."

Matthew walked to the hold. He fought to control his anger, as well as the sick feeling that accompanied these men knowing just how weak the Colfax defenders actually were.

The leader looked up sharply when he appeared. "What do you want? I already told you none of this is your business."

"Perhaps," Matthew agreed calmly, hoping Calhoun wouldn't indicate they knew each other. He couldn't stop whatever was going to happen, but he could make certain Calhoun wasn't alone. "It certainly seems newsworthy, however. Seems the blacks have caused you a lot of trouble down here." He prayed the furious judgment he felt wasn't revealed in his voice. "It could be beneficial to have your side of the story told." He chuckled and shrugged. "I'm a new reporter looking for a good story." He tacked on another lie for good measure. "My granddaddy owned a plantation down here for a while. It wasn't a big one, but he told me how bad things got for everyone before the war."

The leader eyed him sharply. "You ain't just a Yankee."

Matthew shrugged. "Nope. I'm from West Virginia, actually."

The man continued to look at him and then sighed. "This man is Willie Calhoun. Seems to think it's his job to destroy the life of every white man in this area. It's time we taught him a lesson." His features darkened with rage. He turned around to glare at Calhoun, who was sitting in a chair, his arms bound tightly. "I should kill him right now."

"That's right," another man said roughly. "What we really ought to do is hang him. His daddy was a good friend of mine. Meredith Calhoun would be horrified to know what his son was doing."

Matthew pretended to consider what they were saying. "Wait a minute," he said suddenly. "Didn't I read somewhere that William Calhoun is a Louisiana Representative. Is this the same man?"

"He is," the leader acknowledged grudgingly. "He's a disgrace to the state. He deserves to die," he said scornfully. "I suspect even his daddy would agree."

Matthew struggled to think of a way to resolve the situation. He suspected the man was right about Willie's father. The two were vastly different, but the elder Calhoun had given Willie his entire empire and walked away. He was somewhere in Europe, probably blissfully unaware of what was happening in Louisiana. "Perhaps there's a better solution than killing him," Matthew said casually.

The leader glared at him. "I can't think of anything better than killing this traitor to the white race."

Matthew fought to keep his features impassive. "You're certain there isn't a way you can use him to achieve your goals?" He'd heard one of the men call the leader Hooe. If he remembered correctly, Hooe was the owner of the store who had threatened to whip any black who voted in the 1868 election. He was a dangerous Confederate veteran with hatred filling his veins.

"What do you mean?" Hooe snapped.

Matthew remained silent, hoping the other men would provide the answer.

"He might have a point," another man spat. "We know Calhoun controls the blacks. They do whatever he tells them to. We know we can take that courthouse any time we want to, but what if Calhoun could get them to leave? It's going to be nothing but trouble if Kellogg sends troops. Calhoun's letter won't reach him, but it doesn't mean something else won't."

Matthew continued to listen. The men he had met defending the courthouse were strong and determined, but he saw no reason to point that out. It was also true they didn't stand a chance against a large number of armed veterans.

"Yeah," another man blustered, his fat cheeks glistening with sweat from the rising heat inside the boat as the sun melted away the fog. "Let's send Calhoun up to tell the blacks to leave the courthouse."

"And what makes you think I would do that?" Calhoun asked haughtily.

Matthew hid his groan. Calhoun was known for his acerbic personality but now was not the time to antagonize these men. Matthew wouldn't be surprised if one of them whipped out a pistol and did what all of them wanted to.

Hooe narrowed his eyes. "We might let you live long enough to do it, Calhoun. On the other hand, we can shoot you right here. Wouldn't bother me a bit."

Calhoun hesitated for a long moment and glanced at Matthew.

Matthew, fighting to keep his face neutral in order to not divulge their connection, hoped his eyes communicated his message.

Calhoun finally nodded. "Fine," he said curtly. "I don't know what they'll do, but I'll relay a message."

"That might keep everyone alive a while longer." Hooe's lip curled, and he laughed harshly. "Or not. Can't say I care much one way or the other."

Matthew relaxed slightly. They still might kill Calhoun, but at least it wasn't going to be at that moment. It would give him time to continue formulating a plan.

Hooe swung around to stare at him. “You really want a story, Mr. Justin?”

Matthew nodded, wondering what was about to happen. “I do.”

Hooe stared at him for long moments before he eventually nodded, evidently coming to a decision. “You’re coming with us.”

Matthew gazed at him. Being with a group of murdering men who could realize at some point that he wasn’t sympathetic to their cause was hardly appealing to him. However, if he wanted to truly reveal what was happening in Louisiana, he had no choice. “I’ll get my satchel.”

His thoughts turned to Anthony. He had no way to get word to him. He forced himself to not think of Janie or the children. He had made the choice to come to Louisiana. He had to play it out and see what the future held.

“Justin!” Hooe barked.

Matthew turned. “What?”

“You don’t write things the way I like, you might not get out of Louisiana either.”

Matthew stared at him but didn’t respond. He knew Hooe was speaking the truth.

“I just got a report of a large group of armed men waiting for the steamer at the Pineville Landing. Somebody revealed Calhoun would be on the boat,” Ward growled.

Anthony listened closely. “How do you know they were after Calhoun?”

“I don’t,” Ward admitted. “It makes sense though. They hate him but they’re afraid of his power. They don’t want him anywhere near New Orleans.”

"And if they captured him?" Anthony pressed.

Ward's shoulders sagged. "Then we're in big trouble," he said bluntly. "If they get the letter Calhoun is carrying, it will be a massive intelligence windfall. It details how weak our force around the courthouse is, and it reveals I don't believe we stand a chance without U.S. troops to save the day." He grimaced. "It will make the supremacists more likely to attack."

"And if they attack, they'll win," Anthony observed.

Ward met his eyes evenly. "I have some fellas out in the woods keeping an eye on things. I had word earlier today that there's a force of men growing in number at a plantation called Summerfield. The owner has helped them before." He paused. "That plantation puts them three miles from the courthouse."

Anthony knew the situation was dire, but he had a more important matter on his mind. "What about Calhoun and Matthew?" he asked. "If they capture them, what will happen?"

Ward looked away and didn't answer.

Chapter Eleven

"You want me to do *what*, Miss Rose? Now I know you're crazy, for sure." Not even the heavy beard of Jeb's narrow face could conceal his astonishment. He shook his head vigorously. "Do you know what you're suggesting?"

"I know what I'm asking, Jeb," Rose said calmly.

Jeb's wife, Amelia, leaned forward to gaze into Rose's eyes. "Why you asking him to do this?" she demanded. "Ain't none of them Klan will hesitate to kill my husband. Jeb will do anything in the world to keep you safe, just like he been doing for the last years, but why you asking him to keep some Klan member safe?" Her voice trembled. "I don't want to lose my husband."

"You're not going to," Rose said firmly. "The only thing I want him to do is go talk to Alvin."

"That's a big ask, Miss Rose," Jeb protested. "Alvin might be white, but he don't want to get in wrong with the Klan either."

Rose knew that was true. "You've had to save him from the Klan already, Jeb," she reminded him. "Without your help, he would be dead."

"That was more than three years ago," Jeb replied. "They ain't bothered him since."

"Which doesn't mean they won't come after him again," Rose stated. "If they kill Rawlings, it could embolden them to take stronger action." They had known Jeb would be hard to convince, but she stood a better chance at it than anyone. She knew just how close Jeb and Alvin had become. "Rawlings is their Grand Cyclop," she revealed.

Jeb looked at her blankly. "Their what?"

"It's the title the Klan has given to the man who runs the KKK for a certain area. Rawlings is the Grand Cyclop here."

Fear mingled with disgust in Jeb's eyes. "Why you wanting to save a Klan leader, Miss Rose?"

It was a fair question. "I suppose I have mixed motives," Rose admitted. "His children are my students. If their father is killed, it will change their lives forever. And if the Klan will kill him, there's no reason they won't also kill his wife and children."

"Like they will us?" Amelia asked bluntly.

"Yes," Rose said. "It's more than that though. The entire South seems to be controlled by hatred and fear now. You know that Carrie and I went to help Rawlings' youngest son on Christmas Eve when he was accidentally shot."

Jeb narrowed his eyes. "I heard there was a pistol and a threat if you didn't go. That's not exactly an offer to help."

"That's true," Rose admitted. "Carrie initially refused."

"That woman got a death wish," Amelia muttered.

Rose, despite the gravity of the situation, chuckled. "Not really. She didn't want to help the man she suspected orchestrated the burning of the barn."

"Makes sense to me," Jeb muttered. His eyes narrowed again. "Why'd you go help that boy?"

"Because of Abby," Rose said softly. "She told us that you can't fight hate with hate. It turns out that me being there, with Moses, was what made Rawlings realize the KKK is wrong. He left the Klan because he realized his hatred of blacks makes no sense."

Silence fell over the cabin. The newly hatched crickets tuning up outside the open window offered the only sound.

"Jeb, I know I'm asking a lot of you," Rose said. "Those of us on the plantation have talked about it a lot. If we can help Rawlings and his family escape, we might be able to avoid more bloodshed. We hope it will weaken the Klan if their leader simply disappears."

"And you figure seeing him surrounded by a group of white men who ain't Klan members will convince them they're out numbered?"

"Unless our plan to get them out of here without being seen is successful. There's a chance it will work," Rose insisted. "At one point, many of the men we're planning to ask were close to being Klan members themselves. The thing that changed them was having children at the school. If we're going to help the Rawlings, we can't have the plantation men escort them out."

"Cause the Klan won't hesitate to kill every black man they see if they're caught," Jeb said shrewdly.

Rose nodded. She'd said everything she could say. In the end, it would be up to Jeb and Amelia. She would ask him to put his family at risk, but she wouldn't force it.

"You really think your plan will work?" Amelia asked, her voice steady despite her trembling hands.

"I think we have a chance," Rose replied honestly.

"And all my Jeb got to do is go ask Alvin to round up a bunch of white men who have students in your school, and convince them to escort Rawlings out of town?"

Hearing it put so bluntly made Rose hesitate. Even if Jeb could convince his friend, did Alvin really have a chance of talking enough men into helping him?

Jeb was the one who answered her unspoken thoughts. “Anybody who got a child at Rose’s school will do just about anything she asks. They won’t like it, but they’ll do it.”

Rose felt a surge of hope, but she remained silent. The cricket chorus grew louder as she waited.

“I’ll do it,” Jeb finally said. “I still think you’re crazy, but I also see what you’re saying. I can’t say I won’t be real glad to see Rawlings and his family gone. It wouldn’t hurt me none if the man ended up dead, but his wife and children don’t deserve to pay the price.”

Amelia nodded. “I’ve met his wife. She seems like a fine woman. I was gonna ask her to join me at the next Bregdan Women meeting. Don’t reckon that will happen now.”

“You’ll be giving her and the children a chance at a new life,” Rose told her, reaching out to squeeze her hand. “I can’t think of a better gift than that.”

Matthew couldn’t keep from glancing behind them nervously as he and Calhoun trotted the final mile to Willie’s plantation. He expected a posse of men to burst from the dense trees at any moment, guns blazing. From the look on Calhoun’s face, though he stared stoically ahead, he expected the same thing.

Two days earlier, after being captured on the steamboat, they had been bound with ropes in a thicket of trees not far from the landing. Matthew had told Hooe he would accompany them to get a story, but obviously the suspicious man wasn’t convinced of Matthew’s intentions. The message had been clear. He was allowed to join them, but he wouldn't be trusted.

Bugs had swarmed the unprotected parts of their bodies as evening began to fall. Matthew was furious about their situation, but his fear of what could happen if he protested kept him quiet. He knew it would take little for the posse to decide to kill Calhoun. Most likely, if that happened, they would also dispose of him.

Later that night, two horses had been brought into the clearing. With no explanation, Calhoun and Matthew had been untied and ordered to join the men if they wanted to live. They rode through the night, the Louisiana murkiness threatening to swallow them. The only sounds, aside from men cursing, were owls, crickets, and loud bullfrogs. Matthew did his best to ignore the loud rustling that could indicate a cougar or an alligator.

At about two o'clock in the morning, they had stopped at a remote house. Hooe made Calhoun dismount, and then subjected him to the humiliation of a strip search by his men.

Calhoun had remained silent as he peeled his clothes off beneath the glow of the moon, his face an iron mask. Only his eyes glittered with a rage that spurred the men into greater laughter. Their howls of amusement echoed throughout the clearing.

Matthew had ground his teeth in frustration and anger. He knew the men were using their power to amuse themselves, but there was nothing he could do to stop them. If he told them he was going to include their behavior in his article, he suspected they would retaliate on the spot. He was also honest enough to admit he was grateful he hadn't been included in the travesty.

Once they determined Calhoun was adequately embarrassed, they approached the abandoned house, tied their horses, secured their prisoners, and laid down on the porch to sleep for the night. It was only minutes before the men were snoring.

Matthew was awake the entire night, his eyes searching the darkness for more danger, his thoughts absorbed by Janie and the children. He refused to close his eyes and let his guard down. Calhoun, tied to a railing at the other end of the porch, was certainly doing the same thing. Matthew wondered if Anthony had received word of the capture. His friend would be sick with worry.

Deep in thought about the last two days, Matthew wasn't aware they had finally arrived at Calhoun's house.

"You're safe!" Anthony appeared on the porch, his face filled with relief. "What happened?

Matthew told him what had happened on the steamboat and relayed the journey to the remote cabin before he picked up the rest of the story. "The next morning, we got very close to Colfax before we were stopped by another group of men. They told Hooe it was reckless for such a large body of white men to be so close to the courthouse. Evidently, they're still trying to avoid bloodshed."

Anthony frowned. "That was yesterday. Where have you been since then?"

Calhoun scowled. "They weren't willing to let me go. They were afraid I would reveal their whereabouts to the courthouse defenders."

Anthony looked at Matthew. "What about you?"

Matthew shrugged. "They dragged me along. They've decided I'm going to write their story, but they still don't trust me." He smiled tightly. "With good reason."

"Last night was better than our first night," Calhoun continued. "Hooe's men weren't any more comfortable than we were sleeping outside, so they decided we would all stay at the Ice House Hotel in Alexandria." He grimaced. "I can assure you my body appreciated the bed."

Matthew had also been miserable on the wooden porch, but he could imagine it had been far worse for the hunchbacked cripple. The fact that Calhoun had not complained once told him much about the man's character, and just how he had been able to stand against so much hatred.

Anthony shook his head, obviously still confused. "I don't understand why you're here Matthew. If you have been pretending to not know Calhoun, why would they send you off together?"

"I talked with Hooe," Calhoun said. "He agreed to let us return today if I ordered the blacks to lay down their arms and give up the courthouse."

"And if I covered the surrender," Matthew added. "My job is to keep an eye on Calhoun and make sure he does what he promised."

"We boarded the steamboat this morning," Calhoun added. "When we got to the landing, we went to the courthouse, and I did as ordered."

Anthony's eyes flicked between the two of them. "And?"

Calhoun shrugged. "They refused." He smiled briefly, but his eyes were dark with weariness and pain. "I knew they would, but I did as ordered. Matthew watched me do it."

Matthew took up the story. "I was at least able to pick up some intel. The posse Nash is putting together has grown," he said grimly. "Reports have come in that there are at least one hundred men camped out at Summerfield Plantation."

Anthony nodded. "Ward told me about it. He came by yesterday, before he left for New Orleans."

Calhoun looked at Anthony sharply. "Ward has gone to New Orleans? I didn't see him at the courthouse, but I assumed he was out doing reconnaissance."

"When he heard you were captured," Anthony said, "he knew it was up to him to get to New Orleans and request troops. He took a group of men with him."

Calhoun frowned. "I'm afraid Ward made an impulsive and risky decision. He has removed the entire leadership of the men guarding the courthouse. I fear they won't be able to withstand an attack without his leadership."

"He urged the men to hold out until his return," Anthony replied. "His illness is acting up so badly he can hardly walk. One of his friends had to help him mount his horse to ride down to the steamboat. He seems to be in a great deal of pain."

Calhoun scowled. "So, he can't fight anyway." A resigned look settled into his eyes. "If the men who captured me were true about their intentions, Ward won't return in time to fight."

Anthony gazed out into the shadows falling over the late afternoon. His expression was grim. "Ward gave me more information. Alphonse Cazabat wasn't duly elected as the parish judge, but he believes he was. He's determined to take control again. He's told Nash to suppress a riot at the courthouse, even if it takes two hundred men to do it. Nash figures he has legal authority now to arrest or attack the defenders."

Matthew's gut tightened, and his breath caught. "Not to mention all the women and children." He still hoped there would be some way to avoid bloodshed, but his confidence was diminishing by the minute. Ward being gone did nothing but make the odds more insurmountable for the men defending the courthouse.

"Nash is recruiting men by telling them the Grant Parish blacks are going to kill all the white men and take the white women and girls," Anthony said angrily. "They're telling recruits that the blacks are out to create a new race of men through mass rape."

Matthew clenched his teeth. He'd seen what motivating through fear could do. People stopped thinking–they simply acted to protect what they feared losing.

"Utter nonsense!" Calhoun snapped. "I've lived here most of my life, but I still can't believe the level of ignorance that controls people's thinking."

"Will Ward's trip to New Orleans create any positive outcome?" Anthony asked.

Calhoun shook his head. "I doubt it. When Hooe and his men discovered the letter and took me captive, I'm afraid it destroyed our hope of support from the troops. Ward has some influence, but my position in the legislature would have insured that Kellogg listened." His features darkened. "I know our governor. I'm also sure other Democrats have gone to New Orleans to fill his ears with lies. Governor Kellogg will decide that a large force of troops will be unduly provocative at this point."

"He'll let the blacks at the courthouse be attacked?" Anthony demanded.

Calhoun sighed heavily. "It's more likely that he doesn't believe it will actually happen. Though I had a small degree of hope when I decided to take the letter to New Orleans, I'm afraid that Kellogg couldn't get troops here even if he tried. The state and federal government have no steamboats. They depend entirely on the men who own the ones that ply our rivers."

Matthew's breathing grew shallower. "None of the boat captains will bring troops or militia members here," he guessed. "They'll lose their business if they cooperate with the Republicans."

Calhoun nodded but remained silent.

There was really nothing left to say.

Matthew felt the bile rise in his throat. The best thing he and Anthony could do was ride out of the area before the worst happened. Though it would be the wisest action, he knew neither of them would do it. They had become invested in the lives of the defenders.

Calhoun said what Matthew wasn't willing to say. "You and Anthony should leave in the morning. Ride back to the Mississippi River and catch a steamboat home. When I asked Thomas to come here, I had no idea what the reality would be. I won't be responsible for something happening to either of you. There's nothing you can do to stop what will, or will not, happen here."

Matthew knew he was right, but he shook his head. "We can't do that."

"Why not?" Calhoun barked. "Didn't you hear me? There's nothing you can do."

"I agree that we can't stop it," Matthew admitted.

"But Matthew can be the one to tell the truth about whatever happens here," Anthony said firmly. "We're staying to finish what we came here for."

Calhoun hung his head in defeat. "Stay in the back bedroom tonight," he said hoarsely. "There are two beds. Beneath the blue rug, there's a door that will take you down to a hole. It's a small tunnel that dumps you out behind the big oak in the back. It's not much, but it's the only protection I can offer if the posse comes here. If the house is surrounded, you can hunker down until it's over."

"What about you?" Matthew asked. He had grown fond of Calhoun. The man, in the midst of virulent hatred, exhibited a rare kind of courage to do the right thing.

Calhoun smiled briefly, a look of sad acceptance in his eyes. "I suppose I've known all along it would come to this. When they decide to come for me, it will be my time. I might delay it, but they will kill me."

Rose and Carrie were waiting on the porch when Jeb rode up in the dark. They were drinking strong cups of coffee to chase away the weariness from a sleepless night.

Dawn had not yet begun to lighten the sky. Thick clouds obscured the moon and stars, creating a somber mood that increased the sense of anxiety infusing the air.

Jeb pulled his horse to a stop. The lanterns on the porch illuminated his face enough to reveal a nervous gleam in his eyes. "They should be at the Rawlings' by now," he reported.

Rose sagged against the porch column with relief. "Alvin convinced enough of them?"

Jeb shrugged. "Don't know if it will be enough. Last I heard, he talked six men into going along with your scheme. If they get attacked by the Klan, I don't know what will happen."

Rose felt sick that she had put her students' fathers in danger, but it still seemed the best course of action.

"How far are they taking them?" Carrie asked, feeling a deep sense of déjà vu. Anthony had been driving the wagon when they'd helped Charlotte Cummings and her children escape. It had taken her persuasiveness to convince Charlotte to come with them, while Minnie and John helped convince the children it was alright to leave.

"They're doing the same thing you did," Jeb informed her. "They be taking them up to the railroad station north of Richmond. I gave them the money Mr. Cromwell sent for their train tickets. If all goes well, they'll be in Philadelphia sometime tomorrow."

It would be difficult for the family to start over, but at least they would be together. Along with the money, Thomas and Abby had included a letter to Rose's twin, Jeremy, asking him to find a position for Rawlings at the factory. They didn't know if he would be willing to work alongside black employees, but it would be his best chance at a job.

"I got some men watching from the woods," Jeb added.

"What?" Rose asked with surprise.

"I knew you'd want to know if the family got away," Jeb answered. "They be hidin' real good. Even if the Klan shows up to go after Rawlings, they won't see them. There be a hidden trail that follows the main road for a while. They gonna follow along until they get a ways down the road. If the Klan don't know they're leaving, and they don't come after them, there be a good chance they'll make it."

Rose smiled. "You're a good man, Jeb. Thank you."

Jeb's lips tightened. "Ain't no need to thank me yet, Miss Rose. Alvin might have found the whole family dead this morning," he said flatly. "I don't know nothing. We tried to keep it quiet, but not everyone he asked agreed to do it. One of them who refused his request could have talked about our plans. The Klan ain't gonna let them ride out of here if they done caught wind of anything."

"When will we know?" Anxiety tightened Rose's gut again. She knew it was possible the Klan had been tipped off.

"Alvin is gonna send one of the men back with news once they get at least ten miles away." He hesitated. "He don't know I have some of the plantation men watching. I weren't taking any chances on them being exposed."

Rose hated that Jeb had made the right decision. The plantation men would risk their lives easily for Cromwell, but it wasn't fair to ask them to risk anything for a family that had been responsible for so much misery. Alvin had convinced some of the area white men to help with their plan, but they had no way of knowing the connections they might have with the KKK.

Rose took a deep breath. "We've done all we can."

"And now we wait," Carrie said softly.

Rose had just given her students a writing assignment when she heard the clatter of hoofbeats on the dirt road that led past the schoolhouse. She stiffened, well aware it could be a contingency of the Klan coming to mock their effort to protect the Rawlings. Worse, if they had foiled the plan to rescue Rawlings and his family, they could have been emboldened to attack the schoolhouse in retaliation. She exchanged a look with Hazel, the school's other teacher, and carefully edged toward a window so she could peer out.

"Mrs. Samuels?"

Rose looked down to see Bernice, Jeb's ten-year-old daughter, looking up at her. "You should go sit down," Rose said calmly, hoping fear wasn't revealed in her voice.

"Is something bad happening?" Bernice whispered with a trembling voice.

Rose wanted to reassure her, but she knew she might be ushering the children out the back door to safety any minute. She still hadn't looked outside. "It will be fine," she said weakly.

"Is my daddy alright?" Bernice asked.

Rose sucked in her breath but didn't answer immediately. *What did the little girl know?*

Bernice answered her unspoken question. "I heard Daddy and Mama talking last night. They didn't know I was awake. Do you think Rodney is safe? He's my friend. He lets me play with him at lunch."

Rose sighed knowing it was impossible to keep secrets in small houses. She glanced up and realized every child was watching her. "Your father is fine," she assured the little girl.

"What about Rodney?" Bernice asked persistently.

"I hope so," Rose said quietly. She couldn't honestly say more than that. Every student in her school understood fear and loss. She hoped they wouldn't have to endure more.

Her thoughts flew to the adjoining schoolhouse where Phoebe taught. Ever since the Virginia Board of Education had deemed it illegal for black and white students to study together, they had been forced to separate the students. They still played at recess and shared special events together, but the separation meant she didn't know what was going on with the other half of her students. Since it had been white fathers who had helped the Rawlings family, they were in as much jeopardy – perhaps more.

Keeping her hand on Bernice's shoulder, Rose moved to the window and looked out again. She held back a gasp of relief when she recognized Alvin. His war years had left him with half a leg and a missing arm, but he still rode with grace. She watched as he and five other men rode up to the gate.

"All of you stay in your seats," Rose said firmly. "Everything is fine." She looked down at Bernice. "Your daddy is fine. Go have a seat. I'll let you know about Rodney as soon as I can."

Bernice looked like she wanted to protest, but she nodded and obeyed.

Rose slipped from the schoolhouse and ran up to the gate. "Alvin!"

Alvin's thin face was serious, but he didn't look alarmed. "They're gone, Miss Rose."

"They made it safely?" Rose demanded. *Gone* could mean many things.

"Far as we know," Alvin assured her. "We watched them get on the train. I was gonna send two men back earlier to tell you, but it seemed best to stay together."

Rose sagged with relief, knowing how fast they must have ridden to get to the train station and back. "That's wonderful news." She smiled up at the five men. "Thank you. I know I asked a tremendous thing of you." She stiffened suddenly and glanced nervously down the road. "Did anyone see you?" The men could still be in grave danger.

"Not that we know of," Alvin replied, although worry glinted in his eyes. "We rode fast so that we would be less likely to be missed around here. The Klan has eyes everywhere."

"Surely the Klan would have tried to stop you if they saw you helping Rawlings and his family leave," Rose said, praying she was right.

"Maybe," Alvin said slowly. "They might figure they're better off with Rawlings gone anyway since he ain't gonna be in the Klan anymore. That don't mean..."

Rose understood when his voice trailed off. The Klan might be alright with Rawlings leaving, but that didn't mean they wouldn't exact retribution from the men who made it possible. If they hadn't seen him leave though, there would be no retribution to exact. They might simply decide they had lost their chance to kill the KKK defector.

"Only time will tell," Alvin finally said. "We're all gonna go on home. I just wanted to let you know that your plan worked."

"Thank you all," Rose said again, hoping her fervent tone indicated how grateful she was.

Alvin nodded. "Jeb was right. We'll do just about anything for you, Miss Rose." He smiled slightly. "I just hope your next request ain't such a big one."

Rose laughed. "I'll do my best," she promised.

When Rose turned back toward the school, she saw Carrie step out onto the porch of the medical clinic. She smiled brightly and nodded.

Carrie grinned, raised a hand, and then walked back inside.

Rose gazed up into the trees, taking a moment to relish the victory before she went back inside to her students to tell them Rodney was safe, but wouldn't be back.

Chapter Twelve

April 13, 1873
Easter Sunday

Matthew had been pulled out into the early morning by a compulsion he didn't understand. The last few days had been uneventful, but he could feel the tension in the air. Restless and anxious, he needed to go for a walk to clear his head.

Purple wisteria climbed pine trees, its fragrant blooms disappearing into the fog hovering in the woods. He knew the sun would burn it off quickly.-He startled a deer and her fawn drinking from a small stream. They gazed at him wide-eyed and then melted into the overgrowth. Thick ferns created a nearly impenetrable layer on the forest floor. Narrow trails revealed animal routes through the forest.

There had been no communication from Ward. Not one man had been willing to leave the courthouse to deliver news, but there had been no sounds of battle. Not knowing was somehow worse than being in the thick of the conflict.

Calhoun sat on his front porch every day with a rifle resting on his knees and a pistol sitting on the table next to the coffee he never seemed to be without. The lines etched in his face deepened with each passing day. He was grateful for their company, but he had obviously resigned himself to what he believed was the inevitable outcome.

A crackling noise in the woods made him stop short and peer around. He knew he was in a vulnerable position.

"Where are you going?"

Matthew whirled around when the hissed whisper sounded behind him.

Anthony stepped out of the woods.

"What are you doing here?" Matthew demanded, willing his heart to slow down.

"I saw you leave and followed you," Anthony admitted. "Where are you going?"

"I'm going for a walk."

"To where?"

Matthew shrugged. "How would I know? I know I'm not headed toward the courthouse, but I don't know anything about Calhoun's plantation. I just needed to clear my head."

Anthony's expression said he understood. "Mind if I join you?"

Matthew didn't feel like talking, but he welcomed his friend's company. "If you can be quiet."

Anthony grinned. "I can do that."

The two men set off down the narrow trail, their footsteps soundless in the soft green growth that spread out from the surrounding forest.

Matthew walked slowly, taking deep breaths of the cool morning air. With nothing happening over the last few days, he wondered if all the fear and anticipation had been for nothing. Perhaps Nash's posse, intent on taking the courthouse back, had decided it wasn't worth the risk of actually doing it. Perhaps they feared U.S. troops arriving and throwing them in jail. He wondered if he and Anthony should leave the following morning and head home. Just the thought made him happy.

He closed his eyes for a moment and imagined waking up next to Janie and playing with his children in the yard.

"What's that?" Anthony suddenly asked, his voice deliberately low.

Matthew jolted to a stop and opened his eyes. "What is what?" he hissed.

Anthony lifted his head and sniffed. "I smell campfire and bacon," he whispered.

Matthew frowned. "As far as I know, we're still on Calhoun's plantation. There shouldn't be anyone out here."

Anthony responded by moving off the trail and edging back into the wooded cover.

Matthew followed. Now that he was paying attention, he could smell the campfire and bacon as well.

Anthony began to pick his way forward, placing his feet carefully to keep from alerting whatever, or whoever, was ahead.

Matthew followed closely, feeling more vulnerable than ever. He regretted not having his pistol. *What had he been thinking?* A quick look told him Anthony was unarmed as well. They couldn't afford to be discovered.

It took less than five minutes to begin to hear noises. Knowing the sounds would mask their approach, they moved a little quicker, intent on staying out of sight.

Matthew sucked in his breath when he stopped and peered through the undergrowth. His heart sank and then started beating furiously. He was grateful for the sounds of the encampment that would conceal their presence.

Anthony squeezed his shoulder tightly. "We've got to get out of here," he hissed. "We have to warn them what is coming."

Matthew knew he was right, but he couldn't take his eyes off the clearing around what seemed to be an old sugar mill. There were more than a hundred men gathered around cookfires. Their laughter and talk filled the air but couldn't hide the dark danger that hovered over them. Matthew watched as men cleaned and checked their rifles and six-shooters. Every man seemed to be well armed.

Anthony gripped his shoulder again. "Look."

Matthew's eyes followed his pointing finger. His eyes widened with disbelief when he saw a field cannon. He suspected it had been commandeered from one of the riverboats. It wasn't large, but it would certainly give the men an advantage if they could get it close enough to the courthouse.

He thought of all the men, women, and children who believed the courthouse was a haven of safety. Then he looked again at the small army determined to take it back.

There was no haven.

One of the men, obviously a leader, called the others into formation.

Matthew knew they should leave, but he felt compelled to hear what was happening. He had already determined he couldn't stop whatever battle was coming, but he had vowed to make sure the nation would know the truth; that truth involved what was happening in this clearing. He sank down deeper into the overgrowth, slowing his breathing so he could hear more clearly.

The leader leapt onto his horse and rode along the line of men who had settled into a straight-line formation. He asked each of them their name and kept a careful tally in a book he carried.

When he was done, the man led his horse to the middle of the formation and spoke loudly enough to be heard by everyone. "Boys, this is a struggle for white supremacy. There are one hundred and sixty-five of us ready to go into Colfax this morning. God only knows who will come out. Those who do will probably be prosecuted for treason, and the punishment for treason is death."

His words rang out, hanging in the smoke-filled air. A somber silence fell over the clearing.

Matthew watched as emotions played across the faces of every member of the posse. He recognized Sheriff Nash standing to the side, watching the lineup with angry determination. It had taken him more than two weeks to pull together this posse. How many of them would really do battle after what the leader had said?

"You know what you're up against." The man's voice rang out. "If you're afraid to die for white supremacy, now is the time to step out of line."

About twenty-five men, their faces full of fear and hesitation, stepped forward, untied their horses, and rode away at a rapid gallop. Not one of them hesitated or looked back. Obviously, they hadn't been fully informed of what was expected of them.

Still, there was a large force ready to do what was required. The fact they had chosen to stay after what they'd heard, spoke of their fierce belief in their cause and actions.

The leader watched the others go, his face full of disdain, and then turned back to the men still watching him. "There are now one hundred and forty of us. That's plenty to do what we came to do. We ride to protect what is ours. We ride to protect white supremacy. We ride to protect our women and children from the plans of the blacks to violate and steal them!"

Matthew wanted to jump up and protest that every man there was being lied to, but he couldn't tell the truth to the nation if he was dead.

He and Anthony remained concealed as the small army of men mounted their horses and rode away.

"Let's go," Matthew said urgently. No longer worried about stealth, he crashed through the undergrowth and started running down the trail. He didn't know how long it would take the men to reach the courthouse, but he had to be there to bear witness to whatever happened. Anthony was right behind him when they burst out of the woods into Calhoun's yard. A quick glance at the front porch told them he hadn't yet assumed his guard position.

"Let's get our horses," Matthew said. "Calhoun shouldn't be there. Those men are in a killing mood, and Calhoun can't help. He'll be nothing but a sitting target."

Anthony turned toward the back door. "You get the horses. I'll get our guns."

Matthew and Anthony rode side-by-side down the dusty dirt road, their eyes constantly scanning the woods around them. There was still no sound of battle in the distance, but they knew it could change any minute. They also realized there could be men riding to capture Willie Calhoun. The fact that they were staying in his home would make them prime targets.

No one accosted them.

Just as they arrived, they saw a white man ride away from the courthouse encampment. They angled their horses to intercept him. The man, his blue eyes wide with terror, attempted to ride around them.

Matthew and Anthony, perfectly in sync, turned their horses across the narrow road to create a blockade.

Matthew held up his hand. “We’re not here to hurt you,” he said. “We’re friends of Willie Calhoun.”

The man, short and wiry, jerked to a stop and eyed them suspiciously. “What are you doing here?”

“My name is Matthew Justin. I’m a newspaper reporter,” Matthew informed him. “I intend to tell the truth about what happens here today. My friend here is Anthony Wallington.”

The man eyed Anthony. “A reporter I understand. What are *you* doing here?”

Anthony managed a wry smile. “I’ve been asking myself that same question every day.”

The man chuckled briefly before the tension reappeared. “My name is Arthur Valencia. I’m a schoolteacher and salesman from Connecticut who came down to work in this area a few months ago. I’ve been trying to help the freedmen, but they convinced me to leave a few minutes ago. They told me only black men would do the fighting.” He scowled. “I know they’re trying to protect me.”

“Do they stand a chance?” Matthew asked.

Arthur scowled. “Honestly? No. I fought with the Union during the war. I spent the night showing them how to dig a trench around the courthouse for protection, but not all the men are even armed. As far as I can tell, there are about two rounds per man. If there is a true assault, they don’t stand a chance. The trench will offer some protection, but I'm afraid not much. A true trench would have been enforced with heavy timbers and be deep enough for the men to kneel behind. There wasn't time for that. It wasn't until yesterday that they seemed to accept that an attack is inevitable and will most likely happen today." His mouth drooped. "The trench they dug is only about two feet at its deepest point. The dirt pile in front of it is reinforced with two-and-a-half-inch thick wooden planks." He shook his head. "The men worked on it all night. They're exhausted. When I left, there were dozens of them inside sleeping."

Matthew thought about what he'd seen. "There are one hundred and forty well-armed veterans headed this way," he stated frankly. "I'm surprised they're not here yet."

Arthur's face turned white. "I helped the freedmen rig up three improvised artillery pieces, but I doubt they'll even work. When they tried the first one, it exploded. We put the other two up on some dirt piles, but they're nothing more than a diversion." He took a deep breath. "I haven't been here very long, but there are many good men inside that courthouse. They believe they stand a chance."

"They don't," Anthony said sorrowfully.

Once again, Matthew considered turning and riding away. He didn't want Anthony to have to carry the Louisiana memories he would endure for the rest of his life, and he didn't want to expose them to danger, but he knew he couldn't leave. The truth must be told. "You don't have to stay, Anthony," he said fiercely. "Leave now. You'll be at the Mississippi by tomorrow night. You can wait for me there."

Anthony met his eyes. "I'm going to assume you know me well enough to know I'm not going to do that. We're in this together."

Matthew bit back further words. He wouldn't have been persuaded either if their positions had been reversed. Instead, he turned to gaze at the courthouse again. "What's happened with all the women and children?" He was relieved to see they were no longer camped around the building, but that didn't mean they were safe.

"The men sent them away shortly before you arrived," Arthur informed them. "They know they can't protect them from what's coming."

"Where are they?" Matthew asked.

"Back in the woods in a clearing on Calhoun's plantation," Arthur replied. "Most of the women and children are already there. The rest should be arriving now. I don't know how safe it is, but at least they won't be in the direct line of fire." He looked toward the river. "I had hoped Ward would return with the other men he took to New Orleans. Without them, they have only a handful of men with fighting experience."

"And no ammunition," Anthony growled. "Perhaps this could still end peacefully." The expression on his face said he didn't believe it.

Matthew shook his head. "It won't. Nash is out for blood. He won't settle for anything less than complete capitulation by the blacks. They'll have to surrender and give up all their arms."

"That won't happen," Arthur snapped. "There may have been a chance once, but that was before Jesse McKinney was shot in the head in his yard. Jesse's killers are with Nash. If these men lay down their arms, they'll be at the mercy of those killers."

"I'm afraid they're going to be at their mercy anyway." Matthew cast around in his mind for some kind of solution, but the situation had reached a point of no return.

Arthur nodded. "I believe you're right." He looked at Anthony. "I'm headed for the Mississippi. This state is crazy. Are you sure you don't want to join me?"

Matthew knew before the sentence was out of his mouth what his friend would say.

"I'm staying," Anthony said simply.

Arthur turned and rode away.

Matthew and Anthony had ridden away from the courthouse to occupy a higher position on the far side of a cotton field that would soon be destroyed by the posse. Unless they were deliberately attacked, they should be safe.

It was shortly after noon when the skirmish line appeared. Even from a distance, Matthew could see the determined, angry looks on the faces of the men moving toward the courthouse.

The freedmen ran forward and lay down behind the trenches.

The battle was about to begin.

When the posse was about three hundred yards from the building, they called for the cannon. A crew of men rushed forward with the field gun wagon. They put in the gunpowder, followed by an iron slug and some wadding.

Matthew tensed as he watched them pack the missiles in with a ramrod and light the fuse.

Boom!

The first shot landed well in front of the trenches. It kicked up a shower of red soil but did no damage.

"Perhaps the freedmen stand a chance," Anthony said, a hint of glee in his voice.

Matthew didn't reply. Nash's men were just getting started.

The skirmishers began to fire, but the freedmen stayed below the trenches. The bullets zipped over their heads but found no targets. An occasional shot came from the freedmen, but it was obvious they were saving their ammunition as ordered.

"They're going to shoot one of their artillery pieces," Anthony exclaimed. He leaned forward in the saddle as a group of the defenders prepared to fire the makeshift cannon the schoolteacher had helped them build. One man lit the fuse and ran back to join the others, who had retreated to the end of the trenches. They had obviously learned their lesson after test-firing the first one.

Matthew prayed this one would work.

There was the expected boom, but it came from the improvised cannon blowing up.

Matthew could hear the laughter rolling up from Nash's men. He knew the spectacle would do nothing but embolden them.

Nash's men moved the cannon closer, but it still wasn't close enough to reach the trenches. It was obvious they weren't eager to get within rifle range of the defenders waiting for them.

Matthew and Anthony watched for two hours, but the battle was little more than a standoff. Regular fire from Nash's men was met by sporadic gunfire from the defenders, but neither side made progress.

"Perhaps they stand a chance after all," Matthew muttered. "I suspect many of Nash's men aren't anxious to die to protect the courthouse. They might not have ridden off like the twenty-five this morning, but that doesn't mean they're willing to risk their lives."

"What's that?" Anthony asked suddenly.

Matthew looked in the direction he was pointing. Their higher position gave them the ability to see what the courthouse defenders could not. His heart sank as he watched a pair of men scouting the riverbank. Inexperienced in tactical warfare, the freedmen had not thought to protect their flank. The levee that separated the courthouse from the river was completely unguarded.

"There's a gap in the levee," Anthony groaned. "It's behind and to the right of the trench line. If they get the cannon there..."

Matthew didn't finish the sentence for him. He already knew Nash's men would carry the cannon wherever it could be useful. When they fired, the missiles would go straight into the trenches.

They watched as a group of men began to move the cannon. To distract the freedmen from what was happening, the other skirmishers opened fire. They couldn't hit the men in the trenches, but it assured that the defenders were oblivious of what was happening behind them.

Matthew gritted his teeth, helpless to stop what was unfolding. There was no way to broadcast a warning to stop the inevitable bloodshed. "This is going to be bad."

Anthony remained silent. The expression on his face revealed the horror he was feeling.

As the cannon crew rose to load the artillery piece, making them vulnerable to the freedmen if they were spotted, the firing intensified from the rest of the line to cover their actions.

Boom!

Matthew's gut twisted as he watched a hail of buckshot descend upon the oblivious defenders. He heard the screams and cries of pain.

The freedmen panicked with the unexpected attack. Chaos erupted as the men leapt up and dashed for the cover of the courthouse. There were so many trying to force their way in through the narrow door, others had to run in another direction, with nowhere to go.

Nash's men let out a rousing rebel yell and rushed forward, their rifles blazing.

Matthew grimaced. He had witnessed many scenes like this during the war. The Confederacy was alive and well in Louisiana.

It was obvious the battle had turned in Nash's favor. His forces raced forward, stopped at the warehouse next to the courthouse, and continued to shoot at the fleeing freedmen, cheering as more men fell beneath the barrage of bullets.

"They're moving the cannon closer," Anthony said grimly.

Matthew watched as the crew moved the cannon to within about eighty yards of the courthouse and fired four more blasts. A shot from a defender struck one of the cannon men, causing the gun to fall silent, but a full rout was already under way. The cannon was no longer needed.

A group of the defenders, realizing they had lost, raced for the woods, trying to reach their wives and children.

Bile rose in Matthew's throat as about twenty of Nash's posse remounted and raced after the fleeing defenders. There was nothing he could do as he watched them fall beneath a hail of bullets. He watched one man fall and then rise enough to crawl toward the trees. One of the posse members stopped, spun around, and rode back to shoot him several more times. This time, when the man fell, he didn't move again.

Matthew felt a moment's relief when Nash's men stopped short of the woods. Evidently, they were willing to gun down men fleeing in an open field, but they weren't eager to track them through undergrowth and tendrils of Spanish moss.

His relief was short-lived.

"They're going back to the courthouse," Anthony groaned.

Matthew, reliving the memories of all the deaths at the New Orleans courthouse in 1866, could only grit his teeth and shake his head. The courthouse was completely surrounded. He could imagine the scene inside. There were dozens of men crammed into the building. He knew they were terrified.

Nash sat astride his horse, talking to some of his men.

Despite the suffering within the building, a steady barrage of bullets erupted from the windows. The men were hopelessly outgunned and outnumbered, but they weren't giving up. Matthew knew they were all too aware of what would happen if they did.

"Do you think he'll lay siege to the building?" Anthony asked. "The freedmen must be hungry, thirsty, and desperate. I doubt it would take more than a day or two before they're forced to surrender."

Matthew thought about what he knew of the man leading the battle. He was almost certain what he would do. "I don't think so," he said shortly. "He's not the type to wait. He won't risk the possibility of troops arriving."

As he spoke, he saw the beginning of what he had expected to happen. A crew of men set fire to the wooden cistern house adjoining the courthouse. Flames leapt upward, but they didn't extend to the cypress shingles next door.

"They're going to set the courthouse on fire!" Anthony exclaimed.

Matthew nodded, knowing they would devise a method to achieve their goal. The challenge would be accomplishing it without more casualties. After some talk, two of the men ducked into an abandoned cabin and emerged with a long bamboo fishing pole. Another man slashed open a saddle blanket and pulled out wads of cotton. It took only minutes for them to tie the cotton to the end of the pole and then douse it with kerosene and light it.

It flared up in the afternoon air thick with smoke.

One of the freedmen, captured from the first wave of fleeing defenders, was called forward. The man holding the torch thrust it into his hands and pointed him toward the courthouse.

Matthew didn't have to hear the conversation to know the man was being told to set fire to the building…or die. He watched, his heart in his throat, as the elderly black man walked slowly across the clearing. When he approached the building, the man looked up in supplication before he touched the torch to the wooden shingles.

Flames leapt upward immediately.

Even from this distance, Matthew could sense the panic and desperation erupting inside the old stable. He knew they would try to put it out, but there was no water. He watched as several men tried to climb into the rafters to knock out the blazing patch of shingles, but carefully placed shots from the posse drove them back.

It took less than a minute for the fire to spread out of control.

"The roof is caving in," Anthony groaned.

Matthew knew the men inside would have to surrender. What he didn't know was what would happen once they did.

Chapter Thirteen

Matthew couldn't hear anything over the sounds of the battle, but he spied the white shirtsleeve tied to the end of a stick as it appeared from a window. Another hand appeared, waving a white sheet of paper.

"They're surrendering," Anthony said. He looked at Matthew. "What's going to happen?"

Matthew shook his head and kept his eyes trained on the action, not willing to give voice to his fears. More than anything, he wanted to be wrong. He knew the freedmen would have been ordered to put all their weapons down. He prayed they complied.

He watched closely, grateful the smoke had lifted enough to make the doorway visible. He took a breath of relief as he watched a dozen black men appear. They were unarmed, some of them waving pocket handkerchiefs as tokens of their capitulation.

Within seconds, his relief turned to horror.

As soon as the first dozen were clear of the building, the firing began.

"No!" Matthew yelled, the blood seeming to drain from his entire body.

"They're massacring them…" Anthony's face was slack with shock.

Matthew couldn't look away. Six of the men fell on the spot. He watched as six others broke free and ran to the nearest warehouse, hoping to hide. A group of Nash's men ran into the warehouse after them. Moments later, Matthew heard at least a dozen shots. He knew all the freedmen were dead.

He wasn't ashamed of the tears rolling down his face.

The firing continued. Nash's men were arranged around the courthouse in a huge, irregular semicircle, all of them shooting.

"They're going to shoot each other," Anthony growled. "I hope they kill each other off."

Matthew echoed his sentiments but couldn't force words past the boulder in his throat.

He felt a grim satisfaction as he watched five of Nash's men fall, all from friendly fire.

The wind had shifted in their direction. It carried a wave of acrid smoke, but it also bore Nash's words. "Cease firing, men! You're shooting our own men!"

The shooting stopped, and the remaining defenders were rounded up and taken prisoner. A group of them were put under guard at the base of a sprawling pecan tree. The others were marched to a nearby field and placed beneath a downy cottonwood. Desperation hung in the air like a cloud of relentless mosquitoes.

Matthew and Anthony sat like statues on their horses as the afternoon continued to play out. More than anything, Matthew wanted to wheel his horse around and ride away as fast as he could, never looking back and never returning to the state of Louisiana. He sat stoically, trying his best to compartmentalize the emotions rampaging inside him.

Two of the freedmen were ordered to put out the fire that had spread to the next-door warehouse.

Random gunfire announced another defender dead. Nash's men were spread out, seeking anyone they could murder.

By four o'clock, dead men lay scattered all over Colfax. The wounded moaned and screamed as smoke continued to boil up from the courthouse.

Matthew continued to sit and watch. He was barely aware that Anthony hadn't left his side. Part of him was grateful, but another part wished no one else would ever know what he had endured in this state. It would have been easier to pretend the pain wouldn't constantly haunt him. Knowing Anthony would carry the same terrible memories somehow made his own seem even more unbearable.

Anthony spoke only when the sun slipped below the tree line. "What will they do with the prisoners?"

"I have no idea," Matthew admitted. He had suspicions, but he couldn't bring himself to voice them.

"Are we going to stay out here all night?" Anthony asked quietly.

Matthew realized with a start that it was going to be dark soon. "No." He sighed deeply and nudged his horse forward. The only thing he knew to do was return to Calhoun's house. They needed to assure themselves the man was alright, but they also needed a place to spend the night.

"We're leaving in the morning," Matthew said shortly. He wished he could leave that very moment, but it was too dangerous to travel at night and Thomas would want to know Calhoun's fate.

"Fine with me," Anthony muttered. His face was tense as he gazed at the chaos below them. "Are we going to ride through all that to get back to Calhoun's?"

Matthew hesitated, but he didn't know any other way. "Things seem to have calmed down. Nash's men are probably all back at the sugar mill."

"Except the ones guarding the prisoners," Anthony reminded him.

"We'll be alright," Matthew said firmly, hoping he sounded more confident than he felt. "They're not looking for us. I saw Hooe near the courthouse a little while ago. He'll let people know I'm a reporter covering the story."

"And if he asks you how you're going to report it?" Anthony demanded.

"I'll lie," Matthew said bluntly. Only then did he turn to gaze at Anthony. "We're leaving this godforsaken state and going home to our wives."

As they rode through the carnage, Matthew bit his lip to keep from sobbing. Sightless corpses stared up at him. Flies were already starting to swarm around their bodies.

Anthony gasped as they approached one of the victims. "It's Alford," he said hoarsely.

Matthew looked down at the short man's bullet-riddled body. "What a waste," he said bitterly. "All he wanted was to live in this country as a free man. His wife and children will have no one now."

"Let's get out of here," Anthony said, desperation tinging his words. He broke his horse into a canter and surged forward out of sight.

Matthew was more than happy to follow his lead. As he rode, he wondered what had happened to Ronnie, but he averted his eyes from the bodies they passed. He simply couldn't stomach more tragedy.

Early the next morning, Matthew carried a cup of coffee out onto the porch. He and Anthony were eager to head out. He found Calhoun in his usual place, his rifle resting on his lap.

When they had returned the night before, they'd filled their host in on the horrific events of the day. As terrible as it had been for them, Matthew knew it was worse for Calhoun. The man had given everything he could to assure freedom and equality for the people once enslaved on his plantation. In one bloody afternoon, it had all disappeared.

"Did you hear it last night?" Calhoun demanded.

"Hear what?" Once he had finally fallen asleep, Matthew hadn't moved until sunlight filtering through tree limbs had awoken him.

"I don't know for sure," Calhoun replied evasively.

The look on his face told Matthew the man was actually quite certain of what he'd heard. "Hear what?" he repeated grimly.

Anthony stepped out onto the porch. "I heard gunfire last night. What was it?"

Calhoun's face was suffused with a combination of anger and sorrow. "I suspect Nash's men killed all the prisoners," he said hoarsely. If possible, the lines on his face deepened further as he spoke the words.

Matthew felt the blood drain from his face. He had suspected what would happen but had held out a slim margin of hope that he was wrong. "My God..." he whispered.

Anthony suddenly held up a hand. "What was that?"

Matthew listened intently, finally hearing what had alerted his friend. There was something in the undergrowth moving slowly toward them. He reached for the pistol at his waistband at the same time Anthony did. Calhoun picked up his rifle and joined them at the edge of the porch. All their guns were trained on the noise.

The three men stood silently, waiting until the danger revealed itself.

After what seemed like an eternity, Matthew saw a human form dragging itself through the ferns. When he identified the form as a black man, he sprang off the porch and ran toward him. “Ronnie!”

Ronnie gazed up at him briefly before passing out.

Anthony helped Matthew pick up the man’s battered body.

Ronnie had been shot once in the face and twice in the back. “I can’t believe he’s not dead,” Anthony whispered. “How could he possibly survive this?”

Matthew had no answer. “Let’s get him inside.”

Calhoun looked grave as they stepped onto the porch. “Take Ronnie into the back bedroom,” he ordered.

“Can Winnie get us some hot water?” Matthew asked.

“I’m afraid not,” Calhoun said. “Both her husband and son were killed last night. She’s with the other wives and children.”

Matthew set his lips and looked at Anthony. “Let’s get him into the bed. I’ll boil water while you examine his wounds.” He turned to Calhoun. “Do you have any medical supplies?”

Calhoun raised a brow. “Would you know what to do with them?”

Matthew smiled briefly. “Both our wives are doctors. We’ve picked up a few things.” He wasn’t at all sure they stood any chance of keeping Ronnie alive, but they would try.

Calhoun hobbled into the house. "You go boil the water. I'll look for bandages."

Matthew and Anthony carried Ronnie into the house and laid him down on a bed.

His eyes opened to a mere slit before he groaned and passed out again.

"Best thing for him," Matthew said sympathetically. "I'll be back soon."

In the kitchen, he stirred the embers in the stove, added more wood, and then filled a kettle to place on top. He found a large metal pan to accumulate the water, and then rummaged through the shelves in search of clean rags. Once he had a pile, he started opening cabinets, certain Winnie had what he was looking for. He grunted with satisfaction when he discovered onions, garlic heads, and a large jar of honey.

While the water heated, he sliced onions, opened the garlic cloves, and mashed them into a thick paste. Adding honey slowly, he stirred until he was sure he had a poultice Janie would be proud of.

He carried in the pan full of hot water, holding the rags beneath his arm. Anthony had just finished undressing Ronnie's battered body. "How is he?"

"Barely alive," Anthony snapped. "The only good news I have for you is that the bullets went straight through his body. We don't have to attempt to remove them."

Matthew grimaced. "Good thing. I'm afraid that's beyond either of our abilities." He laid down the pan and handed Anthony the rags. "Start cleaning him up. I'll help when I get back with the poultice."

Calhoun appeared at the door. His arms were full of soft cotton cloths that could be used as bandages. He had ripped strips from a sheet that they could use to secure them. “This should do the trick,” he said. “At least, I hope it will.”

Matthew nodded his approval. “That’s perfect.” As he headed into the kitchen, he realized they wouldn’t be riding to the Mississippi that day. He didn’t know if they could save Ronnie’s life, but they were certainly going to try.

Later that evening, Matthew and Anthony joined Calhoun on the porch. They left the lanterns unlit so they could more easily see anyone approaching the house.

“How is Ronnie?” Calhoun asked.

“Alive,” Anthony replied. “I don’t know if he will be in the morning, but he’s still breathing tonight.” He shook his head. “The fact that he lived long enough to get here indicates he’s a strong man with an incredible will to live. He might just make it.”

Matthew looked out into the darkness and then glanced at Calhoun. “I don’t see your gun.”

Calhoun shrugged. “If I need it, it’s just inside the door, but I don’t think I will.”

Matthew and Anthony waited quietly for him to explain.

“Three of the freedmen’s wives came by this afternoon when you were in the back.” Disgust dripped from Calhoun’s voice. “This morning, after all the shooting stopped, the women went to find their husbands. When they got to Smithfield Quarters, they found white men and women plundering and looting their homes. They took all the beds, wagons, mules, and horses. They stole the entire grain supply.”

Matthew wished he could feel shocked. All he felt was a numb acceptance of man's depravity toward other humans.

"The men are still lying where they fell," Calhoun said, his voice cracking as he spoke the words. "They're being eaten by wild dogs and consumed by flies."

Matthew wished he could become accustomed to bile rising in his throat. He blinked his eyes to diminish the images, but it was a futile effort.

Calhoun took a deep breath. "One of the women who came is named Elzie. When she heard the firing last night, she had to know what was happening to her husband. She had seen him corralled with the others beneath the pecan tree yesterday. All through the day she'd held onto the hope he would survive. She crept through the woods and hid in a tall patch of weeds…"

Matthew's throat tightened as Calhoun's voice trailed off. He knew something terrible was coming.

Even the crickets and frogs fell silent as Calhoun struggled to find words.

"Her husband, Etienne, was being marched by. She saw him pulled to a stop and heard him plead for his life. She watched one of Nash's men shoot her husband in the head. Etienne fell almost at her feet. All she could do was crouch in the weeds until they left. She isn't strong enough to pull her husband off the path. He's still lying there."

Calhoun continued in a flat voice. "At least she knows what happened to him. Another of the women told me she saw the posse throwing bodies in the river. They'll most likely never be recovered." He paused. "A few white men came to Elzie today and told her to find men to bury all the bodies."

"So they can cover the evidence," Anthony said bitterly.

"Yes," Calhoun agreed. "Elzie, of course, said she would, but there are no black men to be found. They're either dead or hiding in the woods. Elzie told me there are a group of them still in the pond."

Matthew gasped. "They've been standing in the pond since last night?"

"Safest place for them right now," Calhoun spat. "There's still killing in the air."

Matthew knew he was right. "Why don't you have your gun?"

Calhoun shrugged. "Men from New Orleans will be here soon. It won't be the requested troops, but Governor Kellogg will have to send some type of emissary. Nash knows they'll discover what happened here, so he's not going to allow me to be killed right now. I guarantee you he's trying to figure out a way to come through this and still be the sheriff of Grant Parish."

"Do you believe he will?" Anthony asked incredulously.

Calhoun took a deep breath. "I believe anything is possible around here. I'm leaving for New Orleans in the morning. I'm safe tonight, but I know those boys will try to pin this massacre on me and William Ward. I'm going to make sure he stays away. There's nothing either of us can do at this point, but if we're able to stay alive and out of jail, there might be something we can do in the future."

Matthew thought of Ronnie. He agreed with Calhoun that the man needed to flee, but he and Anthony wouldn't leave until they knew if Ronnie would make it. If he actually survived, some of the women could care for him. He would also be a perfect witness if there was ever to be a trial, which Matthew doubted.

"What's going to happen to Nash and his men?" Anthony demanded heatedly.

Calhoun and Matthew looked at each other, wordlessly communicating their thoughts.

"Honestly?" Matthew answered. "Probably nothing."

"How can you say that?" Anthony protested. "They massacred close to one hundred men. They shot them down like dogs."

"You don't have to tell me how wrong it is," Matthew growled. "I'm only telling you what I think will happen. Not one man was convicted and jailed for the Memphis Riot seven years ago. They killed hundreds and forced thousands more to flee Memphis for the North. No one paid a price for that, despite all the witnesses who bravely told what happened."

"And the massacre in New Orleans that year?" Anthony demanded.

Matthew shrugged, once again feeling the helpless frustration that dogged him. "No one went to jail. Some of the city officers were forced from their positions, but no one was convicted or served jail time." There had been plenty of witnesses to those murders as well.

"Nothing will ever change..." Anthony's voice was thick with defeat.

Calhoun raised a hand. "No one was convicted or served prison time, but that doesn't mean nothing changed, Anthony. While no one paid a personal price, those two riots ignited the country and discredited President Johnson and his policies. Radical Republicans swept the congressional elections that year, obtaining a veto-proof majority. Doing that enabled them to pass the Reconstruction Acts, the Enforcement Acts, and the Fourteenth Amendment that enabled blacks to vote."

Anthony didn't look impressed. "It doesn't seem to be working out so well in Louisiana."

Matthew couldn't find the words to argue with him. Despite all that the Radical Republicans had accomplished, it meant little here in Louisiana and other former Confederate states. Since many Radical Republicans had been defeated in the last elections, the fight for racial equality faced massive headwinds in Congress. The majority of Americans didn't believe in slavery, but that didn't mean they believed in equality for the millions of blacks recently emancipated.

"Perhaps this will wake up the nation to what is happening," Calhoun replied.

Matthew looked at him sharply. "Do you truly believe that?"

Calhoun nodded quickly but then stopped. His eyes dropped and he shrugged. "I don't know what I believe," he admitted quietly. "I want to believe something positive can come from what has happened here. I want to believe men will pay for the murders committed. I want to believe there are enough good people in Louisiana to stand against the hatred of the white supremacists." He sighed heavily. "I suppose only time will tell."

Four days later, Matthew and Anthony finally rode away from Colfax. Ronnie, against all odds, had survived. He would have a long recovery time, but his wife had been taught how to care for him, and she had plenty of supplies. The onion, garlic, and honey poultice had saved Ronnie from an infection that would have ordinarily claimed his life. Other wounded men were also on the road to recovery, at least physically. They would never be able to forget the horror of what they had experienced.

Two U.S. Marshals had arrived from New Orleans two days after the massacre. They would return to New Orleans with their report, but first they had to organize the burial of the corpses that were bloating in the heat. The stench had forced everyone in the area to wear bandanas over their faces.

Individual graves for so many were out of the question. There were only a handful of black men who could be found to do the digging. The solution was to utilize the trench that had already been dug around the courthouse. It was only two feet deep, but the bodies were heaved into the trench and then covered with the red soil of the old Calhoun plantation.

Matthew refused to think about the bodies that would be dug up by dogs, or the bones that would be washed clean by rain.

Without casting a single look behind him, Matthew cantered down the road. He wanted to leave Grant Parish as fast as possible. He hoped that he would find breathing a little easier as they got farther away.

He didn't.

It was several hours before Anthony spoke. "How do you do it?"

Matthew knew what he was asking. "One day at a time," he said, speaking loudly enough to be heard over the drumbeat of hooves. "You will never forget what we've experienced here. You'll never stop having nightmares of what you've seen." He thought about sugarcoating his response, but his friend deserved the truth.

"You still have them?" Anthony asked roughly.

Matthew nodded. Seven years had made what he had experienced in Memphis and New Orleans easier to bear, but now he had Colfax heaped on top of it. He knew the images in his mind were a burden he would carry for the rest of his life.

"How do you do it?" Anthony repeated, this time with an edge of desperation.

Matthew pulled his horse to a stop, waiting for Anthony to do the same, and turned to face his friend. "I wish you hadn't come, Anthony. I wish you hadn't experienced Colfax, but you did. While you'll never forget it, you can also choose to focus on the good things in your life. When the nightmares come, I snuggle closer to Janie. When the images assault me, I play with my children. I write a new story about the good things happening in our country. I walk around the plantation. I go for a ride."

"It helps?" Anthony demanded.

"It helps," Matthew said. "You have Carrie. You have four beautiful children. You have a successful business in Richmond." He remembered something Anthony had told him several years earlier. "When you lost your first wife and child, you didn't think you'd ever get over it."

Anthony's lips tightened. "That's true. I still think about them, but I can remember the good times now." His eyes hardened. "There are no good things to remember about Colfax."

"That's not true," Matthew said, speaking the words for himself as much as he did for Anthony. "Without us, Calhoun could well be dead. Ronnie would be dead for sure. Without us, there would be no one to speak the truth of what happened in Colfax to the nation." As soon as he reached the Mississippi, he would be able to telegraph the

Philadelphia Inquirer that a series of articles would be coming soon.

"Don't you get tired?" Anthony asked. "I don't understand how you've reported on so many tragic events over the years. Why haven't you quit?"

Matthew managed a smile. "I have. Several times." He paused, thinking about the things he'd seen and written about. "Every time I quit something would happen that I believed needed to be told. Like now. I could turn away and refuse to do it, or I could agree to be the voice." He thought about Willie Calhoun and his decision to come in Thomas' place. "It's too late to stop what happened in Colfax, but telling the truth about the massacre could still save Calhoun's life. And William Ward's life."

Matthew thought more deeply. "Years ago, when I was helping Abby fight the businessmen determined to destroy her factories after her first husband's death, she told me something I've never forgotten. She said it was something she hung onto every day." He could feel Anthony's eyes boring into him. "Abby told me that I have one life. One chance to make it count for something. She told me that her faith demands that she do whatever she can, wherever and whenever she can." He paused again. The words felt as powerful and true to him at that moment as they had almost fifteen years earlier, when he was freshly out of college. "She challenged me to do the same, with whatever I have, to try to make a difference."

Anthony nodded thoughtfully. "Do you truly believe we've made a difference here?"

"I do," Matthew declared. Just saying the words made the burden of the images slightly easier to bear. He turned his horse and urged him into a trot. "Neither of us are going to be alright until we get home to our families on the plantation."

Anthony surged forward to join him. "Let's go home."

Chapter Fourteen

Carrie and Susan walked slowly through the horse pastures, stopping to stroke mares nursing their foals, and kneeling down to greet colts and fillies. It was a beautiful spring day, but dark clouds beginning to boil on the horizon warned of an incoming storm.

"The rain will be here in a few hours," Susan said, eyeing the huge nimbus clouds.

"We need it," Carrie replied. "The tobacco seedlings have been planted. What they need now are rain and sunshine." She lifted her face to the sky, enjoying the cool, humid air spiraling their way.

"How are you?" Susan asked quietly.

Carrie stopped and began to stroke a black mare. "Hello, Ebony," she murmured, trying to bring her emotions under control before she answered. The mare's four-day-old filly gamboled around her mother, her perfectly shaped head held proudly. Her tiny hooves pranced in place. She was a stunning replica of her mother but would carry her sire's height. Carrie smiled, absorbing the beauty and energy. "Can you believe it's been almost eight years since Eclipse came to Cromwell? He has sired so many beautiful babies."

"Hmm…" Susan replied.

Finally, realizing Susan was waiting for an answer to her question, Carrie looked up. "It's been almost a month since they left. We've not had one word from them. I'm trying not to imagine the worst, but how can I not?" Desperation tinged her words.

"I know it's getting harder. When you're upset, you get quiet," Susan said gently. "You've been awfully quiet for the last few days." She took Carrie's hand. "I know it doesn't truly help for me to say I understand, but I felt what you're feeling last year, when Harold went to Alabama with Matthew. I was certain I was going to have an emotional breakdown before they returned."

"I know." In a small way, it did help to hear Susan voice what Carrie was feeling. She and Janie talked about it at the clinic, but she knew both of them were verbally diminishing their fears in order to help the other deal with their husbands' continued absence.

Ebony stepped forward and nudged Carrie's shoulder in sympathy.

"Thanks, girl," Carrie said gently. She never tired of how the horses could feel her emotions.

Moments later, Granite galloped over to where they were standing, a shrill whinny announcing his presence before he arrived. He bounced to a stop, his gray head lifted proudly, his tail like a banner unfurled behind him. He pushed Ebony to the side and lowered his head to Carrie's chest.

Carrie laughed. "A little jealous, are we?"

Granite snorted but didn't move.

Carrie stroked his head, reveling in the love she felt flowing from him. Her colt would be a year and a half old soon. The time since his birth on Christmas Eve had flown by.

He remained motionless, seeming to understand she needed his presence.

Carrie felt her breathing ease and the weight on her heart lift. "Thank you," she whispered. When she looked up, she saw Susan disappearing into the barn. Her friend had known being with Granite was what she needed most.

Carrie stood with her colt, watching as the dark rain clouds edged closer.

"It will be rainin' in an hour or two." Miles joined her to watch the approaching storm.

The wind had already picked up, causing the limbs in the oak tree towering over them to dance with the breeze. "That's what I figure." Carrie looked again, noticing the clouds were boiling harder and moving faster. "Do you think it will be a bad one?"

Miles shrugged. "Mother Nature gonna scream a little, but I don't think she will do much damage."

Carrie frowned. "You don't think it will wash away the seedlings?" she asked anxiously.

Miles peered at her. "You feelin' the need to worry 'bout something else, Carrie Girl?" he teased.

Carrie didn't respond as she watched the clouds.

The expression on Miles' face softened. "I be worried about Anthony and Matthew too." He laid a weathered hand on her shoulder.

Carrie appreciated that he didn't insist the men would be alright. She didn't need false promises; she knew how much danger they could be in. It was enough that Miles understood. She sighed deeply. "I'm going to go in the tack room and clean some saddles."

Miles looked at her knowingly. "That be a good idea."

Carrie had spent hours in the tack room when she was a girl on the plantation. The mindless work of cleaning saddles always helped her bring her emotions under control.

Before she could enter the barn, however, she noticed a plume of dust coming down the drive. Someone was arriving and moving at a fast pace. Her heart pounded as she turned away from the barn and waited for their visitor to arrive. Miles, his slender form a steady strength, stood beside her.

"It's Franklin," Miles finally announced. "He went into Richmond for supplies yesterday. There will be wagons following, but he chose to ride his horse. He ain't much for sittin' in a wagon."

Carrie continued to watch, futilely attempting to curb the hope fluttering inside. So many hopeful moments had been dashed with disappointment. This could well be another of them.

When he drew closer, he waved his arm, a smile on his face. "I brought you a telegram, Miss Carrie!"

Carrie hurried toward him. Suddenly, the idea of a telegram was terrifying. Her steps faltered. It could be either good news or terrible news.

Franklin pulled his gelding to a stop and handed Carrie a slim envelope. "It came today. I got back as fast as I could."

"Thank you," Carrie replied. Everyone on the plantation knew Anthony and Matthew had gone to Louisiana. She held the envelope for a moment, wondering if she should carry it inside, in case the news was bad. She probably should, but she couldn't wait any longer. She ripped open the envelope and extracted the telegram.

Miles and Susan stepped up to bracket her with support.

"They're on their way home!" Carrie exclaimed, joy sweeping through her entire being as she read the brief telegram. "They sent this from a landing on the Mississippi. They'll be home in four days!"

Susan grabbed Carrie's hands and began to dance. "That's wonderful news!" she cried.

Carrie threw back her head and laughed as she danced with her friend. When she was gasping for breath, she bent over her knees for several moments, before she looked up at Franklin. He was watching them with an amused expression. "Did Janie have a telegram?"

Franklin shook his head. "There was just the one."

Miles strode toward the barn. "I'll saddle No Regrets for you," he said over his shoulder.

At that moment, Thomas and Abby stepped out onto the porch.

"We saw two crazy women dancing from the library," Thomas called. "Is there something we should know about, or have both of you finally lost your minds?"

Carrie laughed and dashed for the porch. She knew her father would be as happy as she was. She waved the telegram in the air as she ran. "Anthony and Matthew are on their way home! They'll be here in four days!"

Thomas sagged against the porch column. "Thank God!" he said fervently.

Abby tucked her arm through his. "That's wonderful news."

Carrie understood the stark relief on her father's face. He felt responsible for their trip to Louisiana. No amount of assuring him the men had made their own choices could change how he felt. She was certain that he, too, had spent far too many hours imagining the worst.

"Janie is staying late at the clinic today. I'm going to give her the good news."

"Go," Thomas urged her. "She needs to know Matthew is on his way home." He glanced at the sky. "Ride fast. That storm will be here soon."

Carrie nodded and looked at Abby. "You'll tell the children when you see them?"

"Of course," Abby replied. "I already know Annie and Minnie will start planning the celebration dinner immediately."

Janie was locking the medical clinic door when Carrie burst from the woods. She dropped her key into her bag and froze in place. She couldn't see the expression on Carrie's face. Had she come to deliver good news or bad?

Carrie galloped up and slid No Regrets to a halt.

Janie relaxed slightly when she saw her friend's blazing smile. "Tell me!" she demanded.

Carrie waved a slip of paper in response. "Franklin brought this telegram a few minutes ago. It's from Anthony. He and Matthew are on their way home. They'll be here in four days!"

Janie sank down onto her knees and settled back to sit on the porch stairs. Tears streamed down her face. This time, perhaps more than any of the others, she had missed her husband. Regular nightmares had haunted her since he'd left.

Carrie dismounted quickly and ran to put an arm around her. "It's alright, Janie. Our husbands are coming home."

Janie wiped at the tears and managed a wavering smile. "I know." Her voice cracked. "I've been so afraid." She and

Carrie had talked regularly about their husbands, but she had hidden the deepest of her fears – or so she thought.

Carrie hugged her tightly. "We've both had terrible nightmares. It's not hard to imagine what could have happened down there."

Janie gasped. "You knew?"

"I didn't want to talk about it anymore than you did," Carrie confessed. "I learned a long time ago that if I don't give voice to my fears, they don't have quite the same power over me."

Janie glanced at her. "Does it help?"

Carrie shrugged. "I'm told it does," she said wryly. "The truth is that I've been finding it hard to breathe for the last few days. I'm not sure I was consciously deciding to not give voice to my fears. It was more that I was so exhausted from trying to get through each day, that I didn't have the energy to speak."

"That's what I've been feeling," Janie agreed. "I spoke to patients and my children. The rest of the time I stood on my porch and looked west." She glanced at Carrie sharply. "They're really coming home?"

"They're coming home," Carrie said. "The telegram was short, but they were taking the steamboat up the river to catch the train to Richmond."

Janie hesitated. "Nothing about how things went?"

"No."

Janie caught her breath. "It must have been bad," she said flatly before she stood. "I'm going home to my children. They'll be thrilled to know their daddy is coming home."

She hugged Carrie before she mounted and trotted away from the clinic. She was beyond relieved Matthew was coming home, but she knew her husband, already beleaguered by what he'd experienced over the years, would need her more than ever.

She nudged her horse into a gallop. She wanted to be home before the downpour began, but mostly she needed the feel of the air buffeting her body.

Everyone was on the porch, prepared for the show, when the storm hit at sundown. It announced its arrival with a rumble of thunder and jagged bolts of lightning that transformed dusk to bright light. In advance of the rain, the tree limbs whipped wildly. The horses not in the barn were huddled inside the enclosed shelters in the pasture. Built to protect them when the epizootic hit the year before, they were the perfect shelter from storms.

Carrie cringed when a large limb broke off one of the sentinel oaks bracketing the porch. It landed on the ground with a thud but was well away from the house.

"Look at that!" Russell crowed.

"Look at the lightning," John hollered. "I love storms!"

Rose laughed breathlessly. "Your little sister most certainly doesn't share your sentiments."

Hope snuggled close to her mother, hiding her face each time a streak of lightning split the angry clouds. She didn't want to be left out, but it was clear she would rather be anywhere other than where she was.

Carrie knew Rose wasn't enamored by the storms that rolled through the plantation, but she swallowed her fears and pretended to enjoy them for the children's sake.

Bridget waved her arms toward the storm. "More!" Bridget cried. "More!"

Carrie laughed. She'd had to stop Bridget from running down the porch stairs when the storm started. Her little girl had absolutely no fear. That knowledge was both thrilling and terrifying.

Thomas had laughed and nodded his head knowingly when Carrie ran to scoop Bridget into her arms before she could obtain her goal. "Just like her mama," he teased.

"I'm sorry I did that to you, Father," she said remorsefully. She grinned a moment later and tossed her head. "You survived me. I'll survive Bridget. I merely have to keep her safe until she grows up."

"And even after that," her father said. "I worry about you now, as much as I did then."

Carrie knew how true that was.

Another crack of lightning opened the sky like a curtain. The rain began to fall. Huge drops that sounded like kettle drums pelted the leaves and roof.

The children rushed to the edge of the porch, stretching their hands out to catch the rain.

Carrie stared in the direction of the fields.

Thomas read her mind. "Don't worry. It won't hurt the tobacco seedlings. If it turns to hail, we may need to worry, but a hard rainstorm will do the crops a world of good."

Carrie, comforted, was content to hold Bridget in her arms and watch the storm. Anthony was coming home. They had received a telegram from Moses and the girls two weeks earlier. They were busy exploring the city.

Everyone was safe. That's what mattered.

Four days later, while the sun remained high in the sky, Carrie heard hoofbeats in the distance. She and Janie had closed the clinic for the day. Nothing would stop them from being home when their husbands arrived. She quickly untied the mare she was grooming, let her loose in the pasture, and ran to stand on the porch to get a better view.

When she identified her husband's tall, lanky body, flew down the steps and ran toward him.

Anthony slid to a stop in front of her and leapt out of his saddle.

Moments later, Carrie was swept up into his arms, laughing with joyful abandon. "You're home!" she cried. "You're really home!"

Anthony held her tightly for a long moment before he leaned back enough to gaze at her. His eyes devoured her face before his lips lowered to claim hers.

Carrie kissed him fervently, but her heart had skipped a beat when she'd seen the despairing expression in his eyes. She knew instinctively that what she had suspected was bad, was actually quite horrific. They would celebrate his return, but their true time of reunion would come when they crawled into bed together that night.

"Daddy! Daddy!"

Anthony released her and grabbed his children up into massive hugs.

Minnie and Russell laughed with delight as he swung them around.

Bridget, not to be left out of the reunion, was running toward them, her sturdy little legs pumping as hard as they could. "Daddy!"

Anthony swept his youngest daughter into his arms. He held her closely for a long moment before he swung her upward to perch her high on his shoulders.

Bridget waved her arms. "More! More!"

Carrie laughed helplessly. "That has become her favorite word. No matter what we're doing or having, she simply wants more."

Anthony chuckled. "Exactly like her mama."

Carrie grimaced. "You and my father..."

"Frances?"

"She is safely in San Francisco, exploring the city and having a wonderful time," Carrie assured him.

Minnie danced in front of Anthony. "Annie and I have been cooking all day, Daddy. We have a feast ready for you!"

Anthony took hold of her hand, gripping Russell's hand on the other side. "I can hardly wait, honey. Let's go home."

Laughter rolled around the dining room as Anthony regaled them with stories of their time on the steamboat. He described in vivid detail what Louisiana's lush landscape looked like. He talked about the alligator he had seen, and the many snakes he had spied while he was there. He made the children's eyes grow wide when he told them about the thick, mysterious Spanish moss that floated from the trees.

Annie and Minnie loaded the table with Anthony's favorite foods. A huge roast beef simmered with onions, carrots, and potatoes held a place of honor. It was surrounded by bowls of green beans, lima beans, and fresh lettuces.

Minnie kept piling food on her daddy's plate.

Anthony ate voraciously but finally groaned in defeat. "I can't eat one more bite." He pulled his daughter close to him. "That was the best meal I've ever had, honey. Thank you."

Minnie beamed but shook her head. "We're not done yet, Daddy. We haven't had dessert."

"More food?" Anthony asked with mock dismay.

"More!" Bridget yelled, banging her clenched fists on her highchair tray. "More!"

Anthony looked at Carrie and laughed. "I see what you mean."

Minnie turned and disappeared into the kitchen. Moments later, she backed into the dining room keeping whatever she was carrying hidden. "You have to guess what it is, Daddy," she proclaimed.

Annie stepped out from the kitchen and stood to the side. She gazed at Minnie with affectionate pride. "This girl been cookin' all day. You ain't gonna get to eat this if you don't know what it is, so I'd be thinkin' real careful."

Anthony pretended to deliberate. The other children laughed as they watched him grip his chin with his hand and look toward the ceiling. "This is hard," he said solemnly. "Let's see. You and Annie have made my favorite foods."

Minnie nodded but didn't turn around.

Anthony paused again.

Carrie was impressed with his dramatic flair, even while her heart was aching. He'd spoken not one word about his trip. It could only mean the details were too horrific for the children to hear.

"It's May..." Anthony said slowly. "Which means... strawberries are getting ripe."

Minnie began to bounce in place, but she didn't turn around.

"Am I lucky enough to have strawberry shortcake?" Anthony asked hopefully.

Minnie whipped around, a huge grin splitting her face. "Yes!" she cried. "You guessed it!" She hurried over to the table with a tray that held several plates full of thick biscuits, split open and buried beneath mounds of fresh strawberries, and topped with thick whipped cream.

Annie pushed back into the kitchen, returning with two more trays of desserts. The plates were passed around the table quickly. Silence filled the room as everyone devoured the treat.

Carrie exchanged a glance with her father and Abby, who met her eyes solemnly. They were aware of how carefully Anthony was avoiding what had happened in Louisiana. She knew the three of them had endless questions, but they would have to wait for the children to go to bed.

Night had completely swallowed the plantation when Anthony finally claimed one of the rocking chairs. He lowered himself into it, laid his head back, and closed his eyes. The relief on his face was palpable.

Carrie had watched him glance wistfully at the front door before he walked over to where she sat with Thomas, Abby, Rose, Miles, and Annie.

Silence fell on the porch. The nighttime orchestra had tuned up, the crickets and frogs singing in time with the branches that swayed in the wind. The horses nickered and whinnied to each other, with an occasional snort for emphasis.

Carrie heard Anthony heave a deep sigh. She felt, more than saw, the moment when he relaxed. She reached out to grasp his hand. He held hers tightly, bringing it to his lips for a soft kiss.

No one spoke.

An hour passed before Anthony broke the silence. "Thank you," he said. He pushed back and stood, pulling Carrie up with him. "I know y'all have questions."

"They'll wait," Thomas said quietly. "We're glad you're home, son. When you're ready, you can tell us what happened down there."

Anthony looked away with tightened lips and pressed Carrie to his side.

Anthony paused before he pushed through the front door. "Calhoun was fine when we left."

Carrie watched relief fill her father's face.

Carrie was alarmed when she felt the tremor run through Anthony's body. She hoped she could be the strength he needed when he was finally able to talk about his experience. Her thoughts drifted to Janie. Would Matthew find it easier to talk? Had his many horrific experiences made it somehow easier to communicate?

Carrie reached for Anthony as soon as he slipped beneath the covers. "Welcome home, darling."

Anthony pulled her close to his side.

Carrie instinctively knew her husband was afraid to unleash the torrent of feelings he had buried deep inside to get through the evening with his children. "Whatever happened, you don't need to talk about it now. I'm here. I love you."

Anthony rested his head on top of hers. "It was terrible," he managed.

"I know," Carrie whispered. "I know. I wasn't there, but I could feel it. There were nights I couldn't sleep because of the nightmares. I was dreaming it. *You* were living it." She wrapped her arms around him and held him as tightly as she could, praying her love would reach the damaged places.

"I focused on getting home to you and the children," Anthony whispered.

Carrie felt him shake his head. Another long silence passed. The breeze fluttered the lace curtains, filling the room with sweet air.

"I don't know how Matthew lives with what he's seen," Anthony muttered.

"Neither do I," Carrie admitted. "I'm here to listen to anything you're ready to talk about."

Anthony remained silent for several more minutes, his body as taut as an oak limb. He took several deep breaths that seemed to sap his energy. Slowly, he began to speak.

Carrie allowed the tears to stream down her face as he recounted the horrors he had witnessed. She remained silent, stroking his arm and back as he released the memories. She forced back the bile threatening to erupt, knowing how much harder it must have been to actually witness. She wanted to scream at him to stop when he reached the day of the massacre, but she bit back the words and continued to listen.

Finally, Anthony's words ground to a halt. His breathing was shallow, and his skin was hot.

"I'm so sorry," Carrie whispered, her voice forced out between the tears that had never stopped.

Anthony clung to her tightly and let out a mournful groan. Only then did the tears begin.

Carrie held on as his body trembled from the sobs wracking his slender frame. "I love you," she said softly. "I love you."

She refused to tell him it was alright, or that it would be alright. She carried enough of her own horrible memories to know nothing was ever the same after an experience like he and Matthew had gone through. The memories would fade. Life could have joy and goodness, but you never lost the scars you carried. She would not diminish his experience by suggesting anything else. All she could do was love him through it.

The tears finally stopped. When Anthony began breathing evenly, Carrie knew he'd fallen asleep. She kissed his forehead and snuggled in next to his solid warmth.

Within minutes, she was asleep too.

Chapter Fifteen

Janie and Matthew had shared a quiet dinner and put the children to bed before Matthew suggested a stroll. They walked out into the evening, keeping the house in view in case the children needed them.

Matthew had spoken very little since his return. He had kissed her and played with the children, but the haunted look never left his face. The children were thrilled to have him home, but they kept staring at him with anxious expressions. It was obvious they could feel his tension and angst.

Janie vacillated between sorrow and rage. She was angry at whatever had caused the stark despair in Matthew's eyes, but she was also angry with him. Instead of being here on the plantation with her and the children as he had promised, he'd left them again to chase an important story. She respected him and deeply admired his passion to make a difference, but would there be enough pieces to pick up this time? Would her husband come back to her?

She knew he needed to feel the peace of home. She wanted to give it to him but was struggling with her own emotions. She wanted to feel nothing but joy that he was home again—that's what she'd believed she would feel. The power of her anger caught her by surprise.

A steady breeze carried the perfumes of spring as they walked. A quarter moon allowed the canopy of stars to glitter like polished diamonds. Venus and Jupiter were perched above the moon, their brilliance dimming the other stars.

Janie took deep breaths, praying the beauty of the night would calm her emotions.

"You're angry," Matthew said, finally breaking the silence.

They had agreed to always be honest.

"Yes," Janie admitted. She searched for more words but came up empty. "I'm angry."

"I understand," Matthew replied.

Janie whirled on him. She was breathing hard but tried to keep her voice calm. "Do you?" She stared at him, hating the defeat she saw in his eyes. "What do you understand?"

Matthew stopped walking and turned to face her. "You're angry because I'm a mess again. You love me. You're sorry for whatever I experienced, but you're angry that once again you're going to have to put me back together, because I made the decision to leave. You're angry because the children know something is wrong."

Somehow, his honest assessment of her feelings allowed Janie to catch her breath. "Yes," she admitted. She knew she needed to say more, but she couldn't find the words.

"I'm sorry," Matthew said sincerely. He turned away and stared out over the woods toward the river.

A hooting owl split the night. Moments later, the massive shape of a great horned owl with an impressive four-and-a-half-foot wingspan glided by without a sound. There was enough moonlight to see a doe and her fawn step out of the woods, lift their noses to smell for danger, and lower their heads to graze on the thick grass.

Janie bit her lip and took steadying breaths. Despite her anger, she loved Matthew too much not to feel the agony of his sorrow and pain. "Tell me," she invited.

Matthew continued to stare into the distance.

Janie leaned against a nearby tree. He may not speak tonight. It might be weeks before he could find the words to tell her. She would wait...and hope her anger dissipated.

"I don't know how to keep doing it," Matthew finally said, his voice cracking as he spoke.

"Doing what?"

Matthew spun around suddenly. "You have every right to be angry. I made you a promise that I broke. I've come home with memories that will haunt me for the rest of my life, but..." He fell silent as his voice faltered.

"But?" Janie asked gently. The dull agony in his eyes and the hopelessness in his voice did more to dissipate her anger than anything else could have. She loved her husband. She would help him carry the weight of what had happened in Louisiana.

"But coming home to you and the children was the solitary thing that kept me going," Matthew said quietly. He reached out and pulled her to him, embracing her with trembling arms. "Janie, you are my home. I can't possibly make sense of my life without you."

Janie's heart melted. She reached up to stroke his whiskered face and pushed his hair back from his forehead. "I'm here, honey. Thank you for knowing I was angry, but I was merely dealing with feelings. You've had to deal with what happened down there. You saw it. You lived it." She paused to kiss him gently. "What don't you know how to keep doing?"

Matthew pressed his lips to hers and turned to look back toward the woods, keeping her hand tightly in his. "I don't know how to keep having faith in humanity." His voice grew rougher. "Especially in Louisiana. I know there are good people there—Willie Calhoun is one of them—but there aren't enough good people to stop terrible things from happening."

Janie felt the shudder run through him. She stood quietly. Now that he was talking, he would continue, but it had to be at his pace. He would reveal what he was capable of revealing.

The moon rose higher in the sky as they stood in silence.

When Matthew finally began to speak again, he talked rapidly, as if he wanted to get it over with as quickly as possible.

Janie clenched the fist of her free hand, many times pressing it against her mouth to keep from screaming. When Matthew released her and stepped away, she held both hands to her mouth, wishing she could cover her ears instead.

She had a brief thought of Carrie. Was Anthony talking about his experience? They both healed people in the clinic on a daily basis, but rendering medical aid was simple compared to what lay in front of them now.

When Matthew's shoulders began to shake, though he continued to speak, Janie pressed up against his back and wrapped her arms around him, letting her own tears flow. There were no words that could begin to assuage his pain. Her only course of action was to love him.

The anger flared anew, but this anger was different. It wasn't aimed at him. Hot waves of rage rushed through her when she thought of the men who had inflicted such death and destruction.

Horror choked her as she thought of the hopeless fear and agony felt by the murdered men, and by the families left behind to figure out a way to keep living.

Once Matthew finished speaking and took a few minutes to recover, she asked the first question on her mind. "Have you written it?"

Matthew nodded. "Yes. I wrote the articles on the boat and the train. I sent them off to Philadelphia when we arrived in Richmond."

Janie nodded with relief. "You've done the thing that made you go. You've revealed the truth. What people do with it is up to them. You've told me what happened." She rubbed his back gently. "We can talk about it whenever you need to, but it's over. You're home now." She continued to express what she knew was true. "You'll never forget what you experienced. You'll never forget anything that you've experienced over the years, but you know it gets easier with time."

Matthew shook his head. "I know the memories will fade with time, but I don't know if I can ever find my faith in humanity. It's been hard to hang onto it over the years, but I've always found a way."

Janie looked into his haunted eyes, giving him the time to finish his thoughts. When the silence stretched out, she realized he couldn't find words to continue. "Read your books," she said softly.

"What?"

"Read your books," Janie repeated. "You began writing them when you lost your faith in humanity and walked away from being a reporter. You knew you needed to offset the horror with stories of people who were doing good things and were determined to make a difference."

A coyote howl split the night, its mournful sound reflecting the expression she saw on Matthew's face.

"You need those stories more than ever," Janie pressed.

Matthew frowned. "I know you're probably right, but one truth keeps exploding in my mind."

Janie waited for him to continue.

"Not only in Louisiana, but throughout our country, people are determined to deprive others of their human rights. When they do that, they're denying those people of their very humanity."

"I couldn't agree more," Janie said softly. "Did you write that?"

"I did," Matthew said, hopelessness coating his words. "If it matters..."

"Those words might not matter to many, but I believe there are more people who it *will* matter to," Janie replied. "You're telling people they can't really start living until they can move beyond the narrow confines of their own selfish concerns. They can't truly live until they embrace the broader concerns of every human being." She paused. "There will be people who rise to the challenge. That's all you can ever expect your writing to accomplish, Matthew."

Matthew stared at her with admiration. "I wish I had thought to express it that way."

"You did," Janie said. "I learned that from you, honey. You're the only person who can reveal the truth of what happened down there. You did that."

"If it does any good."

Janie cringed at the despair in his voice. "It's not up to you to determine whether it does any good, and besides, how could you even define that? There may, or may not, be immediate results from your articles. The impact may be felt immediately. It may be felt generations from now. It's not up to you to determine that. You went there because you believed the story needed to be told. You ended up being there to tell a story that may well have stayed hidden away from the entire country."

Matthew gazed into her eyes and pulled her close. "How did you become so wise, Dr. Justin?"

"By feeling the same kind of despair you're feeling right now, Mr. Justin. By fighting back against so many medical beliefs and practices, uncertain if things will ever truly change. I want to scream at the number of people dying who don't have to die. I want to make the world pay attention to the number of war veterans addicted to heroin and morphine because they aren't aware of any other treatment."

Janie took a deep breath and squeezed Matthew as hard as she could. "I was angry because I never want to live a minute of my life without you in it. I was angry that you left and took risks that could have taken you away from me and the children."

"Are you still angry?" Matthew said hesitantly.

"I want to be," Janie admitted. "I want you to promise me you'll never do something like this again." She held a finger to his lips when he started to answer. "Don't you dare do it. I can hope that you'll never leave again, but if we truly want things to change, there have to be people who are willing to take the risks necessary to create that change."

The single coyote howl had faded into the inky blackness. Suddenly, an entire chorus of howls rose on the wind. Mournful howls and high-pitched yips sounded around them, feeling as if they were closing in.

Janie grabbed Matthew's hand. "I think I'm ready to go back to the house."

Matthew chuckled. "The coyotes are hunting. They're not coming for us."

"Perhaps," Janie agreed. "That doesn't mean I won't feel much safer and happier in my house with my children." She tugged his hand and walked quickly toward their home. "Besides, I have other ways I want to show you how happy I am you're home again."

Matthew followed willingly.

Janie knew nightmares would become part of their routine, but they would fade with time. In the meantime, she would hold him, love him, and give her husband courage to keep doing the right thing.

Rose sank back in the rocking chair, grateful for a few minutes of solitude. She considered going for a walk, so she could be alone, but didn't have the energy. After a long day at school, she had taken the children for two hours of play on the bank of the James River. The water was too cold to be enjoyable yet, but the warmer days would change that quickly. She had sat with them while they ran up and down the shoreline and played in the trees along the bank. Moses, before he left, had hung a swing in the massive oak tree near their regular swimming hole.

Thoughts of Moses caused tears to sting her eyes. They had not gone for such a long period without seeing each other since the war had separated them. She felt as if a limb was missing. Every day, she thought of things she wanted to tell him. She wanted him to know about the telegram they had received from the Rawlings family, letting them know they were safely settled in Philadelphia. With a start, she remembered he had been gone when they saved the family. He knew nothing.

Hope had looked up at her with big tears in her eyes when she had put her to bed that evening. "Is Daddy ever coming home, Mama?"

"Of course, honey. He and Felicia will be home again."

"When?" Hope demanded. "I found a big rock by the river today. I need to show it to him."

"We'll save it for him," Rose had told her, swallowing the lump in her throat. "We'll make a big collection of everything you want to show him. When he gets home, I promise he'll want to see each and every treasure."

Her promise seemed to mollify her daughter enough for her to fall asleep, but Rose knew the questions would begin again tomorrow.

Rose sighed when the door opened. She didn't feel like talking to anyone. She relaxed when she saw Carrie step out onto the porch.

Carrie took the chair next to her, reached for her hand and held it tightly, but didn't speak.

Through the window, Rose saw the rest of the adults gather in the library. She could hear low talk and laughter coming from the open window. She watched as Thomas and Anthony sat down in front of a backgammon game. Abby settled down on the piano stool and began to play. Instead of being intrusive, Rose found it comforting. She settled deeper into the rocking chair and let the evening air soothe her.

When the waning moon finally slipped from beneath the horizon to float above the treetops, Rose spoke. "He's been gone a month. It could be another two or three months before they're home." Speaking the words almost stole her breath.

"I know," Carrie said sympathetically. "You miss him with your whole heart."

Rose thought about the agony Carrie had experienced while Anthony was gone. "At least Moses didn't go to Louisiana." Despite how much she missed her husband, she knew what could have happened. Carrie had told her what the men had experienced. If he'd joined Anthony and Matthew, he would have insisted on fighting. He would almost certainly be dead now.

"I'm glad for that," Carrie replied.

Rose knew Anthony was being plagued by nightmares. She thought of how many times she held Moses at night when his dreams took him back to the battlefield or to the many years he had been enslaved. "It will get easier," Rose said gently.

"It will," Carrie agreed, but sighed heavily. "I miss Frances terribly."

Rose realized Carrie needed silence and solitude as much as she did. As much as she missed Moses and Felicia, she didn't expect them to come home traumatized. San Francisco was a safe, growing city. She was certain he and the girls were having a wonderful time, but not having them on the plantation left a gaping hole.

Moses stepped down from the carriage, extending his hand to help Mrs. Pleasant, Felicia, and Frances disembark.

Frances looked around with a disappointed expression but remained silent.

Felicia spoke freely. "They are comparing this to Central Park?" she asked with disbelief.

Mrs. Pleasant laughed. "Golden Gate Park is very new. It's been in development for a mere eighteen months."

"It doesn't look like anything like a park. I hope they have a lot of plans for it," Frances said dubiously.

"They do," Mrs. Pleasant assured them. "The developers envision it being as grand as Central Park. Its rectangle shape is like Central Park, but it's about twenty percent larger." She waved a hand in a grand gesture. "It's more than three miles long and about a half mile wide."

Moses gazed around. "I see mostly barren sand and shore dunes. I've been to Central Park. I'm afraid your park will never look the same."

"Not the same," Mrs. Pleasant agreed. "Despite that, it will become a beautiful, spacious public park. I've seen the topographic map prepared by William Hall. He created it three years ago. A little more than a year ago, he became the park commissioner." She smiled. "You can't see it now, but it's going to be magnificent."

Felicia looked around her. "I suppose it's like having the idea for a business. You have to be able to see what it can become. If you focus on what it is the moment you begin, you'll never be able to achieve greatness. You have to see beyond today's reality."

Mrs. Pleasant eyed her with pride. "Exactly, Felicia."

Felicia spun around slowly. "Tell me what it will look like."

"Lush and green," Mrs. Pleasant replied. "The original plan called for a park using native species suited for San Francisco's dry climate."

"That makes sense," Moses said. "As a farmer, I know it's foolish to plant crops not suited for the area you're farming. You have to let the land tell you what will work."

"Not in California," Mrs. Pleasant responded with a laugh. "It perhaps is foolish, but when you have the money that came from the Gold Rush years, you decide you're going to develop a massive irrigation system that will create one of the most lush, green, beautiful parks in the world."

Felicia shook her head. "The Gold Rush years are over," she protested.

"That's true, but there is still a great deal of wealth here."

"Which should be used to help the thousands that are suffering," Felicia stated. "Can't you feel San Francisco is close to exploding? I sense it in the streets every day. People are desperate. Something needs to change."

Moses listened to the conversation with amazement. His daughter had always been outspoken about her beliefs, but the trip to San Francisco had made her more so. Perhaps it was merely that she was growing up. In many ways, he saw her as the child he had rescued, but she was a young woman, a college graduate, and she had goals she was determined to reach.

"Building successful businesses is the only way to help people who are suffering," Mrs. Pleasant countered.

Moses had watched the two of them grow ever closer as they talked, sparred, and matched wits. He knew Mary Ellen Pleasant viewed Felicia as the daughter she never had. She enjoyed the intellectual sparring perhaps more than even Felicia did.

While they had long business discussions, he and Frances would explore the city on foot and by carriage. He recognized the same desperation Felicia felt. San Francisco was a melting pot of more ethnic groups than he had ever experienced, but he couldn't say that proximity had made people embrace their differences. Instead, it was like a powder keg waiting for the fuse to be lit.

Moses walked away to stand on top of one of the dunes, his gaze sweeping out over the Pacific Ocean. Brilliant sunshine cast sparkles on the water reflecting the deep blue sky that merged seamlessly with the horizon. Energized by openness and fresh, salt-filled air, he took deep breaths. The breeze carried the cry of hundreds of seagulls soaring in circles or diving into the water to snatch up fish. A pod of brown pelicans soared in formation above the top of the waves. He loved the pelicans that never tired of their endless quest for fish to fill their big throat pouches. Sandpipers scurried along the beach, dashing back and forth with amazing speed as the waves surged in and out.

Golden Gate Park lacked the beauty of Cromwell Plantation, but at least he wasn't hemmed in by buildings and hordes of people. He closed his eyes and envisioned the tobacco fields. He knew the plants would be at least a foot high now. He could see the rows of bright green plants stretching toward the woods as far as the eyes could see. He could hear his men calling out as they worked the plants, coaxing maximum growth in their pursuit of a successful harvest.

He opened his eyes when his thoughts naturally went to Rose, John, Jed, and Hope. He missed them with a fierce longing that sometimes surprised him with its intensity. He had known he would miss his family when he agreed to accompany Felicia across the country, but he hadn't realized what a constant ache it would be. He dreamed of going home every day, but he wouldn't take Felicia away until she said she was ready. In the meantime, he was focused on helping Frances have the best experience possible.

He glanced at Felicia deep in conversation with Mrs. Pleasant.

Frances had walked away to gaze out over the dunes, searching for new birds she hadn't discovered yet. She was enjoying San Francisco, but he suspected she missed the plantation as much as he did. He also knew she would never acknowledge it.

Moses walked close enough to overhear the conversation. He was learning as much as Felicia was from the wealthy businesswoman.

"Building successful businesses is the only way to provide employment to people," Mrs. Pleasant was saying again.

"I know that's true," Felicia agreed, "but I've read that at least twenty percent of Californians are out of work. The Gold Rush and the silver from the Comstock Mine created incredible wealth, but those years are over."

Mrs. Pleasant nodded. "You're right, but the mines weren't the only things that created wealth. What else made money?"

Moses knew she was pushing his daughter to think.

Felicia closed her eyes briefly. "During the Gold Rush, as much or more money was made from providing what the miners needed. Levi Strauss is an excellent example. He is a Bavarian immigrant who arrived here in 1850. He brought dry goods to sell, but when he heard of the miners' need for durable pants, he hired a tailor to make garments out of tent canvas. Sales exploded." She smiled. "He identified a need and filled it."

"What else?" Mrs. Pleasant prodded.

"Samuel Brannan," Felicia answered promptly. "He was the newspaper publisher who released news of the gold find, but he didn't truly care if it sold newspapers."

"What did he care about?"

"He knew thousands of people would come to search for gold. Before he announced gold could be found, he bought up every shovel, spade, and pick he could get his hands on." Felicia smiled again. "He bought them for twenty cents apiece. When people started arriving, he sold them for fifteen dollars apiece. He made a fortune." She frowned slightly.

"He saw a need and filled it. Does that bother you?" Mrs. Pleasant asked.

Felicia nodded. "It does," she admitted. "I believe in making a profit, but most of the people who came here were desperate for a new way of life. Instead, they found what was the highest cost of living in the country. If you discovered gold, you could pay for it. If not, you didn't have a chance—and you also had no way to get back home."

"That's true," Mrs. Pleasant replied. "We'll talk about that, but I want to continue discussing how wealth was accumulated."

"The stock and money markets," Felicia responded. "That's how you made most of your money to begin with. When you got here in 1852, you worked as a cook and housekeeper."

Moses knew Mrs. Pleasant had been forced to come west because slavers turned her into a much-hunted slave rescuer. She was responsible for freeing hundreds of slaves in the South and sending them north through the

Underground Railroad. That alone endeared her to him. If it hadn't been for the help of the Underground Railroad, he and Rose wouldn't have made it to Pennsylvania when the war started.

"You invested your earnings in stock and money markets. You also lent money to miners and other businessmen at ten percent interest." Felicia stopped, looking to her mentor for confirmation.

"That's true," Mrs. Pleasant confirmed. "One reason I chose to be a cook and housekeeper was my proximity to successful businessmen. While I was serving dinner, I was listening to their conversations. That's how I learned to be a skilled investor."

"That's when you began to help people," Moses said admiringly. "You diversified your businesses to include laundries, boarding houses, and mining enterprises. You began to buy real estate."

"Most of it I continue to own," Mrs. Pleasant told him. "I will sell it one day, but not now."

"Because of what you do with it," Felicia said. "You brought escaped slaves here and helped them get started in homes and jobs. You rescued free blacks that were enslaved illegally in California and did the same thing."

Frances strolled over to join them, overhearing the conversation. "Most importantly," she added, "you have come to the aid of both black and white women who are being exploited by men here in the city."

Mrs. Pleasant cocked an eyebrow in surprise. "How do you know that, Frances?"

Frances met her eyes evenly. "I've talked to some of the women and girls you've helped."

Mrs. Pleasant looked even more surprised. "I didn't realize you even knew about those houses."

Moses decided to step in. "I've been studying the real estate records in San Francisco. When Frances and I are out exploring the city, we walk by the ones you own to get a feel for what might be valuable in your estimation."

"When we went by some of the houses, we saw women sitting on the steps, so we stopped to talk to them," Frances explained. "They told me."

"Why would they tell you?" Mrs. Pleasant demanded. She didn't look upset, simply mystified.

"Because I told them I know what it's like. I could tell they were afraid."

Moses felt his own eyebrows raise. He knew of Frances' history, because Carrie had told him, but he'd never heard her speak about it.

"I'm sorry, my dear," Mrs. Pleasant said tenderly.

"It's alright now," Frances said easily. "I have a wonderful family. I'm safe, and I'll never let anything like that happen again. I was much younger. Mama helped me come to grips with it." She smiled. "I'm glad you've given homes to girls that need a safe place."

Moses saw Felicia staring at Frances with wide eyes.

"You never told me," Felicia said softly.

"There was no need," Frances replied. "It was a long time ago. I was raped when I was on the wagon train to Sante Fe with my family. I'll never forget it happened, but it doesn't define who I am now." She took Felicia's hand. "I hope you'll create homes for girls and women who need help, too. No matter where you decide to do it." She paused, a somber expression on her face. "They're needed everywhere."

Moses hated that she knew that fact, but also acknowledged it was the truth.

Felicia nodded immediately. “I promise.” Her face twisted into a scowl. “Women simply have to get their rights,” she said fiercely. “It’s wrong how many women are at the mercy of men who use and abuse them. We have to be able to vote, and we have to be in control of our own money.”

“I couldn’t agree more,” Mrs. Pleasant responded. She motioned for the carriage driver. “Let’s go home. I’m rather tired. The wind whipping off the ocean is becoming cooler. I won’t be surprised if the fog doesn’t roll back in soon.”

Moses looked toward the west and saw a gray bank moving toward them. He had learned that fog rolled in more quickly from the ocean. Sometimes the fog carried rain; other times it simply enveloped the city. The weather could change like quicksilver. You always had to be prepared.

The carriage was enclosed, but the driver would be miserable if rain hit before they arrived home. Moses helped everyone into the carriage and looked up at the driver. “Mind if I ride with you?”

The driver, a lanky black man with a thin mustache, shook his head. “Not at all, Mr. Samuels.”

Moses climbed up onto the bench seat. “Thank you, Anson.”

“You won’t be thanking me if that storm hits,” Anson replied.

“Yes, I will,” Moses assured him as they began to roll forward. “Being here in the fresh air and open spaces is much better than being suffocated in the city. At least I’m not enclosed in the carriage right now.”

Anson eyed him. “Where you from, Mr. Samuels?”

“A plantation in Virginia,” Moses replied. “It’s the most beautiful place on the planet.”

Anson scowled. “I used to live on a plantation in South Carolina. I reckon some people thought it was beautiful, but it weren’t the slaves.” He looked at Moses sharply. “You always been a free man?”

Moses laughed. “Hardly. I grew up a slave, like you. The second year of the war, my wife and I escaped from my plantation and went north. I served in the army during the war.”

Anson nodded. “That’s good. I escaped my plantation about ten years before the war. The Underground Railroad helped me and a bunch of others get away. Mrs. Pleasant found out about it and paid our way out here.” He smiled with pride. “I been working for her ever since. My wife and I got a small house down in the city. Got me three children too.”

“That’s wonderful,” Moses said warmly.

Anson stared at him with a curious expression. “Why you back living on a plantation? I know there ain’t slaves no more, but why would you want to live that life again? Ain’t it a constant reminder?” He looked uncomfortable but plunged ahead with an additional question. “How does a plantation worker afford a train trip to San Francisco?”

Moses smiled. “I don’t work on the plantation; I own half of it.” He laughed when Anson’s mouth dropped open. He told the story that he had told what seemed to be a thousand times. Retelling the story was tiring at times, but it gave his people hope that things could change, so he would keep telling it.

“So, you a rich man,” Anson marveled.

Moses knew he was, but he imagined it would always feel surreal to him. Because he rarely spent any of the money he made, it seldom felt he was wealthy. Their trip across the country in the Pullman Palace car had changed his thinking a little, but it wouldn't be a regular occurrence. His only interest in his money now revolved around his ability to help Felicia fund her new businesses. In the future, he would make sure the rest of his children could go to college.

The two men fell silent as the carriage continued forward. Both were content with their thoughts.

Moses was jostled from his thoughts as they entered the city, driving more slowly because of the throngs of people and carriages. The smells and smoke assaulted them, but Moses was happier on the carriage seat. The city streets closest to the water were a beehive of business and industry. Street vendors hawked fish and produce, while ragged children dashed among the multitude of carriages and wagons.

"Do you live around here?" Moses asked.

"Up the hill a ways," Anson answered. "I bought a little wooden house. It ain't much, but it's warm and dry. My family is happy there."

"I'm glad," Moses answered, once more grateful his children were racing around on the plantation, not dodging wagons and carriages.

"You planning on staying here?" Anson asked.

"Not a chance," Moses said firmly. "But then, there isn't a city in the entire United States that I want to live in. I love being in the country. The plantation is the most beautiful place in the world to me."

"Miss Felicia likes it here. Least, she seems to."

"She does." Moses agreed, but couldn't bring himself to say more. It was a fact he was uncomfortably aware of. Felicia had said she wanted to stay on the East Coast, but the trip to San Francisco may have changed her mind. He knew she would be well-mentored and safe with Mrs.

Pleasant. He couldn't imagine getting on the train and leaving her behind, but he would support whatever decision she made. He knew Rose would feel the same way. They had talked about the possibility before he'd made the trip.

"You gonna let her stay here?" Anson asked, eyeing him keenly.

"If it's what she wants," Moses managed, searching for a way to change the subject. When he saw the skeptical look on Anson's face, he was compelled to tell him Felicia's history.

Anson's face shone with astonishment. "She watched both her parents be murdered?"

Moses nodded. No matter how many times he told the story, it would always made him sick and angry.

"You would never know," Anson said softly.

"She is quite remarkable," Moses replied. "She's determined to use what she experienced to make things better for our people."

"Which is why she's here."

Moses nodded. "Mrs. Pleasant met Felicia at her graduation from Oberlin College. She offered to mentor her in business."

Anson's eyes shone with pride. "Ain't nobody better than Mrs. Pleasant," he said firmly. "You know she's a millionaire? Not just a millionaire, though. She has a lot of millions."

Moses was impressed but not surprised.

"She's a brilliant businesswoman," Anson continued. "Too bad ain't nothing she owns in her own name."

Moses stared at him, grateful the city noises made their conversation private. "What do you mean?"

Anson looked uncomfortable. "I shouldn't have said nothing."

Moses was burning with curiosity, but he didn't want to put Anson in a precarious situation, so he didn't press.

The carriage rattled on, slowly moving up the hill.

"A black woman ain't got many rights," Anson said abruptly. He had evidently changed his mind about telling him. "I heard her talking one day. Everything she owns is in some white fella's name. It's the only way to make sure it's safe."

Moses wondered silently what could happen if the white man proved to be untrustworthy, but he kept his question to himself.

"Folks around here call her the Mother of Civil Rights in California," Anson added.

"That so? Why?" Moses was enjoying learning more about the woman mentoring his daughter.

"Back in '63, before the war even started, she helped pass a law that guaranteed black folks would have their testimony heard in court."

Moses whistled. His admiration for the successful woman climbed higher. That was an issue throughout the country. In most places, blacks still couldn't have a voice in court.

"That ain't all," Anson continued. "Three years later, she organized a sit-in of our streetcars 'cause they wouldn't let black folks ride. It was supposed to change everywhere, but not all the companies would let us ride. So, Mrs. Pleasant up and sued one of the streetcar companies and won," he announced. "That company had to start letting us ride. They also had to give her five hundred dollars."

Moses' admiration shot up another notch. He decided it was alright to ask Anson a question he hadn't wanted to ask their hostess directly. "I know Mrs. Pleasant is very wealthy. Why is she still a housekeeper?"

Anson smiled. "San Francisco ain't that different from the rest of the country, Mr. Samuels. Ain't many rich women. There be even fewer rich black women. She doesn't care to flaunt how rich she is. That's why she puts everything in other people's names. She knows men would give her a hard time and try to take control of her businesses. She just goes about her business in secret and keeps learning from the rich men she housekeeps for. She told me one time that the folks she works for act like she's invisible. She says she never wants to give up what she learns from hearing them talk."

"I see," Moses murmured. He could understand her position but wondered if Felicia would have to do the same type of hiding. The idea infuriated him. He thought of Abby, who had endured endless abuse from men who felt threatened by. Felicia would carry the extra burden of being black, without family to protect her. He gritted his teeth as he imagined what could happen to his brilliant, beautiful daughter.

Suddenly, a couple blocks north, he saw what seemed to be some type of commotion. "What's going on?" he demanded.

Anson's lips tightened. He pulled the carriage to a stop and began to look around frantically.

Moses could tell he was searching for an alternate route. "What's going on?" he repeated more firmly.

Anson met his eyes. "There's going to be trouble."

Chapter Sixteen

"Why have we stopped?" Felicia asked. "I thought we were going to your home?"

"We are," Mrs. Pleasant assured her calmly. "We'll start moving any minute now. There's probably some kind of obstruction in the road. It happens."

Felicia stared at her. She knew there could well be an obstruction in the road, but she had learned how to identify hidden fear. "What are you not telling us?"

Before Mrs. Pleasant could answer, the door to the carriage swung open. Her father stepped inside, his massive body making the confined space shrink immediately.

"We're going to take another route," he informed them.

"Why?" Felicia demanded. "We're not stupid, Daddy. We can tell when something bad is happening." She took a deep breath, struggling to bring her sudden fright under control. She'd been feeling the tension in the city ever since they arrived. She was grateful when Frances reached out to take her hand.

"Is the powder keg about to blow?" Frances asked. "Mama has always told me that if trouble is coming, it's best to be prepared, not to wallow in ignorance."

Moses managed a smile. Carrie had taught her daughter well. "Your mama is right," he assured her.

"What is it?" Mrs. Pleasant asked. "Is it the Chinese?"

"Yes," Moses admitted. Before he could say anything else, the sounds of a fight floated toward them.

Yells and taunts flowed in through the windows. They could hear things breaking. Screams of pain ripped through the sudden quiet that came from traffic jolting to a halt. Streams of people ran by, obviously fleeing the violence. Faces reflected their despair and fear.

"What are the Chinese doing?" Frances asked.

"It's not what *they* are doing," Mrs. Pleasant said, agony dulling her normally vibrant eyes. "It's what is being done *to* them." She shook her head. "The whites of San Francisco blame the Chinese for their financial woes. Any other ethnic group is also looked down on, but the Chinese bear the brunt."

"Why?" Felicia asked, her gut twisting. The sounds were the same as the ones from the Memphis Riot that had killed her parents. She could feel her breath coming in short bursts as the memories assailed her. It was as if she were back in her parents' home, waiting for the riot to come to them. She closed her eyes as gunshots erupted in her head.

Moses grabbed her hands. "It's alright, sweetheart. We're getting out of here."

Felicia forced her eyes open, gaining strength from her father's presence. "But what about the Chinese?" Her heart was pounding so hard she was afraid it might crack her ribs. "Who is going to help them?"

Moses pressed his lips together tightly and didn't answer.

More screams erupted. The sound of women and children wailing filled the carriage.

"We got one!" a man yelled. "This one ain't getting away!"

"I got one too," another rough voice hollered.

"String 'em up, boys. We gotta take back control of our city!"

Suddenly, the carriage surged forward, swaying as they made a sharp right turn.

"We're getting out of here!" Anson's call floated down to them.

Felicia looked out the carriage window as they turned. It gave her a clear view of the trouble ahead. "Daddy!" she screamed.

Moses pulled her toward him, burying her head in his chest. He held her tightly, smoothing her hair as she shook with horror. He pulled Frances close to his other side, hating that he had brought these girls into danger. "It's going to be alright," he murmured. "It will be alright, girls."

Felicia knew that wasn't true. Things would never be alright for the families of the men who had been lynched in the streets of San Francisco. She would never forget the image of their slender bodies hanging from building eaves.

"Why?" she whispered. "Why?"

Moses sat with Felicia and Frances on the Nob Hill front porch, watching as a glorious sunset unfolded before them. The sky was ablaze with the fire of the setting sun. The puffy clouds left from the storm turned orange and purple, reflecting their color back onto the ocean that had gone calm and flat. Gentle waves, instead of the crashing breakers from earlier, lapped at the shores.

"It's beautiful," Frances murmured. "Sunsets over the ocean are something I've never experienced."

When the sun sank below the horizon, it shot up brilliant golden rays that pierced the clouds.

Moses looked away from the stunning display and allowed his gaze to sweep across the city below. You could see most of San Francisco from their perch on Nob Hill. Mrs. Pleasant's home wasn't one of the luxurious mansions owned by the gold and railroad tycoons, but it was quite impressive.

The ornate Victorian house was a soft blue, its massive bay windows outlined with dusky rose-colored shutters. The wraparound porch boasted white columns that gleamed under the gas lanterns lining the sidewalk and road. Two turrets, rising from the second floor, offered a commanding view of both the ocean and the San Francisco Bay.

Lights glimmered up from the city below. Gas streetlamps blended with glowing house windows. He could hear the noise of the city floating up to them, but at least it was muted by the distance. It was hardly the peace of the plantation on a summer evening, but it helped ease the trauma they had experienced.

Felicia had hardly spoken a word since she'd seen the two lynched Chinese men hanging from a building's eaves. Frances had been equally quiet. The girls had sat inside for the remainder of the afternoon, far from the windows, as they read books chosen from the extravagant library. It was as if they had suddenly grown frightened of the entire city.

Moses had lured them out onto the porch for the sunset but hadn't pushed them to say what they were thinking and feeling. He had seen more than his share of lynchings, starting with his father when he was eleven years old. The image never left your mind.

His yearning for the plantation increased even more. The South was a volatile place, but at least within the confines of Cromwell, he felt safe.

They sat quietly, watching the day come to an end. A rose garden lining the porch perfumed the air. Bright red blooms competed with white and yellow flowers.

"Daddy, I don't understand what happened today," Felicia finally said.

Mrs. Pleasant chose that moment to join them on the porch. "I hope you never can, Felicia."

Felicia stared at her. "Why not?"

"Because if you can understand what happened today, it means that you think the way those men think. Unless you're filled with anger, hatred, and fear, you can't possibly understand what compelled that mob to murder two helpless Chinese men."

Felicia shook her head. "But if I can't understand what happened, how can I change it?"

Mrs. Pleasant sat silently for a few minutes, allowing her gaze to sweep the city. "Do you remember telling me about how that KKK member came to your plantation and demanded your mama and Carrie come take care of his son?" She waited for Felicia's nod and then continued. "Carrie wasn't going to go, because of the destruction he caused on the plantation."

Mrs. Pleasant turned her attention to Frances. "What did your grandmother tell Carrie?"

"That you can't fight hate with hate," Frances said promptly. "Grandma and I have talked a lot about grace and compassion, Mrs. Pleasant." She shook her head. "You can't possibly believe we should simply forget what those men did!"

"No," Mrs. Pleasant said firmly. "We certainly can't forget it. However, I hope I'll never be able to understand what those men feel. If I do, it means I've become like them. I'll fight to change things in the city, but I have to protect my own heart and integrity to do it."

"Aren't you sick of it?" Felicia demanded.

"More than you can imagine," Mrs. Pleasant said somberly, her lidded eyes heavy with emotion. "I'm sick of what is happening to my people. I'm sick of what is happening to the Chinese and other ethnic groups. I'm sick of what's happening to women." Her eyes flashed, alive with anger. "I will never understand why people feel the need to control and subjugate what scares them."

"Why do they hate the Chinese?" Frances asked.

Mrs. Pleasant sighed. "The Chinese have suffered since they first arrived here. They joined the throngs of immigrants who came here after gold was discovered. White Californians were not welcoming, but in the beginning they needed the immigrants because most of them had experience in mining. They taught Americans how to find and remove gold from the streams and hillsides. Once the whites knew how to do it, they rewarded the foreign miners with a hefty state tax and increasing violence and mistreatment."

Moses listened carefully. He wanted to understand as much as the girls did.

"Much worse was in store for the Chinese," Mrs. Pleasant said sadly. "The Chinese make no effort to look and act like Americans. They live together in special and confined quarters. They dress like they did in China. They eat like they did in China. Most of their food, which includes the white rice that is a staple for them, is imported from China."

Felicia shook her head in confusion. "Why would anyone care how they dress and eat?"

"Because people are threatened by what is different. If they can't understand it, it automatically becomes bad. My experience with the Chinese is that they're peaceful and exceedingly industrious. They are also remarkably economical. They spend little or none of their earnings except for necessities that they buy from other Chinese."

Moses suddenly understood. "White Americans don't see any value in their labor because they aren't benefiting."

Mrs. Pleasant nodded. "True. In order to create some kind of value, they imposed taxes that have increased regularly. They passed laws to force the Chinese to leave California, or to make it extremely difficult and expensive to stay. Chinese children have been excluded from public schools."

"That's terrible!" Frances exclaimed.

"The Chinese have fought back against the unfair laws," Mrs. Pleasant continued. "They have succeeded in some areas, but it hasn't changed the hatred and discrimination."

Moses had been listening to the talk on the streets as he and Frances had explored. "The whites resent the Chinese for being willing to work for lower wages."

"Yes," Mrs. Pleasant confirmed. "America was more than willing to exploit Chinese workers for practically slave labor to build the railroad you came in on, but now that the railroad is done, men don't want to compete with them for jobs."

"It's no different for black men," Moses observed. "Whites resent our presence in the work force." He thought about the convict labor Matthew had told them about. "They are enslaving blacks for profit again. They're calling it convict labor, but it's nothing more than slavery."

Felicia sighed. "It always comes back to money, doesn't it?"

"It does," Mrs. Pleasant said sadly. "That's why I said the one thing that can truly change the situation here is for new businesses to employ people. As long as people are hungry and afraid, they're going to find someone to blame their troubles on."

Felicia stood abruptly and walked to the edge of the porch.

Moses watched his daughter, knowing something was on her mind. She would tell them what it was when she was ready.

Darkness had swallowed the ocean and bay. A quarter moon, rising slowly in the east, competed with a blanket of sparkling stars. A breeze had begun to stir. The whisper of trees covered the sounds billowing up from below. Streetlamps had flared to life, outlining the opulent mansions presiding over the city higher on Nob Hill. He had seen some magnificent homes in Philadelphia and New York City, but none that compared with the homes built by the tycoons of San Francisco business.

Felicia finally swung around. "I wasn't trying to eavesdrop earlier today, but I overheard Anson and my daddy talking about something."

Moses swallowed hard. He hadn't realized their conversation had been overheard.

Mrs. Pleasant eyed her. "About me not owning a business in my own name?"

Felicia's face was deeply troubled. "Yes."

"It's not safe to own a business in my name," Mrs. Pleasant said bluntly. "There are too many men who would make it their life's goal to take it away from a black woman."

"Only black women?" Felicia demanded.

"I suppose I'm more vulnerable because of my race, but women as a whole have fewer rights in America when it comes to money."

"That's wrong!" Frances exclaimed. "My mama and Susan own their stables. They own their medical clinic."

Mrs. Pleasant gazed at her with compassion. "Aren't both of those businesses on your grandfather's plantation?" She looked at Moses quickly. "I understand you own half the plantation..." Her voice trailed off, inviting him to finish her statement.

"But if I owned it all, there would be a never-ending effort to take it from me," Moses said heavily. "Thomas and I have talked about that."

Frances stared at them. "Is that the reason my mama left Richmond and came back to the clinic on the plantation?" She frowned. "I know they had a lot of trouble there." Her frown deepened. "She and Janie decided to come home when a group of men destroyed their clinic."

Moses was quick to give her the rest of the story. "Your mama and Janie were going to stay and rebuild the clinic, but they missed being with their families." He smiled. "She wanted to be with you and Minnie all the time, Frances."

"And now Russell and Bridget," Frances said softly.

"She shouldn't have had to make that decision," Felicia stated. "She shouldn't have to worry who might try to take her business. Neither should you." Her eyes flared as she stared at her mentor.

"You're right," Mrs. Pleasant agreed. "However, until women have the vote, and we're able to fight for our rights, it's not going to change. Men aren't eager for us to have any power over our lives, because it will diminish the control they are determined to exert."

"Most men," Moses objected.

"*Most* men," Mrs. Pleasant agreed, smiling at him warmly. "You do realize how unusual the Cromwell men are, don't you? Felicia has told me enough to make me realize the Cromwell men are extraordinary."

"Because our mamas are extraordinary," Frances said firmly.

"Completely true," Moses told her. "Every woman on Cromwell is truly extraordinary."

"Which won't matter until our country changes," Mrs. Pleasant said. She fixed her eyes on Felicia and Frances. "I'm fighting for change. Your mamas are fighting for change. You are going to have to fight even harder."

Frances cocked her head. "Why harder? Hasn't everyone in the women's rights movement been fighting hard?"

"They have," Mrs. Pleasant agreed. She paused. "Have you ever seen an animal backed into a corner?"

Frances nodded. "I saw a racoon who got trapped in the barn one time. When he realized he was trapped, he began to fight like crazy. It was scary."

"Exactly. The men running our country are getting trapped in a corner, girls. When the women's movement first started, I believe they thought it was a phase that would pass. It was something to joke about over drinks and cigars. Women would get tired of the battle and go back to being the submissive women men want them to be."

Felicia snorted.

Mrs. Pleasant, despite the serious conversation, laughed heartily. "My sentiments exactly, dear." She sobered. "The fight is going to become more intense, because men are realizing women aren't going to slink away into the darkness. We're continuing to fight. There are more of us fighting. The more they try to subjugate us, the harder we fight."

Frances' questioning look faded as understanding took its place. "They're backed into a corner."

A long silence fell on the porch. Moses could tell the girls were thinking hard.

Felicia gazed at their hostess. "You're fighting with your money."

Mrs. Pleasant smiled and nodded. "It takes money to fight." She looked at each girl in turn. "I gave thirty thousand dollars to John Brown."

Moses gaped at her. "You financed John Brown's raid on Harper's Ferry shortly before the war started?"

Mrs. Pleasant nodded. "I didn't necessarily approve of all his tactics, but he was a passionate man who fought tirelessly for abolition. He needed money. I made sure he had it."

Felicia's face reflected a battle between admiration and confusion. "I thought you said you couldn't fight hate with hate."

"I did," Mrs. Pleasant replied. "I did *not* say that you shouldn't fight for what you believe is right. Slavery was a rotten stain on our country. It was going to take bold actions to end it. I had done my part in rescuing hundreds of runaway slaves, but it wasn't enough. We hoped freedom could be accomplished without bloodshed. John Brown hoped the same thing. He believed if the slaves were well armed, that when they revolted the whites would be too afraid to fight back. He wanted what he started at

Harper's Ferry to spread everywhere slavery existed. He had a tremendous vision."

"Which failed," Moses said sadly. "It wasn't until I was in Philadelphia that I learned about his raid on the federal arsenal at Harper's Ferry. It was a complete failure."

Mrs. Pleasant lifted a brow. "Was it?"

Moses gazed at her. "His raid failed. Most of his men were killed. He was hanged. That is my definition of failure."

"I agree he was defeated at Harper's Ferry, but his ultimate goal was the end of slavery," Mrs. Pleasant responded. "His attempt was known around the country. It brought the issue of slavery to a head in our nation. One year later, South Carolina seceded."

"And the war started," Moses finished. "Which was the catalyst for the abolition of slavery."

Mrs. Pleasant stared out over the city. "Our plans don't always go the way we envision them going, but that doesn't mean they don't have a massive impact. It's up to us to take the actions we believe we're meant to take. We can't always know what will come from them."

"You don't regret losing your thirty thousand dollars?" Frances asked.

"I don't believe I lost it, dear. I believe the return on my investment came a little later than I initially anticipated."

Early the next morning, Anson arrived for work. He held several newspapers in his hand.

"Oh, good. The weekly newspapers." Mrs. Pleasant reached for them eagerly. She opened the top edition and began to read. Suddenly she stopped, her face stiffening into grave lines, making her wrinkles appear even deeper.

Moses, reaching for another ham biscuit to go with his coffee, eyed her with concern. “Are you alright?”

Mrs. Pleasant took a deep breath and forced a smile. “I’m fine. Merely a bit of bad business news, but nothing that can’t be dealt with.” She laid the paper aside as she looked up to welcome the girls entering the dining room.

“Good morning, Frances. Good morning, Felicia.”

“Good morning,” they parroted.

“I thought today would be a wonderful opportunity to show you some of the luxury hotels in San Francisco. Frances, if I promise to limit the business talk, would you like to join us?”

“I’d love to,” Frances said eagerly. “But you don’t have to limit the business talk. I don’t enjoy a steady diet of it like you and Felicia do, but I appreciate what I’m learning. When Mama and I are running our clinic, I want to be able to make wise decisions.”

Mrs. Pleasant smiled brightly. “Smart girl!” She motioned to the food on the table. “Eat quickly. I’m eager to be on the way,” she said briskly.

Felicia turned to look at him. “Aren’t you going with us, Daddy?”

“Not today, dear.” In truth, Moses had no idea why he wasn’t accompanying them, but he suspected it had something to do with the newspaper article that had upset their hostess. He thought quickly. “I found a book on tobacco farming at the bookstore. I’m going to use the time to learn some new things.”

Mrs. Pleasant raised a brow but remained silent.

Moses knew how ridiculous his quickly made-up excuse was. It was highly improbable, if not completely impossible, that he would find a book on tobacco farming in a state that couldn't grow tobacco. He was relieved when Felicia merely nodded, ate her biscuit quickly, swallowed some tea, and leapt up.

"Let's go!"

As soon as the dining room was empty, Moses reached for the newspaper, his pulse quickening when he recognized the *Philadelphia Inquirer*. He didn't have to look hard to discover what had alarmed Mrs. Pleasant.

Deadly Massacre in Colfax, Louisiana.

The byline was "Matthew Justin."

Moses read the story, bile erupting in his throat. Every muscle in his body knotted with fury and helpless agony as Matthew's writing transported him to the Easter Sunday tragedy.

When he finished reading, he lowered his head into his hands, letting the shudders course through his body. The truth was like an anvil pressing on his heart. If he had gone with Matthew and Anthony, he would be dead. It was a given that he would have joined the freedmen in their battle—except that it wasn't a battle.

The freedmen, hopelessly outnumbered and outgunned, had given up. They had surrendered and done what the posse demanded. Their reward had been a brutal slaughter.

Moses gasped for breath as he envisioned what Matthew and Anthony had experienced. He thought about how vehemently Rose had opposed him going. She'd been right. His death would have served no purpose other than to give Nash's men another target.

Felicia had saved his life.

She had finally admitted to him, during the long train ride, that she had overheard the talk about the trip to

Louisiana. She had done the one thing she could to stop him by choosing to come to San Francisco early.

Moses strode to the front porch. He looked out over the city, watching as ornate carriages rolled slowly up Nob Hill. He watched the bay glimmer on the horizon and looked up as a flock of pelicans soared overhead on their way to the ocean. Suddenly, he threw his head back and laughed out loud.

San Francisco.

What had felt like a prison a few minutes ago, was suddenly his ticket to life. He hated what Matthew and Anthony had endured, but they had come through it alive. He would have been one of the corpses rotting beneath the Louisiana sun. He would have left Rose a widow, and his children would have been fatherless.

He was glad he couldn't understand the hatred that had produced the Colfax Massacre. He never wanted to be able to understand. He wanted to create a better country for his children and the generations that followed.

As the realization of what could have happened to him sank in more deeply, his thoughts turned to Frances. They had received a telegram when Matthew and Anthony arrived in Richmond, before they left for the plantation, but it had said little more than that they were home safe.

His thoughts turned to the girls as he pondered his next actions. He wanted to hide the newspaper, but he knew the one he'd read was the first of many articles that would be written about the Colfax Massacre. In a country where racial violence had become the norm, the horrific event stood out as particularly heinous. With Matthew's eyewitness account, it was sure to raise the ire of equality-minded people around the country.

He sank down into a chair on the porch. He didn't know how long the girls would be gone with Mrs. Pleasant, but he needed to be ready when they returned.

The girls were old enough to know the truth.

How would he tell them?

Chapter Seventeen

"Daddy!" Felicia's eyes were bright with excitement as she walked into the house. "San Francisco hotels are spectacular. They're as wonderful as the ones I've seen in New York City!"

Frances nodded eagerly. "We drove all over the city. You should see them. I believe the Occidental Hotel is my favorite. It's huge! It's four stories tall and absolutely towers above every other building around it."

Moses chuckled. "That is a lot of superlatives." He had not been to the Occidental Hotel, but situated high on Nob Hill, it could be seen from everywhere in the city. At night, he had stared up at its gleaming lights and considered the luxury inside.

"I loved the Occidental Hotel," Felicia agreed, "but we drove by them so many." She ticked them off on her fingers. "We saw the Russ House, the Cosmopolitan, the Grand, the Palace, the Baldwin, and the Lick House." She looked at their hostess for confirmation.

"Very good," Mrs. Pleasant said with a laugh. "I can't believe you remembered all of them."

Felicia shrugged, but her expression was intense. "Do you believe I could own a hotel like the Occidental one day?"

Moses stared at his daughter. He knew she had high aspirations, but he hadn't known exactly how lofty they were.

"Anything is possible," Mrs. Pleasant replied. "It all depends how badly you want it."

"Even for a black woman?" Felicia asked bluntly. "If I own a hotel like that, I'm not going to allow someone else to own simply because I'm a black woman."

Mrs. Pleasant eyed her evenly. "You know what you have to do, Felicia. Until women have the right to vote and make financial decisions for themselves, you will fight an uphill battle."

Felicia scowled. "What's the point of freedom if we're not really free?"

Mrs. Pleasant glanced at Moses.

"Freedom doesn't come in a day, Felicia," Moses told her, knowing even as he spoke that he hated the reality as much as she did.

Felicia shook her head. "How long does it take?"

Mrs. Pleasant smiled. "I think everyone is looking for the answer to that question, my dear. Because we're black, we see freedom through the eyes of having been slaves. Even though President Lincoln granted us emancipation, it will take time for Americans to see us that way." She paused. "I don't know anyone, however, that isn't striving to be free."

Frances looked puzzled. "I don't understand."

"I believe everyone is chained by something," Mrs. Pleasant replied. "The white men who try to control everything do it from fear. They're chained to fear and greed. They believe their freedom will come from controlling everything and everyone around them."

"That's stupid," Frances replied.

"You'll get no argument from me," Mrs. Pleasant answered. "Every woman in America is fighting for freedom. They want political freedom, but they also want economic freedom. They want the freedom to make decisions about their own lives."

"Like deciding whether to stay married to someone who abuses them," Felicia said thoughtfully. "Matthew's wife, Janie, had to divorce her first husband because he was abusive."

"She was lucky to be able to do that," Mrs. Pleasant said. "It's not easy for women to make that decision, and oftentimes they aren't given the right."

"Every worker in the country is fighting for freedom, especially now that corporations control so much of the money and business in America," Moses added. "It's not only black people though. White men suffer. Every ethnic group in America suffers. Our country is fighting to recover from the destruction of the war. Everyone is suffering." As he spoke, he realized the depth of the truth he was communicating. "Most workers are chained by the greed of the wealthy people who run the business they work for."

"Which is why our plantation workers are treated so well," Frances observed. "Grandpa gave many of them land after the war so they could be independent. The others are paid well."

"That's right," Moses agreed. "I hope every man will work on the plantation for a long time, but the day will come when they can't or don't want to. I want them to have enough money to make different choices with their lives when it's time."

Felicia stood and walked to the window. The glass panes mirrored the frustration on her face. "It isn't fair that most of the people in America have to fight the few that maintain control of our freedoms."

"Not simply Americans," Mrs. Pleasant said. "It happens everywhere."

"Why?" Frances burst out. "Why do a few have so much power?"

"Excellent question," Mrs. Pleasant replied.

Moses waited, along with the girls, for her answer. When the silence stretched out, he decided to fill it. "I believe the few have so much power because there aren't enough people brave enough to fight against it. People become complacent in their lives. They don't believe they have the power to change things, so they do nothing. They expect others to do what they're not willing to do themselves."

Moses paused, deep in thought. "In many ways, people are used as pawns by those in power. They've convinced black people that white people are their enemies. They've convinced white people that blacks are their enemies. Or the enemies are Chinese. Or Mexican." His mind whirled as the truth of what he was saying settled in. "Abby has told me many times that the growth of corporations in America is a bad thing. I'm beginning to understand what she means. Because they're so powerful, they have the means to convince people that someone else is to blame for their troubles instead of deciding to face the true opponent – the corporations. I suppose it's easier to blame others for not changing the things you don't have the courage and determination to change yourself."

Mrs. Pleasant nodded. "That is exactly true, Moses!" She stood and moved next to Felicia. "Freedom takes time. I've been fighting for freedom for decades. I suppose I'll be fighting for it for the rest of my life." She turned Felicia to face her so she could gaze into her eyes. "I suppose you will too." She looked across the room. "And you too, Frances."

"That's wrong!" Felicia burst out. Distress was evident in her eyes.

Moses knew how badly his daughter wanted her actions to change things for her people. He walked over to stand next to her, taking her hand in his. "Freedom does take time, Felicia. That doesn't mean, however, that there won't be periods when you see huge improvements. It doesn't mean you won't help our people create better lives for themselves. People fighting for freedom will sometimes take giant steps toward having it, like when we were emancipated. Other times, it won't feel as if you're making any progress, but each step is necessary."

"So, it's like a walk," Frances said softly. "We're walking toward freedom."

Moses smiled. "I like that, Frances. Yes, I believe you're right. We're walking toward freedom."

Felicia remained distressed. "I would rather run."

Moses chuckled. "You and me both, honey. Sometimes we'll be able to." He thought about the miracle of owning a plantation, and the wonder of riding in a Pullman Palace car across the country. Neither of these was something he could have even dreamed about before the war. "Other times we'll walk slowly, pushing against the forces that try to stop us." The images that swarmed his mind made his smile fade.

Felicia stared at him. "What is it, Daddy?"

Moses hesitated, not sure now was the time to tell the girls what had happened.

"Tell them," Mrs. Pleasant urged. "Ignorance is no one's friend. There are many truths I would prefer to not know, but it's better that I know them."

Moses continued to hesitate. He had spent the entire morning thinking about how he would tell them, but he couldn't find the words.

Felicia looked alarmed. "Daddy, you're scaring me."

"I'm sorry," Moses said quickly. The last thing he wanted to do was add to their fear. Ready or not, it was time to talk. "I'll tell you, but first I want to thank you."

Felicia continued to stare at him. "For what?"

"For saving my life," Moses said solemnly. He turned to Frances. "I want you to know your daddy is alright. He is home safe on the plantation, but he and Matthew had a terrible experience in Louisiana." He held up the newspaper. "Probably the best way to tell you is to read the article Matthew wrote when they returned home. It's the first in what will be a series." He paused. "It's going to be hard to hear."

Frances locked eyes with him. "My father lived it. The least I can do is hear it."

Moses knew she was right. He waved an arm for Felicia to join her friend on the sofa. When they were seated, he cleared his throat and began to read.

When Moses was finished, having stopped many times to compose himself, he lowered the paper.

Both girls had tears streaming down their faces.

"That's terrible," Frances said, her voice quivering with emotion. "I can't imagine what Daddy must be feeling."

Moses didn't feel the need to tell her that her daddy was enduring daily nightmares and constant battles against the memories assailing him. "Your daddy is a strong man, honey. He's going to be alright."

Felicia was staring at him with an inscrutable expression. "If you had been there…" Her voice trailed off.

"I would have died," Moses said quietly. "I would have fought with the other men."

"And they would have slaughtered you too," Felicia whispered. "They would have murdered you exactly like they did my parents."

Moses gritted his teeth but didn't refute her statement. He hated that these girls had to face the truth of what was happening in the country, but he agreed ignorance wasn't the answer.

Felicia leapt up and sprang into his arms.

Moses held her tightly, stroking her back gently. "It's alright, sweetheart. I'm alright."

"I know," Felicia cried, gulping back the sobs wracking her body. "But those poor men will never be alright. Their wives will never see their husbands again. Children will never see their daddy again." She pushed back, rage replacing the tears in her eyes. "It's wrong," she said fiercely.

"It is," Moses agreed. There was no way to make the Colfax Massacre anything other than what it was—a horrific tragedy.

"Will they pay for what they've done?" Felicia demanded.

Moses took a deep breath. "I don't know," he said honestly. Felicia knew the policemen who killed her parents had never been charged. She knew no one in New Orleans had gone to jail for the murders there. She knew most white men got away with killing black people. He wasn't going to sugarcoat it.

Until things changed, it was the way it was.

"Grandpa! Grandpa! We're being invaded!"

Miles poked his head out of the tack room, trying to decide how alarmed he should be as Hope's voice rang through the barn. His granddaughter had a knack for drama. Horses snorted and whinnied as she raced through the barn, looking around frantically. Her beautiful face was almost swallowed by her wide, frightened eyes.

Miles' heart pounded. What could cause that kind of fear? Erring on the side of caution, he ducked back into the tack room to grab his shotgun and stepped into the barn corridor. "What seems to be the problem, Hope?" He kept his voice calm, hoping to ease her panic.

"We've been invaded!"

Miles took her hand and walked to the barn door. A quick look outside didn't reveal marauding invaders. He couldn't hear sounds of an attack, but...

"Do you hear them, Grandpa?" Hope demanded breathlessly. "The boys wouldn't come with me. They made me come warn you all by myself." She planted her fists on her hands indignantly.

Miles smiled down at his seven-year-old granddaughter. The last year had wrought impressive changes in her. She looked more like her mama every day, and she had the same quick intelligence and powerful personality. He thanked God this little angel would never know the horrors of slavery. "Are the boys with the invaders?" he asked quietly.

"Yes!" She grabbed his hand and began to pull him. "You have to come see, Grandpa. They're everywhere!"

Suddenly, Miles heard it for himself. He smiled and allowed her to lead him, but he already knew where they were going. As they walked a little farther down the road, the sounds grew louder.

"Grandpa!" Jed jumped to his feet and waved his arms frantically. "They're everywhere! What are we going to do?" His face was creased with worry as he stared at the trees surrounding him and the other boys.

The woods buzzed with the sound of an army of flying insects. They were perched on every bush and tree. About one and a half inches long, they looked like large flies with stout, green or brown bodies, and black markings. Their antennae were unusually short. Miles knew if he got close enough, he could identify the four clear, fly-like wings that were folded over their back like a tent.

When they approached, the bugs rose in a cloud and disappeared into the trees.

"How do we stop them?" John asked.

"We killed some of them," Russell said breathlessly. He looked around helplessly. "There are just so many of them."

"Now do you understand?" Hope demanded. "What are we going to do about the invaders?"

Miles laughed softly and walked over to join the children. "The cicadas done come back."

The children stared at him, obviously mystified.

Miles walked around in a circle, staring up into the trees and out into the open field around them. The cacophonous whine was a sound he could never forget. He had suspected they would arrive this year, but sometimes their breeding grounds changed location.

"There are hundreds of them, Grandpa!" Jed exclaimed. "Maybe a thousand!"

Miles waved an arm. "Millions actually. They be all over the plantation."

His words shocked the children into silence.

Hope was the first to speak. “Millions?” Her whispered voice was full of awe. She scrunched her face with confusion. “How many is a million? Is that a lot?”

“Way more than you can count,” Miles told her. He bent down and examined the branches of some young redbud trees on the edge of the woods. “Do you remember when Grandma told me she was gonna plant a whole bunch of new apple and pear trees in the spring?”

John nodded, his eyes bright with curiosity. “You told her not to,” he said promptly. “You said she should wait a couple months.” He cocked his head. “Is this why?”

Miles continued to explore, examining small trees and woody undergrowth. He finally found what he was looking for. He turned to wave the children over, but they were already clustered closely behind him. “You ain’t got nothin’ to worry ‘bout,” he assured them. “These cicadas ain’t dangerous to nothin’ but young trees.”

John shook his head. “We’ve lived here almost our whole lives, Grandpa. I’ve never seen them before.”

“You wouldn’t have,” Miles assured him. “They only come out ‘bout every seventeen years.”

The children stared at him in astonishment.

“How do you know?” John asked suspiciously.

Miles grinned. “‘Cause I been living here my whole life too. ‘Cept my whole life is a lot longer than yours.” He thought back. “This be the fourth time they been here on the plantation.” He grinned again. “Yep, every seventeen years. It be a mystery for sure.”

The children continued to regard him suspiciously.

“Are you pulling our leg again, Grandpa?” Hope asked. “Grandma says you do that a lot.”

Miles couldn't blame them for their suspicion. He did enjoy teasing them. He knelt down to show them what he'd found. "Look here. See these brown things?"

Hope leaned forward to look but jumped back quickly. "It's more of the invaders. I'm not getting close to them!"

"Don't be a baby," John retorted. He stepped forward to peer down at where Miles was pointing. Suddenly, he leaned closer. "That's not a bug, Grandpa. Sure looks like one though." He edged around it, examining what Miles had pointed out. "It doesn't have wings either. It doesn't look like a cicada."

"It doesn't," Miles agreed. "The best I can tell, the cicadas live down under the ground for a lot of years. When they be ready, they crawl out of the ground and start climbing up things like this tree here. When they come out of the ground, they don't look like they do now. This one here crawled up this tree and got rid of its skin. Once the cicada crawled out, it left this behind."

Russell pushed closer. "It's hollow."

"That's right," Miles replied.

"So, there isn't a bug there?" Hope asked as she walked forward to stare down at the cicada skin. She wrinkled her nose. "Those skins are everywhere!" She spun around. "Are we really surrounded by *millions* of them?"

"Cross my heart," Miles said solemnly.

"They shed their skins like snakes," Russell said, looking impressed.

"And like caterpillars," Jed added.

John stared up at his grandfather. "Are you telling the truth about the seventeen years?"

"Cross my heart," Miles promised as he used his hand to mark a big X over his heart.

John looked at the other children. "When he crosses his heart, he's telling the truth."

"Why every seventeen years?" Russell asked, obviously fascinated.

Miles shook his head. "There may be somebody smart enough to know the answer to that question, but it ain't me. To me, it's been one of those life mysteries I ain't ever gonna understand." He stared down. "I reckon some science guy gonna figure out the answer soon."

"I bet Felicia knows!" Jed proclaimed.

Miles laughed. "That girl probably does, but she ain't here to tell us."

"Why did you tell Grandma not to plant the fruit trees?" John asked.

Miles smiled, glad there was a question he could answer. "Look here," he commanded.

The children, huddled around him, knelt down to stare at what he was holding.

"This here be the branch of that baby redbud tree. See how the slender branch look like it's all cut up?"

"Who did that?" Hope demanded. "Why would they hurt the tree?"

"The cicadas did it," Miles instructed. "The best I can tell, the females use something on their body to cut slits into tree branches to lay their eggs. Now, if you got a big tree, you ain't got nothing to worry about. The little trees, though...they ain't strong enough yet to live through all these cuts. This little tree probably ain't gonna make it." He thought back. "I remember the first time the cicadas came to visit. They must have come the year I was born, 'cause the best I remember, I must have been 'bout seventeen when they came back."

Hope cocked her head. "You lived here when you were my age?" Her eyes were filled with confusion. "Why?"

Miles smiled gently. "I was a slave here, Hope."

Russell frowned. "My grandpa owned you?"

This wasn't the conversation Miles wanted to be having, but he wouldn't dodge their questions. He knew how easy it was to forget things you didn't live yourself. "Well, your grandpa's daddy owned me back then. When he died, your grandpa owned me."

Russell's frown deepened. "Slavery is a bad thing."

"And your grandpa knows that now," Miles assured him.

"Did he let you go free?" John asked.

Miles hesitated but answered honestly. "No. I escaped before the war started with a bunch of other Cromwell slaves. That's when I went up north to Canada and started working there. A few years after the war, I decided I wanted to come back and see if I could get a job here."

"Why?" Russell asked. "Why would you want to come back?"

Miles smiled. "I hated being a slave, but I loved the plantation. It had been home my whole life. I had it better than the slaves who worked in the tobacco fields 'cause I got to work with the horses. I kept learning things. When I was about twenty, your great-grandpa put me in charge of the stables."

The children digested what they were hearing.

"I'm very glad you came back," John finally said. "If you hadn't come back, Grandma wouldn't have fallen in love with you, and you wouldn't be my grandpa."

Miles laid a hand on his head. "I'm real glad about that too," he said softly. He figured that was enough of a history lesson for now. He pointed to the branch he was holding.

"Back to your question… Like I said, this kind of damage happen to a grown tree, it ain't gonna matter much. It happen to a young tree, it's really easy for the cicada to kill it. That's why I told your grandma to wait. When they're gone, she can plant."

"Because they won't be back for seventeen years," Jed said excitedly. His face tightened with concern. "What about the tobacco? Are the cicadas going to kill it? Will they destroy the crop?" His voice notched up with concern.

"No," Miles assured him. "Don't really know why, but they never touch the tobacco. I figure it ain't a good place for them to lay eggs."

"That's good," Jed said with relief.

Miles suspected Jed would be the Samuels child that took over his daddy's part of the plantation one day. He lived and breathed the tobacco plants. John loved to ride around the plantation with his daddy, but he didn't care much about the tobacco.

"How long will the invaders be here, Grandpa?" Hope asked.

"Not too long," Miles told her. "They usually here 'bout a month or so. I've seen them die after a couple weeks. Last time, they weren't gone for 'bout six weeks." He shrugged. "They ain't gonna hurt anything. You'll hear the whining noise for as long as they be here. One day you'll wake up and things be quiet again. They be gone as fast as they came."

Hope looked confused. "If they're going to die, how do they come back in seventeen years?"

Miles smiled. "Excellent question." He held up the limb again. "These eggs being laid right now are gonna be born. As soon as they hatch out, they gonna crawl down and dig back into the ground. They'll stay there until they be ready to come out again."

"In seventeen years," Hope replied. "Now I know why you believe it's a mystery."

Russell stared around him. "So, while we're standing here, there are millions of bugs crawling out of the ground?"

Miles paused. He'd never thought about it quite like that. "Sounds creepy, don't it?"

"Yeah," Russell stated. He turned around to head for the barn. "Now that I know the invaders aren't going to attack us, I'm going for a ride."

Chapter Eighteen

Warren Hobbs, tucked into a booth at the back of a Portland neighborhood bar, nursed a warm beer while he waited for his friend. He gazed around the dark interior, trying to rein in the thoughts he couldn't seem to stop having. He'd lived in Portland, Oregon for six years. His thoughts flashed to the Ku Klux Klan convention he had attended with Matthew, where he'd convinced his Klan buddies that Matthew was one of them. Although he'd been in disguise, knowing the article Matthew wrote days after the convention would throw light on Hobbs, they had put him on a train the next morning with enough money to start over.

"Hobbs!"

Hobbs looked up as his friend Tyson slid into the booth opposite him. "How's it going?" He looked more closely when he saw the scowl on the tall, bulky man's face. "What's wrong?" he asked.

"You haven't heard?"

"Heard what? I don't know what you're talking about."

"The railroad is letting men go," Tyson snapped. "I got my notice today. A whole lot of us did."

Hobbs' breath caught in his throat. He had suspected the firings were coming, but it had happened sooner than he anticipated. "I didn't know."

"You didn't get a notice?"

"Not yet." Hobbs figured it wouldn't be long. "I didn't work the last two days. My notice is probably waiting for me."

"Maybe not," Tyson replied. "Since you work on the trains themselves, they might keep you. They're getting rid of most of the men who laid the tracks."

That didn't surprise Hobbs. "They can only lay so many tracks." He saw the despondent look in his friend's eyes. They had met on the railroad days after Hobbs arrived from Virginia. They'd been friends ever since. "What are you going to do?"

Tyson shrugged. "I have no idea." He took a deep swallow of his beer. "What about you?"

Hobbs put his thoughts into words for the first time. "I might head back east."

Tyson's eyebrows inched toward his hairline. "East? Where in the east?"

Hobbs shrugged. He knew what he wanted to do. He also knew the reasons it wasn't a good idea.

"You figure the Klan will still have it out for you?"

Hobbs shrugged again. During the early months of their friendship, he'd confessed to Tyson why he was there. He had no way of knowing what awaited him if he decided to head back to Virginia. It had been six years, but memories were much longer than that.

"You could go up north somewhere. I hear Chicago and Boston are rebuilding from the fires they had. It would probably be easy to get a job," Tyson suggested.

Hobbs looked at Tyson more closely. "Is that what you're thinking about doing?"

"I'm thinking about it." Tyson took another swallow. "If you don't work for the railroad, you pretty much gotta work in lumber or farming. Neither one of those got any appeal for me."

Hobbs understood his feelings. He had lost half of his leg in the Antietam battle during the war. Working in the train baggage car with his wooden right leg had been alright, but he could never make it in the lumber industry, and he couldn't imagine returning to the farming life he'd known as a boy, even if his leg would allow him. He had no idea if there was a possibility of a railroad job on the east coast, but he was at least certain his options were better.

"Besides, I don't have any desire to stay in a state that doesn't want black people to live here," Tyson stated. "I've gotten away with it so far because I was valuable to the railroad, but now that they're laying off the few of us black men who worked for them, I figure it's best to move on."

Hobbs scowled. "The KKK is bad, but I don't believe it's any worse than the laws they passed here in Oregon to keep black people out. They decided even before they became a state that they didn't want black people here."

Oregon had passed stringent laws before the war. They gave blacks two years to leave, or they would be whipped for continuing to stay. That penalty was eventually lifted, but they passed other laws to discourage blacks from settling in their state. The Fourteenth Amendment had nullified their laws, but Oregonian whites made no effort to hide their disdain for any blacks who lived there.

Tyson shrugged. "Ain't nothing new."

Hobbs felt regret surge through him. He would always carry the guilt of ever being involved with the Klan. He had let his fear and anger control him. Becoming friends with Tyson had helped reinforce his belief that color had nothing to do with character.

Tyson kept staring at him. "You're not thinking about going back to Virginia, are you?"

Hobbs took another swallow of beer. "Maybe," he admitted.

"And you don't think the Klan will come for you?" Tyson eyed his friend. "You don't exactly blend in with a crowd."

Hobbs flushed. He knew his red hair and freckles made him stand out. Combined with a peg leg, if someone had it out for him, he could be putting himself in a precarious position.

"You won't see me anywhere near the South," Tyson proclaimed. "When I ran away from my plantation and headed north, I swore I wouldn't ever be south of the Mason-Dixon line again." He shook his head. "You might somehow escape the Klan's notice, but I surely won't."

"I agree with you there," Hobbs said. Tyson was almost as large as Moses. His size had made him a welcome addition to the railroad crew, but it also meant he stood out no matter where he was. "The North could be a good option. You would be a good addition to a construction crew."

Tyson nodded. "I have to figure out how to earn enough money for the train fare. I haven't been too good about saving money."

Hobbs shrugged. "I can cover us both."

Tyson stared at him. "Where did you get that kind of money?"

Hobbs chuckled. "The same place you did. I just didn't spend mine as fast."

Tyson looked down, shame shining in his eyes. "Isn't much to do besides hang out in the bar after work."

Hobbs didn't comment. He spent time at the bar, but he also spent a lot of time in the tiny house he had rented shortly after arriving. Thomas Cromwell sent him a few books each month, as well as newspapers, so he could stay current on national events. He had read most of them several times. In case his life changed, he hadn't wanted to be at a disadvantage. The Cromwells had convinced him how valuable education was. His lack of schooling didn't mean he couldn't learn everything possible.

"You really thinking about going back to Virginia?"

"I am. I know trouble could be waiting for me, but it was home for most of my life, and I miss it." He thought about how beautiful the countryside was in the spring. He could envision the glowing dogwood trees, the pink redbud blooms, and the wildflowers exploding across the ground like fireworks dispersing their colors.

Tyson, several years older than him, observed him closely. "You weren't more than a boy when the war started."

"I signed up when I was sixteen," Hobbs replied. "I didn't have a clue what war was. If I'd known, I would have stayed on the farm."

"You thinking about going back to see the Cromwell family? Isn't that who you told me about?"

Hearing the name aloud increased Hobbs' yearning to return. "I met them through Lieutenant Borden."

"The officer whose life you saved?"

"Same as he saved mine," Hobbs said. "Then I met Carrie Cromwell. She saved me too." He thought back to the day during the second year of the war when he had been stripped and left alone in the woods by marauding Union troops. Carrie, involved in her own escape from troops that had overrun Cromwell Plantation, had found him, scrounged up clothes from a deserted cabin, and rode double with him back to Richmond on her horse, Granite. "We have a lot of stories together."

Hobbs took a deep breath. "Lieutenant Robert Borden was killed on the plantation during an attack by the KKK. He dove in front of a little black girl to save her life. Robert took the bullet meant for her."

Tyson eyed him keenly. "That's why you hate the KKK. It's hard to believe you were ever part of it."

"I was stupid," Hobbs said fiercely. "You know I regret every minute of it. I'm ashamed I believed the nonsense they told me. They convinced me I was suffering because of black people. When the Cromwells found out, they should have kicked me out of their home, but instead, they helped me understand why I was wrong. Instead of hating me, they gave me a chance to change. I will forever be grateful."

Tyson nodded. "That's the reason you infiltrated that KKK convention."

"Yes. It's one of the few things I am truly proud of."

"Even if it means you can't stay in Virginia?" Tyson pressed.

"Even if," Hobbs said firmly. "I can always head north, or even come back out west."

"When are you leaving?"

Hobbs shrugged, amazed how confident he was of his decision. "No idea. I only decided I was actually going to do it today. I'll send a letter to Thomas Cromwell tomorrow. I suppose I could simply show up, but I feel better giving him advance warning. He'll be able to telegraph me whether I should come." He didn't add that, as much as he wanted to go back to Virginia, he wasn't sure he would be welcome at Cromwell. They had helped him start a new life, but that didn't mean they would embrace a former Klan member on the plantation.

"Without a job, I don't know how much longer I can stay here," Tyson admitted. "They ain't gonna let me stay in the railroad housing since I don't have a job. I moved in there after the fire last December."

"Stay with me," Hobbs invited. "I don't know for sure when we'll leave, but we can make ourselves useful until we do." He didn't know if having a black housemate would make life uncomfortable in the city, but he didn't really care. He was fairly certain Tyson's size would ensure their safety.

"What are we going to do?" Tyson asked.

"I have a friend who works with the fire department. This summer is starting out drier than usual, so they're on alert. After the fire, the mayor authorized a new volunteer fire company. I'm going to join it."

"Do they have enough water in the cisterns now?" Tyson asked. "It's been six months since almost the entire waterfront burned. What have they done to protect the city?"

Hobbs understood his concern. Three days before Christmas, from his house high on one of the Portland hills, he had watched the fire build and spread. Six blocks of the city had been reduced to rubble. The glow had reflected off the Willamette River as the buildings burned and collapsed. The fire had initially been blamed on a Chinese laundryman's careless actions, but further investigation proved the blaze had been caused by an arsonist intent on destroying the Chinese-owned business.

The firemen fed into underground cisterns for their water supply. Water was pumped into the cisterns from central waterlines, but they'd not been able to pump it fast enough for the need. When the cisterns ran dry, the firefighters were forced to retreat from the inferno, moving away from it in hopes of finding a cistern that still had water as the blaze spread.

"They're working on the water situation, but it's going to take time," Hobbs informed him. "They have, however, bought three new steam fire engines and some other apparatuses. They've tightened fire protection and building codes, and they're trying to make sure the roads stay clear in case of a fire."

Tyson scowled. "I hope so. I got burned out of my room that night. The whole building went up in flames. The firemen couldn't put the fire out because the lumber company had piled huge mounds of wood in the street. It ended up catching fire, making the blaze spread quicker. The firefighters didn't stand a chance."

"It was a bad night," Hobbs agreed. He had considered going down to offer assistance, but when a strong wind blew in from the south, fanning the flames higher, he knew it would take more than an extra man to put it out. Thankfully, heavy rain had started around noon the next day, enabling the firefighters to get it under control. The rest of the embers had been doused by a heavy snowstorm that night.

Evidence of the fire remained along the waterfront. Blackened structures and crumbled buildings dominated the area, but at least it hadn't done as much damage as the Chicago and Boston blazes. Hobbs knew, though, that Portland wasn't any better equipped to stop a more destructive fire, especially if things became even drier.

"What are you going to do for the fire department?" Tyson asked.

"Mostly check to see if businesses are adhering to the new codes. I won't be popular, but it needs to be done."

Tyson shook his head. "I don't mind joining in to fight a fire if it comes, but I'm not going out to enforce codes. With my black skin, I'm more likely to get whipped or lynched. White businessmen aren't going to take kindly to a black man checking on them."

Hobbs knew he was right. "We'll get out of here as soon as we can," he promised.

It couldn't happen soon enough for him. Now that he had made his decision, he was ready to move on.

Rose had been sitting on the porch since lunch ended, her eyes glued to the driveway for the betraying swirl of dust that would announce Jeremy and Marietta's arrival. She was so excited she'd hardly slept a wink. She was also nervous. She swallowed, trying to push away the anxiety roiling in her stomach.

Hope pushed out onto the porch. "Are they here yet, Mama?"

"Not yet."

Hope frowned. "Why not? You told me they would be here after lunch. It's after lunch."

"Yes, but only fifteen minutes after lunch ended," Rose said with a smile. "They will be here sometime this afternoon." In truth, she was as impatient as her little girl. She hadn't seen her twin for far too long.

"I can't wait to see Uncle Jeremy and Aunt Marietta," Hope said brightly. "And the twins. Marcus and Sarah are five now, aren't they?"

"Almost. They'll be five in October."

"And we can teach them how to ride this year?" Hope demanded. "I have Patches ready in the barn."

Rose chuckled. "They may want to wait until tomorrow. They've traveled a long way from Philadelphia."

Hope shook her head. "The adults may want to rest, but my cousins will be ready to have some fun." She spoke with complete confidence.

Rose didn't argue. Her daughter was probably right. She wasn't used to her little girl being seven and a half years old. Hope wasn't going to be as big as John, who was determined to grow to his daddy's size as fast as possible, but she was certain to be taller than her mother. Hope was definitely more confident than she had been at her age. Of course, at her age, Rose had moved into the plantation house to be Carrie's personal slave. She was thankful every day that none of her children had to live their life in captivity.

Hope moved to stand in front of her. She cocked her head, her dark eyes large and luminous in her face. "Why do you look funny, Mama?"

Rose shook off the memories and smiled. "I was thinking about how grown up you are. It won't be long before you're not my little girl anymore."

Hope responded by crawling into her lap and throwing her arms around Rose's neck. "I'm always going to be your little girl, Mama." She leaned back so she could stare into Rose's face. "Are you going to have another baby, Mama?"

Rose laughed, caught by surprise. "Where did that question come from?" Rather than wait for an answer, she pushed ahead. "I'm not planning on it. Why? Do you want a little brother or sister?" She didn't know what she would say if Hope responded affirmatively.

"No," Hope replied instantly. "I like being your baby. I think there are enough children in our family. Don't you think four is enough?" She paused, looking thoughtful. "Though, other families have many more children than that." Hope shook her head and frowned. "If you want more children, I guess it will be alright."

Rose bit back her laughter at the disconsolate look on her little girl's face. "I agree with you that four is the perfect number. Besides, I feel like I have many more children because of my students."

Hope's face lit up. "That's good. Sometimes it's hard to always be the youngest, but most of the time I don't mind." She looked back at the driveway. "Besides, Marcus and Sarah are almost here. For the next month, I won't be the youngest!"

"What about Bridget?" Rose asked.

Hope shrugged. "She can't really talk yet, so she doesn't count." Her face clouded. "I suppose it will be a problem when she does, though." Her smile broke through again. "Until then, I'm still the youngest! Until Marcus and Sarah get here," she added quickly.

Rose bit back her laughter, knowing better than to attempt to follow her logic. She also knew it wouldn't be long before Hope would be too large to crawl into her lap. She was determined to savor every moment. "That's right. I know you'll help make sure the twins stay safe and have fun."

Hope nodded vigorously. "I've been planning things."

Thomas and Abby stepped out onto the porch.

Rose interpreted their quick look down the driveway. "They're not here yet."

Abby laid a hand on Rose's shoulder. "That doesn't mean there was trouble," she said gently.

Rose let out her breath. It had been several years since Jeremy and Marietta's last visit to the plantation. On their last trip, Sarah had been threatened by a white man, indignant that a supposedly white couple had an obviously mulatto daughter.

Sarah had been terribly frightened. Her parents had been outraged, stating they would never again expose their children to southern racism. The yearly trips to the plantation had ceased.

Rose understood, and she had no trouble going to Philadelphia to visit, but she also knew how much fun the twins would have on the plantation. They had parks in the city, but nothing that offered the same kind of freedom Cromwell did.

All the children were excited for them to arrive. They had talked of little else for the last week.

Rose chose to not communicate her fear while Hope was snuggled in her lap. Besides, she didn't need to say what she was certain Thomas and Abby were also feeling. The longer their arrival was delayed, the more likely they had encountered a problem in the city.

By three o'clock, everyone in the house had gathered on the porch. Annie brought out a tray full of cookies and glasses of lemonade. It was warm for mid-June, but not uncomfortable.

"They should be here," John announced, his face creased with concern.

Rose stared at him, realizing how much he looked like his father at that moment. He was only ten years old, but his size made him look much older. "They'll be here," she said confidently.

John turned to gaze at her. "You're worried too, Mama."

Rose swallowed. The children knew what had happened at the train station. She didn't want to feed into their fears, but neither did she want to dismiss John's worry.

Carrie, seated next to her, took Rose's hand. "If we're being honest, we're probably all a little nervous, John," she said quietly. "There could also be many other reasons they're late." She squeezed Rose's hand. "Anthony and Jeremy will handle any trouble."

Rose appreciated her statement, but she was growing more nervous by the minute. Jeremy and his family had arrived in Richmond the afternoon before and stayed at Thomas' home for the night. Anthony, in the city for business, was riding back with them. They had promised they would get an early start that morning. Unless there had been trouble, they should have arrived hours ago. She tried to push away the images swarming through her mind.

"Mama!" John pointed toward the line of trees in the distance. "I see dust!"

Rose jumped up and moved to the edge of the porch, her eyes trained on the horizon as the thin plume of dust grew larger.

Everyone moved to the edge of the porch with her, no one speaking as they waited to see who it was.

Far in the distance, a black speck rounded a curve before it disappeared again into a thicket of trees.

Carrie was the first to speak. "It's them!"

Rose frowned. "How do you know? They're so far away."

Carrie grinned. "I would know my husband's lanky body from twice that distance."

Annie grinned broadly. "I'm gonna go get some more cookies!"

Minnie sprang to her feet. "I'll help you, Annie."

Rose watched as Annie hustled inside with her little red-headed shadow. She knew they had been baking for days. The good smells that floated out when they opened the door promised a delicious feast.

Rose turned back to watch the approaching carriage. She was relieved they were here but wasn't ready to release her worry. They were late. One or more of them could be injured or sick. She was grateful when Carrie stepped to her side and put an arm around her waist.

"You'd think we would give up our worrying," Carrie muttered.

Abby joined them, slipping an arm around Rose from the other side. "Perhaps it's our way of showing we care," she said quietly.

Rose stared at both of them. "You've been worried too?" Somehow, the knowledge made her feel better.

"I believe if we ever stop worrying, we need to wonder if we have stopped caring," Abby replied.

"Which means we'll worry about the people we love for the rest of our lives," Carrie said.

"That's exactly what I mean," Abby said matter-of-factly.

The carriage moved closer.

Rose easily identified Jeremy, Marietta, and the twins. She squinted her eyes when she saw another person in the carriage with them. "Who is that?"

Jed was the first person to realize the identity of their extra guest. "It's Vincent!" he yelled happily. Not willing to wait for the carriage to get to the porch, he ran down the stairs and sprinted down the drive.

"Vincent!" Jed yelled, raising his hand exuberantly.

Rose stared in astonishment. Jed had arrived at the plantation in the company of his father, Morris, and Morris' friend Vincent. The two men had survived a brutal attack by KKK members that had killed Jed's mother. In spite of Carrie and Janie's best care, Morris' wounds had been too infected when he arrived, and he died from sepsis less than a month later. Jed had been with his father when he passed away.

Vincent, also gravely injured, had recovered. Eager to be out of the South, he had moved to Philadelphia to work with Jeremy at the factory. He-was also attending college in his free time.

Rose would be forever grateful that Vincent had been agreeable to them adopting Jed. She couldn't imagine life without the twelve-year-old who had developed a passion for the plantation.

She smiled as Jed ran down the driveway.

"What a treat for him to have Vincent here," Abby said warmly.

Rose nodded. "He'll be excited to reconnect with a piece of his past." The nightmares had become fewer since they'd arrived in the fall two years earlier, but they could still sometimes leave Jed sobbing and crying out for his mama. When Rose would go to comfort him, he would wrap his arms around her as if he would never let her go. The haunted look that had filled his eyes was no longer evident during the day, but sleep lowered his defenses and made him vulnerable. She trusted time would help soften the trauma's grip, but he would always carry it with him.

Jed was running beside the carriage, beaming up at his friend as it rolled along the driveway.

As soon as the carriage stopped, Vincent stepped out and swept Jed into his arms. "My goodness, boy, you are growing like a weed down here! Or maybe I should say you're growing as fast as that tobacco you're so in love with."

Rose grinned. The two of them hadn't seen each other since Vincent had left, but they carried on a regular correspondence.

"I'm twelve now!" Jed announced.

Vincent held him back and stared down into his face. A shimmer of tears appeared in his eyes. "Your daddy would be so proud of you," he said softly. "He and your mother both."

Jed's face filled with sadness for a moment but was quickly dissipated by a smile. "Mama says they know."

Vincent glanced up at Rose and smiled broadly. "I reckon she's right."

Rose smiled back and cocked her head. "Welcome to Cromwell, Vincent! Am I imagining that you look quite different?"

Vincent glanced at Jeremy. "I suppose I do. We'll explain that later."

Rose ran down the stairs to be pulled into her twin's strong arms. "Welcome to Cromwell, Jeremy!" Her voice was muffled by his muscular chest.

"It's good to see you, Rose." Jeremy held her at arm's length, gazing down at her with brilliant blue eyes beneath a thatch of blond hair.

"My turn!" Marietta pushed Jeremy aside. "I've missed you, Rose." She hugged her fiercely before she stepped back and looked around. "And I've missed the plantation. It's wonderful to be back."

“We’ve been looking forward to your arrival,” Rose replied. She looked around, grinning as she watched the children embrace the adults and then turn their entire attention to the twins. “How are Sarah and Marcus?”

Marietta chuckled. “They’re more excited than I’ve ever seen them. I thought they would sleep the entire way out here, but neither one closed their eyes for a second.”

“Mostly, they bounced on the carriage seats,” Jeremy said. “Of course, they kept the carriage bouncing so much, we hardly noticed the ruts in the road.”

Rose laughed. “I had the same problem on my end.” Her thoughts turned to how long they had waited. “Did you have trouble on the way out? Or in Richmond? We were expecting you much earlier.”

Marietta shook her head. “I believe I’ll let your twin answer that one. I tried to talk him out of it for today, but he wouldn’t listen to me.”

Rose eyed Jeremy. “What delayed you?”

Jeremy grinned sheepishly. “It wasn’t just me, Marietta,” he protested. “Vincent wanted to train, as well.”

Rose’s puzzlement grew. “Train? What in the world are you talking about? You’re a baseball player. I admit I don’t know the sport that well, but I don’t remember anything about it that would require training during a carriage ride from Richmond.”

Jeremy shook his head. “Not baseball.” His eyes flashed with eagerness. “Have you ever heard of pedestrianism?”

“Pedestrianism?” Rose was completely mystified. “No, I haven’t.”

“That’s what you get for being hidden away out here on the plantation,” Jeremy teased. “It is quite the rage throughout the country right now.”

"A rage your twin is determined to win," Marietta added.

"Win what?" Rose demanded.

Jeremy chuckled. "I'll tell you during lunch. I'm starving!"

Chapter Nineteen

Anthony swept Carrie into his arms and held her tightly.

Carrie's throat tightened as she returned the embrace. She watched their visitors disappear into the house and focused on her husband. Anthony had only been gone three days, but he hadn't wanted to go to Richmond. It was his first time leaving the plantation since his return from Louisiana. He'd not had one night of solid sleep since the massacre. He could only sleep when she was holding him, but nightmares haunted him. She knew he hated how weak it made him feel.

When Carrie finally stepped back to allow the children to hug him, she could see the weariness dulling his eyes. He must not have slept any during his time away. Her heart ached for him, but she knew nothing but time would ease the agony of the memories he carried.

"What took y'all so long, Daddy?" Minnie asked. "We didn't think you were ever going to get home."

Anthony smiled. "Jeremy and Vincent insisted on walking most of the way."

Carrie stared at him. "Excuse me? They walked?" Her curiosity grew. "Was there something wrong with the horses or the wagon?"

"Everything was fine." Anthony chuckled. "Jeremy and Vincent will explain it. Personally, I think they've gone a little soft in the head, but they are quite committed to their pedestrianism."

Annie stepped out onto the porch before Carrie could ask another question.

"All of y'all get on in this house." She glared at Anthony. "I don't know what took y'all so long, but I be real tired of tryin' to keep food hot." She shook her head with mock disgust, her lips twisting with humor. "Get on in here, or I might take it out to the pigs!"

Jeremy settled back in his seat and patted his belly. "Your fried chicken is every bit as good as I remember, Annie. I've haven't had it in eons. Thank you for a delicious meal."

Annie stared at Marietta. "I taught you how to make my fried chicken. You badgered me till I gave in. Are you tellin' me you ain't making it up there in Philadelphia?"

Marietta looked sheepish. "Fried chicken doesn't taste right in Philadelphia. I made it a few times, but eating it while the sounds of the city exploded around us…" She sighed. "It wasn't right." She looked out the dining room window. "A person is meant to fried chicken when they can breathe fresh air and listen to country sounds."

Rose laughed. "We can provide copious quantities of fresh air and country sounds."

Hope frowned. "Copious? What's that, Mama?"

"It means a whole lot," Rose told her.

Hope's face brightened. "Yes, we have plenty of that!"

Rose turned to her twin. "Now, tell us about pedestrianism. Anthony told Carrie that you and Vincent insisted on walking most of the way to the plantation. That was the reason you were late. He also said he thinks you've gone soft in the head."

Jeremy laughed as he shot a look at Anthony. "Thanks for nothing!" He shrugged nonchalantly. "I understand why you're jealous, though."

Anthony threw back his head and laughed out loud. "Jealous? I was quite happy on my horse, watching you plod along the road."

"We were not plodding!" Vincent protested. "We were setting a good pace."

"If you say so," Anthony teased.

"Jealous," Jeremy insisted. "If you're not now, you'll definitely be jealous when one of us wins the ten-thousand-dollar prize."

Rose gasped. "Ten thousand dollars? What are you talking about? It's time you explain yourselves."

Thomas nodded. "I want to know more about pedestrianism too. I've read something about it in the newspapers, but I didn't focus on it…"

"Because you didn't think it was business or political news," Jeremy finished for him playfully. "Actually, it has become a quite successful business."

"Gambling has always been successful business," Abby said ruefully. "Except for those who don't win."

Rose cleared her throat. "Enough. Most of us around this table don't know what pedestrianism is. Before we debate the pros and cons, could someone please enlighten us?"

Jeremy chuckled. "No more patient than you've ever been, sister of mine."

Rose glared at him.

Jeremy laughed harder, holding up his hands in surrender. "Pedestrianism is competitive walking."

Rose stared at him. “Competitive *walking*?” She considered his answer, but it didn’t make sense. “*Why*?”

Vincent was the one to answer. “First, because it’s good for you. You told me I looked different. I’ve lost a lot of weight from walking and training.”

Carrie nodded. “Exercise is wonderful for your health.”

“And something that’s hard to get when you live in the city,” Jeremy responded.

“Only if you have money,” Vincent corrected. “Most of America walks. We can’t afford carriages or horses, so we walk.”

“That’s true,” Jeremy conceded. He smiled. “Most Americans don’t get paid for it, however.”

John leaned forward. “People pay you to walk, Uncle Jeremy?”

Rose held back her laugh at the eager look on her son’s face.

“If I win,” Jeremy responded.

Rose sighed. “Start at the beginning, please.”

“Mama?” Hope said, tugging at her sleeve. “I don’t really want to learn about people walking. Is it alright if Minnie and I take the twins riding?”

“I want to go riding!” Sarah said. Her caramel skin glowed beneath her soft brown curls.

“Me too!” Marcus added. His blue eyes beamed from beneath his bright red hair.

Rose gazed at them with amusement. Jeremy’s twins were as different as she and her brother were. The fact that Jeremy had been born looking white, and she was obviously black, was why they had lived with no knowledge of each other for two decades.

"We want to go riding too," John announced as Jed and Russell nodded. He looked at his Uncle Jeremy. "I'm sure learning about pedestrianism is interesting but..."

"Riding sounds like more fun." Jeremy chuckled good-naturedly. "I understand. I'll join you tomorrow."

"Go ahead," Rose responded. "But," she added sternly. "You are not to put the twins on Patches, or any other horse, unless Miles or Susan is there to help you. Do you understand?"

"We promise!" The children spoke in unison and stood as one group.

Moments later, the room was empty of children.

Rose turned to Jeremy. "Talk."

"I will, but first, have you heard from Moses and the girls?"

Anthony slapped a hand to his forehead. "I'm sorry. I completely forgot I received a telegram when I was in Richmond. There was also a letter waiting at the house." He reached into his pocket and pulled out two envelopes. "Rose, one of them is for you."

Rose reached for the telegram eagerly, ripped open the envelope, and quickly read the brief message. Knowing everyone was waiting, she read it out loud.

"We are doing well. Miss everyone very much. Learning a lot. Many stories to tell. Can't wait to come home."

Immediately, her heart felt lighter. "They're fine." It didn't diminish the missing, but it at least alleviated the worry.

Anthony handed the second envelope to Thomas.

Thomas opened it, a broad smile erupting on his face as he read. "It's from Warren Hobbs."

"Hobbs?" Carrie asked eagerly. "How is he doing in Portland?"

Thomas held up his hand as he continued to read. When he finished, he took a deep breath. “Hobbs wants to leave Portland. The railroad is laying off workers. More importantly, though, he wants to come home.”

“Back to Virginia?” Carrie asked with a frown. “Is it safe?”

Thomas shrugged. “I don’t know. He claims to be willing to take the risk. He misses home.”

Anthony had a quizzical look on his face. “Is Warren Hobbs the soldier Robert fought with during the war?”

“Yes. He was like a little brother to Robert,” Carrie told him. “Robert was his hero.” She quickly explained why Hobbs had moved to Portland, realizing she’d never given Anthony all the details.

“Do you think the KKK still has it out for him?” Anthony asked.

“Six years isn’t that long,” Thomas answered. “It’s his choice, however.” A worried look crossed his face. “He wants to come to the plantation.”

Rose interpreted his expression. “You’re afraid him being here will infuriate the KKK and make us more susceptible to attack?”

“I didn’t think anyone local attended that convention, Father.”

“They didn’t,” Thomas confirmed. “They talk, though. They could have put out the word to keep an eye out for him if he ever returns.”

Carrie nodded thoughtfully. “Still…”

“Hobbs is family,” Thomas said firmly. “I’ll send a telegram with the next man who goes to town. He’ll know we’re looking forward to his arrival.”

“Actually,” Carrie interrupted. “Rather than a telegram, I’d like to write him a letter.”

Thomas nodded. "I'll let you take care of it."

Rose waited until she was certain the Hobbs issue had been resolved before she turned to Jeremy. "Let's try this again. Pedestrianism?"

Jeremy looked toward Annie. "Do you think it would be possible to get some more dessert first?"

Rose glared at her mother-in-law.

"Boy, you ain't getting' nothin' till you done enough talkin' for your sister to be happy. I don't know why you puttin' off talkin' 'bout it, but if I be you, I would start flapping them lips," Annie said bluntly.

The room erupted in laughter.

"You're right. You're right," Jeremy replied. "However, I hope there will be more dessert when I've satisfied my sister's curiosity."

Annie stared at him stonily.

Jeremy laughed. "You don't change, Annie. You can scare me with a look."

"I'll be scaring you with more than a look," Rose said flatly.

Jeremy laughed harder. "You win!" His voice grew serious. "Pedestrianism is competitive walking. In the last few years, it has become the most popular spectator sport in America."

"More popular than baseball?" Rose asked. "I thought baseball is America's pastime."

"It is," Jeremy answered. "But managing a baseball league is complicated—and expensive. The number of people who can attend is limited."

"And there aren't many people who bet on baseball," Abby added wryly.

"That's true," Jeremy admitted without a hint of remorse.

"Why are people betting on walking?" Rose pressed.

Jeremy took a big swig of tea and settled back in his chair. "Pedestrianism began in England. In 1809, a chap named Captain Barkley made a wager with an acquaintance who bet him he couldn't walk one mile an hour for one thousand consecutive hours—almost forty-one days. If he could do it, he would win one thousand guineas. If he lost, he would have to pay his friend one thousand guineas."

Rose thought about what she was hearing. "Who would agree to such a crazy wager? Who could possibly walk one mile an hour, around the clock, for forty-one days?" She shook her head. "Why would anyone *want* to?"

"The typical worker in England earned about one guinea a week," Jeremy explained. "The answer to who could possibly do it, is Captain Barkley."

Carrie stared at him. "He actually walked a mile an hour for forty-one days? No one can go that long without sleep."

"He slept," Jeremy replied. "Barkley, besides being an extraordinary athlete, is also quite intelligent. He devised a rather ingenious strategy. He decided to walk one mile at the end of one hour, and the next mile immediately after the beginning of the following hour."

"He walked two miles at a time," Anthony observed.

Jeremy nodded. "That way he could sleep for more than an hour before setting off again."

"One hour of sleep at a time?" Carrie demanded. "For forty-one days? Sleep deprivation is a cruel form of torture. It can impair speech and vision. It can cause nausea and hallucinations."

"No argument from me," Jeremy said. "I'm merely telling you what the wager was and telling you that

Barclay won the bet. He actually walked one mile an hour for one thousand consecutive hours." He paused for another drink of tea. "The crazy thing was how many people came to see him during the final days. They figure tens of thousands of people poured into his village to watch him."

"Why?" Rose asked. "He was just walking."

"He wasn't *just walking*," Jeremy retorted. "He was doing something most people couldn't do."

Rose didn't refute his statement. She could tell her lack of enthusiasm was hurting Jeremy's feelings. "Alright. What happened next?"

"Barclay's feat spawned a competitive walking craze in England," Jeremy answered. "Walkers came up with all kinds of ways to compete. Some races lasted hours, many lasted days, or a whole week. Huge amounts of money were wagered. Newspapers would list the results of the matches."

"And now it's here in America?" Anthony asked.

"Now it's here," Jeremy confirmed. "The first well-known walker is Edward Weston."

"Wait a minute!" Thomas exclaimed. "I remember reading about him. He lost a bet that Lincoln would become president."

"Right," Jeremy replied. "He thought Lincoln would lose the election. He was so certain of it, he made a wager with a friend. If Lincoln won, he would walk from Boston to Washington, DC in ten days so he could attend the inauguration."

"How...?"

Jeremy finished Rose's question before she could ask it. "He had to walk almost fifty miles a day."

Anthony whistled. "On dirt roads that were barely passable that time of year."

"In ice and snow," Jeremy added. "It was a brutal undertaking. He didn't quite make it because he got lost the day before he got there. He arrived in Washington, DC five hours after Lincoln was sworn in, but it didn't really matter. He had become a national hero. There were throngs of people in each town he went through. The newspapers covered his trip, and the telegraph company sent news of when he would arrive in the next location."

"Did he sleep more than an hour a day?" Carrie asked.

"Three or four hours a night," Jeremy answered.

"He captivated the country because they empathized with him," Abby said quietly. "An increasing number of people are moving into the city, but thirteen years ago, when he was walking, at least eighty percent of the country lived in rural areas. They were used to trudging many miles over dreadful roads in harsh conditions."

Thomas looked thoughtful. "The people who flocked to watch him realized one percent of the population sits when they travel. The other ninety-nine percent walk."

"That's exactly it!" Jeremy exclaimed. "Weston stopped walking during the war years. He served in the Union army as a messenger."

"Did he start walking again as soon as the war was over?" Carrie asked.

Rose could tell her friend was fascinated.

"Not until two years later, when he got into financial trouble," Jeremy answered. "He trusted the wrong people and ended up badly in debt. A friend suggested he should walk for money, so he decided to go professional. He contacted a prominent gambler, who agreed to back Weston in a wager with another gambler." Jeremy smiled.

"Weston bet ten thousand dollars that he could walk the twelve hundred miles from Portland, Maine to Chicago in thirty consecutive days. Except Sundays."

Rose raised a brow. "Except Sundays?"

Jeremy's smile broadened. "Evidently, his mother was quite upset with him for walking on a Sunday during his trip from Boston to Washington, DC. He promised her he would never walk competitively on the Sabbath again."

Rose was intrigued now. "Did he manage to do it?"

"He got there a day early," Jeremy proclaimed, a touch of awe in his voice. "When he reached Chicago, there were at least fifty-thousand people waiting for him. It was about a fifth of the entire population of the city! He was surrounded by fifty police officers to give him protection, and a thirty-piece marching band led the way. Once again, he was a hero throughout the entire country."

Carrie shook her head. "Why don't we know anything about it?"

Jeremy shrugged. "You were rather buried in medical school six years ago. Rose and Moses were in college. You were rather preoccupied."

"That's true," Rose acknowledged. She had more questions. "What are you and Vincent going to compete in?"

"A roller-skating rink," Jeremy replied.

Rose stared at him. "Excuse me?"

Jeremy laughed at her befuddled expression. "It's true. Before the war, enclosed semipublic spaces were practically nonexistent. There was no place for large groups to gather that was out of the weather. Since the war, however, large buildings have been constructed to accommodate public events."

"You're talking about exposition halls," Anthony said.

"Yes. They're becoming America's first big sports arenas."

Rose was more confused than ever. "You said you were competing in a roller-skating rink."

"I did, but I predict the day will come when pedestrians compete in the big arenas," Jeremy replied. He looked at Carrie. "In the meantime, you've been roller-skating, haven't you?"

Carrie nodded. "We took the children during our last visit to New York City. We had great fun!"

"They're being built across the country," Jeremy informed them. "Roller-skating has become increasingly popular."

Carrie cocked her head. "Roller-skating rinks are large flat surfaces. They would be perfect for..."

"Walking!" Vincent exclaimed.

Jeremy grinned. "Weston understood the profit potential of the skating rinks. He started touring three years ago, performing walking exhibitions in rinks from Indiana to New York City."

"It would certainly be more comfortable than walking outside," Anthony observed.

"Lucrative too," Vincent added. "People throng to the indoor venues. Weston has charged up to fifty cents for the pleasure of watching him walk."

"And people *pay*?" Rose was trying to understand, but it seemed rather far-fetched to her. "They pay to watch him *walk*?"

"*Thousands* of people pay," Jeremy told her. "Weston doesn't merely walk, though. He walks against time. He'll cover one hundred miles in twenty-four hours."

Rose shuddered. "I can't even imagine."

Carrie was thinking differently. "Skating rinks are large, but it must take a lot of laps to accomplish a mile."

"There are rinks where he has to do fifty laps to attain a mile," Vincent answered.

"I would be bored out of my mind," Thomas said. "I couldn't possibly sit there and watch anyone walk around a skating rink for twenty-four hours."

Jeremy smiled again. "Not many people are there for the whole time. They'll show up for the beginning, and the last several hours to discover if he actually accomplishes the feat, but it can be quite tedious to simply watch. Which is why Weston often hires a band to entertain the audience. He's a musician himself, so there are times when he plays the cornet while he walks."

"He is also quite the dandy," Vincent added. "He wears ruffled shirts and carries a riding crop or cane."

"It's become his trademark," Jeremy said eagerly. "He understands the event is as much about entertainment as it is about athletics."

"Remarkable," Rose murmured. Despite her skepticism, she was getting caught up in the pure entrepreneurial genius of what Weston was doing. "People bet on him?"

Jeremy grinned. "Someone bet him he couldn't walk one hundred miles in twenty-two hours. Most of the people who came to see him betted against him as well. He succeeded, with twenty minutes to spare, and walked away with twenty-five hundred dollars."

"Not bad for a day's work," Anthony acknowledged. "Still, he earned it. That would be a brutal twenty-two hours."

"There were five thousand people crammed in the rink to cheer him on," Vincent said proudly. "Two years ago, he walked four hundred miles in five days."

"That's insane," Rose burst out. "Why would he do that?"

"To win five thousand dollars in wagers and gate receipts," Jeremy replied.

"Is that why you're doing it?" Thomas demanded. "Are you in financial trouble, Jeremy?"

Jeremy shook his head. "Far from it, Thomas. The factory is doing well, and I get paid more than any other factory manager in Philadelphia."

Rose looked at him keenly. His voice was confident and reassuring, but there was something in his eyes that made her suddenly uneasy. She pushed aside the thought as soon as she had it. Jeremy was right; the factory was doing well, and he was well paid.

"There's a contest between the factories," Vincent told them. "The contests are happening across the country. City businesses are competing against each other."

"Who is providing the ten thousand?" Abby asked.

Jeremy raised a hand. "Don't worry. None of the factory money is going into the pot. It comes from the spectators who pay to watch, and from their bets."

"How many men are walking?"

"Two from each factory," Jeremy answered. "Close to one hundred people will start out, but it's not only men. Women compete as well."

"And blacks," Vincent said. "It's the one thing I know of that allows blacks and women to compete on an equal basis. It doesn't matter what your gender or your race is. It's about the walking."

"Extraordinary," Rose said, her interest growing. Anything that allowed equality was something she wanted to know more about. "When is your race?"

"The end of July," Jeremy answered. "Which is why we have to train."

"Are you training to walk, or to stay awake?" Carrie asked. "I would imagine there are very fit people who simply can't handle the sleep deprivation."

"That's true," Jeremy acknowledged.

Marietta had stayed silent until now. "I no longer go to sleep with my husband, nor do I wake up with him," she said forlornly.

"It's only until the race is over." Jeremy smiled tenderly at his wife.

"More than a month to go," Marietta said sadly, but then smiled. "I'm planning how I'm going to spend the winnings, though!"

"Don't plan too much," Vincent said calmly. "I don't plan on sharing *my* prize money with you."

Laughter rippled through the dining room.

Rose knew two people couldn't win. She hoped it wouldn't cause a rift between Jeremy and Vincent if one of them was victorious. "How many miles a day are you and Vincent walking to train?"

"We're aiming for twenty miles a day," Jeremy answered promptly. "The plantation is a beautiful place to train. Would you like to join us?"

"Certainly," Rose replied.

"*Certainly*?" Carrie echoed in surprise.

Rose grinned. "Now that school is done for the summer, I've been wanting to ride more. You know better than to think I would walk!" If riding her mare, Maple, twenty miles a day would give her time with her brother, she was up for it.

She still missed Moses with every fiber of her being, but having Jeremy, Marietta, and the twins here would make the time go faster.

Chapter Twenty

Carrie sighed, gripped Anthony's hand tighter, and settled back into the rocking chair. The porch was her favorite place in the world to spend a summer evening. The heavy sweetness of honeysuckle hung in the air. Rose bushes were in full bloom, providing their own wonderful fragrance. She was content to sit quietly as she watched the fireflies begin to blink their lights in the darkening woods. The raucous laughter of the children playing tag was like music to her ears.

"Can't catch me!" Minnie yelled, her laughter rippling almost as fast as her feet moved.

The boys had made it their mission to catch her during their nightly games. They rarely succeeded.

"She's fast," Marietta murmured.

"I'm glad I don't have to try to catch her," Anthony said. "The more she runs, the faster she gets. It's too bad she can't be a professional runner."

"She could compete as a pedestrian," Jeremy said lazily. Slumped back in a chair, he had downed what must have been his tenth glass of water.

"She's eleven," Carrie reminded him.

"There's that," Jeremy agreed. "Of course, as she gets older, she could become famous."

With a start, Carrie realized that was true. "Do me a favor and don't mention that to her."

Jeremy raised a brow. "You wouldn't let your daughter be a pedestrian if that's what she wanted?"

The porch fell silent as everyone waited for her response.

Carrie laughed, knowing there was but one answer to that question. "I will support whatever my daughter wants."

"Good answer," Thomas said encouragingly. "Once again, I will have the joy of watching you deal with what I went through when you decided to become a doctor."

Carrie wanted to protest that it was hardly the same, but she knew that a woman pursuing anything considered typically male territory would entail an uphill battle. "If she races, she'll win," she said confidently.

"You can't catch me!" Minnie taunted the boys again. Her red braids flapped hard against her back as she darted in and out of the trees. Her speed appeared to match the blink of the fireflies and seemed to be synchronized with the orchestra of frogs and crickets.

"That girl wants to cook," Annie said staunchly.

"There ain't no reason she can't cook *and* run," Miles said. "Or walk. She's so used to running now, I don't figure walkin' will be any big deal."

Jeremy nodded, watching her fly around the yard. "I would love to have that kind of speed and energy."

Carrie had seen Jeremy and Vincent head out early each morning as the sun was rising. Most days, Rose joined them on Maple. They wanted to get their miles in while it was coolest, but also early enough so they could be with the family the rest of the day. "Aren't you and Vincent exhausted?"

Vincent shook his head. "Twenty miles isn't really so bad."

"We're going to start adding to the distance next week," Jeremy replied. "It's only a month until the race."

Thomas shook his head. "Do you think the other competitors are training as much as you two are?"

"I hope not," Jeremy said wryly. "I'd like to believe our commitment is giving us the edge."

"But we're not taking anything for granted," Vincent added. "We're training hard to win. I'd hate to think someone trains a little harder, and then beats us."

"People have to work," Anthony reminded them.

"Not the competitors," Jeremy answered. "The competition between the businesses is intense. The walker who wins will keep the money, but the business will have bragging rights."

"And they'll use the victory for advertising," Abby observed. "In the world of marketing, it's actually quite genius. The successful walkers become American celebrities."

"Exactly!" Jeremy replied. "If we win, it will mean a tremendous amount of new business for the factory."

Carrie watched Abby closely. There was something on her face she couldn't quite identify. "Is something wrong, Abby?"

Abby shook her head but then stopped. "I don't want there to be."

"What is it?" Anthony asked.

Carrie remained silent as everyone waited for her mother's answer. There wasn't a person on the porch that didn't appreciate and respect Abby's business acumen.

Abby looked out over the plantation for several moments before she turned back to them. "Warren Hobbs' letter confirms what I have been suspecting. The railroads have grown too quickly. I fear the level of debt they must be carrying. If they're laying off people, it means they're worried too."

"You're afraid the economy is going to crash," Anthony said quietly.

Jeremy interrupted before Abby could respond. "I don't believe you have any reason to be concerned, Abby. Business is great. The factory is strong," he said confidently.

"Yes," Abby agreed.

A long silence stretched out.

"You still believe the economy could be in trouble?" Anthony asked when Abby didn't say anything.

Carrie knew her husband had tremendous respect for her mother. She would often hear them talking in the library, having in-depth conversations about business. Jeremy respected Abby as well, but he carried a confidence in his own business skills she wasn't certain was justified. He was an excellent factory manager, but that did not automatically make him a good businessman. In a time when the economy seemed to be booming, caution was not a popular position.

"I do," Abby conceded.

Anthony turned to Thomas. "And you?"

Carrie knew Abby wouldn't be offended by Anthony asking for confirmation on such a strong assertion.

Thomas took a deep breath. "If my wife says the economy is on the way to trouble, I believe her. She hasn't missed one yet. While I was down here running a plantation, she was enduring the economic struggle of operating her late husband's factories. The American economy struggles on a regular basis, but if it crashes now, it could be different."

"Why?" Carrie asked. She and Susan would also have to make decisions for Cromwell Stables based on the strength of the economy. If a slump hit before the current foals went to their new homes, they could well end up with horses people couldn't afford to buy. If that happened, it would be a substantial hit for them.

Abby met her eyes. "Because there has never been so much money at play in the country. The war changed things in the North dramatically. The South will fight for a long time to recover. The Industrial Revolution changed things. The massive number of immigrants has changed things. The advent of corporations has changed things tremendously." Her eyes were bright with concern.

Annie cleared her throat. "I hate to interrupt such a fun topic, but I got somethin' to tell y'all."

Carrie was more than happy for the topic of conversation to change. The economy had not crashed yet. Until it did, there was nothing she could do. At least not tonight. "What is it, Annie?"

"I reckon I done found homes for ten children from the city." Her voice was casual, but Annie's eyes shone with excited pride.

"What?" Carrie exclaimed.

"That's wonderful!" Abby cried. "How did you do it?"

Annie shrugged. "Miles took me around to houses where I heard they could be wantin' a child. All of them be real sad they didn't get one of the first batch of bridge children." Her expression softened. "Every one of them children is real special." Her eyes followed Russell and little Bridget as they ran laughing around the yard. "They was happy when I told 'em we could bring more out here."

"From the orphanage," Abby said softly. "What a wonderful thing for the children who can leave the city and come out here."

"That's what I figure," Annie agreed.

"When?" Carrie asked eagerly.

Annie shrugged. "Every family be ready right now. There be a few who know they want a boy or girl. The rest don't care. They just want a child."

Carrie laughed happily.

Rose walked out onto the porch. "What are you laughing about?"

Carrie told her quickly.

Rose rushed over to hug her mother-in-law. "Annie, you're a miracle worker!"

"That she be," Miles said proudly. "My wife for sure be a miracle worker."

"When will they be here?" Rose asked.

"As soon as we want to go into town and get the children," Carrie told her. She looked at Annie. "You'll join us. You can help choose which ones are adopted."

Annie shook her head. "My home be here. I don't need to be traipsing into the city. Too many people and too much noise. Besides, I trust y'all to choose them children. If I was gonna go into that orphanage, I would come back with every single one. Nope," she said firmly. "I ain't going."

Carrie opened her mouth to protest but saw Thomas and Abby both shaking their heads behind Annie's back. She bit back her laughter. She realized they didn't want Annie to ever meet May, the cook at their Richmond home. If the two women ever started comparing notes, each would realize the other had been proclaimed the best cook in Virginia. Carrie certainly didn't want to be in the middle of *that* conversation. "You'll be missed," she said quietly.

Annie shrugged. "Ain't no reason for me to leave here. Them children be comin' here no matter what. I'm gonna tell ever'body they can come get their new child right here. That way, I can make sure there be a big feast waitin' for them when they get here."

"That sounds perfect!" Rose said warmly. She looked at Carrie. "Jeremy, Marietta, and the twins will be here for two more weeks. How about if we ride into Richmond with them? We'll take two wagons and bring the children back."

Carrie nodded. "That should work. The children will want to go with us. They'll love a trip to Richmond, and their presence will make the children from the orphanage more comfortable. Especially Russell and Bridget," she added softly.

"Mind if I tag along?" Abby asked.

"We're expecting you to tag along!" Carrie told her.

"I don't think I want to be left behind," Thomas protested.

Carrie laughed as she shook her head. "We'll all go!"

Miles watched them. "Y'all head to the big city. Me and Annie gonna stay right here and pretend we own the place." He grinned. "We gonna sit on this porch every night. Least I won't have to worry for a few days 'bout them children eatin' all of my wife's cookin' before I get any."

As if summoned by his words, the children dashed up onto the porch, breathless and sweaty. Broad smiles covered their faces.

Annie rose and headed for the house. "Y'all come on inside. I got a big platter of cookies and lots of cold lemonade in the kitchen."

"We're starving!" Their voices rose in unison.

Annie shook her head. "All y'all ate enough for an army not too long ago."

"We ran it off, Annie!" Minnie proclaimed. "At least the boys did while they were trying to catch me." She smirked. "*Trying* to catch me."

"Are you boasting?" Carrie asked.

"Of course," Minnie said innocently. "You always tell me women should be proud of their talents. Doesn't that apply to girls, as well? Besides, it's not boasting if it's true."

Carrie tried to contain the laughter bubbling inside. "Who told you that?"

Minnie glanced at Abby. "Grandma."

Carrie knew when she was defeated.

"I did say those words," Abby said hastily. "I don't believe, however, that I meant you should taunt the boys with it."

Minnie maintained her innocent expression. "It's not my fault they get upset when they can't catch me. Besides, they tease me all the time." She frowned quickly, but her eyes danced with fun. "Are you saying I shouldn't tease them because I'm a girl?"

Abby threw up her hands and laughed. "I'm certainly not saying that."

Thomas chuckled. "I thought Bridget was going to be your biggest challenge, Carrie. I'm realizing Minnie will also give you a run for your money."

Carrie nodded proudly. "I'm thrilled with the fact that my girls refuse to conform to societal norms."

"Does that mean we can go in for cookies and lemonade now?" Russell demanded. "I may not be able to catch my sister at tag, but I can most certainly beat her to the cookies!" Without waiting for permission, he dashed across the porch and through the door. His feet pounding through the dining room sounded like a herd of horses were now in the house.

"Hey!" Minnie yelled, looking at Carrie wide-eyed.

"Let them go," Rose moaned. "I need peace and quiet."

Moments later, the porch was empty of children. They could hear laughter and talking through the open windows, but the peace had returned.

Moses had a destination in mind when he and Felicia started out that morning. The first week of July had been beautiful and clear. The day before them promised more of the same. The blue waters of the bay were as clear and sparkling as the sky presiding over it. It was disconcertingly easy to forget, if only for a few hours, the poverty and discontent that surrounded them.

Felicia tucked her hand through his arm and smiled up at him.

Moses, at that moment, knew the trip had been worth it. He and his daughter had always been close but had developed an even closer relationship in their three months away from the plantation. He longed for Rose and the other children, but he would stay until Felicia announced she was ready to go home. If she did. He did his best to not think about the very distinct possibility she might choose to stay in San Francisco.

"I can't believe Frances wanted to stay at the house," Felicia said. "It's a beautiful day."

Moses loved Frances like his own daughter, but he was glad for some time alone with Felicia. "She has spent much more time exploring the city than you have. Frances comes out with me every day. I know she's happy to spend a day at the house reading. Mrs. Pleasant will be in meetings today, so she has the house to herself."

"I suppose," Felicia said doubtfully. "Regardless, I like having you to myself. Where are we going today?"

"Clay Street," Moses answered promptly. He knew he hadn't kept the excitement from his voice when Felicia gazed at him curiously.

"What's on Clay Street?" Felicia asked.

"What is going to be the first wire rope street railway," Moses answered.

"That tells me nothing."

Moses laughed. "You're right. I didn't know what it was when I first heard the name either. It's kind of like a train, but it doesn't operate like a train. It's being built on Clay Street because the hill is too steep to use horses."

Felicia frowned. "I've seen horses pulling streetcars on these hills." Her frown deepened. "I've also seen how much they struggle. I've even seen horses beaten when they can't make it up the hills," she said angrily.

"I agree that it's terrible," Moses replied. "So does Andrew Hallidie. He came up with the idea for his invention when he witnessed a streetcar being drawn by horses slide backward on wet cobblestones, killing the horses."

"That's terrible!" Felicia said with a gasp.

"Hallidie saw the whole thing. He was appalled and decided to do something about it. His father is an inventor in Great Britain. He has a patent for wire-rope cable. When Andrew migrated here in 1852 during the Gold Rush, he decided to put it to use. He developed a cable system to haul ore from the mines, and also to build suspension bridges to reach the mines. He decided to use what he knew in order to help the horses."

Felicia looked impressed.

"Hallidie and his partner began construction of his new invention in May. My understanding is that Hallidie is the promoter. William Eppelsheimer is the engineer. I'm eager to see how far they've progressed. Their contract states the line has to be operational by August first, so they should be pretty close to completion."

They walked in silence for a few minutes, letting the congestion of the city swirl around them. Moses was more used to it now, but it didn't change his longing for the plantation. He would stand on the porch of Mrs. Pleasant's house early each morning, pretending he was gazing out over the plantation in preparation for a day in the tobacco fields. When the sun started to rise, melting away his pretense, he tucked away his longing to the back of his mind and prepared for a new day.

"Here we are," he announced as they approached a sign for Clay Street.

"It's very crowded," Felicia said quietly, gripping his arm more tightly.

"The entire city is crowded," Moses muttered. He knew Felicia was thinking about the Chinese she had seen lynched several weeks earlier. Violence was commonplace in San Francisco.

He smiled down at her. "On Clay Street, however, it's congested at the bottom." He pointed at the incline before them. "The hill is so steep that it isn't feasible to build higher up. My understanding is that the wire rope street railway will change that."

Felicia gazed in the direction he was pointing. "That hill looks dangerous."

"Not with Hallidie's invention," Moses said eagerly. He pointed to the middle of the road. Railroad tracks ran straight up the middle. "Before they put the tracks in, they dug a deep trench and put an endless wire rope beneath the ground in a tube."

"Endless?" Felicia asked. "How is that possible?"

Moses grinned. "I talked with one of the workers when I was last here. There is a steel wire rope, three inches in circumference and eleven thousand feet long, in a steel tube beneath the street on a pulley system."

Felicia looked intrigued, if slightly befuddled.

Moses knew he needed to keep it simple. His daughter was brilliant, but her passion was business, not engineering. He thought about Russell. The boy would be demanding to know every detail. When he got home, he would have an eager audience. Until then...

"What operates it? What makes it move?" Felicia asked.

"A powerful steam engine." Moses had been allowed to see it the last time he was here.

"Is the wire cable truly strong enough to keep a car full of people moving up a steep hill?"

Moses obviously needed to reassess Felicia's engineering prowess. She might never want to know how to operate a cable car, but she clearly had a grasp of what it took for it to be successful.

"The principle is simple," Moses explained. "The cable car is equipped with a grip, which is essentially a three-hundred-and-twenty-seven-pound pair of pliers. The grip extends through a slot between the rails and grabs hold of the cable to pull the car along." He decided not to go into deeper detail, though he had read everything he could find about it. "When the driver wants to stop the car, he releases the grip lever. That makes the grip completely let go of the cable. When he applies the brake, it stops the car."

Felicia looked thoughtful as she gazed up at the incline. "I think coming down would be even more nerve-wracking than going up. What if the cable can't stop the car at the bottom of the hill?"

"It's a good question," Moses answered. "I suppose the answer is that they've developed the mechanization to keep it from happening. The braking system is almost as impressive as the endless wire."

"They hope," Felicia said skeptically.

Moses laughed. "Ever the practical one."

Felicia raised a brow. "Have you ever seen a train on an incline like that? The railroads are smart enough to lay tracks on as flat of ground as possible. If I decided to ride such a contraption, I would consider its ability to stop to be merely an intelligent consideration."

Moses laughed harder. He knew he could never win a debate with Felicia. It was best to let her win and move on.

As they stared up the hill, two men stopped next to them, deeply involved in conversation.

"It's time to buy," one man insisted, his narrow face atop broad shoulders making him look out of balance.

"It's premature," his stout friend replied as he gripped the lapels of his obviously expensive suit. "You don't know for certain this contrivance will work."

"It will work," the first man said confidently. "I know both the inventor and the engineer. Even if they run into problems, they'll resolve them. It won't be long before this wire cable street railway will make it feasible for people to reach houses farther up the hill. The cost of land will explode in value."

"Perhaps," the other man said doubtfully.

"You mark my words," his friend replied. "I'll try to not rub my success in your face when I'm selling my land for many times what I buy it for."

"Let's go, Daddy," Felicia said suddenly, tugging at his arm.

Moses eyed her. "Where are we going?"

"To the San Francisco real estate records office," Felicia whispered, her mouth close to his ear.

Later that evening, when Mrs. Pleasant had returned home and they'd finished dinner, Felicia brought up the topic Moses knew she'd been thinking about since that morning.

"What do you know about the wire rope street railway going in on Clay Street?"

Mrs. Pleasant took a sip of tea and gazed at her. "I know Andrew Hallidie is a brilliant man. I was privy to an entire conversation one night at a dinner I was serving. He came to San Francisco nearly penniless and found great success in the gold mines. He attributes it to the system of cables he ran to transport the ore. He said it made his mining efforts much more effective. He went into great detail about why it worked. His father is a brilliant inventor whom he learned much from." She paused for another sip.

"Will you get on it?" Felicia demanded.

"If he claims he can make a streetcar run up that hill by steam engine, I believe him." Mrs. Pleasant smiled. "At least enough to give it a try when it's open to the public." Her smile turned into a chuckle. "I might not be on the first car, however."

"What do you know about the real estate available on the hill?" Felicia asked next.

Mrs. Pleasant put down her cup of tea. "What an intriguing turn in the conversation. What are you proposing, my dear?" Her interest was obvious.

"That you buy as much of the land as possible on that hill." Felicia relayed the conversation they'd overheard. "Daddy and I went to the real estate records office today. The land can be bought quite cheaply. Even if it doesn't go up as much in value as that man said, it will certainly increase enough to create a nice profit."

Mrs. Pleasant looked impressed.

"This is all her idea," Moses said. "I was completely immersed in the engineering aspects of Hallidie's creation. I never once thought about profits from what will become accessible when he succeeds."

Mrs. Pleasant nodded. "It's due to be tested on August first?"

"And operational by September," Felicia answered. "That man wasn't careful about who could overhear their conversation. I'm sure others will pursue the real estate."

Mrs. Pleasant chuckled. "And now you have learned the lesson of discretion in business, Felicia. Many fortunes have been lost by loose lips." Her gaze turned serious. "How many properties are available?"

"I viewed records for about fifty parcels. They've probably thought for years that they'll always be saddled with unusable land. It won't dawn on many of them that the new system will change things. It's hard to know how many owners would be willing to sell, but if you move quickly, I'm certain you could obtain some of them."

Mrs. Pleasant eyed her closely. "If *we* move quickly, my dear."

Moses felt his heart catch in his throat. This was it. He'd never imagined taking Felicia to view the new railway would create an opportunity for her to partner with their hostess on a venture of her own creation.

He shouldn't have been surprised.

He wanted to walk from the room, but he needed to hear the answer.

Felicia gazed at Mrs. Pleasant. "Not *we*," she said firmly. "I have loved my time here in San Francisco, and I've learned more than I thought possible, but it's not my home."

Mrs. Pleasant didn't try to conceal her disappointment. "It could be, Felicia, in time. You will have opportunities here that you might not have elsewhere."

Felicia shook her head. "No, this city is chaos. Your home is here. You love it, but I want to return east." She reached out to grip Mrs. Pleasant's hand and smiled warmly. "One thing you've taught me is that opportunity can be found anywhere if you know how to look for it. Today, overhearing that conversation, is a perfect example. I will find the right business opportunities no matter where I decide to live."

Moses stifled his broad grin. Mrs. Pleasant was gravely disappointed. He knew how much she had hoped Felicia would stay. He, however, was breathing much easier.

Frances, not bothering to hide her grin, was clearly elated. "I'm beyond thrilled you're coming home with us!"

"What will you do?" Mrs. Pleasant asked. "I'm certain you'll be successful no matter where you go, but do you know?"

Felicia shook her head. "I don't. I think I had hoped San Francisco would be my answer. Now that I know it's not, I'll have to decide what is."

Moses remained silent. It was enough that Felicia was coming home with them. What happened next was not his worry. At least her decision to come back east would ensure she was closer.

"How much longer will I have the pleasure of your company?" Mrs. Pleasant asked.

Felicia squeezed her hand. "I was hoping I could be with you when you check into the properties on Clay Street. I'm certain I will learn a great deal."

"Of course," Mrs. Pleasant replied. "That would be wonderful."

Felicia's eyes turned to her father. "I'm thinking we could leave in a few weeks?" She paused. "I have a request, however."

Moses raised a brow and waited, knowing he would probably be willing to do anything. He also knew it would be wiser to wait before he unilaterally agreed.

"I would like to take a different route going home. I may never return to the West again. It would be fabulous to see more of the country."

Moses grinned. "That's a simple request and a good idea. I'll make reservations for three weeks."

He was already writing the telegram to Rose in his mind.

When Moses stepped out onto the porch later, he found Felicia in one of the chairs staring out over the ornate railing. He joined her but remained silent. He imagined she was pondering her decision and how to make the most of her remaining time in San Francisco. He was happy to sit quietly, breathing in the salty air and gazing at the glowing lights below. At night, you would never guess the suffering going on in those streets.

"I know you can't be objective, Daddy, but do you agree with my decision to return to the east coast?"

Moses paused, wanting to be as objective as possible. "You're a brilliant young woman, Felicia. I believe you're right that you'll find opportunities wherever you go. I also believe you understand you'll face more challenges without Mrs. Pleasant to guide and partner with you."

Felicia looked at him sharply. "Do you think I've made a mistake?"

Digging deeply, Moses considered her question. "No," he said after several moments had passed. "You're used to challenges. There are some who would be too frightened to move forward without a mentor constantly at their side. You're not like that. Besides, you have me as a financial partner. You have Abby as a constant mentor. You have Thomas who will keep directing you to the information and knowledge you'll need." He wanted to ask her where she thought she would go, but he knew his daughter truly didn't know.

"Regardless," Moses said thoughtfully. "You fulfilled your ultimate objective in deciding to come here now."

Felicia met his eyes. "To keep you alive."

Moses nodded. "That's right. I'll always be grateful."

Felicia leaned in close to his side and nestled her head on his shoulder. "Not as grateful as I am," she said quietly. "Living in constant chaos has made me think so much of Memphis. It's brought up so many painful memories. Without you and Mama, I probably wouldn't be alive. If I was, I would certainly not be a college graduate and living the life I'm living now."

Moses knew that was true. "You'll figure out your future one step at a time."

Felicia stood suddenly and walked to stare out over the cityscape below. "I'm walking toward freedom, Daddy." She swung around to stare at him. "Every black person in America is doing the same thing. Every woman is."

When Felicia paused, Moses knew she was remembering the Chinese man she had seen lynched from a building.

"Every person is, I suppose," she said quietly. "Everyone is bound by some kind of chains."

Moses rose to stand beside her. "You're right. Every person I know struggles with something. They're looking for the freedom to live their lives the way they long to."

Several more minutes passed as Moses let Felicia process her thoughts.

"I want to help women walk toward freedom, Daddy. I've been given a good mind and opportunities that most women will never have. Now, it's my responsibility to open doors for other women."

"You will," Moses assured her. "Of that, I have no doubt."

There was no need to discuss the uphill battle she would face.

Felicia already knew.

Chapter Twenty-One

Carrie stepped into the barn and inhaled deeply. It was going to be a hot, muggy July day, but the early morning air was delicious. She laughed when Granite stuck his head over his stall door and snorted loudly. "Ready for some fun?"

Granite bobbed his head vigorously and snorted again.

Carrie quickly saddled No Regrets, lead her outside, mounted, and trotted smoothly down the road. Granite cavorted behind her.

A quick glance back revealed Jeremy and Vincent leaving the house. They would still be walking when she had finished her ride and opened the clinic. Carrie was impressed with their discipline but didn't envy them. They both seemed to enjoy the walking, but she also knew they carried a great deal of pressure to win the pedestrian contest coming up in two weeks.

She pushed aside her thoughts, leaned low over No Regrets' neck, and urged her into a gallop. She whooped with joy as the wind whipped her braid into disarray. She knew without looking back that Granite was right on their heels. No Regrets was fast, but Carrie already knew her nineteen-month-old colt was faster. He would gain even more speed as he matured.

When Carrie pulled the mare back to a slow trot, she gazed across the tobacco fields. The rains and summer heat had worked their magic. There was little she loved as much as watching the tobacco grow from tiny seedlings to towering plants. The vibrant green was topped with millions of pink flowers spreading over the plantation.

The men were already hard at work, weeding and cutting back plants to allow for stronger growth in the coming months before harvest. Tobacco worms were plucked off, thrown into cans, and disposed of. Now that school was out, many of Rose's students had joined their fathers, eager to earn income until classes started again. The plantation rule was that no one of school age could work the fields during the school year.

The year-round nurturing of the fields was what made Cromwell tobacco crops successful. The application of oyster marl and the richness of winter cover crops restored the soil between plantings. This was the first year more land had not been cleared for tobacco.

Moses had offered his men's strength and time to clear more land for three additional horse fields. They had been cleared and seeded with tall fescue three months ago. Carrie was thrilled with the results so far. Tall fescue had begun to appear in seed catalogs three years earlier. She and Susan had done their research and decided to give it a try.

The fescue was growing thick and strong. They weren't ready to turn horses into the pastures yet, but by the end of summer she thought they would be ready.

Carrie turned away from the fields and started down a well-worn trail. She laughed when both No Regrets and Granite snorted their delight. A few minutes later, they broke out onto the bank of the James River.

Granite immediately plunged in, pawing at the water and dipping his head to catch the spray.

Carrie dismounted and untacked No Regrets so she could join her offspring. Settling onto a log along the shore, she watched with joy as the horses splashed in the river. They drank deeply and lowered themselves into the water to roll. When they finally stood, they shook vigorously, spraying diamond droplets that turned into rainbow prisms.

Carrie was tempted to join them, but she had a full day ahead of her at the clinic. Besides, she would be swimming that afternoon at the going-away picnic for Jeremy and his family before they left the next day.

Annie was determined to outdo herself, though how she possibly could was beyond Carrie's imagination. Even in the heat, Annie had continued to create extravagant spreads for everyone. She claimed it gave her complete joy to feed them.

Carrie leaned back against the log and gazed up into the clear sky. The wooded trail opened to a small field ablaze with wildflowers. Eastern tiger and zebra swallowtails dipped and flew from bloom to bloom. Thick bunches of purple asters contrasted sharply with the yellow and orange black-eyed Susans. Tall milkweed provided a feeding place for the monarch butterflies she loved so much. Bluebirds darted through the plants, while hummingbirds drank deeply from their chosen flowers.

Carrie took a deep breath as a sudden rush of missing Frances filled her. Her daughter would delight in the morning beauty and would be entranced by the birds enjoying the flowers. "Two more weeks," she said softly. At least she knew when Moses would be bringing her daughter home.

Rose had slumped with relief when Moses' recent telegram had announced Felicia would return with them. She had been prepared for Felicia to stay.

They had celebrated when they learned she was coming home. No one expected her to always live on the plantation, but she would be closer than California. That was something to be grateful for.

Carrie remained silent as Granite and No Regrets emerged from the river and wandered over to the field to graze. When the mare was dry, she would saddle her and ride back. Until then, she would let the wonder of the morning fill her soul.

Her thoughts turned to Anthony. Her husband had not gone a single night since returning from Louisiana without terrible nightmares. She'd watched helplessly as fatigue joined with the heat to sap his energy. From talking to Janie, she knew Matthew was experiencing the same thing. Each night, Carrie held him tightly until the nightmares ended. There were times she couldn't wake him, when all she could do was listen to his whimpers and wipe away the tears rolling down his face.

This morning, with him finally sleeping soundly, she had slipped out of bed to come to the river. Janie had told her only time would help Anthony and Matthew deal with the trauma from their time in Louisiana.

Time and love.

The only way Carrie could give him the love he deserved was to give herself time alone when she needed it. She knew with every fiber of her being that Anthony loved her, but he was rarely able to show it since his return. Most of the time he seemed to be in a different world, guarded and tense. He would sometimes play with the children like he used to, but mostly he sat in a rocking chair on the porch. She knew the children were confused.

Anthony hadn't been to the workshop with Russell. He held Bridget each night, but he no longer tickled her and made her giggle. He thanked Minnie when she brought him delicious treats, but the superlatives and compliments had disappeared. He had left a devoted father and husband. He had returned a shell.

Anthony had apologized several times, but even his apologies were full of the pain he couldn't release. It was easy to assure him that she understood. Her journey of recovery from losing Robert and Bridget had been different, but grief was grief. Everyone had to deal with it in their own way. She could give him the time he needed.

Granite wandered away from the field and approached her on the log. As if knowing she was hurting, he lowered his head, nudged her shoulder, and gently rested his muzzle for her to stroke.

Carrie let her tears fall. She would give Anthony all the time he needed, but that didn't mean she wasn't lonely. Granite stood quietly, letting his love wrap around her as she released her pain.

"Is it that bad?"

Carrie gasped and spun around when the deep voice sounded behind her. Lost in her pain and tears, she hadn't heard Anthony ride up. Granite shied backwards but didn't leave. "Anthony!"

Anthony, his green eyes warm with concern, joined her on the log. "Why are you crying?"

Carrie considered making something up but decided truth was her best option. "I'm lonely," she confessed. "I know you need time to deal with Louisiana. I'm happy to give it to you, but I miss you." She gazed up at him. "I miss us."

"Me too," Anthony replied. "Something happened this morning..." His voice trailed away.

Carrie remained silent, waiting for him to finish.

Anthony pulled a sheaf of papers out of his pocket. "I found this next to the bed this morning."

Carrie stared at the papers. She hadn't realized she'd left Biddy's letter out after she'd read it last night before Anthony came to bed.

"I read it," Anthony said, his voice growing hoarse with unshed tears.

Carrie had read the letter so many times after Robert and Bridget's deaths that she had almost memorized it. "Did it help?" she asked softly. Anthony knew about the letter, but he'd never read it. Susan, after her miscarriage, had been the only other person she'd shared it with. It was like a special treasure she couldn't bear to have diminished by other eyes seeing it.

Anthony held the letter out to her. "Will you read it to me again?" Hope mixed with the pleading in his eyes.

Carrie, knowing its power, cleared her throat and began to read.

My Dearest Carrie,

I have asked Abby and Rose not to give you this letter until the end of July, because I don't believe you will be ready to hear anything I have to say until then. You may still not be ready, but I fear waiting any longer would not help you.

You know my story, so there is no need to remind you while you are buried in your own grief.

Carrie paused in her reading. Though she had read it the night before, it never ceased to impact her just as powerfully. Biddy, now gone from the earth, had lost her husband, her sons, and all but one of her grandsons to the war. It made Carrie happy to know Biddy was with them again, though she would always miss her dear friend.

"You've told me how many of her loved ones died during the war." Anthony's eyes were trained on the whitecaps the wind stirred on the river. "She lost so much."

"She did," Carrie answered, before she turned back to the letter.

I'm sure at this point you are wondering how I survived it all, because you are questioning why you should survive your own loss.

No one's grief is alike, Carrie. All of us have a different life, and we are all different people. We all lose our loved ones in different ways. There are many who are certain they understand your grief, but those are the ones who probably understand it the least. I certainly understand grief, but I'm not so arrogant to say I understand your *grief. You do not need to explain your grief to anyone. It is mostly important for you to know your pain is unique to everyone else's. You can merely do the best you can to survive it.*

Anthony held up his hand to stop her. "Thank you for never saying you understand what I'm feeling. I don't understand it myself, so how can anyone else?"

Carrie remained silent but nestled one hand inside his for a moment. This was not a time for her words.

She kept reading.

There will be people in your life who may feel you have grieved long enough, or that it is time for you to move on with your life. They will think about the strong Carrie they know and expect you to behave in a certain way. Sometimes, my dear, our very strength means our grieving is even deeper because our hearts are so passionate about everything. It can be both a blessing and a curse. Most days, four years after the loss of my final grandson, I can walk through life fairly normally, but then something will happen that awakens all the pain and makes it all seem fresh and new. All I can do is grit my teeth, wait for the worst of the agony to pass, and pray for my breath to come a little easier. Carrie, no one can dictate how you deal with the loss of Robert and Bridget. We all must find a way to embrace life again, though I'm quite certain that seems impossible to you right now. For so long, I simply didn't care to try to make meaning or sense of all the death. There is no real sense in it, after all, but humans strive to find a way to move on since we are the ones still alive. You never truly get over it, because the deaths leave a hole in your life that nothing else can fill.

There are people who will tell you that you have to let go of your loved ones. What rubbish!

Carrie couldn't help the smile that trembled on her lips as she envisioned Biddy's bright blue eyes snapping with indignation. She could hear her Irish accent clearly through the written words. Now, though Anthony would never know her delightful accent, Biddy's words were reaching her husband.

I've never told anyone that I have Faith fix birthday cakes every year for my husband, my sons, and my grandsons. The children in Moyamensing have no idea why Faith bakes so many cakes, but they know what the smells from the kitchen mean, and they are always lined up to eat them. Many would tell me I'm being maudlin, but it is simply my way of honoring their existence in my life. I treasure the memories of each one, even while I strive to live life each day and move into the future, however much more of it I have left. The day is coming soon when I will be with all those I have lost. You do not have that same knowledge, so do whatever feels right to you to honor the lives of Robert and Bridget.

Now, I'm going to tell you something I am quite sure you don't want to hear, and you may not be ready to hear it, but still I am going to say it. We are enough alike that I know your first thought is to shut everyone out and endure the pain on your own. Carrie, my dear, you will never move through your grief unless you experience it. Hiding it or denying it will only prolong it. Talk about it, Carrie. Talk about it with Abby. Talk about it with Rose. Talk about it with anyone who will listen—even Granite, who may be the best listener of all!

Carrie chuckled.

Anthony eyed her. "Were you talking to Granite when I arrived?"

Carrie nodded, her heart flooding with gratitude. "He always listens," she whispered.

Anthony slipped his arm around her waist, pulling her close. "Keep reading."

Carrie closed her eyes for a moment. Other than the first night he returned home, Anthony had not shown the affection she'd grown accustomed to. She held him every night during the nightmares, but when he woke, he withdrew back into his shell. The feel of his strong arm around her filled her with both delight and longing.

Talk, Carrie. Talk about Robert. Talk about Bridget. Talk about the pain ripping through you. Talk about how you feel like you are a failure for not saving them. Talk about how you believe it is your fault.

I already know what you are thinking, Carrie. How do I know you believe it is your fault? I know you, dearest one. I've watched you go long, sleepless days and nights to save everyone you can possibly save. I've watched you fight the grain of society to help others because you believe it is the right thing to do. I watched you save so many here in Moyamensing from cholera. How it must ache that you could not save your husband and daughter. I'm not going to try to convince you it is not your fault, though it is most assuredly not. I'm just going to tell you to talk about it. Every time you do, you will breathe a little easier. It's okay that you don't believe me, but I urge you to at least try. You have so many people who love you so deeply. Let them love you, Carrie. Please let them love you.

Carrie could feel Anthony's shoulders shaking as he tried to swallow his tears.

I fear I may have already tried to say too much, but I don't know how long it will be before I see you again. I wish we could sit in my parlor and talk for hours, but I understand why you don't want to leave the plantation. Grieving is a process, dear one. There will be days when it doesn't hurt quite so badly, and then it will come roaring back with an intensity you are sure will destroy you. There are days when sadness consumes you, and then anger will make you want to lash out at every person around you. You will feel crazy at times. There will also be days when you will almost feel normal — but then you will feel guilty, because how could you ever hope to feel normal again? The spiral of feelings will seem to spin you around until you feel there is no life within you.

Now, do I believe it will get better? Yes. Though I will never quit missing the loved ones I have lost, my life is also full and good. The things I am doing will never replace what I have lost, but I have wonderful people that make the loss not quite so terrible. You are one of them. I have no idea how long it will take for you, Carrie, but there is one thing I encourage you to do. Every time you think of Robert dying in your arms, also try to pull forth a memory of you dancing together. Remember your first kiss. Remember laughing together. Accept the pain of the horrible memory but also welcome the other memories that make you miss him so very much. Remember him the way he is hoping you will remember him.

I love you, Carrie. You are constantly in my thoughts and prayers.

Biddy

Carrie lowered the pages and waited for Anthony to speak.

The moments turned into minutes. She knew he was struggling to control his emotions. She wished he wouldn't, but he would have to be the one to choose to release his pain.

Granite returned to grazing.

Carrie gazed out over the water, praying Biddy's words would help Anthony as much as they had helped her.

Reading them now, as it had last night, helped her accept his grief.

"Does it impact you as much every time you read it?" Anthony finally said.

"Every time," Carrie answered.

Anthony fell silent again and took a shuddering breath. "It was horrible."

Carrie remained silent.

Slowly, Anthony began to speak. He had told her about what happened in Colfax the first night he had arrived home, but it had been more of a report of the situation. Now the details poured forth. What he'd seen. How he had felt. The sounds he'd heard. The smells that had assaulted his senses. The blood. The sightless eyes. The wails of the survivors. The children who lost their fathers.

Carrie tightened her arm around his waist and let him talk. She had heard similar stories from survivors in the war. It never grew less horrifying, but she knew there was healing in the telling. Anthony had not fought in the war, nor had he seen the aftermath of battles. There had been nothing to prepare him for the horror of Colfax. Even while she thought it, she knew nothing *could* have prepared him. She was glad. Matthew had experienced many horrors, but instead of being numb to them, each one seemed to carve a bigger piece from his soul.

When Anthony ran out of words, he sat gasping for air as if he might never breathe again. Only then did the tears begin to flow. Sobs took their place, wracking his slender frame as he lowered his head into his lap.

Carrie stroked his back, letting her tears flow with his. She hated that he had experienced the worst of what humanity had to offer.

Gradually, the sobs lessened.

"I don't know how Matthew stands it," Anthony finally said.

"He doesn't," Carrie told him. "He has the same nightmares every night."

Anthony looked almost hopeful. "He does?"

"Janie holds him, like I hold you."

Anthony sat quietly before he turned to gaze into her face. "Does it really get better?"

"It gets better," Carrie replied, but she was determined to be honest. "You'll never forget it, however. There will always be things that make the memories come alive again."

"What helps?" Anthony demanded.

"This," Carrie said simply. "I'm here to listen every time you need to talk." She took a breath. "The children will help you."

Anthony frowned. "I haven't been much of a father since I got home."

Carrie wasn't going to deny the truth. "You can start fresh. The children don't understand what you've been through, but they love you with all their hearts. Their love will help you."

Anthony gripped her hand. "I haven't been much of a husband, either."

Carrie turned to him. "You can start fresh with that too. I'm right here with you. I understand."

Anthony's eyes glowed as he lowered his head to meet her lips.

Carrie pressed into him and returned his passionate kiss. Her heart soared as her hard core of loneliness dissolved and melted. "I missed you," she whispered when Anthony lifted his head.

"I'm so sor—"

Carrie pressed her finger to his lips. "Please don't apologize again. I understand. I have missed you, but I know how easy it is to get swallowed by grief." She stroked his cheek softly, gazing into eyes that gleamed with love again. "I'm glad to have you back."

Even as she spoke the words, Carrie realized there would be more times when the pain caused him to retreat behind his wall. Still, he would eventually return to her and the children each time.

The afternoon air rang with laughter, talk, and squeals of delight.

Rose, drying off beneath the sun after a long period of swimming, leaned back against the log beside Marietta. She watched Carrie playing in the water with Anthony and the children. The two of them looked happier than they had since Anthony's return from Louisiana. She and Carrie would talk about it soon, but she already knew Anthony was beginning to heal.

Rose turned her attention to her sister-in-law. "I can hardly believe you've been here a month. It seems more like a week."

"It's flown by too quickly," Marietta said sadly. "It will be hard to go back to Philadelphia in the middle of summer. I'm going to miss the plantation, the horses, and the river." Her eyes settled on the sprays of water erupting from the river. "Not to mention these wonderful children."

Rose watched the children playing and splashing in the water. The twins, at first shy of the river, were now swimming like fish. They laughed and splashed as hard as any of them. "It's been so good to have Marcus and

Sarah here." She hated the idea of them being trapped in the city again.

Marietta was evidently thinking the same thing. "If I wouldn't miss them so terribly, I would ask if they could stay. My mother's heart, however, couldn't stand it."

Rose completely understood. "At least Philadelphia has parks," she offered.

Marietta smiled. "Nice try. I know parks are better than nothing, but there's not a park in the world that can compare to Cromwell Plantation."

Rose wouldn't try to debate the obvious. "You'll come back," she said instead.

"We plan on it," Marietta replied. "We're still nervous about bringing Sarah to the South, but not bringing her seems more difficult—especially now that they're old enough to understand how wonderful the plantation is. I anticipate them asking about their cousins every day when we're home again." Her eyes settled on the flash of red hair in the water. "And Minnie. She's been so wonderful to them. They're both riding now, they love to swim, and they're even cooking."

Rose chuckled. The twins spent time in the kitchen, but she was certain the four-year-olds were doing more taste-testing than actual cooking. Her thoughts grew serious. "You truly never worry about their safety in Philadelphia?" Rose asked.

Marietta met her eyes. "Of course I worry about them. Philadelphia is better than Richmond in many ways, but there is a great deal of prejudice toward black and mulatto children."

"And adults," Rose reminded her, though she knew Marietta needed no reminding of what Jeremy dealt with for his open acceptance of blacks and mulattos. He no longer tried to hide who he was, but his blond hair and blue eyes helped keep him from being an obvious target.

"Mama!" Marcus and Sarah dashed from the water and ran toward them. "Come swimming with us!"

Marietta shook her head. "Not today."

Sarah scowled and formed her lips into a perfect pout. "That's what you said yesterday."

"And the day before," Marcus protested. He planted his fists on his hips. "Please, Mama? We're leaving tomorrow."

Rose knew swimming wasn't one of Marietta's preferred activities. She'd been in the river a couple times, but she didn't look forward to it.

"Daddy!" Marcus called. "Mama won't come swimming."

"It's our last day!" Sarah yelled. "Come help us, Daddy!"

Jeremy grinned and strode out of the river, the water droplets on his broad chest glistening in the sun. "They're right, you know. It's the last day."

"I'm enjoying it from here," Marietta said weakly.

Rose, knowing what was coming, bit back her chuckle.

"You'll enjoy it more from the water," Jeremy announced as he leaned over and scooped her into his arms.

"No!" Marietta shrieked.

"Yes!" Marcus yelled with delight. He ran toward the water, Sarah right on his heels.

Jeremy ran past them, holding Marietta tightly as she struggled. He plunged into the river, continuing to run until the water was deep enough to lower his wife into the sparkling water.

Marietta shrieked again but was laughing, as well. Her dress floated up around her like a fluffy cloud. She pushed it down and began to splash her children, her laughter ringing out even louder than theirs.

Annie shook her head. “I hate to think of them children back in that big city.”

“Me too,” Rose confessed. “I know it’s their home, but I wish we could be together more often.”

Jeremy strode to the edge of the river and looked in their direction. “Are you going to make me come get you, too?”

Rose waved her hand dismissively. “I’ve been in the water most of the afternoon. I’m quite comfortable here.”

Jeremy narrowed his eyes. “I want my twin to come swimming with us.”

“When did you start to believe I would be swayed by what you want?” Rose teased.

“You’re in trouble now,” Annie declared.

“Like waving a flag in front of a bull,” Abby predicted.

“It’s time for battle!” Jeremy yelled.

Anthony broke away from playing with Carrie and the children.

Thomas stood from where he had been seated on the shore. “I thought you would never give the call.”

Rose stared at the men. “What…?”

It took only a second to know the men had planned this moment in advance.

Abby and Annie, recognizing the same thing, stood and began to back away.

“We’re not going swimming right now,” Abby proclaimed.

“I ain’t goin’ swimmin’ at all!” Annie insisted. “What you fools think you be doin”?”

The men continued to advance, their eyes gleaming with determination and amusement.

Annie stood her ground. “You lay one hand on me, and you won’t eat nothin’ on this plantation for the rest of your life.”

Jeremy laughed loudly. “Empty threats.”

Annie snorted. “Ain’t a single one of you big enough to get me into that water.”

“True,” Jeremy agreed easily. “That’s why there are three of us.”

For the first time, Annie looked alarmed. “I ain’t ever been in that river. I ain’t startin’ now.”

“There’s a first time for everything,” Anthony announced.

Annie started to back up more quickly. “You ain’t gettin’ me in there!”

The three men descended on her and began to corral her toward the water.

“You fools get away from me!” Annie hollered, though her expression revealed she knew she was outnumbered. “Where’s that son of mine when I need him!”

Thomas chuckled. “It wouldn’t take three of us if Moses were here. He would do the job himself.” He glanced toward the other women. “We’re coming back for you.”

“It’s futile to resist!” Carrie called.

Rose laughed and beckoned to Abby. “We might as well go in.”

Abby grinned. “It seems the easier option.” She ran forward and grabbed one of Annie’s hands.

Rose dashed forward, grabbed her mother-in-law’s other hand, and pulled her onward. “Let’s go swimming.”

“Oh, for Pete’s sake!” Annie yelled. “All of you be plum crazy!”

The children were yelling now, urging Annie to come swimming with them.

Annie quit resisting. Accepting the inevitable, she yelled loudly and plunged into the water. She shrieked when it closed around her, but she couldn't hide the delight in her eyes.

Rose doubled over laughing. She wished Moses was here to see his mama in the James River.

The children rushed over, jumping up and down around her, but not splashing. They seemed to know Annie wasn't quite ready for that level of exuberance.

Annie gazed at them, laughed loudly, and did what none of them anticipated. She whipped her arms back and heaved mountains of water at Jeremy, Anthony, and Thomas. "Get them!" she yelled to the children. "Make them pay for what they done!"

The children cheered as war broke out.

The sun was setting as the last crumbs were consumed. Fireflies blinked on and off in the darkening woods as a lone owl hooted.

"What a perfect day, Mama."

Rose smiled as Hope snuggled sleepily into her side. She was glad they had brought the wagon. The children would be asleep before they got back to the house. "Yes, it was," she said softly.

As the sun sank beneath the far tree line, it shot brilliant rays into the pink and purple clouds clumped above it.

"The sun is celebrating," Hope murmured.

"I believe you're right," Rose agreed. She hated to see Jeremy and his family leave, but they had created memories that would last a lifetime. Sadness and joy mingled together in her thoughts.

"Them new chillun gonna love this place," Annie stated with satisfaction. "I figure by the end of summer we's gonna have a picnic for all them new families."

"That's a wonderful idea," Carrie replied as she looked down at Bridget nestled in her arms. Minnie and Russell cuddled next to Anthony, their faces content as they watched the setting sun.

Rose watched them. It was difficult to imagine Russell and Bridget had once lived under a bridge in Richmond, always on the verge of starvation. The orphanage children at least had food, but she knew it was a hard place. There were simply too many orphans and abandoned children to receive the care and attention they needed and deserved. Thanks to Annie, ten more were going to know what it felt like to have a family.

She could hardly wait until tomorrow.

Chapter Twenty-Two

Anthony pulled the front wagon away from the train station after the children waved their final goodbyes to Jeremy, Marietta, and the twins as they boarded the train that would take them north.

Thomas pulled the second wagon behind him. It was loaded with baskets of food that Annie had insisted on sending with them. It had been added to by May. Determined not to let the plantation cook outdo her, May had cooked all last night into the early morning hours. It had already been decided the extra food would be left behind at the orphanage.

Rose sat quietly, envisioning how much ten children's lives were about to change.

Abby sat with the children. She looked like a queen, perched on top of the mountain of blankets they had piled high to keep her comfortable on the long ride.

"You're certain they will let us take the children?" Russell asked anxiously.

Abby reached for his hand. "The Friends Asylum for Colored Orphans is going to be beyond thrilled to see us arrive," she said confidently. "The Bregdan Women have been supporting them for the last eighteen months. I've met Lucy Brooks, the founder. She's quite a remarkable woman. Her mission is to make sure every child in her care has a good life. She's told me she wished every child in the asylum could end up on the plantation. She's told me how thrilled she is with how well your friends from beneath the bridge are doing."

"They're not coming to the plantation, though," Russell reminded her. "Only Bridget and I get to live there, Grandma."

"That's true, but Mrs. Brooks knows we would only allow the children to go to good homes."

Rose watched Russell smile and relax. Every bridge child had written a letter to Lucy Brooks, telling her about their new lives near the plantation. Though they were the bridge children were all white, their happiness was proof of everyone's commitment to making sure they went to good homes. Now it was time for ten black children to begin a new life. Rose was already looking forward to teaching them.

Russell suddenly frowned. "What if the children don't want to come with us?"

Rose thought it was a fair question. After the lives they had lived on the streets, the orphanage might have truly become home to them. They might not want more upheaval.

"They'll come with us," Minnie said confidently. "By the time you and I tell them how wonderful life is at home, they'll be begging to come."

Rose hoped that was true.

Minnie continued. "We'll tell them about school, about good food, and swimming in the river."

Rose smiled. She didn't know how many of the orphans had ever been swimming, but she knew they would be excited about plenty to eat.

The wagons pulled up to the newly erected building at 112 West Charity Street. The three-story white building was surrounded by tall boxwoods and a white picket fence that encased the grounds.

Rose heard sounds of play coming from behind the house. Her heart sped up as they piled out of the wagons.

The lady who opened the door raised her eyebrows in surprise when she saw them but smiled pleasantly. "Good morning. How may I help you?"

Abby stepped forward. "My name is Abigail Cromwell. Is Mrs. Brooks available?"

The woman eyed her closely. "Are you the one from Cromwell Plantation? Your Bregdan Women send money from the quilts they make?"

Abby nodded. "Yes."

The woman stepped back and held the door open. "Come right in. We appreciate what you've done for the children."

"We'd like to do more," Abby replied. "That's why we're here."

"That right?" The woman pointed them toward the parlor. "Make yourselves comfortable. Mrs. Brooks got here a little bit ago. I'll get her for you."

Rose was impressed with how quiet and well-behaved the children were while they waited. She knew from their curious expressions that they were wondering what it would be like to live in an orphanage. The pensive look on

Russell's face revealed he was thinking about how grateful he was to have landed on the plantation before this was a reality for him. The building was large, but with fifty children inside, there was limited space.

A short woman in a dark, conservative dress, her braided hair pulled back into an austere fun, moved toward them. Her face was transformed by a smile that bloomed when she saw Abby. "Abigail Cromwell! What a delight to have you visit."

Abby stepped forward and grasped both of the woman's hands warmly. "It's wonderful to see you again, Lucy. How are you?"

"I'm well," Mrs. Brooks responded. "Our new building has become home to many of the city's orphans. The city officially recognized us last year. The area churches provide much of what we need. Your Bregdan Women continue to be a big help." She peered at Abby. "How can I help you?"

"I'm hoping we can help *you*," Abby answered. "Or at least some of the children."

Mrs. Brooks cocked her head. "I'm listening."

Rose stepped forward and explained what Annie had done. "We have ten families waiting for children," she finished.

Mrs. Brooks clapped her hands together with delight. "I'm thrilled beyond words!" she exclaimed. "We won't turn children away, but we're more than full." She paused. "Are you looking for particular children?"

Rose shook her head quickly. "No. There is one family who wants a girl and another who wants a boy, but the others simply want a child. We've decided you and your staff should choose which children."

"I see," Mrs. Brooks murmured. She looked toward the woman who had welcomed them at the door. "Simone, please come here."

The slender woman with graying hair and warm eyes hurried over to them. "Yes, ma'am?"

Mrs. Brooks explained the reason for their visit.

Simone's eyes widened. "You're ready to take ten children today?"

"If that's alright," Rose replied. "We understand more time might be needed. We can stay here in the city for a few days if that would be best." She knew families would be disappointed if they had to wait longer for their children, but they would be together soon.

Simone glanced at the clock on the wall. "It's only nine o'clock," she said with surprise.

"We know it's early," Rose said hastily. "We saw some family members off at the train station and came right here."

"How far is it to your plantation?" Simone asked.

"Four hours," Rose answered. "We have baskets of food in the wagon for the children." She smiled. "Our cooks went rather overboard. In fact, we're going to leave some of it here with you. It would take fifty children to consume the food we have." She smiled. "The families wanting to adopt them will be waiting on the plantation for their child. They're rather eager."

Simone returned her smile. "In that case, I don't know why the children can't go with you today." She hesitated when she looked at their large group.

Rose didn't need to be told what she was thinking. "The children can stay here while we go outside" she said quickly.

"Anthony and I will stay with them," Thomas offered. "We'll be fine."

Simone led the way out into the large backyard, where children played tag or sat under the shade of a single oak tree large enough to provide respite to everyone, talking and laughing.

Rose immediately wanted to take each one of them home with her. She was grateful they wouldn't have to choose. The expressions on Carrie's and Abby's faces revealed they felt the same.

When they appeared in the yard, many of the children stopped talking. Their eyes filled with curiosity as they waited to see what was about to happen.

"It's been a long time since anyone left here," Simone said quietly. "There are so many children in need, but far fewer families willing to take them in."

"I wish we could take more than ten," Rose said sadly. She had already begun making plans to convince more families to claim one of these children. Without asking, she knew each of them had painful stories of what led to their being at the orphanage. She thought of Felicia and Jed. Without her and Moses, they would have ended up under a bridge or in an orphanage.

"Ten children will be very happy very soon," Simone told her gently. "The others will be fine. We take good care of everyone here."

"I'm quite certain of that," Rose said.

Simone waved her hand toward a bench tucked up against the house. "Y'all wait right there. I'll talk to the children."

Rose watched intently as Simone moved among the orphans. Soon, ten children moved away from the group and hurried into the large house. Their eyes were bright with both excitement and anxiety.

Simone approached them again. "You can go back inside now. It won't take the children long to get their belongings together. When they come down, I'll introduce them. I've also got paperwork on them, revealing what we know." She frowned. "We don't always know much, though."

Rose stood but couldn't take her eyes off a girl huddled beneath the tree. She looked to be eight or nine, but it was hard to tell because she was so slender and petite. Her curly hair was pulled back from her caramel-colored face. Even from here, Rose could see the blue eyes that revealed she was mulatto. She was turned away from the rest of the children, her shoulders tense and guarded. "Who is that little girl under the tree?"

Simone's face grew serious. "That's Penny," she said. "She's been with us less than a week."

"What's her story?" Rose asked, continuing to watch her.

Simone frowned. "We're not sure. She hasn't spoken since she arrived. One of the men from Ebenezer Baptist Church found her alone on the streets and brought her here."

Rose could feel the fear engulfing the little girl. It hung over her like a black cloud. "She's been hurt."

Simone scowled. "Yes. The man who brought her here said she had been attacked. Her cuts and bruises are healing, but she won't say a word." She hesitated. "It could be she was…" Her voice trailed off as if she didn't want to give words to the sexual assault they suspected.

Rose's heart swelled with sympathy. Unbidden, Hope's question about whether she was going to have another child came to mind. At the time, it was not something Rose was considering. They had a full house already.

"Rose?" Carrie appeared at her side with a questioning look.

"That little girl needs a home, Carrie."

"She does," Carrie agreed.

Rose smiled. "Am I crazy?"

Carrie shrugged. "Of course. That's what makes you special."

Rose chuckled. "Without even asking Moses?"

Carrie shrugged again. "You know what his answer would be, don't you?"

Rose did.

As if pulled by their thoughts, the little girl finally looked up and met Rose's gaze. A mixture of fear and hope ignited in her eyes, but she looked away quickly, pulling her shoulders together even more, closing herself up like a turtle.

"Simone." Rose held out a hand to stop the woman from entering the house. "We would like to take Penny with us, as well."

Simone looked startled. "You said you only had families for ten children."

"My husband and I will adopt Penny," Rose said. "We have four children, two of whom are adopted. Our youngest, Hope, is seven."

"The smallest one with you today," Simone said with a smile. "She's beautiful."

"She also has a loving heart," Rose told her. "She'll love having a sister, and I'll love having another little girl."

"I'll get her," Simone replied.

Rose held out her hand again. "Please. May I get her?"

Simone nodded. "She ain't going to talk to you, though."

Rose was already moving toward the little girl. When she reached her, she settled on the ground, mindless of her dress. "Good morning," she said.

Penny gazed up at her for a moment before she looked away and down to the ground.

Rose's heart constricted when she saw the little girl begin to tremble. "I'm not going to hurt you," she said tenderly. "I'd like to give you a home and be your new mama. If that's alright with you."

Penny gasped, clenched her fists, and shook her head decisively.

Rose was startled. Her mind began to whirl. She thought about what Simone had told them. Penny had arrived the week before, after being attacked. What if she hadn't been alone on the streets? What if someone was injured and not able to look for her? Penny was thin, but she didn't look uncared for.

Rose decided to follow her instincts. "Or help you find your mama." Something about the little girl's reaction told her there was much more to her story than anyone knew.

Penny's eyes shot up to meet hers, but she remained mute.

Rose suspected whatever trauma she had endured had also taken her ability to talk, but intelligence shone brightly in her eyes. "I live out in the country, but you and I will stay here in the city to look for your mama." She didn't know where her words were coming from, but they felt right. Her instincts were confirmed when Penny continued to meet her eyes. "Would you be willing to come with me to another house in the city? We have found families for ten of the children, but you and I will stay there and look for your mama."

Penny's eyes filled with wild panic. Her breath began to come in short bursts.

"I promise I won't take you away from the city," Rose assured her. She wanted to reach out and hug the little girl, but she suspected it would frighten her more. "I don't know what has happened to you, but I would like to help."

Penny's panic gradually subsided to a wary caution.

Rose thought about what she was doing. The children would be fine going back to the plantation with everyone else. May, Spencer, and Micah would be happy to have her and Penny stay longer at Thomas' house. Rose had no idea how to go about finding a woman that may, or may not, exist in a city bursting at the seams, but the flare of hope she saw in the little girl's eyes said she was doing the right thing. If they couldn't find her mama, she would take Penny home to the plantation.

Penny stared into her eyes for several more moments, and then nodded slowly.

Rose stood and reached out for her hand. Penny took it but kept her gaze on the ground.

"I can't believe my eyes," Simone whispered as they passed by her.

Rose suspected she needed to stay close to Penny. "Let's go get your things," she said. "You lead the way."

"Mama, I'm staying here with you."

Rose took a deep breath, fighting a smile as she gazed at Hope standing in front of her defiantly, her tiny fists bunched on her hips. "I don't know how long I'll be here, honey. You need to go back to the plantation with everyone else."

The wagons were full of children, belongings, and supplies. Anthony and Thomas were on the driver's seats, ready to leave. As they were lifting their reins to urge the horses forward, Hope had jumped out and run back to where Rose stood.

Penny was inside with Simone, waiting.

"I'm staying," Hope said stubbornly. "Didn't you say you were staying here to look for Penny's mama?"

Rose nodded.

"And that if you couldn't find her you would bring Penny to the plantation?"

"I did," Rose agreed.

Hope narrowed her eyes. "Then that means Penny could become my sister. What kind of sister would I be if I didn't help her find her mama?"

Rose chose not to point out that if their search was successful, Penny would not be her sister.

Hope wasn't done. "Penny is scared. She needs a little girl her age to make her feel better. I can sleep with her. It doesn't matter that she can't talk. I can still tell her about the plantation. If you don't find her mama, she'll already know how wonderful it is and it won't be so scary." She took a deep breath. "You're a good woman, Mama, but Penny needs a little girl."

Rose opened her mouth to dispute her daughter's words, until the truth of what she was saying sank in. She nodded slowly. "I believe you're right, Hope. I would like you to stay."

Hope's eyes widened. "Really?" She clapped her hands with delight.

Rose walked to the wagons to explain the change in plans.

Carrie was already holding out Hope's small luggage. "You'll be needing this," she said before Rose uttered a word.

Micah raised his eyebrows with surprise when he opened the door. "Miss Rose!" He looked past her toward the street, where a carriage was pulling away. "Is everything alright?" He looked down and saw Hope and Penny standing next to her. "Well, hello girls." He held the door open and beckoned them in. "Come on inside."

Rose sniffed the air as they entered. "You're in luck," she told Penny. "May told me this morning she was making a blackberry cobbler. From the way it smells, I believe it's just out of the oven."

"That's right," Micah said with a chuckle.

Hope bounced up and down. "Miss May makes the best blackberry cobbler in the world. Just wait until you taste it."

Penny gazed around the house, her eyes wide with wonder.

Rose suspected the little girl had never been in a house so grand. Thomas had bought this house during the war and then decided to keep it for times when the family needed it. Micah and May, once his slaves, were now valued employees and family members.

Micah was looking at the girl with a gentle smile on his kindly face.

Rose would explain the situation once she got the girls settled. She leaned down. "Would you like to stay in Hope's room with her tonight?"

Penny nodded, keeping her eyes on the wooden floor.

Hope filled in the silence. "You're going to love my room," she gushed. "I usually share it with Minnie and Frances, but it's great that it will just be the two of us. Sometimes, I get real tired of always being the baby," she confided. "It's nice to share it with someone my own age!" She glanced up at Rose. "*Are* you my age, Penny? I think you are, but I don't really know."

Penny remained silent, her shoulders bunching together again.

Rose squeezed her hand, suspecting Hope's chatter was overwhelming her. "Let's go upstairs, girls." She turned to Micah. "We'll be down for lunch soon, if that's alright."

"Of course," Micah answered.

Hope's room was right next to Rose's. Penny's belongings fit in a small pillowcase. Her clothing, ruined during the attack, had been replaced with two worn dresses, some undergarments, and a pair of shoes. Rose would remedy that over the next few days.

When they were ready to go downstairs, Rose held out her hand. "Are you hungry?"

Penny took her hand, not quite so hesitantly this time, and nodded. When she looked up, there was a question in her eyes.

"We're going to look for your mama," Rose promised. "Mrs. Brooks gave me the name of the man who brought you to the orphanage. I'm going to try to find him today." It wasn't much to go on, but it was a start.

Hope eagerly grabbed her other hand. "Let's go eat!"

Penny allowed herself to be led downstairs.

Penny scarfed down the food May placed in front of her. She wasn't willing to talk, but she was more than eager to eat the roast beef, mashed potatoes, and fresh green peas set before her. When she was done, she looked hopefully toward the kitchen door.

May interpreted her look. "Are you ready for some blackberry cobbler, Penny?"

Penny nodded eagerly, but then gasped and shook her head just as quickly.

Rose was the one who interpreted this time. "Go ahead and get the cobbler, May." She turned back to the little girl. "It's not bad for you to eat good things, honey," she said gently. "Your mama would be happy to know you're eating so well."

Penny frowned.

"You're going to have to trust me on this one," Rose told her. "I'm a mama too. If anything were to happen to me, I would want to know all my children were safe and eating well."

"I bet I can eat mine faster!" Hope challenged as she picked up her spoon.

Penny looked doubtful but didn't draw back when May placed the cobbler in front of her. She sniffed and picked up her spoon as the delectable aroma drifted up. Once she started, she finished the dessert as quickly as the rest of the meal. She glanced at Hope, allowing herself a tiny smile when she finished before Hope did.

At this rate, it wouldn't take long for Penny to fill out.

Rose also noticed Hope had deliberately let Penny win the contest. Her heart swelled with pride for her compassionate daughter.

"Where is Spencer?" Rose asked. She had already learned that neither Micah nor May knew the man who had delivered Penny to the orphanage. May's husband was her best bet of finding him.

"He had a job this morning," May answered. "He was planning on being home for lunch, but he's running late."

Just then, they heard the screen door in the back of the kitchen slam closed.

May shook her head. "I don't know how many times I got to tell that man not to slam the back door."

Rose saw the glimmer of amusement in Penny's eyes. Wherever she was from, she'd obviously been scolded for slamming the door. It was good to know she had once had a home.

Spencer pushed in through the swinging door. "I'm starving!" he announced.

He stopped dead in his tracks when he saw Rose and the girls. "Rose! What are you doing here?" His eyes narrowed. "Is everything alright?" His gaze swept over Penny. "Where did this beautiful little girl come from?"

"That's why we're here." Without going into a lot of detail, Rose explained she was helping Penny look for her family. For all she knew, there may also be a father and siblings who didn't know what had happened to her.

"You know the name of the man from Ebenezer?" Spencer asked.

"Parker Homestead," Rose said. "Do you know him?" She held her breath as she waited for his answer. She knew the odds weren't favorable. Richmond's population had exploded since the end of the war, and it grew every year.

A look of wonder crossed Spencer's face. "As a matter of fact, I do. He works down at the brick factory. He's a real good man. Deacon in the church."

"Can you help me find him?"

"I reckon I can do that easy enough," Spencer replied. "Tonight? The brick factory changes shifts about seven o'clock. You want me to bring him here?"

Rose shook her head. "I'll come with you to the factory." She needed to be able to talk to the man privately. There was no way of knowing how much of the attack Penny remembered. If something had happened to her mama, Rose wanted to be the one to tell her.

Rose felt Penny tug at her dress. She knew the little girl wanted to join her, but she wasn't willing for her to hear what might be brutal details. "Will you look after the girls when I leave, May?"

"Of course," May replied, glancing at Penny with soft, compassionate eyes.

Rose put her arm around Penny's shoulders. "It will be better if I go by myself, Penny."

Hope stepped in. "I'm glad you're going to be here with me. We can play out back until the fireflies come out." She looked up at May. "Can we catch some in a jar?"

May smiled. "Of course you can. Since it's a special day, I reckon you girls can have some extra blackberry cobbler tonight." She paused enticingly. "I might make some whipped cream to go with it."

"Yes!" Hope squealed as she spun in a circle of delight.

Spencer stepped forward and held out his hand to Penny. "Will you come out back to the garden and help me pick vegetables for dinner, girls? May won't feed me unless I do work around here," he teased.

Penny stiffened, pulled into Rose's side, and buried her face in her dress. She could feel the little girl trembling.

Rose didn't blame her for being frightened. Spencer was one of the gentlest people she knew, but his size was imposing. "Why don't we all pick vegetables?" she suggested.

Penny peeked up at her and nodded.

The sun had begun its slow descent when the wagons drew close to the plantation, but there were many hours of daylight ahead.

Carrie smiled with delight when she saw the throng of people standing on the driveway in front of the porch. She had taken over driving the wagon two hours earlier. Anthony had taken the horse tied to the wagon and ridden ahead to make sure all the families knew the children were coming.

Russell, John, Jed, and Minnie had regaled the orphans with stories of the plantation and school. Even the most frightened children had slowly relaxed. They ate copious quantities of food as they rode, their faces turned to the sun as they devoured the beauty of the countryside.

Carrie knew many of them had been trapped in the crowded city for their entire lives. They had either been born in Richmond or come there shortly after their births. Former slaves had brought their families to the city when the end of the war had granted them emancipation. Many families were thriving. Many more were barely surviving.

Abby and Carrie had read the children's reports from the asylum on their way out of the city. Four of the children were truly orphans. Their parents had died of disease, most likely caused by poverty-stricken conditions. The other six had been dropped off at the orphanage by parents who couldn't care for them. Carrie could imagine the anguish of parents releasing their children in hopes they would have a better life. She hoped they would somehow learn their dreams had come true.

As the wagon drew closer, the sound of cheering wafted up on the breeze. The words became clearer as they approached the house.

"Welcome! Welcome!"

The children stared at the smiling faces waiting for them. Their anxiety returned with the reminder they weren't simply on a fun ride into the country. Their lives were about to completely change.

Carrie, from her perch on the wagon seat, listened to the children.

"Look at that house! I ain't never seen nothin' that big before!"

"Are them folks gonna be our new families?"

"This place sure is pretty."

She looked back and smiled warmly. "This place is called Cromwell Plantation. I grew up here. And, yes, the people waiting are your new families. Every one of them is very happy to have you. They're here to take you to your new homes. You're about to begin a brand-new life. I hope you love it here."

The children, now silent, stared up at her with wide eyes.

When the wagon pulled to a stop, Abby stepped down to address the waiting families.

Annie, her face wreathed in a huge smile, had removed her apron in honor of the occasion. She was watching over the proceedings like a proud mama hen. As well she should. Without her efforts, the children wouldn't be here.

Annie raised her hand to draw attention. "Any of you children be hungry?"

Abby laughed. "Not a chance. They've been eating from those baskets ever since they left Richmond. You sent enough for an army."

Carrie hid a smile. They had been careful to leave the food May had prepared back at the orphanage; Annie would have spotted any basket that wasn't sent by her in an instant. The important thing was that every child remaining at the orphanage had received a special treat today.

Abby turned back to the children. "The wonderful woman on the porch is Miss Annie. She single-handedly runs this huge house. She was the one who made the delicious food you ate today, and she is also the angel that arranged for you to come to a new home."

Annie beamed as the children smiled up at her shyly. "We be real glad to have all of you here!"

At that moment, with the sun shining on her white dress and glowing face, she did indeed look like an angel.

Chaos reigned for the next thirty minutes as families were introduced to their new child. Annie made sure to send food home to every family. She had prepared a feast that wouldn't be eaten at that moment, but it wouldn't go to waste.

When the last wagon disappeared down the road on their way home, Annie turned to Carrie. "Where are Rose and Hope?" she demanded.

Carrie's thoughts were finally free to turn back to the city. "Trying to save a little girl."

Chapter Twenty-Three

Rose was grateful for Spencer's imposing presence as men poured from the brick factory set on the outskirts of town near the river. The random admiring whistle or bold glance was abruptly cut short when Spencer glared in the direction of the offender.

Most of the men didn't bother to look their way. Eyes down, they walked slowly away from the factory. The heat of the summer day, combined with the flames of the brick kilns and the steam necessary for the machinery to press the bricks into wooden molds, was brutal and draining.

These men were eager to get home and relax after a long, twelve-hour shift.

Spencer suddenly stood up and waved his arm. "Parker! Parker Homestead!"

A middle-aged, muscular man with very dark skin and graying hair lifted his head wearily. He smiled when he spotted Spencer and changed direction to join them.

"Howdy, Spencer. What are you doing here?" His voice was tired, but his eyes sparkled with curiosity. The curiosity deepened when his eyes settled on Rose. "Hello, ma'am. How are you?"

Rose liked the man on sight. His lined face crinkled with kindness when he smiled. She was glad he had been the one to find Penny. A sudden question sprang into her mind; one she hadn't thought of until now. The little girl didn't speak. How did she get her name?

"Hello, Parker," Spencer said. "I know you're on your way home. You got a minute you can spare?"

Parker nodded. "What can I do for y'all?"

Spencer gestured toward Rose. "This is Rose Samuels. She has some questions for you."

"That right?" Parker asked easily. "I'll help if I can."

Rose smiled. "You saved a little girl five days ago."

Parker's smile disappeared behind a frown. "I did. That was a real bad night." His frown deepened. "Is that little girl alright? I took her over to Mrs. Brooks at the Colored Asylum. I didn't know what else to do with her."

"She's fine," Rose said. She briefly explained why she was in Richmond.

A bright smile flared on Parker's face. "Ten of those children have homes now? I've heard of Cromwell Plantation. I know what's going on out there for black folks. I reckon those children couldn't have gone to a better place."

"They'll have good homes," Rose assured him.

"Is that where Penny went?"

Rose shook her head. "Not yet. That's why I'm here, Mr. Homestead. I was going to take her with me to the plantation and adopt her, but she's not ready to come."

"Why not?"

Rose chose her words carefully. "Penny isn't talking, but I get the idea she believes her family, or at least her mama, is still here in the city. I'm hoping, if that's true, you can help us find her. I know it's a long shot, but you might know something that can help us."

Parker sighed. "That little girl still isn't saying anything? She didn't say a word to me once I found her." His face tightened. "She was a mess. Whoever attacked her left her behind a building down on Broad Street. I wouldn't have seen her, except for a little whimper I heard when I walked past the alley. I went back and found her in a heap on the ground."

Rose stiffened with fury. She couldn't imagine the terror Penny had experienced.

"Did you look to see if anyone else was around?" Spencer asked. "Seems odd for a little girl to be out by herself at night."

Parker looked thoughtful. "Come to think of it, I didn't do that. All I could think about was getting Penny some help. I picked her up and took her home to my wife. We talked about keeping her, but we got more mouths to feed than we pay for already," he said apologetically.

"I understand," Rose said. "You did the best you could for her by taking her to Mrs. Brooks. I have another question, though. If she hasn't spoken since the attack, how do you know her name is Penny?"

"I don't," Parker admitted. "One of my children named her. He came home real excited that night because he done found a penny on the road. He decided that since I had discovered the little girl on the road, he would call her Penny." He paused. "I'm hoping she'll start talking again and can tell us who she really is."

Rose hoped the same thing. "Can you tell us where the alley is that you found her?"

"It be down off Broad Street, right next to the First National Bank on Main Street. You can't miss the alley. I figure that little girl was about fifty feet in."

"Thank you," Rose answered. "We appreciate your time."

Spencer read her mind. "We'll head there now, Rose. We've got enough daylight to at least look around a little." He tipped his hat at Parker. "Thank you."

"I hope you find out who she is," Parker said sympathetically.

"If we don't, she'll go back to the plantation with us," Rose promised. Truthfully, she was hoping they wouldn't find the little girl's family. She had fallen in love with Penny, and she knew Hope would adore having a sister close to her age.

Broad Street was busy when Spencer guided the wagon onto it, but it was a fraction of the throngs of traffic that were typical earlier in the day. It took only a few minutes to reach the First National Bank, one of the first buildings erected after the fire at the end of the war. The bank, housed in a four-story stone building, had played a substantial role in helping provide resources to rebuild the city. Spencer pulled the wagon to the side of the road and set the brake. "Let's take a look."

Rose was already climbing down.

She hesitated when they reached the narrow alley swathed in dark shadows. Once again, she was grateful for Spencer's presence. On her own, she wouldn't have had the courage, or the stupidity, to walk into possible danger.

Spencer took the lead, walking forward slowly, his eyes scanning the area.

Rose followed him, searching for anything that would help them understand what Penny had experienced that night.

After several minutes of searching, they both admitted defeat. There was nothing to be found. The only thing in the alley was piles of rancid trash.

"I wonder..." Spencer said slowly. He stared toward the end of the alley. "There are some houses back behind the bank, Rose. Somebody there might have seen something."

Rose started in that direction but stopped. It could well be total darkness when they returned. "We should take the wagon around the block. I'm not eager to walk through this alley at night, even with you."

"Smart thinking," Spencer replied. "I might be big, but enough men could take me down. I don't aim to put you in any danger. Besides the fact you're my friend, Moses would hunt me down when he comes back from San Francisco. That husband of yours makes me look small!"

Rose chuckled and walked quickly back to the wagon, pushing aside the intense longing that Moses' name had conjured. He would be home soon. For now, she had other things to focus on.

A few minutes later, they stopped in front of a row of tiny clapboard houses, their bare dirt yards shaded by oak trees that must have been there since the founding of the city. Black faces stared at them from the porch of every house. It was too hot to be inside. Being outside gave them the chance of capturing whatever breeze might be blowing.

Rose approached the first dwelling, formulating words in her mind to explain why they were there. "Hello," she said pleasantly. "My name is Rose Samuels."

A man stepped from the house with an expression of surprise. "Howdy, Spencer. What you doin' here?"

Rose sighed with relief and waited for Spencer to speak. She was glad they wouldn't be seen merely as strangers.

"Hello, Benji. I didn't know you and your family lived here."

Benji, a short, thin man with tight black curls and snapping dark eyes, grinned. "Ain't much, but it's home.

It's a lot better than we had on the plantation before the end of the war." He waved his hand toward the porch. "That there be my wife, Sonja, and my children, Ben, Gary, and little Sonja." His voice grew serious. "We thank God every day that can't nobody take this place from us. Not so long as we can pay for it."

Spencer nodded solemnly. "It's the best feeling in the world to be free. That's for sure."

Benji eyed him. "What you doing here? I don't reckon you just droppin' in to say howdy."

"I'm not," Spencer confirmed. He introduced Rose and then got down to business. "You know Parker Homestead?"

"Course we do," Benji answered. "He be a deacon at our church. A real fine man." A frown appeared. "Something wrong with Deacon Homestead?"

"He's fine," Spencer said quickly. He pointed behind the house. "Five days ago, Deacon Homestead found a little girl in that alley right there. She'd been beaten real bad. He rescued her and took her to the Colored Asylum for children. She ain't talking, so we don't know who she is or what happened to her." He paused while they made sympathetic sounds. "Rose wants to adopt her, but first we have to be sure what happened to her mama."

"Her mama?" Benji asked sharply.

Spencer nodded. "Hard to believe a little girl was out all by herself at night. Other than hurt real bad, she didn't look like she'd been living on the streets. She might have been taken from her home by whoever beat her, but there's a chance her mama was also attacked. Deacon Homestead didn't think to look for anyone else. Since these houses back up to the alley, we thought maybe you might've heard or seen something."

Benji narrowed his eyes. "Five nights ago?"

Rose felt a surge of hope. "That's right. Do you remember anything?"

"Not me," Benji replied. "I heard something at work, though, the very next day. Denny lives three doors down. I overheard him say something about his wife taking care of somebody she done found on the street."

"Where on the street?" Spencer pressed.

Benji shrugged. "Don't know more than what I told you."

Rose looked down the road. "Is the woman still there?"

"Don't know," Benji replied.

"I think maybe she still be there," Sonja said. "I ain't seen no one outside but Denny and his family, but she might be too hurt to come outta the house."

Rose met Spencer's eyes.

"Thank you," Spencer said. "We're going down to check things out."

A few moments later, Spencer and Rose walked up to the family standing on another porch.

"Are you Denny?" Spencer called.

Denny gazed at them. "Who's asking?"

"Spencer Blackstone and Rose Samuels. We ain't here to cause any trouble for you. We're looking for someone."

Denny didn't return his smile. "That right? What makes you think I know something about who you lookin' for?"

Rose decided to step in. She understood his hesitancy to speak to strangers. "We don't have any reason to expect anything, Denny, but we're hoping you do." She explained why they were there. "Benji said he overheard that you had taken in a woman who was hurt. I'm hoping she might be this little girl's mother."

A slight woman with a worn flowered dress and a matching bandana around her head rose from the straight-backed chair she was sitting on. "Denny, let them folks up on this porch," she commanded. "They don't mean us no harm."

Denny looked chastened and stepped back. "Sorry," he mumbled.

Spencer shook his head. "Ain't no reason to be sorry, Denny. Times are hard for black people in this city."

"What happened to Alice has reminded us," the woman replied.

Rose stepped up onto the porch, resisting the urge to dash inside the house. "Is Alice the woman you saved?"

"She is," the woman confirmed. "My name is Gertrude. It's nice to meet you folks."

Rose smiled warmly. "Hello, Gertrude."

"You say there's a little girl?" Gertrude asked. "Alice been talking 'bout a little girl ever since she woke up two days ago. She ain't out of bed yet, but her mouth works fine."

Rose felt both disappointment and joy surge through her. "What is the little girl's name?"

"Gloria," Gertrude answered. "That be the little girl you be talking about?"

"I don't know," Rose admitted. "She hasn't spoken since she was found. I don't know if she has ever spoken, or if the trauma of the attack made her stop. They gave her the name Penny, simply because they don't know who she is."

"How old?" Gertrude asked.

"Eight or nine would be my guess," Rose answered. "She could be a year or two younger or older. It's hard to tell."

"If it's Alice's girl, she's eight," Gertrude answered, a gleam of excitement shining in her eyes.

"How is Alice?" Rose asked.

Gertrude frowned. "Not good. Whoever attacked her, beat her real bad. She's got a broken leg and a broken arm. She was unconscious for two days, so we don't know where she come from. We ain't got no money to take her to a doctor, but we found someone who set things the best they could. She's got two swollen eyes and a bunch of cuts, but they ain't so bad now. I treated them and packed them with honey and garlic. I think she's gettin' better, but it be a while before she be back to normal." She frowned. "Actually, I'm afraid she might not be doing too good," she admitted with a sigh. "I don't mean to be confusing. I reckon she was better yesterday than she be today. I don't know what else to do for her."

Rose's heart clenched with pity and anger. Someone had tried to kill both Alice and her daughter.

Denny shook his head. "Alice dragged herself out to the end of the alley. Still don't know how she did it, but she was lookin' for her little girl. A couple of us went back into the alley to look, but we didn't find nobody else."

Rose nodded. "Deacon Homestead must have already found Gloria and taken her with him." She was already certain Penny and Gloria were one and the same. "Can we talk to Alice?"

Gertrude opened the screen door. "Of course. Knowing her little girl is alright – if this girl is Gloria – will do more to make her better than anything could."

Rose stepped into the house. It was small and sparsely furnished but neat as a pin. A thin sheet had been hung across one end of the main area.

Gertrude pointed toward the sheet. "We gave her the little privacy we could." She walked over and pulled back the sheet.

Rose smiled down at the woman gazing up at her. She immediately knew Alice's wounds had become infected. Her eyes were glazed with fever, a sheen of perspiration over her face. The combination of fever and the heat in the house must have been making her truly miserable. Rose rapidly formulated a plan.

"Who are you?" Alice whispered.

Rose knelt down next to the bed. "My name is Rose Samuels." She thought about what she had been told about Penny from Deacon Homestead. "Was your little girl wearing a pink dress the night you were attacked?"

Alice stared at her hard. "How you know that?"

"Gloria is alright," Rose said softly. "Your little girl is safe."

Alice's fevered eyes glimmered with tears. The look on her face was a mixture of skepticism and joy. "How you know that?" she repeated.

"Because I have her," Rose answered. She explained what had happened since the attack.

Alice listened closely but looked confused. "Why didn't Gloria tell them folks at the asylum what happened?"

Rose chose her next words carefully. "Gloria hasn't spoken a word since the attack, Alice. I believe the trauma of what happened to her took away her voice."

Alice stared at Rose. "My girl ain't talking? That can't be. She don't never stop talking." Her eyes hardened. "What they do to my little girl?" Her voice faltered. "What they do to my Gloria?" she pleaded in a shaky voice.

"Nothing is broken," Rose replied. "She had cuts and bruises, but they're healing."

Alice regarded her steadily. "What else?"

Rose fell silent, searching for a way to answer the woman's question, while knowing what the truth would do to her.

Alice shook her head defeatedly. "You ain't got to say it. Not a black woman alive that don't know what most white men think we're good for." Her eyes grew dull. "I wish they'd done it to me, instead of my little girl. I tried hard to protect her."

Rose wasn't sure if she should ask what happened in the alley.

Alice solved the dilemma for her. "I don't usually go out that late. My husband died a few months back in an accident at one of the factories, so it's just me and Gloria now. One of our neighbors took real bad sick, and asked me to go to the store. I shoulda gone the next day, but I had a chance to work, so I went that night. I didn't wanna leave Gloria alone, so I took her with me." She shook her head. "I started to run when I saw them men following us. I could tell they were trouble." Fresh tears started to stream down her face. "I seen them men before. They didn't like it much that my husband be a white man. I figure they had it out for me and Gloria now that he be gone."

"I'm so sorry," Rose whispered.

"Gloria couldn't run fast enough to get away. One of them men grabbed her up when they caught us..." Her voice trailed away.

Rose wanted to stop her from reciting the story, but suspected the woman needed to tell it.

"I fought to reach her. That's when they started beating me. I felt my arm and leg break... I heard Gloria screaming for me..."

The agony in her voice was almost more than Rose could stand. Tears streamed down her face as she listened. She reached down and grabbed the hand on Alice's good arm.

"I couldn't get to her. At some point I blacked out. When I done come to again, the men were gone, and I couldn't find my girl. I crawled out of that alley looking for her." Her eyes found Gertrude. "These kind folks took me in. They looked for Gloria, but she be gone." Alice stared at Rose again. "She's really alright?"

"She is," Rose said firmly. "She's going to be thrilled to see you." She didn't know when, or if, Gloria would find her voice, but she hoped it would return in time.

Rose had finalized her plan while Alice was talking. She turned to Gertrude. "I'd like to take Alice with me. My best friend is Dr. Carrie Wallington. I live outside the city about four hours from here. Dr. Wallington operates a medical clinic there."

She turned her eyes back to Alice. "You've got an infection, Alice. Dr. Wallington can help you." She pushed aside the image of Jed's father dying of sepsis because his infection was too severe when he reached the plantation. They would be able to help Alice much sooner. "She can also set your broken bones better. Instead of splints, she'll give you casts. Your leg and arm could be as good as new."

Alice narrowed her eyes. "That be the Dr. Wallington who ran the Bregdan Clinic here in the city a few years back?"

Rose gasped. "You know her?"

"I know *of* her," Alice corrected. "One of the ladies I was cleaning for back then went to her right regular. Used to talk about her a lot. She was real sad when they closed that clinic and left. She a good doctor?"

"The best," Rose assured her.

Alice frowned. "What about my Gloria? I ain't gonna leave her here."

"Of course not," Rose said. "Gloria will come with you. The two of you can stay on the plantation for as long as you need. You'll have a chance to heal and make some decisions about what comes next."

Alice stared at her. "Why you doing this?"

Rose smiled. "Because I can. I don't know anybody that doesn't have troubles of some kind, but black women carry more than our share of them. We have to stick together. I believe I found Gloria at the orphanage for a reason." As she spoke, she realized how true her words were. With Gloria refusing to talk, the mystery may have never been solved. If Spencer hadn't known Parker Homestead, she could have been searching the city for days, with no assurance of finding him.

Alice nodded decisively. "When we gonna go?"

"Tomorrow morning," Rose said promptly. "Early." Alice badly needed medical attention. The news of her daughter's safety had given her renewed energy, but Rose knew the infection would continue to eat away at her. It was imperative she get treatment quickly. The ride out to the plantation might be agony, but it was the best place for her and Gloria.

Rose stood and went out to the porch. "Spencer, please go to Thomas' house and get as many blankets and pillows as you can."

"We bringing Alice back to the house." It wasn't a question.

"Yes. We can't transport her without a way for her to be comfortable."

Spencer nodded. "Be back as soon as I can."

Denny stepped forward. "I reckon I'll go with you."

No one on the porch needed to be told that two black men together would be safer than one.

Alice stared up at the elegant brick home when the wagon pulled to a stop. "This where we staying tonight?"

Rose had watched the woman courageously battle pain and fear as the wagon rumbled along the roads. She was lying on a mountain of soft blankets and pillows, but there was no way to protect her completely. "Yes. I'll explain it all another time. Right now, I want to reunite you with Gloria and get you settled in a bed."

Alice nodded wearily. "She know I'm coming?"

Rose shook her head.

"She in the house?" Alice asked, her eyes trained on the front door.

"Gloria is in the back catching fireflies with Hope," Spencer informed her. "Least ways, that's what she was doing when I left to come get you."

A soft smile bloomed on Alice's face. "That's nice. We been living in a tiny room since she been born. Weren't nowhere for her to go outside and catch them fireflies." She shook her head. "I hated being a slave, for sure, but at least I got to see the fireflies at night. My girl ain't never had that."

"She'll have plenty of it at Cromwell," Rose promised. "And lots of children to play with." She wasn't adopting Gloria, but at least she was able to give her and Alice a new beginning. There was great joy in that knowledge.

Spencer let down the back of the wagon and carefully carried Alice to the house.

Alice moaned but didn't cry out.

Rose hurried ahead to open the door.

May was already there. "I went down in the basement and got some remedies," she said. "I ain't a doctor, but Miss Carrie has taught me a lot. You take Alice upstairs to the room next to yours. Micah already took up a basin of cold water to bring her fever down, and a hot one to clean her wounds. I'll be up to take care of her."

Alice's eyes searched the rooms she could see from the foyer. "Where is my Gloria?"

Micah appeared in the doorway. "Hello, Alice. I'm Micah. I'll go get Miss Gloria. You let Spencer carry you upstairs. You want to be settled in before I bring your little girl to you."

Rose, watching Alice's face, knew the woman understood that Gloria didn't need to be any more frightened than she was. Seeing her mama lying in a bed would be much easier than seeing her unable to walk.

Thirty minutes later, Alice had been bathed, her wounds had been treated, and she was wearing one of May's nightgowns. A light sheet covered her as a steady evening breeze blew cooler air into the room. She gazed around with wonder. "I ain't never been in a place as fine as this."

"We're glad to have you here," May assured her.

A sound down the hallway brought a smile to Alice's face. A moment later, Gloria burst through the door with wide, searching eyes.

"Mama!"

Rose's eyes filled with tears at the sound of Gloria's sweet voice.

"Mama!" Gloria cried again. "You're here!"

May held her hand out to stop the little girl from leaping onto the bed. "Yes, Gloria, it's your mama, but she's hurt. You have to be very gentle."

Gloria stopped immediately, her eyes growing grave with concern. "Mama? You alright?"

Alice reached out and stroked her face. "Hi, honey. I can't tell you how happy I be to see you." Tears glistened in her eyes.

"Why you crying, Mama?"

"Because I'm happy," Alice whispered. "I didn't know if I would ever see you again." She continued to stroke her daughter's face and reached down to grasp one of her hands. "I love you, honey."

"I love you too, Mama," Gloria said. "I didn't know if I would ever see you again, either." Her voice trembled. Bright tears appeared in her eyes.

Alice's face crumpled with emotion. "I'm sorry you was hurt, Gloria."

"You tried to stop them," Gloria said softly.

Rose could tell she was reliving the attack. Once again, fury and pity raged through her. Nothing but time would offer healing to either of them. She stepped forward. "Why don't you snuggle with your mama for a little while."

Gloria looked up with wide, hopeful eyes. "I can do that? It won't hurt her?"

"Not if you're careful," Rose assured her. "Just lie right here and be real still."

Gloria nodded seriously and climbed slowly into the bed.

Alice gazed at Rose with deep gratitude and then leaned down to kiss her little girl's head. "I love you, sweetheart."

"I love you too, Mama."

Rose's heart ached when she saw the deep fatigue and pain etched into Alice's face the next day. "We're almost at Cromwell," she said encouragingly.

Alice managed a weak smile.

Gloria stood up in the wagon and clutched the wagon seat so she could peer over Rose's shoulder. "I ain't never been out of Richmond before."

Rose smiled. She wasn't sure how many times Gloria had made the same statement during their drive out. It didn't matter though; she was simply thrilled to hear her voice.

Spencer had insisted on driving them in the wagon. Rose had eagerly accepted. The injured woman could never have ridden in one of the River City carriages. Even with the mountain of blankets and pillows, the rough road had been agony for her.

"Gloria will be in my room, right, Mama?"

Rose had also heard this question what seemed like hundreds of times. Patiently, she recited the same answer. "I don't know, Hope. We'll have to decide the best place for Gloria and her mama to stay." She suspected, because the house was so full, that a room in the guest house would be best, but she didn't want to disappoint Hope.

Rose smiled when she saw Spencer looking forward eagerly. He seldom left Richmond. He'd been to the plantation several times when he was driving for Carrie during and after the war, but it had been a few years since his last visit. She was grateful the dark clouds on the horizon had not enveloped them in rain yet. They would be home before the afternoon storm hit.

It had taken longer than she hoped to get to the plantation, but they'd had to stop often to give Alice a break from the jostling and bumping of the wagon on the rough road. Rose knew the trip was brutal on the injured woman, but she also believed the plantation was the best place for her. They had started her on homeopathic remedies for the infection and fever. She would soon be able to rest and heal, without having to worry about Gloria.

"Mama! Look!" Gloria yelled. "We finally be here. It's Cromwell!"

Alice lifted a hand weakly but was unable to lift her head.

Rose's heart constricted with sympathy. She wanted to urge Spencer to drive faster, but she knew it would only make the bouncing worse. She hoped Carrie was home for the day. She'd thought of taking Alice straight to the medical clinic, but she didn't believe the woman could endure much more pain.

Rose pointed toward the patch of woods to the right of the plantation. "Take the wagon there."

Spencer squinted against the sun. "That's something new."

Rose nodded. "As big as the house is, we've outgrown it. When we have visitors, they stay in the new guesthouse. It was built two years ago."

Hope appeared at her side. "Gloria and her mama aren't staying at the house?" Her eyes brimmed with disappointment.

"We don't know yet," Rose said gently. "We have to see what Carrie says about what Gloria's mama needs." She paused. "I know you want what's best for her, don't you?"

Defiance flared in Hope's eyes but disappeared quickly. "Yes, Mama." Her voice dropped to a whisper. "Is her mama going to be alright?"

Rose wouldn't make a promise she didn't know she could keep. Keeping her voice low enough so that Gloria couldn't hear, she responded honestly. "I hope so, honey."

Chapter Twenty-Four

Carrie climbed the steps to the house later that evening. It had been a whirlwind few hours, but Alice was settled in the guesthouse. It had been decided, much to Hope's delight, that Gloria would stay in the big house with the girls until Alice was mostly recovered.

Carrie had sent Anthony to the clinic for needed supplies while she examined Alice's broken bones and cuts. One of Moses' men had gone for Janie and brought her to the house, as well.

When Carrie had what she needed, she used chloroform to anesthetize Alice, so she could reset the bones that had been poorly splinted. When she was satisfied they were in position, she and Janie had put casts on the broken arm and leg. Her entire leg was encased in plaster because the thigh bone had been badly broken. Her fractured forearm was in a partial cast.

Next, they had turned to her cuts and open wounds. Infection had started to set into several of them. It had been necessary to debride the wounds to get rid of the dead tissue, but since she was asleep, Alice hadn't felt the pain—it would have been too much for her in her weakened condition. Fresh ointments and bandages had finished out the work.

Carrie had waited for Alice to come out of the anesthesia, assured her she would recover fully, and left her to sleep. The exhausted woman needed rest more than anything else.

"Will Alice be alright?" Abby asked when Carrie stepped onto the porch.

"I believe so," Carrie answered, sinking into a rocker next to Anthony, and reaching for a glass of lemonade. She looked at Rose. "You were right to bring her here. If we hadn't reset her bones, she would never have been able to use that leg and arm very well." She frowned. "Any longer, and the infection from her wounds could have killed her like it did Morris." She forced a smile through her weariness. "It will take time, but I truly believe she'll recover one hundred percent."

"And then what, Rose?" Abby asked.

Rose shrugged, looking a little sheepish. "I have no idea," she admitted. "I couldn't leave either of them in the city. Alice was going to die in Denny's house. Gloria would have been without a mother. The only thing I was certain of was that Gloria would be safe here on the plantation until Alice heals."

"You love that little girl," Abby said softly.

"I do." Rose smiled as she looked out at the yard where Gloria played with the children. Her open smile and joyous laughter were a song to her heart. "Until Alice can care for her again, I will."

"All of us will," Annie said firmly. "That little girl done been through a horrible time."

Gloria split away from the game of tag, dashed up onto the porch, and stood in front of Carrie. Her dark eyes were piercing and direct. "Is my mama gonna be alright?"

"She is," Carrie assured her, grasping both of Gloria's hands, and gazing into her probing eyes. "It's going to take her time to get better, but she's going to have the best care possible."

"Me too?" Gloria asked, her voice hesitant now. "You gonna take care of me?"

"You too," Carrie told her gently. "As far as we're concerned, you're one of our children now. We'll take care of you and make sure you have everything you need. You'll get to spend time with your mama. She won't be able to walk for a while, but we'll bring her outside every day so she can get fresh air and sunshine. You can be with her."

A relieved smile bloomed on Gloria's face. "That be real good."

"What does your mama do in Richmond?" Rose asked.

"She cleans houses for rich white people," Gloria said. "Before that, she be a cook."

"In Richmond?" Rose asked.

Gloria shook her head. "No, ma'am. She cooked when she be a slave. Back before the big war." She looked thoughtful. "She told me she misses cooking, but she ain't found nobody in the city that wants her to cook. So she cleans." She smiled brightly. "We don't have much money, but sometimes when we get a little, my mama will cook us a real good meal. It's like we be eating in heaven!"

Carrie chuckled along with everyone else, but her mind was spinning. Though Annie would never admit it, she was getting older. At the same time, there were more and more people to cook for. Minnie was a big help and loved to cook, but only when she wasn't in school or playing with the other children. Perhaps when Alice was healed, she could help Annie in the kitchen. It was beyond time.

It would require strategic planning to convince Annie to share her kitchen, but they had time. It would be several months before Alice could use her arm and leg freely again. Once the bones healed and the casts were removed, it would take time for her to regain mobility and strength.

"Do you know how to read?" Rose asked.

Gloria hung her head and looked ashamed. "No," she whispered. "My mama wanted me to go to school, but I usually help her clean houses. We need the money real bad."

Rose smiled tenderly. "I completely understand. Would you like to know how to read?"

Gloria's eyes widened. "Yes, ma'am! Hope told me you be a teacher. You think you could teach me how to read?" Her face tightened with a frown. "I ain't very smart."

"Who told you that?" Rose asked, keeping her voice gentle.

"Them men," Gloria said, her voice dropping to a whisper. "When they grabbed me away from my mama, they said they could do what they wanted with a stupid little nigger girl."

Carrie gasped and felt the tears rise to the surface.

Rose pulled Gloria to her in a tight embrace. "They were the stupid ones," she said fiercely. She held the little girl away and gazed into her eyes. "You are a beautiful, smart little girl, Gloria. Don't you ever let anyone make you think otherwise. You survived a terrible time because you're smart. Even though you couldn't talk, you made sure I looked for your mama. That was very smart."

Gloria peered up into her face. "Really? I ain't stupid?"

"You're *smart*," Rose repeated. "I'm going to teach you how to read and write."

"I'm going to teach you how to ride a horse," Miles promised.

"And I'm going to teach you how to make the best oatmeal cookies on the planet," Annie added in a choked voice.

Anthony, not to be outdone, chimed in. "And I'm going to teach you how to swim."

Gloria gazed around the porch, her eyes as wide as saucers. She turned and looked out over the plantation. The sun had been swallowed by the tree line, but the encroaching darkness was kissed with a rosy hue. The evening was sultry, but a soft breeze carried the perfume of honeysuckle onto the porch. The horses grazed peacefully in the pasture. She swung back to gaze at them, her face filled with awe. "Is this heaven?"

Rose chuckled. "Sometimes I believe it is, Gloria. Sometimes I believe it is."

Moses finished his meal and sat back with a sigh of contentment. His mother would always be the best cook he knew, but the meals served on the Chicago, Rock Island and Pacific Railroad were delicious. He found it astonishing that the train had a kitchen capable of putting out such a high caliber of food.

Felicia took the final bite of her chocolate cake and groaned. "I'm stuffed."

Frances shook her head. "You say that after every meal. I don't know how you eat so much food."

Felicia grinned. "I can eat whatever I want and never get bigger. You're merely jealous."

"Absolutely true," Frances said ruefully. "If I ate like you do, I wouldn't fit into any of my dresses by the time we get home. It's not fair," she complained.

"You're right," Felicia said sympathetically. She reached for the untouched chocolate cake beside Frances' plate. "Would you like me to eat your temptation?"

Moses laughed. "My daughter has a cruel streak."

"I was simply attempting to be helpful," Felicia protested, her eyes dancing with fun.

Frances shoved the cake in her friend's direction and turned to Moses. "Where are we now?"

"We're somewhere in Iowa," Moses replied. "We should be in Chicago tomorrow night."

Frances stared out the window of the dining car. "Iowa is pretty."

At almost seven-thirty, the sun had exited the day, but there was enough light to see the sprawling, lush, green countryside. Houses were sparse, obviously homesteads for area farms. A wet summer had created tall corn as far as the eye could see.

Moses nodded. "It will do."

The conductor, a man named William Smith, stopped to look down at him. "You don't like Iowa?" Brown eyes gazed at him from beneath a black-brimmed conductor's cap.

"On the contrary," Moses said easily. Over the last few days, they had spoken with the conductor several times. "It's beautiful, but I like Virginia better."

"You going home?" Smith asked.

"Yes, we are," Frances said excitedly. "We've been gone from home for three months. San Francisco was interesting, but there is nowhere as beautiful as Cromwell Plantation."

Moses knew Frances had grown increasingly homesick in the last month. She had never complained, nor even talked about it, but he could see the longing in her eyes.

"Is that right?" Smith asked. "You live on a plantation?"

"We do," Moses responded.

Smith looked confused for a moment. "All of you live there?"

Moses smiled. "That's right. I co-own the plantation with Frances' grandfather."

Smith's eyes widened slightly but his only overt response was a casual nod.

Moses bit back his grin. The conductor was well trained to treat every passenger equally. He was sure there was talk of the black man and the two young ladies in Pullman's finest sleeping car. While he didn't feel the need to flaunt his success and wealth, he secretly enjoyed disrupting white people's perceptions and stereotypes.

Felicia had no such compunctions. "My daddy owns the most successful tobacco plantation in Virginia," she said proudly. "He employs close to one hundred men during the planting season. He pays them very well."

"I see," Smith murmured. His expression was a mixture of skepticism and jealousy.

Moses decided it was time to change the topic of conversation. "I know we're in Iowa. How far are we from Des Moines?"

"About fifty-five miles," Smith answered promptly. "We're about twenty miles from Adair. It shows on the map as a little town, if you can count eighteen people as a town."

Frances' eyes widened. "Eighteen people?"

Smith smiled. "There's not much there, but it has a place on the map. We'll stop there for water." He paused, checked his pocket watch, and evidently decided he could talk longer. The dining car was almost empty, with coach passengers already back in their seats. "Do you mind me asking what you were doing in San Francisco?"

Moses was silent, giving Felicia a chance to answer.

"I graduated from Oberlin College last December," Felicia said. "I'm going to be a businesswoman. I was in San Francisco to be mentored by an extremely successful woman there."

Moses understood the surprise on the conductor's face. It was probably more about Felicia's age than her color.

Felicia noticed his expression too. She decided to answer his unspoken question. "I'm eighteen." She didn't offer any more information.

Smith looked at her with increased respect and turned to Frances. "Are you a college graduate as well, Frances?"

Frances laughed. "No. Felicia isn't like normal people. She always has to be several steps ahead of mere mortals like me."

Felicia shook her head. "Hardly. Conductor Smith, Frances is going to medical school in the fall."

Smith looked impressed. "You're going to medical school, young lady?"

"I am," Frances answered. "However, I wouldn't be too impressed. America's medical schools aren't impressive."

Moses stared at her with surprise. "What do you mean?"

"It's true," Frances stated. "I had time in San Francisco to do more research. American medical schools are privately owned, have very few entrance requirements, and most provide no clinical training."

"But your mom…"

Frances cut off Moses' protest. "My mom was very lucky when she decided to go to the Woman's Medical College of Pennsylvania. They did a better job than most, but it was insufficient. She told me her best decision was when she left her medical school and transferred to the Homeopathic School of Philadelphia."

Felicia was staring at her friend as well. "I thought you were going to medical school where your mom started? You told me it was better."

Frances shook her head decisively. "I'm not. I'm not sure where I will decide to go, but I want a good education."

"Most doctors aren't well trained?" Smith asked.

"Hardly," Frances responded. "Most doctors learn through apprenticeships with practicing physicians. It gives the doctors extra income and cheap labor, but it hardly trains skilled doctors." She shook her head. "There used to be very few medical schools, until people figured out running medical schools was quite lucrative. There are more than seventy medical schools now, but the quality of education has decreased even further. All it takes to open a school is to have a place to meet and a group of physicians willing to lecture. Students buy tickets for the lectures, and the physicians make a hefty supplemental income." Her frown deepened. "They're graduating doctors who have no idea how to help people."

"I had no idea," Felicia murmured. "When did you learn this?"

"This summer," Frances answered. "Your focus was on learning business practices. It wasn't something I needed to talk about." Not waiting for Felicia to answer, she continued. "Most medical schools have no admission requirements. Medical students are unruly and undisciplined." Her lips tightened. "Many are illiterate. To make it worse, there is no clinical practice — students sit and listen. It's a terrible way to learn."

Conductor Smith was staring at her. "You sound as if you have some doctoring experience already."

Frances smiled. "My mama is Dr. Carrie Wallington. She's the best doctor I've ever seen. She went to medical school, but she's also a specialist in homeopathy and herbal cures. She was probably the only woman in the South to operate on patients during the war. On top of that, she did a surgical internship with the top surgeon in Philadelphia." She paused. "She runs the medical clinic on the plantation, but she could work anywhere in the country."

"This is important, Frances," Felicia stated. "You're supposed to start medical school in a few months. What are you going to do?"

Frances shrugged casually, though her eyes didn't match her gesture. "I don't know yet. I'm going to talk to mama about it when I get home."

"She'll support whatever you decide," Moses offered.

"I know," Frances agreed. She hesitated for a long moment. "I may go to Boston," she said slowly.

"Boston?" Felicia exclaimed.

Frances nodded. "Do you remember when we met Dr. Rebecca Crumpler in Richmond? The one who was treating patients through the Freedmen's Bureau?"

"Of course," Felicia answered. "She left Richmond and returned to Boston because of the poor treatment she received in the South. It was bad enough that she was a woman doctor. Being a *black* woman doctor was more than Richmond could handle," she said sarcastically.

"Dr. Crumpler went to school at the New England Female Medical College in Boston," Frances said. "They were the first medical school to graduate a black female physician. This year, the medical school is joining with

Boston University. They will become the first accredited coeducational medical school in the country. Their requirements are much more stringent." She smiled. "Besides that, Elizabeth is in Boston, running the homeopathic practice with her father. I would have the best of both worlds."

Moses was fascinated by the conversation, but he feared Conductor Smith was feeling trapped. "We enjoy talking to you, but don't feel you have to listen if you have work to do."

Smith smiled slightly. "I do. I will leave you to your conversation. We should be pulling into Adair in less than ten minutes."

Moses watched him walk away, swaying with the movement of the train. He realized nightfall had claimed the countryside while they were talking. He could hear the engine roar, gathering steam to power its way up an incline. "Girls, let's go back to our car." He had some reading he wanted to do before they slept, and he had promised Felicia a game of backgammon.

They both nodded and pushed back their chairs to stand up.

Moses frowned when he heard the engine roar even louder. Suddenly, they were thrown to the floor as the train abruptly slowed.

Seconds later, he heard the sound of wrenching metal and a loud crash.

Chapter Twenty-Five

July 21, 1873

"Daddy!" Felicia screamed.

Moses half-stood, determined to reach the girls, but a powerful jolting motion knocked him to the side. His head struck a table as he was thrown to the floor again. He looked for something steady to grab onto, but everything was moving sideways.

Plates clattered to the floor, breaking into pieces when they hit. Glasses crashed down, shattering into shards. Silverware clanged and flew through the air.

Moses ducked just before a glass shard hit him in the face. "Protect your faces, girls!" he yelled as he was thrown against the side of the train. At last, there was something to hang onto. He reached up, grabbed the edge of a windowsill, and tried to heave himself to his feet.

That's when the gunfire started.

Moses threw himself back on the floor as a bullet shattered the glass over his head. He caught a glimpse of the girls' faces. No longer screaming, their expressions were rigid with fright. Felicia's eyes were glued to him, waiting for direction.

Moses' brain raced as he tried to figure out what to do.

Felicia had blood running down her face.

Frances had a ragged gash on her neck. Blood had already darkened the edge of her dress.

Moses remembered the day Felicia's parents were murdered in front of her. He had been hiding in the alleyway across from her house. He had caught her eye and motioned for her to run to him. That day, he saved her life. He was determined to save both girls today.

In the brief moment he'd been able to look out the window, he'd seen that the engine and the two cars directly behind it had derailed. The engine laid upside down in a creek bank, the other two cars almost on top of it. Steam was pouring from the smokestack.

He began to hear screams from the coach cars behind them. They had been the only people in the dining car. He knew there were a hundred people on the train, but he had no way of knowing how many were injured or dead.

More gunfire erupted.

Moses held his finger to his lips, hoping that if they stayed quiet, whoever was attacking the train wouldn't find them. He couldn't tell how many attackers were outside, but he was certain there were at least four men firing rifles and pistols. Now that the train was still, he crawled slowly across the floor to the girls, brushing aside shattered plates and glasses as he went. It seemed to take forever, but he finally reached them.

"Daddy!" Felicia whispered.

"Stay down and stay quiet," Moses ordered in a low voice. "The train must be under attack."

Both of the girls' eyes widened, but they remained quiet.

Moses wanted to stand up to see what was going on, but he didn't want to alert anyone to their presence. He could hear yells in the distance that were slowly getting closer.

Suddenly, Conductor Smith appeared in the doorway, his clothes torn and askew. Blood ran down his face and stained the sleeves of his jacket. His eyes looked wild. "Have you got a gun?" he asked urgently.

Moses shook his head. "No. What has happened?"

"The train is being robbed by men with white hoods over their faces."

Moses felt a new fear grip him. Any kind of attack was bad, but if the Klan found black passengers on the train, they would be more brutal. He looked around desperately. They could do what they wanted to him, and Frances would probably be safe because she was white, but he had to hide Felicia.

Smith, not bothering to say more, pushed through the dining car, and disappeared into the connecting coach car.

Moses suddenly spied what looked to be some type of closet. Staying on his knees, he grabbed Felicia's hand and started pulling her across the floor. He could hear the sound of voices drawing closer. His breathing quickened as he moved faster. Finally, he reached the doors and pulled them apart, wincing when the sound of squeaking metal ripped through the air. He gasped with relief when he saw a closet just big enough for his daughter. "Get inside," he whispered.

Felicia shook her head. "No. What about you, Daddy? And Frances?"

"Frances will be alright," Moses assured her. "So will I."

"I'm not going to be the only one hiding from the Klan," Felicia said stubbornly. She turned and started crawling back to Frances. "We both know *you* won't be alright."

Moses gritted his teeth and considered forcing her into the closet.

Felicia, seeming to feel his thoughts, turned her head to peer at him over her shoulder. "I'm not a little girl anymore, Daddy. You don't have to save me this time." Her last words were delivered with a tender smile.

Moses opened his mouth to protest, but his words were cut off when the door at the end of the dining hall slammed open.

He stood to block the two hooded men striding toward them. He hoped his size would give them pause, although they might become more dangerous if they felt intimidated by a black man. He could feel their stares through the white hoods' slitted eye holes. Steady breaths gave him a measure of control over the fury roaring through him.

"Where are the passengers?" one of the men shouted.

Moses quickly realized the invaders thought he was a waiter on the train. It wouldn't dawn on them that a black man could afford train travel, much less the finest sleeper car. He motioned to the girls behind his back to remain quiet.

"Coach car, sir," he said in what he hoped was a deferential tone. He felt a twinge of guilt for sending them back to other passengers, but he also knew they were going anyway. His sole concern was keeping the girls safe.

"Get out of our way, boy!" one man spat as he pushed past.

Moses stepped back and watched the two men disappear into the next car. Fresh screams and crying erupted as the men started shouting. Listening carefully, he realized the Klan members were demanding cash and jewelry from the trapped passengers. He thought of the five hundred dollars in his inside coat pocket and felt a moment of bitter amusement. The robbers had walked right past the person who probably had the most money, simply because they couldn't believe a black man might be wealthy.

More gunshots rang out, but they didn't seem to be coming from the coach. He could hear pounding feet on the railbed outside the window. Moses sank down to a sitting position. He leaned against the side of the train, pulled the girls in next to him, and used his feet to drag two tables over to partially conceal them. It was the best he could do in the moment.

"Daddy?" Felicia whispered.

"We're alright," Moses said, hoping he sounded reassuring. "They think I work on the train. They won't pay us any attention." He prayed he was right.

"What are they doing?" Frances demanded, her voice equal parts fear and outrage.

"Robbing the train," Moses answered. He decided not to tell the girls the train had been derailed. Even when the men got what they wanted and left, they would be trapped with no way to get to their next destination.

The railroad company would send another train when it discovered the trouble, but there was no way of knowing when that would be. Since the dining car hadn't jumped the track, he was sure the remainder of the train was on the metal rails. If they survived, they would at least have a place to sleep tonight. They would be much better off than everyone else.

The three of them sat quietly. Eventually, the gunfire stopped, and the yelling ceased.

After a brief silence, they heard a loud Rebel yell that pierced the night, followed by the sound of pounding hoofbeats.

Screams dissipated but were replaced with crying and pleas for help.

"People are hurt!" Frances said urgently. She pushed herself up from the floor and started toward the coach car.

Moses reached up to stop her. "*You're* hurt, Frances."

Frances shook her head. "I'm fine. It's not a deep cut, and it's already quit bleeding." She turned and stared at him. "I'm going to help those people, Moses."

Despite his anxiety, Moses couldn't control his grin. "You sound like your mama."

"Thank you," Frances said softly. Her face set into stubborn lines. "Mama taught me that you help people when you have the chance."

"You don't have any supplies," Felicia said as she pushed herself to her feet.

"I'll do what I can," Frances said stubbornly.

"I'm coming with you to help." Moses knew it was useless to try to stop either one of them. The only thing he could do was assist.

Conductor Smith appeared at the door again. His questioning gaze settled on Frances.

Frances spoke before he could voice his question. "I'm coming to help whoever I can." She paused. "Is there a medical kit on the train?"

Smith shrugged his shoulders. "I should know that, but I'm afraid I don't."

"I know where one be, Miss Frances."

Moses smiled with relief when Burt, the porter for their sleeper car, appeared behind the conductor. "I'm glad you're alright."

Conductor Smith eyed the slender man, sharply attired in his porter uniform. "What are you doing here, George?"

Moses sighed. "His name isn't George. This is Burt."

"I came to check on my passengers," Burt said, standing up straighter when Moses used his real name.

His face creased with concern when he saw Felicia and Frances. "You girls are bleeding!"

"It's nothing," Frances assured him. "Will you take me to the medical kit?"

Moses stepped closer. "You came through the coach cars, Burt. How many people are hurt?"

"Hard to tell," Burt said grimly. "I didn't see nobody dead, though. Just lots of folks scared out of their minds."

"I'm glad nobody died," Felicia exclaimed. "The gunfire was terrifying."

Moses was watching Conductor Smith as she talked. He saw the flash in the man's distraught eyes.

"Go ahead and tell us, Smith," Moses said. "We'd prefer to know the truth."

"Engineer Rafferty is dead," Smith said heavily. "He was killed when the engine flipped over. I was able to creep up and see what happened. As far as I can tell, the fireman who was feeding the boiler when the attack happened is still alive, but I don't know for how long. He's badly hurt and burned."

Moses tightened his lips. "Will someone go for help?"

"Somebody is on the way," Smith assured him. "It won't take him too long to walk into Adair to send a telegram."

"And then?" Moses asked.

"They'll have to get some other trains out here to get everyone." Smith sighed. "I don't know how long it will take, but it won't be quick. New trains will have to come in from Des Moines."

Moses gazed at the darkness. He realized the man going for help might be waylaid by the bandits. There was no way of knowing when help would come. His thoughts jumped ahead to Rose. All he could do was send a telegram, when possible, to let her know they wouldn't be in Richmond when planned.

Frances stepped forward. "The medical kit, please?" she asked. "I can't do anything about dead men, but I can help with the wounded."

"Come with me," Burt replied. "I don't know how much the medical kit will help, but you can have it."

Frances and Felicia followed Burt as he walked quickly through the coach cars.

Frances was relieved to see that most of the passengers were unharmed. They were talking among themselves in frantic whispers, keeping their eyes trained on the windows, though the darkness made it impossible to see if the bandits were approaching again. Many of the women and children were crying.

"Do you think they'll be back?" Frances whispered when they reached the platform at the end of the second car. Her eyes scanned the dark woods, knowing any number of men could be watching them at that very moment.

"No," Burt said confidently. "Them white-hooded idiots got what they wanted. The train crashing made a lot of noise. There's no tellin' how long it will take for help to arrive, but them men aren't gonna want to be anywhere around here. I heard their horses galloping away when things finally got quiet."

His announcement made Frances feel marginally better. She forced herself to keep her thoughts on the wounded passengers but had a fresh perspective of how her mama must have felt during the war. Hearing the stories was one thing; experiencing something like it for herself was entirely different. She had already decided she would never go anywhere again without carrying a medical bag.

When they entered the baggage car behind the sleeper cars, Burt opened a compartment and pulled out a thick bag. "This is what we got," he announced.

Frances reached for it eagerly. When she saw a mound of bandages and tubes of ointment, she felt better. It wasn't everything she needed, but it would do. "I can work with this." She gripped the bag handle and hurried back to the coach cars, Felicia on her heels.

When she reached the first one, she raised her voice so she could be heard above the noise. "My name is Frances. This is Felicia. Who is injured? I'm here to help."

The train fell silent for a moment as eyes stared at her dubiously.

The first response was from a stout man in a seat close to her. "What are you planning on doing, young lady? You're just a girl."

Frances had prepared herself for resistance. "I happen to be a girl who has worked in a medical clinic for the last four years, treating all types of injuries," she said loudly, making sure everyone could hear. "If you don't want my help, I'll go to the next car. However," she said, knowing her confidence would help the passengers believe in her, "unless there is a doctor on board, I'm the best you're going to get." She didn't add that she was probably *superior* to any doctor who might be there.

The man who had challenged her looked at her with surprise. "You don't say..." He gazed around and then made a decision. "My wife hit her head when the train crashed. I think I've stopped the bleeding, but I can't do anything else."

Frances stepped toward him and knelt in front of the frightened woman seated next to him. "Hello, ma'am," she said softly. "What's your name?"

"Beth," the woman whispered. She was holding her husband's handkerchief to her head. Once white, it was now crimson red. Her blond hair had turned a rusty color.

"Hello, Beth." Frances kept her voice low and comforting, imitating her mama as best as she could. "Can I see your injury?" She held out her hand toward the woman's head. "I can't treat it until I can see it."

Beth pulled her hand away slowly, gripping the handkerchief tightly.

Frances was relieved when she saw the cut. It needed attention but wouldn't need stitches. She knew how to stitch a wound, but she didn't want to do it here on the train, and she doubted the medical kit had supplies for it.

Burt appeared at her side. "Is there anything I can do to help, Miss Frances?"

It was a heady feeling to realize she was in charge. Before, she had always merely assisted her mama. Now, she was the one giving the orders. The heady feeling dissipated when she realized she now also bore the responsibility.

Moses materialized as well. "You tell us what you need."

Frances took strength from his steady gaze. She knew it would take time for help to reach them. She looked outside at the darkness and thought of Burt's assurance that the robbers were gone. "Felicia and I can handle things in here, but we need hot water," she said. "The only available water is in the creek bed. I can't use it until it has been boiled."

Moses nodded and turned to Burt. "Do you have anything we can use to boil water?"

Conductor Smith stepped forward. "The dining car has a large metal pot."

The woman's husband stood. "I'll help build a fire." He leaned down and spoke tenderly. "You're in good hands, Beth. I'll be back."

Beth turned her blue eyes to Frances.

"You're going to be fine," Frances told her, astounded by the trust she saw in the older woman's eyes. She may be young, but she was only two years younger than her mother had been when she was operating on soldiers during the war. She could do this. "As soon as we have hot water, I'll clean up the wound and bandage it." She tossed the bloody handkerchief aside and pressed a fresh bandage against the cut. "Keep pressure on the wound until I come back."

Frances moved down the aisle, stopping when someone raised their hand for help. Thankfully, there were only six passengers in need of care. No one was gravely injured – mostly cuts and bruises.

Conductor Smith appeared at the door between the cars. "Miss Frances, can you come now?"

Frances was alerted by the anxious tone in his voice. She picked up the medical bag and hurried toward him. "What's wrong," she asked quietly.

Conductor Smith stood on the platform, keeping his voice low as he answered. "It's Mr. Royce. He's the Superintendent of the Iowa Division of the Rock Island Railroad."

What he did hardly mattered to Frances. Her mother had taught her to treat all patients the same, no matter their title or wealth. "Is he hurt?"

"He was in one of the baggage carts that derailed. From what I can tell, his face collided with one of the stanchions. He's bleeding so badly it's hard to tell exactly where the wound is. He insisted you treat the passengers first, but if you're done here..."

Frances sucked in her breath. If he had been bleeding badly since the train wrecked, he could be very close to death if it wasn't stopped. She glanced toward the second car, hoping no one there was badly injured, but knowing she needed to treat Superintendent Royce first. "Take me to him."

As she started forward, Moses appeared with a large pot. "I have hot water for you." He looked back over his shoulder at the first coach car. "I heard about Mr. Royce. You go to him, and I'll get another pot of water. Felicia and I will clean the wounds of the passengers you've checked on."

Frances nodded gratefully as Smith took the pot. "Thank you."

"This way," Smith said.

Frances had her first glimpse of the wrecked train as they stepped outside. The blaze of the fire built for boiling water created a glow captured by the overhanging trees. She gasped at the sight of the massive iron engine lying on its side in the creek bed. She knew the engineer's body was encased inside what was now a metal tomb. The two baggage cars that had been pulled from the tracks by the wounded engine lay at a thirty-degree angle on the bank. Baggage spilled from the open doors. "Why did they do this?" she whispered in a shocked voice.

"I spoke with one of the express baggage agents," Smith said angrily. "Two of the robbers demanded he open the safe. When he did, they took out about seventeen hundred dollars, then demanded to know where the rest of the money was. They believed there was going to be more."

"Should there have been?" Frances asked.

Smith lowered his voice. "This train was supposed to be carrying a hundred thousand in gold. My friend said the shipment was changed to a later train at the last moment."

Frances scowled. "So good people are dead and injured because they were after *gold*?"

"Life is rough in this part of the country," Smith said flatly. "Bank robbers. Armed robbery of all kinds. Murder. Things are so spread out, it's tough for anyone to enforce the laws."

Now, more than ever, Frances was ready to go home. But first, she had patients to care for. "Where is Mr. Royce?"

Smith led her to an elegantly attired man, his suit now bloodied and crumpled, huddled against the side of the first baggage car. He looked up with eyes that were already close to swollen shut. He held a thick cloth to his face that was bright red and dripping blood.

"This is Frances, Superintendent Royce. She's been helping the injured passengers. She works for her mother who is a doctor and owns a medical clinic in Virginia."

Royce moved the cloth enough to allow him to speak. "The fireman," he said hoarsely. "He's hurt worse than me. Go to him."

Smith shook his head slowly. "There's no use," he said sadly. "He's dead."

Frances grimaced. Two dead. "That's terrible," she whispered.

Smith looked like he might be ill. "He was badly burned. It was a mercy that he died."

Frances gritted her teeth and turned to the person she could help.

Thirty minutes later, Superintendent Royce's broken nose had been cleaned and bandaged. The bleeding had stopped.

Royce glanced up at Smith. "Were all the passengers robbed?"

"No sir," Smith replied. "I talked to one of the passengers who foolishly stuck his head out of a window to talk to one of the robbers."

"Fool man," Royce muttered. "He could have been shot."

"Yes," Smith agreed. "He asked the robber if they meant to kill innocent women and children. He was told to put his head back inside and he wouldn't get hurt. The man told him they weren't petty robbers. They were big robbers."

Royce grunted but didn't say anything.

"Seems the robbers only take from the rich because they can afford to lose it. They take it for the use of the poor." Smith shrugged. "From what I hear, only the passengers who looked wealthy were robbed."

"Well, that's something," Royce muttered. "The James Brothers aren't known for their compassion."

Smith stared at him. "You're saying those men were the James Brothers? One of them was Jesse James?"

Royce nodded. "I believe so."

"The James Brothers and their gang are bank robbers," Smith protested.

"It seems they've expanded their trade," Royce said wryly. "I guess they couldn't resist the allure of a hundred thousand dollars' worth of gold."

"It's awful risky to derail a train," Smith stated. "They're going to have an army of lawmen after them."

"Lawmen and every man we can get who will form a posse," Royce said. "I'm sure they're already long-gone, however. No one's been able to catch them, because when they rob a bank, they hightail it out of there before a posse can be mounted to go after them."

Frances was intrigued by the conversation. She, along with most of America, had heard of Jesse James. His bank-robbing exploits were often front-page news. "How did he know there was supposed to be gold on the train?"

Royce gazed at her. "Good question, miss. Somebody working for the railroad has loose lips. We'll try and find out who it was, but it's more likely we'll never know." He sighed. "We're lucky the shipment was delayed."

Frances looked at him closely, noting the pain radiating in his eyes. "You need to rest, Superintendent Royce," she said firmly. "No more talking for you."

Royce raised a brow. "That sounded remarkably like an order, young lady."

Frances flushed but didn't look away. "You can take it any way you want to," she said calmly, once again imitating her mother. "If you want to increase your pain level by continuing to talk, it's entirely up to you."

Royce chuckled, waved his hand, and laid back.

Frances left him on a makeshift bed of blankets and boxes, and then headed back to the second passenger car. Weariness sat on her like an anvil, but she was determined to press through.

"You were wonderful today," Felicia said admiringly.

Frances yawned, grateful for the soft bed and plush pillows waiting for her. Burt had treated her like royalty when she had finally stumbled into the sleeper car. "I'm grateful I could help those people. Thank you for your help today."

Felicia continued to stare at her with a strange expression.

"What?" Frances muttered, fighting to stay awake, when all she wanted to do was sink down into oblivion.

"I've watched your mama and Janie treat people ever since I've been on the plantation. It's what they do. I know you help them at the clinic, but today..." Felicia paused thoughtfully. "Today you acted like an actual doctor. There was no one to tell you what to do. You simply started doing it."

Frances felt a warm glow of pride. She couldn't wait to tell her mama what had happened.

"Are you truly going to Boston?" Felicia asked.

Frances realized that somewhere in the midst of the day's chaos, she had reached a decision. She wanted to be the best trained doctor she could be, in all areas. "Yes," she said firmly, amazed at her sudden decisiveness after weeks of uncertainty. "I'm going to Boston."

"I'm coming with you," Felicia stated.

Her weariness forgotten; Frances bolted straight up. "What did you say?"

Felicia chuckled. "I'm coming to Boston with you. If it's alright, that is." She looked thoughtful. "I've been thinking about it ever since I decided not to stay in San Francisco. It's going to take Boston a long time to recover from last year's fire. There will be a lot of opportunities for me and Daddy to invest in real estate and businesses. I learned so much from Mrs. Pleasant. I'm ready to apply it now… after a few more months at home," she added hastily.

Frances clapped her hands. "Elizabeth and Peter are in Boston. They're like family."

"I thought about that too." Felicia hesitated. "So, what do you think? Do you want to go to Boston together?"

"Of course I do!" Frances said happily. "I can't imagine anything I would like better."

"I can't imagine anything your parents would like better either." Moses' deep voice sounded into the darkness.

Frances had totally forgotten Moses was listening to their conversation, but she was thrilled to have his approval. She was certain her parents would agree as well.

It was mid-afternoon the next day before the first train backed up to transfer the stranded passengers. On such short notice, the railroad hadn't been able to divert a train with enough cars to carry them all. The dining car, though, had managed to create enough simple meals to feed everyone on the train for breakfast and lunch. Crying and despair had changed to smiles and laughter as everyone ate, roamed around outside the train in the sunshine, and talked nonstop about their ordeal. Their survival had become excellent fodder for stories that would be told over and over to family and friends.

Frances stood next to Conductor Smith and watched the stream of people enter the new train cars. She, Moses, and Felicia were going to wait for the second train that would arrive in a few hours. Several of the passengers, bandages indicating she had treated them, waved to her before they were swallowed by the train.

"You did good, Miss Frances," Smith said huskily. "It was a lot to ask of you to take care of everyone, but you did it."

Frances thought of her mama. "You do what you have to do when the time comes, Conductor Smith. None of us thinks we're capable of big things until we're required to do them. It's then that we discover we're capable of doing more than we ever dreamed."

Smith cocked his brow. "That's a lot of wisdom from someone your age."

Frances laughed. "That comes straight from my mama."

Chapter Twenty-Six

Hobbs walked as fast as he could back to his house, cursing the wooden leg that meant he would never run again. Still, he had learned to maneuver with it better than he imagined he could when he woke up from surgery during the war and discovered his leg was missing.

He was breathing hard when he climbed the stairs to his narrow porch.

Tyson met him at the door, his eyes darting around nervously. "What's wrong?" he demanded.

Hobbs grinned and pushed in through the door. Not yet able to speak, he held an envelope up triumphantly, struggling to catch his breath. When he could talk, he waved the envelope again. "The letter came."

A month earlier, he had received a brief telegram from Thomas Cromwell.

COME HOME. LETTER TO FOLLOW.

"Sure took a long time," Tyson replied.

Hobbs shrugged. "The train makes mail faster, but any number of things could have happened to slow it down. Thankfully, we didn't have to wait for it to come by a wagon train or the Pony Express."

"What's it say?"

"I'm about to find out." Hobbs sank down in a wooden chair at the table and opened the envelope carefully, his eyes going immediately to the signature. "Carrie wrote it!"

he exclaimed. He pulled out the two sheets of paper, scanned them, and began to read out loud.

Dear Hobbs,

What a joy to hear from you. I know Father has written that you're welcome to come home, but I asked him to let me write the letter to you.

I have missed you deeply since you left for Portland. I know it was the safest decision for you at the time, but I've missed you. Robert and I loved you so much. Losing Robert, and having you leave the same year, was hard.

I know Father has kept you informed of things that have happened, but letters can never do justice. I am doing well. I'm remarried to a wonderful man, Anthony Wallington. We now have four children.

"What?" Hobbs exclaimed with alarm. "It's not safe for Carrie to have children after losing her first daughter." He returned to reading.

I can see the astonishment on your face, even from here in Virginia.

Hobbs chuckled before he turned back to the letter.

All four of the children are adopted. Frances just turned seventeen. Minnie, my red-headed dynamo, is eleven. Russell, adopted just last year, is also eleven, though he seems much older. Bridget is almost two – a curly, black-headed bundle of joy.

I never imagined I would have a family. It only makes what I have that much more precious.

We have talked a lot about your returning to the South. I don't know what you're planning on doing, but we would like you to consider working with us here at Cromwell Stables. We are growing steadily. Clint, the stable manager, is excellent at his job but could certainly use more help.

If you decide it's not a good fit for you, we'll do our best to help you find a position that will suit you better. We simply want you to be happy.

I could write for days about things that have happened, but I would much prefer to sit out on the porch with a glass of tea and tell you about them. Everyone here feels the same way.

Send a telegram to let us know when you'll arrive.

Sincerely,

Carrie

Hobbs put the letter down slowly. Reading Carrie's words had made the longing to return home even stronger.

"You're a lucky man," Tyson said quietly.

"I am," Hobbs agreed. He had buried memories of home when he'd arrived in Portland. His decision to betray the KKK had closed that door to him. It was better to not dwell on the memories. To have that door open again, and in such a wonderful way, was almost more than he could fathom.

"Are you going to take her up on that offer?"

Hobbs hesitated. He was fairly confident he would be safe on the plantation, but he also knew the KKK was active in that area, and he knew the Klan hated the way Cromwell Plantation operated. Going back to the South was a risk. He might as well be doing something he loved. "Yes."

"Yes?" Tyson eyed him. "You reckon it's gonna be safe?"

Hobbs shrugged. "Living life ain't safe. I did the safe thing when I came out here. I don't reckon I regret it, because I'm alive and I've been able to save some money. I'm tired of merely being safe. It's time to live where I want to live and do the things I want to do."

Tyson shook his head. "That might be the best way for a white man to live, but it don't work that way for a black man."

Hobbs wanted to argue the point, but he knew Tyson was right. He ran the risk of danger if he was recognized by a Klan member. Tyson's life was in danger every moment, simply because of his color. "Where are you going to go?"

"I been thinking about it," Tyson replied. "I'm gonna go as far as Chicago. I figure there be a lot of jobs there 'cause they be rebuilding from that big fire. I know some other black folks that live there. They say it's better than the South."

"That sounds like a good plan," Hobbs replied.

"When we gonna leave?"

Hobbs grinned. "Now that I have the letter, I don't see any reason to stay around here. We'll leave in four days."

Tyson cocked his head. "August fourth?"

"Yep." Hobbs' heart raced with excitement. "August fourth."

Jeremy and Vincent looked at each other and grinned nervously.

Jeremy gazed across the arena and spotted Marietta and the twins. They had come to see him begin the race at eight o'clock in the evening. They would be back the next day to see him walk the last two to three hours.

If he was still walking.

He gazed around at the throng of almost one hundred pedestrians lined up to begin the race. There were fifty Philadelphia factories represented in the group of competitors. As he eyed them, he wondered if they had trained as hard as he had. He wondered if they had deprived themselves of sleep as much as he had. Pushed themselves as hard as he had. His mind traveled back to the plantation. It had been the perfect place to train. Before they left, he and Vincent had walked fifty miles in one day.

In the two weeks he'd been back in Philadelphia, he had walked as much as possible, but it hadn't been the same. There were no long stretches of open land. Whenever possible, he had switched from walking to running, hoping the added exertion would make up for the lesser distance. He had been able to go to a couple of parks, which gave him more freedom, but he was concerned his fitness level had diminished.

"Stop worrying," Vincent hissed. "You can't do any more than you've done. You're going to waste good energy worrying about what happens in the next twenty-four hours."

Jeremy knew he was right, but it did nothing to settle his nerves.

"What are you going to do with the money if you win?" Vincent asked.

Jeremy looked at his friend and employee sharply. That was the one thing they had never talked about. They both seemed to know the topic was off-limits. Why, he wasn't actually sure. It was simply something they never discussed. Perhaps it was because they were competing against each other. It was best not to know the motivating factor.

Vincent held up a hand. "Forget I asked."

Jeremy shook his head. "It's just something we never talked about. I don't mind you asking." He paused, making certain he was willing to disclose his motivation for pushing so hard. "It will pay off my house."

"Pay it off?" Vincent echoed.

Jeremy understood. Vincent couldn't yet afford even the smallest house in the city. When he could, the house would most likely cost a couple thousand dollars. It would be almost impossible for him to imagine buying a house like the one he and Marietta lived in. Jeremy was buying the house from Abby. It had been her home when she lived in the city. The terms were lenient, and he knew she would be patient if he ever hit hard times, but he didn't want to take any risk of losing their home. His gut tightened when he thought of the risks he had already taken.

Vincent's eyes narrowed suddenly. "You doing alright?"

Jeremy tensed, hating that he had revealed his reason for walking. "I'm fine," he insisted.

Jeremy wasn't about to reveal that while he was training for his own race, he was also betting on other pedestrian events. He knew it was stupid, but he couldn't seem to help himself. His initial wager was a lark. He had won a little money but intended to be done. Slowly, over the last year, he continued to return to the races, increasing his bets each time. Organizers made sure the races began and ended in the evenings, ensuring working men and other spectators could attend. What they earned from ticket sales and bets must be impressive.

Marietta would be appalled if she knew how much of their money he had wasted on gambling. He had lost more than he'd won, yet he kept betting, hoping he would hit it big. It never happened.

His wife was not like most women. She took an active interest in their finances and talked often about how much they had in the bank. She didn't know the truth. What he told her was their bank balance, and the actual amount, were significantly different. Lying about it was as disconcerting as the truth that would come to light at some point.

When he found out about the factory race, he had seen a way to put things to rights again. Instead of betting, he would use his athletic abilities to compete. If he won, the money would go into the bank immediately. If Marietta examined it closely, she would realize it was replacing money, not adding to an already healthy amount, but he would be less ashamed to admit what he'd done.

His betting days were over. At least...after this race.

He had placed a large bet on his winning.

He had to win.

Forcing himself to stop thinking about it, he looked at Vincent. "What about you? What are you going to do with the money if you win?"

"Start a business of my own," Vincent answered. "I've dreamed about it for years. Don't misunderstand me," he added hastily. "I enjoy working at the factory, but I want something of my own."

Jeremy understood more than Vincent could know. He and Marietta had also talked of owning a business of their own. Abby and Thomas paid him well, but he liked the idea of being his own boss. The money they had been saving was meant for that very purpose. The thought of having lost most of it by gambling made him sick to his stomach. He forced his thoughts away from his problems. "What kind of business?"

Vincent shrugged. "Only so many things a black man can do in this town. I believe education is the key to everything, so I want to start a school."

Jeremy stared at him. This was definitely something they had never talked about. "A school?"

Vincent nodded. "I'm a year away from having my college degree. There's enough money in Philadelphia to support a good school for black students."

Jeremy's thoughts flew to his friend, Octavius Catto. The founder of a school here in the city, Catto had been murdered almost two years ago, during a violent election day. Jeremy had held his dead body in his arms. "I see," he murmured. There was scarcely a day that went by when he didn't miss his friend.

"All competitors take your places."

The loud call boomed out over the mass of people assembled to watch the beginning of the race. They were here to view the walkers, but mostly they were in attendance to watch the band hired to entertain the audience. They would eat and drink while the walkers began their endless circling of the arena. Pickled eggs and roasted chestnuts were in abundance.

Jeremy smiled and waved at Marietta and the twins as he took his place. He listened as the organizer reiterated the terms of the race that he knew by heart. He was determined not to lose because of a mistake on his part. He had analyzed what it would take to succeed and decided his strategy.

If he were to walk the entire twenty-four hours, he would have to cover four point two miles an hour for the entire time. If he walked faster, he could take breaks to rest. However, if he rested and faltered toward the end and couldn't maintain the necessary pace, he would lose the race. He would walk hard and fast for as long as he could, stopping enough to drink water and have food to maintain his energy. He had practiced eating and drinking while he walked. He wouldn't stop to rest unless he absolutely had to.

The stakes were too high to not give it everything he had.

"Go!"

The order for the race to begin rang out through the building.

Jeremy strode out confidently. He had determined he would ignore everyone else around him. He would simply walk. He wasn't interested in talking to other competitors. He wasn't interested in cute gimmicks that endeared other walkers to the audience. He wasn't dressed in fancy clothes. He didn't carry a musical instrument.

He was there to walk.

He had to win.

Rose arrived in Richmond on a Thursday afternoon. She had promised the children a shopping trip before their father arrived on Saturday. Their excitement was running high as they ran into the house, eager to see what May had cooked for them.

Micah, his face grave, was waiting alongside Abby and Thomas when Rose reached the porch.

Rose took a deep breath when she saw his face, held her hand to her heart, and walked up the steps. The magnolia tree standing to the side was adorned with glorious blooms perfuming the early afternoon air. "What is it?" she asked calmly, despite her racing heart.

"It's a telegram for you, Rose," Micah said.

Rose reached for it, willing her hand to stay steady.

Abby stepped up next to her and slipped an arm around her waist while she opened the telegram.

TRAIN WAS DERAILED AND ROBBED. WE ARE FINE. TRAIN DELAYED. IN RICHMOND ON MONDAY.

"The train was derailed and robbed!" Rose exclaimed. "But everyone is alright," she added quickly.

"Thank God!" Abby said. "The girls must have been terrified."

Rose was certain Moses had been equally terrified — frightened more for the girls than himself. She could hardly wait to hear the details.

"I'm glad they be alright," Micah said. His eyes flashed with excitement. "I reckon they're gonna have quite a story to tell."

"I'm sure they are," Rose agreed. As much as she hated the two-day delay to be with Moses, she knew the children would be thrilled to spend extra time in Richmond. "Their train is arriving on Monday. We'll head back to the plantation on Tuesday."

Thomas smiled. "The children will have time to do everything they wished for, after all."

Rose rolled her eyes and groaned. "If I can keep up with them."

"Oh, please," Abby said playfully. "We may be old grandparents, but we can take the children places. It will be tremendous fun. I'll probably see things I've never seen before in Richmond."

Rose shook her head. "Whatever word I would use to describe you and Thomas, it would not be *old*."

May stepped out onto the porch. "Well, I'm old," she declared. "Too old to want the lunch I worked on all morning to be ruined by y'all standing out here on this porch gabbing."

Abby chuckled and embraced her friend. The two women had grown extraordinarily close when Abby had first moved to Richmond years earlier. "If I'm not old, neither are you."

May was the one to roll her eyes this time. "Deny it all you want, Abby, but we are two old women."

Laughing, the women entered the house behind Thomas and Micah.

Rose stood on the porch, looking west. She was relieved to know Moses and the girls were alright, but questions swarmed through her mind. *Were they really alright? Were they injured? Had they been robbed?*

Once she had exhausted thoughts of Moses and the girls, her thoughts turned to Jeremy. He had started walking last night at eight o'clock. The race would be over in seven hours. *Was he still walking? Was he winning?*

Abby's face appeared at one of the windows, her voice clear through the screen. "You can drive yourself crazy with all the questions you're asking yourself right now. You won't get any answers until Moses and the girls are home. If I were you, I would come inside and eat the delicious lunch May prepared."

Rose laughed, shook her head to cast aside the unanswerable questions, and entered the house. "For your information, I was also thinking about Jeremy. His race will be over in seven hours."

"Marietta promised to send a telegram with the results," Thomas reminded her.

Rose smiled. "Do you truly think that keeps me from thinking about it every minute until I hear from her, brother of mine?"

Thomas grinned. "I know better than that." He glanced north. "I can't imagine walking one hundred miles in twenty-four hours. Personally, I think he's out of his mind to attempt it."

"I hope he wins, though," Abby added. "He's worked so hard."

Jed popped his head in from the kitchen, obviously listening to their conversation. "So has Vincent," he stated. "I want Vincent to win."

Rose completely understood his loyalty to the man who had helped save his life in South Carolina and would always be a connection to the father he had lost. "I'll be thrilled if either one of them wins," she said warmly. "They've both worked hard."

Jed gazed at her for a moment with a satisfied expression and slipped back into the kitchen.

Rose went in search of the children. Gloria was excited to be with her new friends, but Rose was afraid being back in the city was going to be traumatic for her.

The children were playing a game of tag in the backyard. They needed to run off the unreleased energy from the long wagon ride into town.

Her heart quickened when she saw Gloria standing alone beneath the large oak tree. She looked sad and lonely.

Rose joined her and slipped an arm around her waist. "How are you, Gloria?"

Gloria shuddered. "Scared."

"I understand that."

Gloria turned her dark eyes up to stare into Rose's face. "You do?"

"I do," Rose responded. She sank down onto the ground and gently pulled Gloria down beside her. "Are you afraid the men who attacked you will find out you're back in the city?"

Gloria nodded, her face tightening with fright. "What if they do?" she whispered.

"You'll have us to protect you," Rose said firmly.

Gloria still looked frightened. "My mama couldn't protect me. What if you can't either?"

Rose knew it was a fair question. It was one she had already been asking herself. If the men who had attacked Gloria saw her again, they may be compelled to finish the job so she couldn't identify them.

A large figure appeared beside them, blocking out the sun and casting a huge shadow.

Gloria gave a cry and shrank against Rose's side.

"You don't have to be afraid, Miss Gloria."

Gloria gazed up slowly. "Mr. Spencer? Is that you?"

"It sure is." Spencer sank down on his heels and lowered himself to sit next to the little girl. "You ain't got nothing to be afraid of while you're here in town, young lady. I'm going to be with you every minute you're away from the house." He chuckled. "Don't you reckon I'm big enough to scare away anybody that might want to hurt you?"

Gloria nodded slowly. "You're right big," she acknowledged.

Spencer smiled gently. "Will you be my little girl while you're here? It would mean a lot to me if you'd let me take care of you and keep you safe."

Rose's heart swelled with gratitude. Spencer had fallen in love with Gloria during. the time they'd spent in the house. She understood. The shy little girl was easy to love.

"I reckon I could do that," Gloria replied softly. When she looked up, the fear in her eyes had been swallowed by a confident gleam. "Ain't nobody gonna mess with me if you be around."

"No, they won't," Spencer said.

Rose felt better, but she wasn't completely convinced. A group of angry, scared white men wouldn't hesitate to shoot Spencer if they believed he posed a threat to them. Had she made a grave error by bringing Gloria back to Richmond? The little girl hadn't wanted to be left behind, but perhaps Rose was putting both Gloria and Spencer in danger by her reckless decision.

"Y'all get in here!" May appeared at the back door. "If you want to eat, that is!"

The children whooped with delight and ran toward the house.

Hope stopped beside the tree and held her hand out to Gloria. "Let's go eat!"

Gloria grinned and jumped up to join her.

Spencer laughed as the two girls dashed into the house. "They've become best friends."

"They have," Rose agreed. "Hope is disappointed Gloria isn't going to be her sister, but she's adjusting."

"How is Alice?"

"Getting better," Rose told him as they walked toward the house. "Her wounds are mostly healed. She's still in her casts, so she can't walk yet, but she's outside every day and is getting stronger. All of Annie's cooking is good for her."

Spencer chuckled. "Annie's cooking is good for anyone."

Rose eyed him. "I wouldn't let your wife hear you say that."

Spencer grinned. "May is the best cook in Virginia," he said firmly. "But that don't mean Annie isn't a wonderful cook."

"Spoken like a true diplomat."

Spencer nodded. "I'm getting more involved in Richmond politics. I'm told I need to be diplomatic. It don't come naturally, but I'm learning." He stopped before they entered the house. "Isn't Jeremy racing today?"

"He is," Rose answered. Once more, her thoughts flew north. She wanted her twin to win the race, but more than that she wanted to know what had created the shadow she'd seen in his eyes when he was at the plantation. He had evaded her questions, but her instincts told her something was wrong.

Chapter Twenty-Seven

"Jeremy!"

Jeremy was relieved beyond words when he heard Marietta's voice call out to him. The twins' shrill voices rose above the roar of spectators in the rink. He wasn't sure how many thousands of people had crushed into the building in the last couple hours, but he was certain the organizers were thrilled.

A band played in the back of the building. Smells of food hung in the air.

Jeremy was only vaguely aware of any of it. At some point in the last five to six hours, he had stopped feeling or hearing much of anything. He was surprised Marietta's voice had penetrated his fog, but it was exactly what he needed.

He was not alone.

He was exhausted, aching, and hungry, but he wasn't alone.

Jeremy focused on putting one foot in front of the other. He had quit wondering about the other walkers. He didn't have the energy to care about anyone but himself. In truth, he couldn't say he cared about anything, including the outcome of the race.

All he could do was keep walking.

He had lost track of Vincent hours ago. He didn't know if his friend was in front of him or behind him, or in the rink at all.

He didn't have the energy to lift his head to see who remained in the race.

All he could do was keep walking.

Suddenly, he heard Marietta's voice close to him. Jeremy jerked his head up and saw her face smiling at him over the railing. He saw both alarm and pride in her piercing gaze. He could only imagine what he must look like after twenty-two hours.

"You're in the lead, Jeremy!"

Marietta's words cut through the fog surrounding him. *He was in the lead? He was winning?*

His moment of jubilation waned quickly. He might be in the lead, but if he didn't achieve one hundred miles, it wouldn't matter. No one would win the race. He wanted to know how many miles he had covered, but he couldn't force his lips to form the words. He had long ago given up trying to keep track of the number of times he had circled the rink.

All he could do was keep walking.

He used a slight motion to pull up his pocket watch so he could see it through blurry eyes. Two hours to go.

No one could hear the moan of pain that erupted from his mouth. Was it possible for him to keep walking for two more hours? Could he keep his feet moving?

In his wildest imaginations, he couldn't have foreseen how difficult it was to walk for twenty-four hours. As he had planned, he hadn't stopped to rest. He'd slowed enough to grab food and water but kept walking.

His plan to maintain a certain pace for the required hours had dissipated in a mist of weariness. He was moving, but he had no idea how fast he was going or if he was even close to reaching the goal of one hundred miles.

His body craved one thing. Sleep. He knew if he stopped that he would probably fall asleep where he stood. He was somewhat surprised he hadn't fallen asleep while he was walking.

"You can do it, Daddy!"

"Go, Daddy, go!"

Jeremy felt a spurt of energy when he heard the twins cheering. The thought of his gambling losses had spurred him on for the first eighteen hours. After that, he no longer cared. The twins' voices reminded him he had something bigger to walk for. His family.

Somewhere during the long hours, he had decided he would tell Marietta the truth. No matter if he won or lost, he would be honest with her. If he lost, he would work harder to recoup the money he had gambled away, and he would never gamble again.

At one point, once he had come to that decision, he had almost stopped. What did it matter?

He had looked up–long enough to see other walkers, their faces set in determination, circling the rink. At that moment, it became a point of pride. He was an athlete. He had started this race to finish. To win.

He didn't know if he was going to win, but he was most certainly going to finish.

All he could do was keep walking.

"You can do it, Daddy!"

"Go, Daddy, go!"

Jeremy raised his hand slightly and managed to shape his lifeless lips into a resemblance of a smile.

"I believe in you, Jeremy!"

Marietta's voice, more than any other, was what Jeremy needed to keep going. To his surprise, his legs felt stronger, and he started walking a little faster.

One hour to go.

Jeremy fought the fatigue encasing his legs in bands of steel. Every step was taken through what felt like thick mud. He could feel his legs tremble. He was no longer certain he was walking straight.

He set his eyes on the rink floor in front of him and kept walking — or at least moving. He was no longer sure he was moving fast enough to call it walking.

All he could do was keep moving.

He fought to formulate thoughts in his head. He thought about Marietta. About the twins. About playing baseball. He thought about Octavius Catto. About the factory. About gambling.

He thought about everything except the pain wracking his body.

Suddenly, Marietta was there beside him, leaning far out over the rink wall. She thrust a glass of water at him. "Drink this, Jeremy."

Her tender voice cut through the darkness threatening to close in around him. He reached for the water, willing his hand to grasp the glass, put it to his lips, and drank. The cool liquid eased down his throat. How long had it been since he stopped to eat or drink? He no longer knew.

All he could do was keep moving.

Walk.

Move.

Walk.

Move.

"We have a winner!"

The booming voice of the announcer somehow cut through the yells and cheers from the sidelines. "We have a new Centurion!"

The crowd fell silent, waiting for the results.

Jeremy stumbled to a stop. *Who had won?* He peered around the rink, trying to identify who was being cheered as the winner. Two hours earlier, Marietta had told him he was in the lead, but he could have been surpassed.

"Jeremy Anthony is our new Centurion," the voice called. "He has walked one hundred miles in twenty-three hours and twenty minutes!"

Jeremy stared around him, not certain of what he had heard. Perhaps he had heard his name in a delirium.

"You won, Daddy!"

"You won!"

Somehow, Marcus and Sarah's voices sounded above the cacophony of the wild cheering that had erupted throughout the roller rink.

Jeremy shook his head. He'd actually *won*?

The announcer made his way down to his side. "Congratulations, Mr. Anthony!"

Jeremy blinked his eyes to get rid of his blurry vision. "I won?"

"You won," the announcer assured him.

The man reached over and raised Jeremy's right arm high in the air. "Ladies and gentlemen, Jeremy Anthony has won ten thousand dollars!"

The cheering erupted again. Jeremy was vaguely aware of men, eager to claim their winnings, pushing their way toward the betting counter. Others stomped their feet on the wooden floor and cheered. He was surprised the noise didn't lift the roof off the roller rink.

"You did it, Jeremy!"

Marietta's voice broke through again. He looked over and saw the broad smile on her beautiful face. The fatigue lifted enough for him to smile back. Suddenly, he could feel his legs again. He could think again.

He had won!

Only then did he think of Vincent. He looked around the rink, searching for his friend. It took a few moments, but he finally spotted him seated on the ground, his head hanging between his knees, the picture of exhaustion and despair.

Jeremy shook the announcer's hand, thanked him again, and walked slowly to Vincent.

Vincent looked up when he saw Jeremy's feet appear in front of him. "Congratulations," he croaked.

Jeremy, ignoring the pain in his legs, squatted in front of his friend. "Thank you," he said quietly. "I couldn't have done this without you training with me."

Vincent shrugged. "You earned your victory, Jeremy."

Jeremy shook his head. "I think *we* earned it, Vincent." He pulled a piece of paper from his pocket. "I placed the last bet of my life on this race." He opened Vincent's hand and put the piece of paper into it. "I'd like you to claim the winnings."

"I didn't win the race," Vincent protested.

It was Jeremy's turn to shrug. "You helped me win, my friend. I want you to have your new business. Go claim your winnings."

Vincent stared up at him. "My new business? How much did you bet on you winning the race?"

Jeremy smiled. "Enough. Go claim your winnings."

His gambling days were over.

He forced himself to his feet, aware Marietta and the twins were coming toward him.

Marietta wrapped her arms around him and squeezed him tightly. "Congratulations, honey! I thought your training was ridiculous," she said sheepishly. "But you did it! You actually won ten thousand dollars!"

Jeremy grinned as the twins wrapped their arms around his legs. He allowed himself to feel the triumph rushing through him. He'd never done anything as difficult in his life, but it had been worth it.

A man standing next to the edge of the rink yelled over to him. "Will you race again, Mr. Anthony?"

Jeremy laughed and shook his head. Once was enough. He had no intention of becoming a professional walker.

Marietta gazed at him proudly. "Let's get you home to eat. You've earned it."

"Sleep," Jeremy mumbled. "All I want to do is sleep. I'll eat after I sleep." Saying the words made him realize anew how exhausted he was.

Rose had kept herself busy with the children to distract herself from the reality that it was Saturday, and Moses wasn't home. The last three months had been interminably long, but to have been so close to feeling his arms around her, only to have it snatched away, had been the hardest to bear. She knew it was only two extra days, but they would feel the longest.

She listened and smiled as the children talked nonstop about the fun they'd had that day. The wagon was going to be filled with new clothing, books, and tools.

Minnie had bought a new cookbook for Annie. She was excited to experiment in the kitchen with her.

Russell had bought new tools for his workshop, talking endlessly about the new projects he was going to create with his daddy.

Bridget had climbed into Thomas' arms when she was too tired to walk anymore, exclaiming over each exciting new thing she saw.

Jed, after being forced to try on new clothes, had focused on new candies to taste from the confectionery store. He was proud of the large bag he had filled.

John had claimed he didn't need or want anything, but in the end, he bought new baseball gloves, a bat, and balls so everyone could play.

Rose knew he had missed his daddy the most. All the children longed for him to return, but Moses and John shared a special bond. She had taken care of buying new clothes for her son, who was growing like a weed. At ten, he was already wearing men's clothing. Just as with Felicia, she had to constantly remind herself he was much younger than he seemed.

Gloria had accepted new clothes, but she hadn't been satisfied until she bought her mama three new dresses and books they could read together. She had made great strides in learning to read. Hope had helped her pick out the books.

Rose was also teaching Alice to read, spending at least an hour with her each day. The woman had progressed from embarrassed shame about her inability to read, to great pride in reading the simple books Rose brought her. No one had mentioned her working in the kitchen with Annie when she was better, but she and Annie spent time every day talking about new recipes and the secrets to

Annie's cooking. The two women were forming a fast friendship.

When the talking had died down and the children were absorbed in their bowls of blackberry cobbler, Spencer turned to Thomas. "What can you tell me about the tobacco tax?"

Thomas scowled. "I can tell you it's ridiculous. It's as if the government is trying to restore their coffers after the war almost entirely from taxing southern tobacco. I thought it would ease up after a few years, but they show no inclination of giving us a break."

Spencer nodded. "There are a lot of men hurting in Richmond. They're closing lots of the tobacco factories because there ain't as much tobacco coming in. Men can't feed their families because they don't have jobs." He looked at Thomas closely. "Are you having trouble on the plantation?"

Thomas sighed. "Not yet. But if things don't change, there won't be a tobacco farmer in the area that will be able to make it. We're alright because we saved money during the good years, but if there's trouble with the economy, we'll feel it."

"White folks here in Richmond believe Virginia is being taxed so much because they're being punished for slavery," Spencer added.

Thomas listened closely. "I understand how they feel, but I don't believe that's the case. White and black tobacco farmers are being taxed the same."

"Except most of the black farmers can't afford taxes like that," Spencer pointed out. "The taxes are putting them right out of business. That's the reason there's not as much tobacco coming in. They can't afford the taxes, so they stopped growing it."

"That's true," Thomas said. "I hate what is happening."

"It's just one thing that is bad," Spencer continued. "The Republican GOP is trying to make it impossible for a black man to have any say in this city at all. They got real nervous when we organized so well after the war. I reckon they thought we were too dumb to do it. While we was celebrating our new political rights and power, they been coming up with ways to *contain* us," he said bitterly. "That's the word they used."

Rose listened closely. She freely admitted there were times when the real world seemed far away. Her life was on the plantation, but she knew she needed to understand what was going on in Virginia and in the country. When the Virginia Board of Education had passed laws saying she couldn't have both black and white students in her school, it had come as a complete shock. They had dealt with it and found ways to integrate their students, but she realized it was merely one sign of how the state was trying to diminish black rights.

"The city council did some fancy gerrymandering here in the city. When they was done, there were six districts. One of them, Jackson Ward, is down where I used to live. It's where most of the black folks live. The other five have mostly white folks. They're aiming to make sure we don't got much power." Spencer scowled. "Even the GOP ain't doing much to help us. We started out thinking they was gonna get us the rights we deserve, but that ain't happening. They see us as nothing but brainless workers who they gonna use to get what they want."

Rose understood Spencer's passion. She also realized that when he was worked up about something, he reverted back to what he called his *slave speak*. He had worked hard over the years to improve his speaking so that he would be viewed as the intelligent man he was, but it was easy for him to slip back into what he had known most of his life.

"We's getting real tired of voting for white men only. We be told to wait over and over. They tell us our time will come, but ain't none of us see it coming." Spencer's eyes flashed with frustration.

"There are blacks being voted into office," Rose protested. "It may not be happening here, but it is in other places."

"Some," Spencer agreed. "But they's putting things into place to make sure it don't happen no more. I don't reckon most of those men will be in office by the next election. Besides that," he continued, "the police be harassing us real bad. The wife of a friend of mine was beat up bad by the police. She weren't doing nothing but walking home."

Rose watched Thomas, dismayed when he didn't refute what Spencer was saying. She knew he and Abby were deeply involved in national politics. She had a sudden urge to snatch up the children and return to the plantation where she knew they were safe.

"That's terrible!" Abby exclaimed.

"It's just one example," Spencer replied. "The police got it out for us. We sent up three men to the city council, but they didn't do nothing but ignore us. It's like we ain't got no power anymore. Them white men in the GOP used us to get where they are, and now they be turning their backs."

Thomas eyed him sympathetically. "It didn't help when the Conservative Party swept the elections in Virginia a year and a half ago."

Spencer grunted. "Sure hard to live in a city controlled by Democrats. They started a war they couldn't win, and now they be back in control again." He shook his head. "I can't even understand how that happened."

"I don't understand why we have to talk about politics," Russell stated, wiping the last of the blackberry cobbler from his lips. "We've had a fun day. Why ruin it with politics?"

"Yeah," Jed added. "Politics is boring." He took one final bite of his cobbler. "I'd rather go outside and play."

Thomas smiled, but his tone was serious. "Do you know you can go outside and play *because* of politics, Jed?"

Jed cocked his head. "What are you talking about?"

"Many people think politics is boring," Thomas answered. "I happen to believe politics is an essential part of our everyday lives. Because of that, it can never be boring."

"And politics influences everything in our world," Abby added. "Most people think politics is about who runs the country or who gets elected president."

"Isn't it?" Russell demanded.

"Yes," Abby conceded. "It's so much more than that, though. It's really about how power and influence are used to shape our lives."

"Why can't people run their own lives?" Russell asked. "It seems like things would be a whole lot better if people didn't think they could control how others live."

Rose was impressed with the boy's observation. "I agree with you, Russell. Unfortunately, it doesn't work that way."

"Why not?" Minnie asked.

Thomas answered her question with another question. "You know that Grandma and I spend a lot of time in the library writing letters to people around the country?"

Minnie nodded. "Of course. Mama says you're doing important work."

"We think so," Thomas replied. "Many people believe politics is mostly about who gets elected in whatever election is coming up next. It's much more than that. Your Grandma and I believe politics is a way of making decisions about how power is used."

Minnie nodded thoughtfully but shook her head almost immediately. "I don't know what you mean."

"And why do I get to play outside because of politics?" Jed asked again, clearly confused.

Rose decided to step in on this question. "Your daddy used to be a slave, Jed, right?" She waited for his nod before she continued. "I was a slave until I was nineteen. So was Moses."

Jed nodded. "I think I knew that. You were a slave on Cromwell?"

"Yes," Rose replied.

"I was a slave too," Spencer said somberly. "For a whole lot longer than your mama and daddy."

"And me and Micah were slaves for longer than anyone," May added. "We were born slaves. We weren't free until we were fifty years old."

"What's that got to do with me being able to play?" Jed remained befuddled.

"Because politics made you free, Jed," Abby said gently. "Without politics, you would be working the fields somewhere for whomever owned you."

"Playing ain't something you feel like doing after you been working out in the hot sun all day," Spencer said.

"You for sure wouldn't be riding around the plantation with your daddy," Thomas added. "And he wouldn't be part owner of Cromwell."

John looked at Rose. "You've told me you used to be a slave, but I'm beginning to understand what that means."

Rose was glad her son didn't have a comprehension of slavery, but it was important he understood where he came from. The workers on Cromwell were black, but they were paid well and treated fairly. It was clear she needed to teach more about slavery in school. Her students could never become complacent about the lives their families had lived. If *their* children were so unaware of how their families had lived, what would it be like in a hundred years? Two hundred years? They needed to know the price paid for their freedom.

Jed's expression had grown serious. "How did politics make me free?"

Thomas looked at Abby. "You should be the one to answer that, dear. You did more than any of us here to make it happen."

Abby smiled at him lovingly. "From the beginnings of slavery in the United States, there were people who believed it was wrong, Jed. Most of the states in the North abolished slavery very early, but the Southern states believed slavery was necessary to run their large plantations and farms. They got used to not having to pay people to work for them."

"My daddy told me once that his daddy was also a slave," Jed said soberly. "He was brought over by a big boat from Africa."

"It goes back a lot of generations," Abby said sadly. "The slave trade started in Africa. Unfortunately, slaves were taken all over the world, not merely to the United States. It's true, though, that America has had more slaves than any other country."

Jed shook his head. "Why didn't people do their own work? Or pay to have it done? Like on Cromwell?"

Thomas smiled. "That's a very good question, Jed. I wish it had been done that way."

"There were a lot of people who believed it should be done that way," Abby said. "Almost fifty years ago, people started fighting for the slaves to be freed."

John looked at Rose. "Those were the abolitionists. Right, Mama?"

"That's right," Rose answered. "Abby was a very active abolitionist. She helped a lot of slaves gain freedom." She was thrilled the children were getting a lesson in politics in the best way possible. It wasn't simply something to learn in school; it was something that had impacted people they knew and cared about.

"If abolitionists started fighting to free the slaves fifty years ago, why did it take so long?" Minnie asked.

"Good question," Abby responded. "Do you remember when your grandpa said that he and I believe politics is a way of making decisions about how power is used?"

Minnie nodded.

"Well, one group can't make decisions about how every person acts, as much as we want to. The South didn't want to give up their slaves because it would change how much money they made. It takes time to change people's minds about how they use their power."

"How did the abolitionists change the slave owners' minds?" Jed asked.

"They didn't," Spencer replied. "That's why there was a big war. The South decided they wanted their slaves more than they wanted to be part of the United States, so they chose to leave. Only, the North wasn't going to let them leave, so they fought the war over it. The war started the year you were born."

Rose smiled to herself. The answer was incredibly simplistic, but it was also a very succinct description of what had happened.

Russell had looked thoughtful during the entire conversation. "Is that why blacks are treated so badly now? Politics didn't change how people think down here. When the North won the war, it just forced them to do something they didn't want to do. Now they're trying to take their power back so they can run things the way they want to."

Rose understood the thunderstruck expression on every adult face in the room.

"That's exactly right," Thomas answered. "You've taken a very complex situation and explained it very clearly. There are, however, a lot of politicians who believe blacks should be treated equally and fairly."

Russell stared at him. "That may be, but Daddy told me more about what happened in Louisiana, Grandpa. It doesn't seem like the Northern politicians have any more power now than they did before the war. There are a lot of terrible things happening to blacks." He shook his head. "What's it going to take to change how people use their power?"

Rose sighed. "That's an excellent question, Russell. It's one that people all over the country are trying to figure out the answer to. Even though it doesn't seem like it, there are many people in the South who believe blacks should be treated equally."

Russell looked dubious.

"Like Grandpa and me," Abby told him. "And your daddy and mama."

"And Matthew and Janie," Rose added. "Harold and Susan."

"And the white Bregdan Women," Abby said. "They're committed to making things better for all the black women who have become their friends."

"And you," Thomas said. "You, and Minnie, and Frances. You three will play a part in changing how people think, and how they use their power."

"That's true," Russell conceded, but he wasn't done with his questions. "Why is it so hard?"

"People don't like to change," Abby said with a sigh. "You and I have talked before about how much I love history. I don't care about events and dates as much as I care about the *people* involved. In my opinion, history is the study of human nature. *Why* do people do what they do?"

"Good question," Russell muttered. "It's hard to understand."

Rose wondered if he was thinking of the difficult times he had experienced living under the bridge when he'd lost all his family, and been forced to fend for himself.

"People act from fear, Russell," Abby continued. "The South opposed ending slavery because they were afraid their prosperous lifestyles would disappear if they let the slaves go. Men fight against women voting because they're afraid they'll lose their power over them. I don't believe the majority of white people hate black people. They've been taught to be afraid that giving black people equality will somehow diminish their own rights and freedoms."

"That's stupid," Jed said bluntly. "And I don't think you're right. The KKK hates people. They killed my mama and daddy, and they tried to kill Vincent."

"And they killed my mama's first husband," Minnie added.

"And they killed all those people down in Colfax," Russell said.

Rose was impressed with the children's ability to challenge what they didn't believe. Their freedom to do so was another example of how much the country was changing. When she was a child, she could never have questioned what a white person did or said.

"That's true," Abby said gently. "I happen to believe the KKK is the best example of what I'm saying. Yes, I certainly think there are some people that just hate, but I don't believe they were born hating. They were *taught* to hate. In the case of the KKK, when the South lost the war, the men who started the Klan had lost everything in a war they were either convinced they would win easily or didn't understand why they were fighting in the first place. When they lost, they didn't know how to deal with it. They were afraid and angry and needed a target. They saw the blacks as an easy target."

"My daddy wasn't an easy target!" Jed burst out. "He tried to fight back! He tried to save my mama!"

Rose stood and went to her son, pulling him into her arms. She understood the pain and anger etched into his face.

"I know he did," Abby said soothingly. "What happened to your parents was so horribly wrong, Jed. I am not for one second condoning what the KKK did to anyone. I'm simply saying they are afraid and angry. Their anger should actually be aimed at the government. It was politicians that kept slavery alive in this country. It was politicians that allowed the war to happen. Politicians have made Reconstruction even more difficult. Politicians have made decisions that have resulted in too many people dying."

"Why isn't the KKK mad at *them*?" Minnie cried.

"I'm sure they are," Abby replied. "They feel powerless to change things, though. The only way they know how to lash out is to brutalize people they feel power over."

"Us," John said flatly. "Black people."

Rose wished she could shield her children from the reality of this conversation, they needed to know the truth of the world they lived in.

"Yes," Abby said sadly.

Thomas held up his hand. "I read a story I found fascinating. If you put one hundred black ants, and one hundred red ants in a jar, nothing will happen. They'll all be in the jar together, without hurting each other.

However, if you shake the jar hard, the ants will start killing each other. They see the jar shaking as a threat to their survival. The red ants will consider the black ants their enemies because they're different. The black ants will consider the red ants their enemies."

The children listened closely.

Thomas continued the story. "The real enemy is the one who shakes the jar, but the ants have no way of knowing that. They have no way of attacking the person who shook the jar. The same thing happens in human society. The moral of the story is that before we attack each other, we should think about who is shaking the jar."

"Politicians shook the jar of this country," John said slowly. "But they're safe because they aren't inside the jar where all the killing is happening."

"That about sums it up," Thomas said. "There are some politicians who are paying the price of fighting for black equality, but they are certainly the minority. Willie

Calhoun is a perfect example. Trying to help him was the reason Matthew and Anthony went to Louisiana. Calhoun is a good man."

"What will it take to change things?" Russell asked. "Talking about the problem is alright, but fixing it is the only answer."

Rose understood how he thought. Russell clearly had an engineer's mind. He viewed things as a problem to be fixed. He created things in his workshop that were a solution to a problem or could make life better.

Abby took a deep breath. "People with enough courage to keep demanding change until it happens. People with enough conviction to refuse to give in when things get hard." She paused. "Abolitionists started fighting to free the slaves in 1820. It took forty years for that to happen. By making people understand how wrong slavery was, the politicians finally realized they had to do something. Because the North was demanding the end to slavery, the South decided to secede. Their choice started a war that lasted four years." She took a deep breath. "I hate that so many died in a senseless war, but I'm glad it culminated in the end of slavery."

"Freedom ain't all we wanted it to be, though," Spencer said. "We thought when we got freedom that we would be real Americans. We thought we could do all the things we dreamed about doing while we was standing out in fields working and getting beaten." He shook his head. "It ain't that way."

"Yet," Rose said firmly, wanting to make sure her children held onto hope. "It isn't that way *yet*."

"Yep," Spencer agreed. "You're right, Rose. Things aren't so good right now, but we're not giving in and walking away. We're gonna fight. We're gonna keep right on fighting until things change. We ain't slaves anymore. White people might not want us to be free, but they can't take that away from us."

Rose bit her lip to keep from saying what she was thinking. Emancipation had supposedly given freedom to slaves, but her people were being enslaved by the prison system in the South, and they were being terrified and controlled by white supremacist groups. Blacks might be walking toward freedom, but they were far from achieving it.

"How are you fighting things?" John asked Spencer.

Spencer grinned. "I figure on getting more involved in politics. I used to be like you kids. I thought politics was stupid. *Boring.* That was before I realized it was the only way I could help change things. I'm learning all I can and getting involved every way I can."

"Do you like it?" Russell asked keenly.

Spencer regarded him. "Like it? Nope. Can't say I do. I get real frustrated because we seem to be going backward more than we're going forward. But I don't have to like it. I just got to get to the end of each day and know I fought hard to be part of the solution, not just part of the problem." He looked around the table at the children. "I wasn't ever much of anything. That is, until Carrie started treating me like a real human being during the war. She made me think I could be somebody."

"You are an incredible man," May said. "You're the best man I know."

"I appreciate that," Spencer said, a glow of love shining brightly in his eyes. "But you got to say that because you're my wife. With the rest of the world, it's only my actions that will tell what kind of man I am. When my time is done, I want folks to say I did everything I could to make sure black folks be treated right."

Rose smiled. "I think Carrie will say that you treated *all* people right."

Spencer's expression softened. "Yep. That be right." He looked around the table at the children again. "I want folks to say I treated *everybody* right."

Chapter Twenty-Eight

Jeremy slept for fourteen hours straight. When he woke up, Marietta fed him all the food he could stand to eat. When his stomach was full enough to burst, he fell asleep again. When he woke six hours later, he could finally think clearly.

"What time is it?" he mumbled when he woke in the dark.

Marietta's voice was sleepy but amused. "Two in the morning. I wondered if you would sleep through the night. Are you hungry?"

Jeremy shook his head before he realized she couldn't see him in the dark. "No." He took a deep breath, the decisions he had made while walking, front and center in his mind. "I'd like to talk, though. If you can," he added hastily. "I know it's the middle of the night."

"You sound serious," Marietta said.

"I am," Jeremy replied. He heard the scratch of a match and watched while Marietta lit the lantern in their bedroom.

Marietta's concerned blue eyes regarded him steadily as she settled back into the bed, her body propped against the headboard. "What's wrong, Jeremy?" She hesitated. "Are you finally going to tell me what's been bothering you for the last several months?"

Jeremy sucked in his breath. "You knew?"

"Knew that something was wrong? Of course. What it is? I have no idea. I kept hoping you would tell me." Her expression grew tender. "I'm glad you finally can. I'm your wife. Whatever it is, we'll figure it out."

Jeremy shook his head. "You might not feel the same way when you learn what I've been hiding."

Marietta's tender expression didn't change. "Try me."

Jeremy suddenly wished she would turn off the lantern. He would rather confess to his gambling in the dark. He didn't want to see the disappointed expression on her face, nor the hurt he knew would shine from her eyes. "I've been stupid," he finally said.

Marietta took his hand but remained silent.

Slowly, Jeremy told her everything. The beginning of the gambling. How bad it had gotten. How he felt totally out of control. How he had diminished their bank account without her knowing.

He watched a myriad of expressions cross her face. He pushed on, telling her why he decided to compete in the race. That in his desperation, he had bet on himself to win, and given the winnings to Vincent.

"I'm putting the money I won into the bank," Jeremy finished. "You have my word I will never gamble again. I'm sorry beyond words that I spent our money and hid what I was doing from you."

"How much money did you take from the bank?" Marietta asked quietly.

Jeremy wanted to make up a number, but he was done lying to his wife. Besides, she would discover the truth anyway. He hated that he would probably lie if he could get away with it. "Three thousand dollars," he replied.

Marietta's eyes widened. "You gambled away three thousand dollars?"

"Yes," Jeremy admitted. He wished he could say something that would justify his actions, but he knew there were no valid excuses.

"And you're putting the entire ten thousand into the bank?"

"Yes," Jeremy promised again. "Every penny."

Marietta cocked her head. "How much did Vincent win with your ticket?"

Jeremy looked away, wondering if she was upset that he had given his winnings to Vincent. "Nine thousand dollars."

"You would have won nine thousand dollars?" Marietta asked with a gasp.

"Yes." Jeremy suspected he should add something, but he didn't know what else to say. Simple answers seemed the best option at the moment.

Silence fell in the bedroom. The only sound was the occasional noise of a horse and carriage going down the cobblestone road.

"So, we're seven thousand dollars richer," Marietta said.

It was impossible for Jeremy to ascertain her emotions in the short statement. "Yes."

"Then we're better off than when we started," Marietta stated.

Jeremy stared at her. "You're not furious with me?"

"I was when you first started talking," Marietta admitted. "I'm glad you told me before I discovered it on my own. I appreciate you finally being honest. I also appreciate that you're sorry, and I'm grateful you'll never gamble again."

Jeremy understood from the stern gleam in her eye that he would not get off so easily if he were to lapse from his promise. "You have my word," he said.

Marietta gazed at him for a long moment. "I believe you, Jeremy." Her expression softened. "I have made many mistakes in my life. They didn't cost us three thousand dollars, but a mistake is a mistake. If I want you to forgive me for mistakes I will make in the future, I must forgive you for your gambling."

"Thank you," Jeremy said, hardly able to believe she wasn't yelling at him or walking out the door. "I know how stupid it was."

"Good," Marietta replied. "Now, what was it like to walk for twenty-four hours?"

Jeremy stared at her. He realized she was telling him the subject was closed. She had forgiven him and was ready to put it behind them. It might come up again in the future, but he was going to accept the gift she was offering him now. "Something I never want to repeat," Jeremy stated.

"But you won ten thousand dollars," Marietta protested. "If you won a few more races, we could do anything we wanted."

Jeremy was relieved to see the playful glint in her eyes. He had already thought of that, but he never wanted to push his body that hard again. "I tell you what, wife of mine," he said slowly, drawing out the suspense as he paused. "If you walk it with me, I'll do it again."

Marietta laughed. "Not a chance," she retorted. The playful look disappeared behind an expression of tender caring. "I almost cried when I saw you near the end of the race. I scarcely recognized you. There's not a thing we need that would make it worth you repeating one hundred miles in twenty-four hours."

"I'm glad you feel that way," Jeremy replied. "There's a lot we can do with ten thousand dollars, though."

"They never thought they would have to pay it out, you know," Marietta told him.

"What?" Jeremy was confused by her statement. "What are you talking about?"

"The factory owners association never thought they would actually have to give that money to someone," Marietta revealed. "I heard a group of men talking when I got there a few hours before the end of the race. There were no professional walkers in the race, so they didn't think anyone would be able to actually walk one hundred miles. They were planning on keeping the money themselves."

Jeremy scowled. "I'm not surprised they would do that." Then he grinned. "I'm thrilled I destroyed their plan!"

"Me too," Marietta said heartily. "You may have been stupid about the gambling, but you were brilliant with how you trained for the race."

Jeremy smiled his gratitude and asked another question. "How did Vincent do?"

"He was in second place," Marietta answered. "You only beat him by three laps." She paused. "I hate gambling, but I'm glad you made the final bet that gave Vincent nine thousand dollars. He's a good man."

Jeremy couldn't have agreed more. "He's going to start a school for black children," he revealed. "He told me about it right before the race started." He knew Marietta, who had been a schoolteacher for black children in Richmond when they met, would be thrilled.

"That's wonderful!" Marietta said. She looked at him more closely. "You look tired again."

Jeremy, now that he had unloaded the burden he'd been hiding for months, felt the weight of fatigue pressing down on him again. "I think I could sleep more," he admitted.

Minutes later, Marietta snuggled into his side, Jeremy was sound asleep.

Carrie ran a soft brush over Granite's velvety coat. He sighed and closed his eyes with pleasure. As she brushed him, she hummed quietly. She missed the children and the sound of their laughter, but the plantation was different when it was quiet. It felt even more like a haven of peace.

Anthony was in Russell's workshop, preparing a surprise for him. Not even she knew what he was doing.

A flock of yellow finches had settled in a nearby tree. Their song was a background orchestra to the peace. It was too early for the treefrogs and crickets, so there was nothing to compete with their glorious song. The occasional nicker or whinny provided unexpected percussion.

Carrie smiled as she brought even more of a gleam to Granite's coat. Her father had sent a rider to alert them to the train robbery, so they wouldn't be alarmed by the delay. She was concerned about Moses and the girls, but the telegram had stated everyone was fine. Until she had a reason to think otherwise, she would believe what Moses had said.

Much to her delight, there had been an additional telegram. Hobbs was leaving Portland on August fourth. He was expecting to arrive in Richmond on the twelfth. He'd come to the plantation from there.

Susan strode into the barn, her swollen belly leading the way. "It's so quiet."

"Isn't it wonderful?" Carrie said with a grin.

Susan's pregnancy was going smoothly. Her baby was due in about a month. There had been no indication of trouble. Though the others had taken over the heavy duties, Susan came to the barn every day. She positively glowed with vitality and health.

Susan stroked Granite's muzzle. He sighed and pushed his head into her hand. "This is one spoiled horse."

Carrie shook her head. "He is most certainly not spoiled. He is well loved."

Susan grinned. "Everyone knows you spoil Granite."

Carrie tossed her head. "Everyone is simply jealous." She leaned forward and kissed Granite's neck. "Let them be jealous if they want to, boy." She stared at Susan. "Neither of us cares what anyone thinks."

Susan laughed. "Oh, we figured that out eons ago."

Carrie unsnapped Granite's lead line from the wall and led him out of the barn. "My well-loved horse and I are going for a walk," she retorted.

Susan's laughter followed her a long distance from the barn.

Felicia sat back with a sigh and pulled her shoulders up close to her ears to release the strain in her neck.

"Finished?" Moses asked.

"Yes." Felicia felt a surge of satisfaction. A glance at a nearby clock told her they were less than thirty minutes from Richmond. She could hardly wait to see everyone and be home again, but she'd wanted to finish the poem that had been rolling around in her head ever since they left San Francisco.

Frances entered the sleeper car with a smile. "We're almost home!"

Felicia nodded. She had missed home, but Frances had been like a fish out of water in San Francisco. Her friend had made the most of her time and explored the city for hours, but she knew Frances had missed the plantation every minute they'd been gone. "How are you going to handle being in Boston?" she asked.

Frances sank down into a chair, a thoughtful expression on her face. "I'll have a purpose in Boston," she replied. "Don't take this the wrong way, but I had no purpose in San Francisco. You were there to learn about business with Mrs. Pleasant, which kept you absorbed the entire time. I went along because I wanted to cross the country and experience something I never had. After our second week in San Francisco, I'd done that."

Felicia stared at her. "We've been gone for more than three months."

Frances met her gaze. "I know," she said quietly. "For the last two and a half months, I've felt like I didn't have a purpose. I did the best I could," she added hastily. "I read many books, but I couldn't find any medical books in the city that deserved to be read. What I found was nothing more than quackery nonsense. I learned about other things instead."

"Like the pitiful state of medical education in the country," Felicia reminded her.

Frances grinned. "Exactly. For that alone, I'm grateful I took the trip. Without so much spare time, I'm not certain I would have done enough research to discover the truth. I could have wasted a lot of time in Philadelphia before I realized I didn't want to be there."

"You've seen things that most people could only dream of seeing," Moses said.

"I will always be grateful," Frances replied. "Seeing America was fascinating. The West is beautiful but..." Her voice trailed away.

"But?" Moses asked.

"It's not *my* kind of beautiful," Frances admitted. "The towering mountains and the endless miles of open plains are lovely, but I prefer thick forests, endless green fields, and lakes and rivers everywhere. I need to be in a world that's green, not mostly brown."

Felicia understood. "I agree. The entire country has its own kind of beauty, but I need the type of beauty only the east coast can offer, too."

Moses cocked his head. "The middle of the country is lush and green, girls."

"It is," Frances agreed, "but it doesn't have the ocean." Her eyes gleamed. "I loved being in Boston when I was there with Mama. My favorite part was the wharves on the ocean. One day we rode out to where there were waves crashing onto a beach. I'll never forget that." She paused. "Somehow it made me feel bigger inside, but also smaller. I don't know how to describe it, but I want more of it."

Felicia grinned. "You'll take me there when we get to Boston?"

"Of course I will," Frances answered. "We're going to have many wonderful adventures."

Moses cleared his throat. "I've never been the first, you know."

Felicia raised a brow at the rapid shift in the conversation. "The first at what, Daddy? I don't know what you're talking about."

"The first person to read one of your poems. Your mama is usually the one to show it to me after she reads it." Moses paused. "It seems to me that taking you across the country for three months entitles me to be the first, for once?"

Felicia grinned. "I suppose you have a point." She'd never really thought about it, but he was right. She always shared the poems with her mama first. This one, especially, should be read by her daddy first. It was his willingness to take her on this trip that had led to her understanding of what it meant to walk toward freedom.

Moses held out his hand. "We have twenty minutes before we arrive in Richmond. Hand it over, please."

Felicia laughed at his determined expression and handed him the sheets of paper she'd been working on since they'd gotten on their replacement train three days ago. There were parts she knew almost by heart.

where do I belong? me & my black skin

the blackness of my skin mimics the vacuum of my mind —
a void exists as my eyes gaze over my surroundings and
questions haunt my sleep,
questions taunt my waking.

where does my black skin belong?
where do I belong? me & my black skin . . .

my journey is not unique for all colors of skin desire to live

my journey is not alone for all colors of skin dream of home
my journey is not solo for all colors of skin deserve peace
and
my journey is not exceptional for all skin nightmares from the savagery of white man.

my black skin is yellow Chinese skin — hanging dead from the eaves by white man's hand
my black skin is white Irish skin smoldering — smoked by white man's fire
my black skin is brown Indian scalp skin dripping blood — oozing by white man's knife
my black skin is black Negro skin blotched and blotted — glass lashed from white man's whip

my black, yellow, white, brown skin is skin ravaged in violent brutality — raped by white mans greed

my black, yellow, white, brown skin is skin hated by white man fear

my black, yellow, white, brown skin is skin illiterate to white man equality

my black, yellow, white, brown skin is skin impoverished to white man law.

today —
the blackness of my skin is all skin. tomorrow —
the blackness of my skin is all skin.

questions haunt my sleep — questions taunt my waking.

how does my black mind shine in the whitewashed shadow land?
how does my black mind burnish white man command?
how does my black mind flash affluence to white man's control?

how does my black mind afford freedom?
freedom to desire, freedom to dream, freedom to deserve?
how does my black, yellow, white, brown body dare emancipation o'er white man's nightmare?

how does my black, yellow, white, brown body, skin, mind live in freedom?
oh yes, I ask once again —
how does my black, yellow, white, brown body, skin, mind live in freedom?

the black void of my skin mimics the vacuum of my mind —
and yet, yet, yet, yet
drifting & sifting within the arcane abyss of my spirit — I hear.
the arcane abyss of my spirit encompasses fierce perceptive voices
voices of my black, yellow, white, brown skinned ancestors

my ancestors declare:
their black, yellow, white, brown blood drips through my veins
their black, yellow, white, brown thought dwells in my brain
their black, yellow, white, brown strength rises in my hands
their black, yellow, white, brown voice lays in my throat
their black, yellow, white, brown heart beats in my chest
their black, yellow, white, brown courage walks within my feet.

black, yellow, white, brown in body
black, yellow, white, brown in skin
black, yellow, white, brown in mind
black, yellow, white, brown, black ancestors.

the ancestors blood drips through my veins: they usher my autonomy
the ancestors thought dwells in my brain: they escort my resolutions
the ancestors strength rises in my hands: they shepherd my strength
the ancestors voice lays in my throat: they guide my proclamations
the ancestors heart beats in my chest: they lead my principles
the ancestors courage walks valiantly within my feet: they shepherd my full freedom.

and now I know. I know. I know.
I know now
where my yellow Chinese skin belongs
where my white Irish skin belongs
where my brown Indian skin belongs

where my black Negro skin belongs —
I belong: Everywhere.
Everywhere: I belong.
I belong everywhere for I am a living ancestor.

Moses took a deep breath. He would have to read Felicia's poem many times before he fully absorbed and comprehended it. What he was stunningly aware of was his daughter's talent. He was stunningly aware of the power of her brilliant mind and the cutting edge of her words.

He gradually became aware of her piercing gaze as she waited for his reaction. He fought for words that would begin to do it justice. "I've never read anything so powerful," he said. "You have taken the reality of generations of people's lives and somehow communicated it in this poem." He stared down at the sheets of paper again. "Thank you," he said softly.

Felicia looked satisfied.

"Can I read it?" Frances asked.

Moses waited for Felicia's nod before he handed the poem to her friend.

The clack of the train wheels was the only sound as Frances read. Shafts of light flashed in through the window as they passed through tunnels of trees, moving closer to Richmond and the end of the trip that had bound the three of them so closely together.

When Frances finished reading, she turned and stared out the window for several minutes.

"You didn't like it?" Felicia asked tentatively as the silence drew out.

Frances swung around to stare at her. "How could I not love it? Your daddy is right – I've never read anything as powerful."

Moses couldn't miss the troubled look in her eyes.

Neither could Felicia. "Then what's wrong?"

Frances stared at both of them, her eyes shifting between them. "I hate that I'm ashamed to be white," she confessed. "White people have done such horrible things."

Moses had suffered greatly under the power of white people, but he knew Frances' feelings were wrong. Just as he never wanted to be ashamed for being who he was, he didn't want her to be ashamed for who she was.

He reached forward and encased her slim white hand in his massive, strong black hand. He stared at their hands for a moment, wishing the whole world could experience such an easy blending of colors. "You should never be ashamed of who you were created to be, Frances," he began. "God didn't make a mistake by creating you to be white, any more than it was a mistake for me to be black."

"But..."

Moses held up his hand to stop Frances from interrupting. "It's true that white men brought blacks from Africa to be slaves, but it was Old Sarah who told me the truth about how that happened."

Both the girls stared at him. "What do you mean?" Felicia asked.

"Your grandmother was brought to America by white slave traders, but they weren't the ones who captured her. Other Africans stole her, along with dozens of others, from her village. They forced them to walk to the wharves where the white slave traders waited and sold them."

"Is that true?" Frances demanded.

"It is," Moses answered. He'd had long conversations with Sarah about the millions of slaves residing in America. After she'd been captured, she had been forced to wait in a large cage on the wharves for weeks. She saw thousands of men, women and children herded into other cages.

"Slavery existed in Africa long before the white man came. It was different, though. In many African cultures, it was an accepted domestic practice, but slaves had far more rights, and they were often treated like true family. They were adopted by the family and became part of their lineage." His lips twisted. "Not that they wouldn't have rather been in their villages with their own people, where they were truly free, but at least they had some rights and protections under the law."

"But why sell them to white people?" Felicia asked.

"Sarah told me she was taken during a time when many African states were at war with each other. They needed guns," Moses said.

Frances stared at him with disbelief. "The Africans sold each other so they could buy guns to kill each other?"

Moses nodded. "Guns were the deciding factor in the slave trade. European whites knew they had something the Africans wanted. Still," he added, "Sarah told me she doesn't think many of the African kings and chiefs would have sold their people if they had understood the brutality of slavery here in America."

"So, it all comes back to the brutality of white people," Frances declared.

"The brutality of *some* white people," Moses stated. "When you see something bad happening, it's easy to blame an entire race or culture. The truth, however, is that only *some* of the people are greedy and evil. The vast majority are simply people who want to live in peace. They want a home and food. They want to love their family and live a good life." He squeezed Frances' hand. "That is true for any race. Yes, there are greedy white people. There are also incredibly wonderful, generous, and loving white people – like your family. White people are who ended slavery in America."

"But..."

Moses held up his hand again. He had more to say. "There are greedy, evil black people who sell their people into slavery. There were black slave owners here in America."

Frances stared at him. "Black people owned other black people?"

Moses nodded again. "They did. Not many could afford to own slaves, but if they could, there were many that did. Frances, I believe that slavery is more about power than about the color of your skin. Africans have owned slaves for thousands of years — probably since the beginning of their existence. People have always wanted others to do the things they prefer not to do."

"You don't," Felicia burst out.

"No,' Moses agreed. "But that's because I know how horrible slavery is. I lived it. My family lived it. My father died because of it. My little sister was killed. I watched others tortured and beaten because of it." He paused, determined to be brutally honest. "In another time, perhaps I would have owned slaves."

"That's not true," Felicia cried. "You're not like that!"

Moses looked at her tenderly. "Felicia, none of us knows what we're truly capable of until we are in the situation. People are controlled by human nature. Everyone wants to believe they're superior to someone.

Everyone wants to have power over someone. We want to believe we're better than we are. I'd like to think I would never have become someone who would own a slave, but I can't know that for sure."

Felicia and Frances were both silent for a long moment.

"It still doesn't make any of it right," Frances said.

"I couldn't agree more," Moses replied. "The whole point of this conversation is that you shouldn't feel ashamed of being white. There are people who should be ashamed of their actions or their attitudes, but they should never be ashamed of the color of their skin." He thought hard. "I think every person, no matter the color of their skin, should choose to use how they're created to make the world better."

"Use how you are created to make the world better," Felicia said softly, repeating what he'd said.

Frances peered up into Moses' face. The trouble finally disappeared from her eyes. "I can do that," she declared. "I can use my white skin to make the world better."

"And I can use my black skin to make the world better," Felicia added.

A long shrill whistle cut into their conversation.

Frances leapt up. "We're home!"

Chapter Twenty-Nine

Rose could hardly contain her excitement as they caught sight of the smoke from the train in the distance. They couldn't see the actual train yet, but they could hear the rumble of the wheels, and the tracks were beginning to hum.

Hope began to jump up and down as the boys leaned out over the tracks so they would see the train as soon as it rounded the far curve.

Thomas, Abby, and the other children were seated on the benches against the shaded side of the station, sequestered from the heat of the sun. Gloria sat with them. The shy, uncertain expression on her face revealed she didn't believe she should be part of the family reunion.

"I see it!" John hollered.

"Me too!" Jed yelled.

Moments later, the entire group crowded together on the platform, watching as the train rolled to a stop in front of them.

Rose's heart was beating so fast she was sure everyone on the platform could see it.

John stood close beside her, already a full head taller than she was. He leaned down to talk to Jed and Hope. "Let Mama see Daddy first."

Hope frowned. "He's my daddy. I should see him first."

John smiled. "He'll want to see you, Hope, but Mama is his wife. She should get to hug him first. She missed him even more than we did."

Rose stared at her son with astonishment. When had he matured enough to understand what he was saying? "Thank you," she whispered.

"Alright," Hope said dejectedly, her lower lip quivering.

Rose kissed her velvety cheek. "I promise you won't have to wait long, honey."

Jed took his little sister's hand. "It's alright, Mama." He gazed down at Hope. "Besides, Hope, we'll be the first ones to hug Felicia."

Hope's expression brightened. "That's good. I've missed Felicia too!"

Just a few minutes after the train stopped, the door to the Pullman sleeper car opened.

"Moses!" Rose took three steps forward and fell into his arms. She didn't bother to hide her tears of joy as she felt his strong arms engulf her and pull her to him. It didn't matter that she could hardly breathe. His presence was all the air she needed.

"I missed you." Moses' voice was rough with emotion. "I missed you so much."

"I missed you too," Rose answered, her voice muffled against his broad chest. She pushed back so she could look up into his face and smiled brilliantly. "Welcome home."

Moses threw his head back with a laugh, pulled her off her feet, and swung her in a circle, mindless of the crowd on the platform. When he put her back down, he kissed her soundly. Only then did he turn to the children.

With a cry, all three of them fell into him, laughing and talking at the same time.

Rose watched them for a moment, her heart swelling with more feelings than she could identify.

"Mama?"

Rose spun around and swept Felicia into her arms. "Welcome home, honey! I can't wait to hear about everything. I missed you!"

Felicia held onto her tightly for a long time.

Rose finally held her away so she could look into her eyes. "Are you alright, Felicia?"

Rose, focused on her daughter, was vaguely aware of Frances being greeted by her family. Rose knew Frances would understand Carrie and Anthony staying behind to keep an eye on Susan and the plantation, but she also suspected she would be disappointed. She had a letter for her from Carrie in her pocket. She would give it to her when they were back at the house.

Felicia nodded. "I'm proud of you, Mama."

Rose cocked her head, surprised by the declaration. "Thank you, but..."

"I'm proud of you for choosing to be such a good person."

Moses stepped over and slipped his arm around Felicia's waist. "You'll understand what she means when you read the poem your brilliant daughter finished just before we arrived."

Rose smiled, thrilled to know there was a new poem. "I can't wait to read it."

"As long as you know I got to read it first," Moses said smugly.

Rose laughed. "That's been bothering him for a long time," she confided to Felicia. "I'm thrilled you put him out of his misery."

Minnie appeared, holding hands tightly with Frances. "Let's go home! May has lemon chess pie waiting for all of us!"

Laughing, they turned to head for the carriages waiting for them.

"Not so fast."

Rose jolted to a stop as a towering white man stepped in front of their group, his eyes latched on Gloria. Instinctively, she stepped in front of the little girl, holding her close behind her body. "What do you want?" she snapped. She had told Spencer to stay home, thinking they wouldn't need protection at the train station.

Moses looked confused but stepped next to Rose, his immense height overshadowing the man who had confronted them.

The white man eyed him, his anger seeming to intensify as he glared at Moses. "Who are you?"

Moses remained calm. "I don't know that it matters. The bigger question is who are you, and what do you want?"

"Where did you get that little girl?" the man growled.

"What does it matter?" Rose tried to match Moses' calm, but she knew her voice was edged with anger and fear. She regretted bringing Gloria into Richmond. She could feel the little girl's body trembling with terror.

"What is going on here?" Thomas appeared at their side.

Rose relaxed a tiny bit. He had been in the carriage but must have realized there was trouble. She had no doubt Moses could beat this man in a fight, but a black man fighting a white man in Richmond would lead to nothing but trouble and jail time.

"What's it to you?" the man snapped.

Thomas stared daggers at the man.

Abby stepped up next to him.

Frances joined them.

Then Russell.

Then Minnie.

John, Jed, and Hope followed, forming a solid wall of humanity between the man and Gloria. Without knowing what was going on, they were going to protect the little girl who had become a sister to them.

They looked frightened, but their faces were defiant.

The white man scowled. "I have business with that little girl."

"I doubt that very much," Thomas replied sternly. "She's eight years old." He looked thoughtful. "On the other hand, you may very well have business with the Richmond police. Police Chief Major John Poe is a friend of mine. Perhaps we should head down to the station and discuss the rape and attempted murder of a little girl and her mother in an alley a few weeks ago," he said cuttingly.

The man's features stiffened as he took several steps back. "That's not necessary," he protested. "I don't know what you're talking about."

Thomas took several steps forward until he was face to face with the man. "I'll give you two seconds to get out of here. If we ever see your face again, I will make sure Chief Poe knows what you did," he growled. "As it is, you're not worth the waste of my time."

A flash of anger appeared in the man's eyes, but he turned and stalked away.

Rose watched him go, wishing she could believe the trouble was over. She turned and pulled Gloria into her arms. "It's alright, honey. He's gone."

Gloria, tears rolling down her cheeks, huddled against her, trembling violently. "That was one of the men who hurt me and Mama!"

"He's gone now," Rose said softly.

Gloria stayed plastered to her body but looked up with wide, frightened eyes. "Will he come back?"

Thomas squatted down so he could look into her eyes. "No, honey. He won't bother you again."

"How do you know?" Gloria whispered.

Rose wanted to ask the same question but remained silent.

"Because men like that are cowards," Thomas said, his voice belying the anger sparking in his eyes. "Now that he knows you're protected by people who are friends with the chief of police, he won't dare to come near you."

Gloria peered up at Rose. "Is that true?"

Rose, pushing aside her own doubts, nodded. "Yes, honey. You're safe," she said.

Gloria finally straightened, her eyes darting around the platform as she searched for more danger. "Can we go home?" she whispered.

Moses stepped forward and swept her into his arms. "We're going home right now," he promised.

Rose watched, wondering if she would be frightened of Moses since she'd just met him. Instead, Gloria smiled up at him and snuggled into his arms.

Frances grinned when she saw the envelope waiting on her bed. She sat down eagerly and ripped it open.

Dearest Frances,

It's excruciating for me to not be on that train platform when you arrive today. I know, however, that you will understand why I couldn't leave Susan when she's close to giving birth. It does help to have a daughter who plans to be a doctor!

I have missed you every minute you've been gone but comforted myself with the knowledge you were having a wonderful adventure — one I have long dreamed of having. I'm excited to spend hours with you, hearing about your adventures and learning what changes have happened in you. No one can go three months without changing. It's even truer when those three months have been spent so far from the life you know.

I love you, honey. I'm counting the minutes until you're with me again!

Mama

Frances read the letter several more times, folded it carefully. and put it in her pocket. The ache of disappointment to not see her mama on the platform had been erased completely. She also realized moving to Boston, once again being so far from her family, was going to be extremely difficult. She was confident it was the right decision, but that wouldn't make it easy.

Rose appeared at the doorway. "Good letter?" she asked with a smile.

"The best letter possible," Frances replied.

Rose peered at her more closely. "Then why do you look sad?"

Frances hesitated. Felicia hadn't had time to tell Rose about their plans, but she quickly realized it didn't matter. She was free to talk about her own decisions. She had wanted to tell her mama first, but Rose was her second mother. There was no need to hide it. "It's going to be hard when I leave for Boston. I'm going to miss everyone terribly!"

Rose raised her eyebrows and walked into the room to sit next to her. "Boston?"

Frances nodded. "I'll tell everyone more about it, but I've decided Boston is the best place for me to go to medical school. I wanted to tell Mama first, but..."

"I see," Rose said slowly. "Your mama will understand, as long as you provide her with every detail that you don't tell anyone else." Then she smiled. "Elizabeth and Peter are there. They'll be thrilled to have you in the same city."

Frances smiled. "I know. That makes it easier." She didn't mention that it would be even easier since Felicia would be with her.

Dinner had been a raucous affair. Everyone was laughing and talking at the same time, but it was so joyous, no one seemed to mind. As time went on, they would hear all the stories.

Gloria had chosen to sit next to Moses and had gazed up at him adoringly while they ate.

Rose knew Moses made the little girl feel safe. Their children had clamored to sit next to him but had quickly conceded when they saw the expression on Gloria's face. Even Hope had realized how much Gloria needed to be near him after her earlier scare.

Rose knew he would play with them outside until they were ready to go to bed, so each of the children would have time with him. They would soon be riding the tobacco fields on the plantation again. Moses was going to be thrilled with the lush crop waiting for him.

From her place in the parlor, after dinner, she could hear the yells of delight and the giggles that erupted from Moses tickling the children when he caught them.

"Mama?"

Rose looked up when Felicia walked into the parlor. "Hello, honey." She gazed at her lovingly, thrilled beyond words to have her home again.

"Can we talk?"

"I would love that," Rose said. She patted the sofa next to her.

Felicia settled down and laid her head on Rose's shoulder. "I'm glad to be home."

"Not as glad as I am to have you home," Rose said as she stroked Felicia's head. "I know we have much to talk about, but first, I want to know if the trip was worth it."

Felicia sat up and nodded enthusiastically. "It was a wonderful trip. I learned more than I dreamed I would from Mrs. Pleasant." She paused. "I also learned I don't want to live in San Francisco."

Rose smiled. "Is it alright to say I'm thrilled by that realization?"

Felicia grinned. "I would be disappointed if you weren't."

When Felicia's smile faded, Rose braced herself. She could feel another big piece of news about to be revealed. "Go ahead and tell me." As she spoke the words, she prayed her reaction would be what Felicia needed it to be.

"I'm going to tell you, but you have to promise to let Frances tell Carrie first."

Rose nodded solemnly, certain of what was coming.

"Frances and I are going to move to Boston," Felicia said, her eyes gleaming brightly. "With Boston rebuilding from the fire, I'm confident there will be wonderful business opportunities. You and Daddy will invest in some of them, and Mrs. Pleasant has already told me she would like to be my partner in some of my ventures. That way, she can earn profits without having to leave San Francisco. If I'm wise with my spending, I'll soon have enough profits to make my own investments, while you and Daddy also make money."

"And Frances will go to medical school there."

Felicia took a deep breath, shook her head, and laughed. "Frances already told you."

Rose didn't miss the disappointment lurking in her eyes. "Not about you going with her, honey. Just about her decision to move to Boston." She took Felicia's hand. "She didn't betray your confidence. I'm hearing your plans for the first time."

Felicia relaxed. "What do you think?" she asked eagerly.

"That it will be much easier to visit Boston than San Francisco," Rose said immediately. She squeezed Felicia's hand. "I'm thrilled for you. I always knew you wouldn't stay on the plantation. That's not what you're meant to do. Boston is a wonderful city. I believe you'll love it there."

"I can go to the ocean, too," Felicia said.

Rose laughed. "That you can!" She loved the anticipation glowing in Felicia's eyes. She also recognized a deeper maturity and confidence than she'd had before the trip. "San Francisco was good for you."

Felicia nodded. “It was, Mama. I learned a lot, but mostly I learned how much I already know.” Her shoulders straightened. “I’m ready for this,” she said firmly.

Moses walked into the parlor. “Are you ready to read your poem to your mama, as well?”

Thomas, Abby, and Frances entered the parlor almost on his heels.

“There’s another poem?” Abby asked eagerly.

Frances nodded. “The best one yet, Grandma.”

Abby sat down next to the fireplace and faced Felicia. “Is it too much to ask for all of us to hear it?”

“*Hear* it?” Felicia said hesitantly. Being a public speaker and telling her story was different from reading a new poem out loud. “I only finished writing it today. What if all of you just read it?”

“You told me you practically had it memorized,” Moses reminded her. “No one can read it like you can, Felicia. It needs to be read in your voice, and with your heart.”

Felicia took a deep breath, emboldened by his encouragement. “I suppose I can. Let me get it.”

Moses reached into his pocket. “I happen to have it right here.” He laughed at his daughter’s surprised look. “Did you really think you could get through the night without reading it?”

Felicia laughed. “I suppose not.” She reached for the sheaf of papers, cleared her throat, and began to read.

where do I belong? me & my black skin

the blackness of my skin mimics the vacuum of my mind —
a void exists as my eyes gaze over my surroundings and
questions haunt my sleep,
questions taunt my waking.

where does my black skin belong?
where do I belong? me & my black skin . . .

my journey is not unique for all colors of skin desire to live
my journey is not alone for all colors of skin dream of home
my journey is not solo for all colors of skin deserve peace
and
my journey is not exceptional for all skin nightmares from the savagery of white man.

my black skin is yellow Chinese skin — hanging dead from the eaves by white man's hand
my black skin is white Irish skin smoldering — smoked by white man's fire
my black skin is brown Indian scalp skin dripping blood — oozing by white man's knife
my black skin is black Negro skin blotched and blotted — glass lashed from white man's whip

my black, yellow, white, brown skin is skin ravaged in violent brutality — raped by white mans greed

my black, yellow, white, brown skin is skin hated by white man fear

my black, yellow, white, brown skin is skin illiterate to white man equality

my black, yellow, white, brown skin is skin impoverished to white man law.

today —
the blackness of my skin is all skin. tomorrow —
the blackness of my skin is all skin.

questions haunt my sleep — questions taunt my waking.

how does my black mind shine in the whitewashed shadow land?
how does my black mind burnish white man command?
how does my black mind flash affluence to white man's control?

how does my black mind afford freedom?
freedom to desire, freedom to dream, freedom to deserve?
how does my black, yellow, white, brown body dare emancipation o'er white mans nightmare?

how does my black, yellow, white, brown body, skin, mind live in freedom?
oh yes, I ask once again —
how does my black, yellow, white, brown body, skin, mind live in freedom?

the black void of my skin mimics the vacuum of my mind —
and yet, yet, yet, yet
drifting & sifting within the arcane 'of my spirit — I hear.
the arcane abyss of my spirit encompasses fierce perceptive voices
voices of my black, yellow, white, brown skinned ancestors

my ancestors declare:
their black, yellow, white, brown blood drips through my veins
their black, yellow, white, brown thought dwells in my brain
their black, yellow, white, brown strengths rise in my hands
their black, yellow, white, brown voice lays in my throat
their black, yellow, white, brown heart beats in my chest
their black, yellow, white, brown courage walks within my feet.

black, yellow, white, brown in body
black, yellow, white, brown in skin
black, yellow, white, brown in mind
black, yellow, white, brown, black ancestors.

the ancestors blood drips through my veins: they usher my autonomy
the ancestors thought dwells in my brain: they escort my resolutions
the ancestors strength rises in my hands: they shepherd my strength
the ancestors voice lays in my throat: they guide my proclamations
the ancestors heart beats in my chest: they lead my principles
the ancestors courage walks valiantly within my feet: they shepherd my full freedom.

and now I know. I know. I know.

I know now
where my yellow Chinese skin belongs
where my white Irish skin belongs
where my brown Indian skin belongs
where my black Negro skin belongs —
I belong: Everywhere.
Everywhere: I belong.
I belong everywhere for I am a living ancestor.

When Felicia stopped reading, silence filled the parlor.

Rose understood. She had read all her daughter's poems, many of them powerful, but never had she heard one that knocked the breath from her and made her question her existence.

"I'm speechless," Abby finally managed.

"As am I," Rose murmured, searching for words to do the poem justice.

"You have quite a gift, young lady," Thomas added. "I've read poetry my entire life, but you give voice to ideas and thoughts in a way I've never read before." He shook his head. "I know you'll be a wonderful businesswoman, but I hate that you won't spend your life as a poet."

Felicia smiled. "I'm glad you liked it."

"I told Felicia I've never read anything so powerful," Moses interjected. "She's taken the reality of generations of people's lives and-communicated it in this poem."

"That's exactly it," Rose said fervently.

"When I first heard the poem, it made me ashamed to be white," Frances confessed.

"I will admit to feeling that too," Abby said quietly. "There have been so many wrongs done to people."

"There have," Frances agreed. "Moses showed us, though, how terrible wrongs have been done by every race.

He helped me understand I shouldn't be ashamed of being white."

"Or of being black," Felicia added. "There are people who should be ashamed of their actions or their attitudes, but they should never be ashamed of the color of their skin."

"Exactly," Frances said. "Every person, no matter their race, should choose to use how they are created to make the world better." She took a deep breath. "No matter what has happened in the past, I can use my white skin to make the world better."

"And I can use my black skin to make the world better," Felicia said. She turned to Rose. "That's why I thanked you earlier for being a good person, Mama. You use your black skin every day to make the world a better place."

Tears welled in Rose's eyes. She looked around the room, gazing at the people she loved most in the world. Her eyes locked with Moses. "All of us do," she said quietly. Her thoughts flew to her own mother. "Your grandmother taught me that when I was young." Her mind flew to the last line of the poem. *I belong everywhere for I am a living ancestor.*

Rose gazed at her brilliant and talented daughter. "You're right, Felicia. I belong everywhere, for I am a living ancestor." Rose's gaze swept the room. "*All* of us are living ancestors."

Chapter Thirty

August 1, 1873

Hobbs walked slowly through the Portland streets. He was eager to leave but actually doing it, six years after Portland had offered its refuge to him, was proving more difficult than he thought. He walked slowly down the wooden sidewalks on Front Street, past the First National Bank. Past Buchtel's Gallery and Union Insurance Company. The street was dry and dusty, plumes of dirt spiraling in the air with the force of the Chinook winds blowing down the Columbia River Gorge. Brick buildings with metal roofs competed for space with the wooden buildings that had survived the fire the year before.

Hobbs let the memories swarm through him as he walked.

Steamers plied the waters between Portland and the coast, carrying tens of thousands of goods and imports. Soon, hundreds of thousands of salmon would force their way upriver, returning to their original spawning streams to begin the new cycle of life.

He strolled down Washington Street, northwest of the Willamette River. Huge brick buildings in Corinthian, Victorian, and Second Empire style rose in front of him. He'd fallen in love with this part of Portland, dreaming of the time he might live in something so luxurious. On the outskirts of the wealthy section were the more modest houses of the middle class. Further out, the direction he was headed, were the tenements of the poor.

As Hobbs walked through the tenements, he nodded to many that he knew.

"You leaving soon, Hobbs?"

Hobbs stopped to speak with one of the city firemen. "Day after tomorrow, Charlie."

Both men frowned when a gust of wind sucked up a tornado of dust. On the outskirts of town, a bigger plume was picked up and spun through the air. The entire Pacific Northwest was in the grip of a severe drought.

"Wind has to be blowing close to seventy miles per hour," Charlie muttered. He pulled out a handkerchief to wipe his forehead. "It's too blazing hot."

Hobbs nodded, knowing both of them were thinking about the risk of fire. He looked around at the wooden tenements that would be destroyed completely if another blaze took control of the city. He was suddenly eager to get home to his house high above Portland. There were times the walk uphill had gotten tiresome, but it was always worth it when he sat on his porch and gazed out over the city and the sparkling waters of the mighty Columbia and Willamette Rivers. Mountains stretched far into the distance, with snow-covered Mount Hood a constant, even in the middle of a hot summer.

"We're gonna be in trouble if another fire starts," Charlie said darkly. "Eight months ago, we had a big rain to put out the fire. Not to mention, we didn't have the heat we do now. It's the only reason we could stop it at only two blocks of the city destroyed. If a fire started now, it could destroy all of Portland."

Hobbs knew he was right. "We've done what we can to prepare for it." Even as he spoke the words, he was aware it hadn't been enough.

"Nonsense," Charlie growled. "I know you've been working to keep the roads clear, and you're checking to make sure businesses are trying to better prepare, but the city ain't no more ready for a fire than it was last year. The hydrants still ain't pressurized. I reckon there ain't enough water in the cisterns, either. Not with this drought."

Hobbs wanted to refute his statements, but he knew they were true. "Surely, we wouldn't have a fire so soon again," he protested lamely. He wanted to believe that something so terrible wouldn't strike the city again, that somehow the gods would spare them.

"The city is *talking* about doing a lot of things," Charlie said derisively, obliterating the slight hope he held onto. "Far as I can tell, the only thing they've done is put up a bigger bell."

"We have more volunteer firefighters," Hobbs pointed out.

"Won't matter how many we got if they can't get water."

Again, Hobbs couldn't argue the truth. Instead, he searched for another positive. "We have three new fire engines."

"That we got to pull to a fire ourselves," Charlie snorted. "By the time we get it where the fire is burning, we're exhausted. Seems they could at least get a few horses to pull the engines. They want us to act like animals, but we're men."

Hobbs took a deep breath. He was done trying to find something good. He prayed he was gone before something bad happened.

Hobbs jolted awake. He listened closely, wondering if someone had broken into the house. He heard Tyson snoring, but other than the relentless howling of the wind, it was quiet.

A quick look at his watch told him it was four forty-five. Soon, the glow of the sun would begin to lighten the horizon, but for now, the sky was brilliant with stars. It was a cloudless night with no hint of the rain they so desperately needed.

Hobbs rolled over and tried to go back to sleep, but he was too restless. He tossed and turned for several minutes before he gave up and threw back the thin sheet, the only cover he could stand in the heat. He padded to the sink to get a glass of water, glancing out the window as he did.

"Tyson!"

Hobbs ran back to his room and pulled on clothes as quickly as he could. "Tyson!" he shouted again.

His friend appeared at the door to his room, his voice groggy with sleep. "What are you hollering about? It's the middle of the night."

"Fire!" Hobbs said hoarsely. "The city is on fire."

Tyson cursed and crossed the room to stare out the window. A moment later, he was rushing to his quarters.

Hobbs was part way down the hill when he heard Tyson clatter down the steps behind him. He was moving as fast as he could with his wooden leg, but Tyson would have no trouble catching up to him.

"Go on!" he gasped when Tyson reached him. "I'll get there as fast as I can."

Tyson nodded grimly and kept running.

It would take every man in town to stop the fire.

If it could be stopped.

Hobbs groaned when he reached the city limits. He gulped for breath as he tried to determine where he should go first. The fire bell was clanging, barely heard above the sounds of people yelling and screaming. Men rushed into the streets, pulling on their clothes as they ran.

The nightmare was coming true.

From where he stood, near the intersection of First Avenue and Taylor Street, he could see that what had once been the furniture shop of Hurgren and Shindler was already crumbling to ashes. The blaze must have started there. He could well imagine how fast the fire had burned when it found the barrels of varnish.

The flames had already devoured a block, shooting through a livery and harness-makers shop on its way to destroy the three-story Metropolitan Hotel, the Multnomah Hotel, and the Patton House. Every building was already engulfed in flames.

He leapt back as the heat of the consuming fire created its own punishing wind. It felt as if his skin was being scalded. He pulled up his bandana to cover as much of his face as possible. He shoved his hat tightly to his head, hoping it would create a barrier from sparks seeking to set his hair on fire.

Pushed northeast, the flames hurtled across Front Street to the levee. As Hobbs watched, the fire ran north, eating up the wooden structures along the Willamette River, and also turning up Second Avenue.

Hobbs stared in horror. How could the fire possibly be contained?

Tyson appeared beside him. "There's no way the volunteer fire department can put this out!" He looked around wide-eyed. "How can we help?"

"Come with me!" yelled a man running past, pulling on suspenders as he sprinted toward a burning building. "They've already called for help," he yelled over his shoulder. "A steamer is coming down from Vancouver! More help is coming from Salem on the train."

Hobbs followed the man, knowing it would take far more than additional resources to put this conflagration out. With the way the winds were raging, massive amounts of the city would be consumed before anyone else arrived. Four engine companies and one hook and ladder company had leapt into action at the sound of the fire bell. Thirty-two cisterns were scattered around town, but there was no way of knowing exactly how much water they contained. He was sickly certain they would run dry under the demand.

He stopped when another building exploded in front of him. One minute it was a store, the next minute it seemed to be nothing but a single flame roaring like a monster. Hobbs was stunned by the ferocity of the fire as it ate the city.

"Over here!" a firefighter yelled. "Come man this hose!"

Hobbs leapt forward and grabbed the hose. Tyson snatched the one next to him. Even as they trained streams of water onto the flames, Hobbs realized the futility of their effort. He could practically see the heat of the fire turn the water into steam as soon as it got close.

Still, they had no choice but to fight the enemy.

The streets were full of people fleeing for their lives, their arms overflowing with the few possessions they could grab. People jostled him, some running through the stream of water as they raced down the streets.

Tears choked his throat as flames devoured livery stables full of screaming horses. He wanted to turn away and be sick, but he tightened his lips and kept fighting.

Massive explosions rent the air as warehouses full of accelerants blew up, spewing hot ash and liquids through the air, igniting even more fires as the ash spread to other buildings.

The fire was a living thing, breathing death and destruction everywhere it turned its gaze.

Hobbs gritted his teeth against the heat and fear, focused on doing the job he had been given to do. His hose seemed to be making no difference, but it was all he could do.

He had no idea how much time had passed, but it was going to be a very long day.

"Get over there and work!"

Hobbs looked up in time to see a group of Chinese men herded at gunpoint toward one of the burning warehouses. They weren't volunteer firefighters. Hobbs had no trouble with every man in town being conscripted to fight the fire, but he could tell with a single glance that the Chinese were being forced to do what no white man was willing to do.

"Get water on those warehouses!" a man yelled.

Hobbs could see the terror and pain on the faces of the Chinese men. He could feel his own face burning from the heat of the flames, and he wasn't nearly as close as the men being forced forward. He gritted his teeth with anger. He'd seen firsthand, more times than he could count, how badly the Chinese were treated. Because of his work with the railroad, he knew the hatred extended up and down the entirety of the West Coast.

He'd seen what irrational hatred and fear of blacks could do in the South. The same people who had turned their noses up at slavery were treating the Chinese with equal amounts of contempt and hatred. It was a constant mirror, reflecting back to him his attitude toward blacks when the KKK had recruited him.

He watched as streams of water were pointed toward the Chinese men as they worked to pull burnable debris away from the buildings. The heat was so intense, they had to be hosed with water to keep them alive so they could continue to work.

Knowing the attempt to save the building he was hosing down was completely pointless, he turned his hose toward the suffering men, hoping to alleviate at least some of their pain.

"Get up there!"

Hobbs whirled around as he heard a man scream for mercy. Armed with a bayonet, a soldier was prodding a Chinese man to walk barefoot over a burning boardwalk.

Hobbs roared with anger, dropped his hose, and hobbled as quickly as he could toward the soldier. Mindless of danger, he snatched the bayonet out of his hand, and waved for the Chinese man to run.

Barely able to walk, the man shot him a grateful look and disappeared down the road, quickly swallowed by smoke that hung thickly in the streets.

"What are you doing?" the soldier yelled furiously.

Hobbs glared at him. "Keeping you from being even more of an idiot than you already are. We're here to put out a fire, not torture innocent people."

"For all I know, that man is the one who started the fire," the soldier snarled. "I've been telling people the Chinese will destroy our city. And now it's happening!"

"You're a fool," Hobbs snapped. "There's no way of knowing who started the fire. You're looking for someone to bully and torture."

The soldier advanced on him. "You love the Chinamen, do you? Perhaps *you're* the one who started this fire," he taunted.

Hobbs snorted, too angry to feel any fear. "You're more of a fool than I first thought."

"Give me my bayonet. I have work to do," the soldier ordered.

"What you were doing could hardly be called work," Hobbs retorted as he drew his arm back. He threw the bayonet as hard as he could, watching with satisfaction as it landed in one of the burning buildings. "You don't need it."

The soldier bellowed and raced toward Hobbs with a murderous glint in his eyes.

Hobbs braced himself and raised his fists.

Suddenly, three volunteer firefighters appeared at his side. They were men he'd worked with for the last several weeks. Charlie was among them.

"Get away from him," Charlie growled. "We're here to put out a fire."

The soldier jolted to a stop. He opened his mouth to protest but spun around and ran. Within moments, he couldn't be seen.

"You alright?" Charlie asked.

"I'm fine," Hobbs answered. He wasn't at all sure they would have come to his aid if they'd seen him save the Chinese man. Irrational hatred was everywhere. His only concern now, however, was the fire. He rushed forward and grabbed another hose. "Let's get back to work."

"It's too late," one of the firemen said. "There's no saving any of the businesses on this road. We have to move forward and find something we can save."

Hobbs was so exhausted he could hardly stand, much less think clearly, when word was passed down that the firemen could rest. He didn't know what that meant, but it gave him permission to slump to the ground, careful not to sit in smoldering ashes.

A glance at his watch told him it was four thirty in the afternoon. Twelve hours had passed since he had looked out his window.

Was the entire city gone?

Had the firefighters been able to save anything?

Throughout the entire day, every time they thought they were making progress, the wind would change direction, blowing sparks and flames on fresh fodder, causing the fire to explode in a new place. Support had arrived, but he didn't know if it had done any good.

He looked around through blurry eyes. For as far as he could see, there were nothing but blackened skeletons of buildings or smoking piles of ash. He watched, unable to stand, as firefighters slowly made their way down the street.

"Let's go, Hobbs."

Hobbs looked up at Charlie, who was as blackened and exhausted as he was. "Is there anything left?"

Charlie grimaced. "I don't know. We ain't gonna find out until we get out of here."

Hobbs struggled to his feet and joined the file of spent, soot-blackened men walking slowly and painfully down devastated roads.

He counted the blocks as he walked.

Two blocks.

Four blocks.

Six blocks.

Eight blocks.

Not able to stand the realization, he quit counting.

Every street they moved down was completely destroyed.

His despair grew as he walked. If the train station was still standing, he would be leaving the destruction soon, but that didn't keep his heart from going out to the thousands who would fight to rebuild their lives.

Tyson emerged from the smoke and joined the throngs of firefighters retreating from the battlefield.

"You alright?" Hobbs asked wearily.

Tyson nodded. "As alright as any of us can be."

As they walked away, a throng of militia took their place. The militia would guard the city against looters, though Hobbs couldn't imagine there was anything left worth taking.

"Ain't sure I can make it up the hill," Tyson grunted.

Hobbs wasn't sure either, but he was desperate to make his way out of the smoke. At least he had a haven above the smoke-filled roads. He knew just how lucky he was. "We can do it," he said grimly. He lowered his head and kept walking.

Darkness had not yet fallen when Hobbs and Tyson stumbled the last few yards to their house. They stepped onto the tiny porch and turned to stare out over Portland.

Hobbs gazed down with disbelief. Even in the dwindling daylight, they could see the glow of small fires continuing to burn. The advance of the fire had been stopped only because it had reached the six blocks of destruction from the December fire. With nothing to consume, the fire had collapsed in on itself. If the burned area had not been there to stop its advance, the fire would still be raging.

On the way up the hill, they had stopped and gathered information from women and children who had climbed higher during the day to escape the flames.

Twenty-two blocks of Portland were gone.

Simply gone.

Somehow, the jewel of the city, the St. Charles Hotel, had been saved. A firefighter brigade from Salem had risked their lives to keep it from burning. Every building around it had been consumed, but the four-story brick hotel with the metal mansard roof had survived.

It was reason for celebration, but the devastation was too great to feel much joy.

The fire had consumed two engine houses, two sash factories, three foundries, four mills, five hotels, one hundred retail stores, and two-hundred and fifty homes.

As Hobbs walked up the hill to his house, hundreds of homeless families had been making their way to set up camp in the city park. There was no way of knowing how long before they had shelter.

Tyson stood motionless, gazing out over the devastation. "I reckon I'm even more glad to be leaving here," he finally said.

"Me too," Hobbs admitted. "Part of me thinks I should stay to help rebuild, though." He acknowledged, even as he spoke the words, that he wasn't going to stay. He could tell from where he stood that the train depot had not been destroyed. He would be on the train in two days.

"Not me," Tyson said firmly. "I'm done here. I helped build the railroad. That's enough for me. I'm heading to a new life in Chicago."

"Which is recovering from an even more terrible fire," Hobbs reminded him.

Tyson shrugged. "Chicago is a new place, with a new beginning. I've had enough of Portland and the state of Oregon." When he looked at Hobbs, he had a tortured look in his eyes. "Did you see what they were doing to the Chinese men?"

"Yeah. It made me sick." As he thought about it, his rage burned almost as fiercely as the fire had earlier.

"There's so much hatred," Tyson said thickly. "The Chinese aren't here to hurt anyone. They want to live, same as I do." He shook his head. "Do you think there's any hope?"

Hobbs shrugged. "I reckon I think so. Look at you and me — a white man and a black man, best of friends. I reckon that's a lot of hope."

Tyson looked thoughtful. "Yeah, I guess you're right." He turned and opened the door. "All I want to do is get out of these clothes, wash off some of the grime, and get some sleep."

Hobbs stood on the porch a few minutes longer. The last beams of the sun reflected off the thick layer of smoke covering the city. The fires still burning caused it to glow from below. The sunlight cast a golden glow from above, catching on the rising wisps of smoke. It would have been beautiful, if it hadn't been so tragic.

He turned to walk inside. He was ready to return to the South. It was time.

He longed for the fresh, clean air on Cromwell Plantation.

Two days later, Hobbs and Tyson stepped onto the train headed east. They weren't looking forward to a week of sitting up in coach, but it was what Hobbs' could pay for. On the other hand, they were completely exhausted from the last thirty-six hours. They had labored, with only snatches of sleep, to help clear debris from Portland streets. It would take years for the city to return to some semblance of what it had been, but the work had already begun.

"I predict we sleep the first twelve hours," Hobbs said as they stowed their luggage in the baggage car.

"Fine by me," Tyson responded. "The last forty-eight hours have been something I hope I never repeat." He yawned and stepped into the train car.

Hobbs found their seats, stowed the bag of food he had brought, and sank down. He wouldn't call it comfortable, but it would do. He had learned during the war that he could sleep anywhere. He closed his eyes, lay his head back, and fell sound asleep.

Chapter Thirty-One

Carrie stood on the edge of the porch, relishing the air sweeping across the plantation. It was still hot in the third week of August, with no hint of fall in the air, but a front the night before had pushed most of the humidity from the area. She was grateful for the relief.

"He should be here by noon," Thomas predicted.

Carrie nodded. "Hobbs was probably on the road before the sun was up. He hasn't been in Oregon long enough to forget how hot it can be here. He would want to ride while it was the coolest. I'm glad he has this wonderful breeze. If he'd gotten here three days ago, when we could practically drink the air, he might have turned around and gone back to the Pacific Northwest."

Abby laughed. "I've had thoughts like that this summer. I know Oregon weather is much different this time of year. Has it been hotter here than usual, or am I just getting older?"

Thomas shook his head. "Did you read the newspaper Matthew brought a few days ago? Portland caught fire and almost completely burned to the ground. Their summer has been brutally hot and dry, and they're in the midst of a drought. I'll take hot humidity over that any day."

"True," Abby conceded. "Thank you for that explanation, dear. I noticed how neatly you walked around the question of whether I'm getting older."

Thomas winked. "I've not reached this age without also getting wiser. Besides, I'm older than you. If I acknowledge your age, it means I have to acknowledge my own. I'm not interested."

"Both of you stop," Carrie scolded. "Neither one of you acts your age, so I don't see how the number of years matters at all. I can only hope I act as young as the two of you when I'm your age."

"Very diplomatic," Thomas said wryly.

"If you'd rather, I could address you as Old Man Cromwell from now on," Carrie teased.

"Not if you treasure your life," Abby retorted.

The three were laughing when Frances arrived on the porch.

Carrie smiled brightly, hoping the smile would hide the heartache she felt. She was completely in agreement with Frances' decision to go to Boston for school, and she would enjoy making the trip to visit her, but she wished she could keep her home for a longer time. Frances had been back on the plantation for less than three weeks. She couldn't imagine watching her and Felicia depart on the train in two weeks, but she would do it with a smile. She at least had the memories of the long talks they'd had since she returned.

Frances had always been mature for her age, but the trip to California had matured her even more. Stepping in to act as a doctor after the train crash had made her realize the extent of her capabilities. She was now a young woman full of confidence about her future.

Frances walked over and slipped an arm around Carrie's waist. "I can hardly wait to meet Hobbs," she said. "I've heard so many stories about him. It will be wonderful to see him in person."

"It will," Carrie agreed, pushing thoughts of her daughter leaving out of her mind.

"Do you think he'll be here soon?" Frances asked.

Carrie glanced at her father as he pulled his pocket watch out.

"He'll probably be here in less than an hour," Thomas proclaimed.

"So, we have time to talk about something?" Frances asked.

Carrie turned her eyes to her daughter. "I know that tone of voice. This is serious."

"It's nothing bad," Frances assured her. "But I have a request."

"Let's hear it." Carrie was already certain she would do whatever Frances asked. Her daughter hardly asked for a thing. When she did, it was only because it was very important to her.

"Will you go to Boston with me to help me find a place to live and get settled in?" Despite all her newfound confidence, Frances' voice was hesitant.

Carrie laughed happily. "I've been dreaming you would ask me," she confessed. "I can't think of a single thing I would rather do!"

Abby looked delighted. "Do you mind if your grandmother rides with you as far as New York? I've been wanting to visit my friend Nancy Stratford."

"Of course, Grandma!" Frances turned to Carrie. "Could we stop in New York for two days? I would love to see the Stratfords, and I know you and Rose would love to show Felicia and me more of New York City."

Carrie raised a brow.

"Felicia is asking Rose right now," Frances admitted. "We can't think of a better way to start our new lives in Boston."

Carrie clapped her hands like a child. "You have made me the happiest mama in the world, my dear!" She pulled Frances to her in a tight hug. "Thank you!"

Carrie's mind whirled with her thoughts. There was nothing she would rather do than travel to Boston with Rose in order to settle their daughters into new lodging. She could visit Elizabeth and Peter, as well as discover how Boston was coming back to life after the devastating fire the year before.

"Mama," Frances said. "Where's Daddy?"

"In the workshop with Russell."

Frances frowned. "Those two are always out there."

Carrie smiled. "I won't deny that. They're having tremendous fun."

Anthony had bought woodworking tools for Russell as a surprise. Their first project was a secret, at least to everyone except Carrie. She knew they were making a cedar chest for Frances to take to Boston with her. Frances was going to feel guilty for complaining about the time they spent in the workshop, but Carrie wouldn't ruin the surprise.

"I hardly ever see Daddy," Frances complained.

"They promised to stay home tonight," Carrie told her. "They'll be here soon to meet Hobbs and have lunch." She could tell by the expression on Frances' face that she was hurt by the realization that Anthony would return early to see Hobbs, but not to spend time with her.

"Your daddy adores you, honey. I'm not going to spoil anything, but I *can* tell you they're doing something very important in the workshop. It might even be a surprise for you."

Frances brightened. "Really? I guess that's alright then."

Susan walked through the barn slowly. She was still coming to the stables but was no longer riding. Harold brought her over in the carriage each day.

"Ouch!" Susan stopped and held a hand to her stomach.

Amber dropped the brush she was using to groom Eclipse and rushed toward her. "Are you alright?"

Susan took a deep breath. "This baby had better be a boy. If it's a little girl who is giving me bruises by kicking so hard, I might be scared to raise her."

Amber laughed. "My mama told me I kicked her so hard she was certain I was a boy."

Susan sighed. "Well, if I end up with a daughter as wonderful as you, I'm happy for her to continue to kick me."

Amber smiled with delight. "You're going to have a wonderful daughter," she said confidently. "Because you're such a special woman."

Susan flushed with pleasure. "Thank you, honey." She rubbed her hand on her protruding belly. "I'm so glad I'm on the plantation for the pregnancy."

Amber nodded. "Abby told me what it's like in the city, especially in high society. I would hate to be pregnant in that world." She grimaced. "I can't imagine having to wrap a tight corset around my body. It would be painful, but it's also terrible for the baby."

"You're right. Many women miscarry because they tighten their corset to attempt to hide their pregnancy." Susan scowled. "Women are the only ones who can provide children, but they're punished for it. Women, especially in factories, lose their jobs as soon as their bosses realize they're pregnant. They're afraid it will slow down the woman's productivity, so they get rid of her. That's one reason women hide it for as long as possible."

Amber shook her head. "That's wrong!"

"It's horrible," Susan agreed. "On the other end of the spectrum, wealthy women also wear the ridiculous corsets. Society frowns on women appearing in public when they're pregnant."

"Why?" Amber demanded.

"Because women are expected to be petite, quiet, and demure at all times. Not to mention, pure. Even when they're married," she added scornfully. "If a pregnant woman appears in public, it's evidence she's involved in sexual conduct, which makes people uncomfortable."

Amber stared at her with disbelief. "Don't white people understand how babies are made?"

Susan laughed. "You had the benefit of your mama being a midwife. Polly has been delivering babies since before you were born."

"Having a baby is a sacred honor," Amber said fiercely. "Women should be celebrated for providing children, not hidden away until the evidence has disappeared." She narrowed her lips. "White people think they're superior, but that is simply dumb."

"You're absolutely correct," Susan replied with a laugh. "I can only hope that women fighting for their rights will end the stranglehold the Victorian mindset has on our country."

"This is one time I'm happy to be black," Amber replied. "No one sees us as pure anyway, so they aren't alarmed when black women are pregnant."

"Which is wrong on a whole other level," Susan answered. She stroked Eclipse's gleaming neck thoughtfully. "I dream of a different life for women in America. I have to believe it will come." She moved her hand down to her stomach. "I have to believe life will be different for the little girl who may be waiting to enter the world." She paused. "If I have a little boy, I'm going to teach him how to treat women."

"He'll have the men here on the plantation to teach him, as well," Amber replied. "We're lucky to be surrounded by men who don't limit us."

"He's here!" Carrie yelled when the plume of dust in the distance turned into the silhouette of a man on horseback.

"Right on time," Annie said with satisfaction. "It's a good thing that boy ain't gonna ruin the special meal we made for him."

Carrie grinned. She had walked into the kitchen earlier and seen Annie, Minnie, and Alice hard at work.

She had taken Alice's cast off her leg and wrist a few days earlier. It would take time for Alice to rebuild her muscles and strength, but she was determined to help in the kitchen as much as possible. She'd been sitting at the kitchen table, chopping vegetables furiously.

As Annie's friendship with Alice had grown, so had her willingness to share the kitchen with her. She actually seemed to look forward to her presence.

Hobbs cantered the last hundred yards to the porch, dismounting as quickly as his leg allowed him to.

"Hobbs!" Carrie cried. "Welcome home!"

Hobbs looked older, but he had the same shock of rusty hair, the same bright blue eyes, and the exact same boyish grin.

"Carrie! It's so wonderful to see you!" Hobbs swept her into his arms and hugged her tightly.

Carrie laughed and returned his embrace. Seeing him brought back swarms of memories. Of him. Of Robert. Of the war years.

"Should I be worried?"

Carrie laughed when an amused voice broke into their reunion. She pulled back and grabbed Anthony's arm. "Warren Hobbs, meet Anthony Wallington, my wonderful husband."

Hobbs smiled but appraised the other man carefully.

Carrie knew he was measuring Anthony against Robert.

Hobbs finally grinned his approval. "It's real nice to meet you, Mr. Wallington."

"Anthony. We don't adhere to formality around here." He held out his hand. "It's a pleasure to meet you, Hobbs. We've heard endless stories about you."

Hobbs laughed. "I'll do my best to clear up the bad ones."

Thomas hurried down the steps. "Welcome back to Cromwell Plantation, Hobbs!"

Hobbs shook his hand firmly. "I can't tell you how wonderful it is to be here, Mr. Cromwell. It's a dream come true to be back on Southern soil."

Carrie could tell from the fervent expression on his face how much he meant it. The next weeks would reveal whether he would truly be happy on the plantation or if he would go elsewhere, but for now, he was home.

"Carrie!"

Carrie whirled around at the sound of Amber's panicked yell.

"It's Susan! Come quickly!"

Carrie took off running. "Anthony, go get Harold!"

She grabbed Amber's arm when she reached the barn. "Get your mama. We might not need her, but I'm not taking any chances."

Carrie dashed in through the barn door to see Susan slumped on the floor against the side of the tack room. "Susan!" She ran over and knelt by her friend. "What's wrong?"

"Wrong?" Susan asked, her face creased with pain. "I'm not sure anything is *wrong.* My water broke." She peered up at Carrie. "Does it hurt every woman this much?"

Carrie felt a twinge of sorrow. She should be able to tell Susan from personal experience, but she had given birth to her stillborn daughter when she was unconscious. She had to rely on book knowledge and others' experiences. "If it didn't hurt like the dickens, it would be men having the babies," she said with a grin.

Abby appeared beside her. "Do you need help? Thomas and Moses are with me."

"Let's get her inside," Carrie said calmly. "Susan has gone into labor."

"It's time," Susan said in wonder, gasping when another contraction hit.

"It's time," Carrie agreed happily.

Moses stepped beside her, put his hands under Susan's arms and lifted her to her feet, slipping his arm around her to hold her steady when she was standing. Thomas took a place on her other side.

Susan managed to grin. "I feel like a bloated whale. How can you lift me so easily?"

Moses grinned back. "It's the least I can do. I'm glad it's not me giving birth."

"As if you could," Abby scoffed. "I don't know a man alive who could bear a child."

Thomas laughed. "I, for one, am perfectly content with that." He patted Susan's shoulder. "We'll be waiting to celebrate with you."

The next several hours passed in a blur.

Susan's contractions were painful, but Carrie was confident the baby wasn't in trouble, merely not in a hurry.

Polly confirmed her analysis when she arrived. Her presence ushered in a deep sense of calm. Polly had delivered more babies than she could count. She'd quit trying to keep track of them years before. "This little one gonna come into the world just fine, Susan. Don't you worry."

Susan's smile turned into a grimace as another contraction gripped her. "Ooohhhhh…"

Polly patted her shoulder. "Keep breathing real steady." She stepped down to the foot of the bed and gazed beneath the sheet. She looked up with a grin. "It won't be long now."

Carrie's examination had revealed the same thing.

"One more second is too long," Susan groaned.

Polly laughed and waved her hand dismissively. "I was in labor with Amber for thirty-six hours. There wasn't anything wrong, she just wasn't eager to enter the world. Seems like she knew it was going to be a cold place for her."

"Thirty-six hours?" Susan gasped. "I can't imagine doing this for thirty-six hours."

"Your baby taking it easy on you this time," Polly said confidently. "It won't be long. I can already see the head."

"Where's Harold?" Susan asked, her eyes frantic.

"Downstairs," Carrie assured her. "Anthony went to get him as soon as Amber called for me. He's waiting for you."

Carrie took another look beneath the sheet. "When the next contraction comes, Susan, I want you to push as hard as you can."

"I *am* pushing as hard as I can," Susan said weakly.

"Nonsense," Carrie retorted. "I know exactly how strong you are, partner. Your child needs you to be that strong. Don't be a baby!"

Susan glared at her as another contraction struck.

"Push!" Carrie ordered.

"Push!" Polly echoed. "Push as hard as you can. Harder even."

Susan took a deep breath and bore down with all her strength.

Her scream echoed throughout the house before she collapsed against her pillow, completely spent.

Carrie caught the baby as it slipped from Susan's womb.

Tears blurred her eyes. The miracle of birth never ceased to amaze her. Having four children made it easier to accept she would never experience it herself, but the reality would always sting.

She pushed aside her own feelings as joy for her friend pulsed through her. Holding the baby up, she proclaimed. "You have a perfect little girl!"

Susan slumped against the pillows and laughed with delight. "I have a daughter?" Wonder replaced the exhaustion in her eyes.

Polly stepped forward and wrapped the baby in a soft cloth. "That you do, Susan. A beautiful little girl with her daddy's red hair. We're going to get her cleaned up, but I have a feeling this one came out hungry."

Dusk was busily swallowing the day when everyone was finally gathered on the porch again.

Susan and Harold were upstairs in a room with their new daughter. They would stay at the plantation until Susan felt ready to return home.

No one spoke as the final glow of the sun was claimed by the dark cobalt night sky. The moon slipped above the horizon, joining the myriad of stars painted across the inky canvas. Late summer fireflies danced through the woods as the frogs and crickets began their nightly chorus. A lone owl, seated high above them in the oak tree, hooted its nighttime song. Too far above to be seen, the honk of passing geese rang through the night.

Hobbs rose from his rocker and stepped to the edge of the porch. "I've missed this," he said quietly. "The Pacific Northwest is beautiful, but there is nothing quite like a summer night in the South."

"I couldn't agree with you more," Thomas said. "I'm sorry your homecoming became rather chaotic."

"Are you kidding?" Hobbs demanded. "Susan giving birth was the perfect welcome. The whole ride here on the train, all I could think about was the power of new beginnings."

"Jessica Susan Justin is certainly a new beginning," Carrie agreed. She joined him and slipped her arm through his. "You've got a new beginning here, Hobbs. If you want it."

Hobbs laughed. "I'm not going anywhere," he said firmly. "I'm going to stay here on the plantation for as long as you'll have me. I don't ever want to live in another city. Working with horses has always been my dream."

His expression changed as he gazed at the fields full of horses. "Robert dreamed of this day," he said softly. "We spent hours on the battlefields at night talking about how he would build the best stables in the South." He took a deep breath. "He began it, but y'all made it happen. I know how happy he would be."

Carrie gazed around the porch.

Frances and Felicia would soon be off to a new beginning.

She and Rose were facing the first of their children leaving the nest.

Alice and Gloria were experiencing their own new beginning on the plantation.

"New beginnings," Carrie murmured. "I suppose all of life is nothing but a symphony of endings and beginnings." A rush of love swept through her.

"Here's to new beginnings for all of us."

To Be Continued...

It's Coming!

However, I can't give you a release date yet. I'm fighting health problems, but I WILL write it!

Make sure you sign up for my BLOG at www.BregdanChronicles.net to receive notice!

Would you be so kind as to leave a Review on Amazon?

Go to www.Amazon.com

Put Walking Toward Freedom, Ginny Dye into the Search Box.

Leave a Review.

I love hearing from my readers!

Thank you!

The Bregdan Principle

Every life that has been lived until today
is a part of the woven
braid of life.
It takes every person's story to create
history.
Your life will help determine the course of
history.
You may think you don't have much of an
impact.
You do.
Every action you take will reflect in
someone else's life.
Someone else's decisions.
Someone else's future.
Both good and bad.

The Bregdan Chronicles

1 - Storm Clouds Rolling In

1860 – 1861

2 - On To Richmond

1861 – 1862

3 - Spring Will Come

1862 – 1863

4 - Dark Chaos

1863 – 1864

5 - The Long Last Night

1864 – 1865

6 - Carried Forward By Hope

April – December 1865

7 - Glimmers of Change

December – August 1866

8 - Shifted By The Winds

August – December 1866

9 - Always Forward

January – October 1867

10 - Walking Into The Unknown

October 1867 – October 1868

11 - Looking To The Future

October 1868 – June 1869

12 - Horizons Unfolding

November 1869 – March 1870

13 - The Twisted Road of One Writer

The Birth of The Bregdan Chronicles

14 - Misty Shadows of Hope

1870

15 - Shining Through Dark Clouds

1870 – 1871

16 - Courage Rising

April – August 1871

17 – Renewed By Dawn

September 1871 – January 1872

March 1872 – September 1872

October 1872 – January 1873

Many more coming... Go to DiscoverTheBregdanChronicles.com to see how many are available now!

Other Books by Ginny Dye

Pepper Crest High Series - Teen Fiction

Time For A Second Change

It's Really A Matter of Trust

A Lost & Found Friend

Time For A Change of Heart

Fly To Your Dreams Series – Allegorical Fantasy

Dream Dragon

Born To Fly

Little Heart

The Miracle of Chinese Bamboo

All titles by Ginny Dye

www.BregdanPublishing.com

Author Biography

Who am I? Just a person who loves to write. If I could do it all anonymously, I would. In fact, I did the first go 'round. I wrote under a pen name. On the off chance I would ever become famous - I didn't want to be! I don't like the limelight. I don't like living in a fishbowl. I especially don't like thinking I have to look good everywhere I go, just in case someone recognizes me! I finally decided none of that matters. If you don't like me in overalls and a baseball cap, too bad. If you don't like my haircut or think I should do something different than what I'm doing, too bad. I'll write books that you will hopefully like, and we'll both let that be enough! :) Fair?

But let's see what you might want to know. I spent many years as a Wanderer. My dream when I graduated from college was to experience the United States. I grew up in the South. There are many things I love about it, but I wanted to live in other places. So I did. I moved 57 times, traveled extensively in 49 of the 50 states, and had more experiences than I will ever be able to recount. The only state I haven't been in is Alaska, simply because I refuse to visit such a vast, fabulous place until I have at least a month.

Along the way I had glorious adventures. I've canoed through the Everglade Swamps, snorkeled in the Florida Keys and windsurfed in the Gulf of Mexico. I've white-water rafted down the New River and Bungee jumped in the Wisconsin Dells. I've visited every National Park (in the off-season when there is more freedom!) and many of the State Parks. I've hiked thousands of miles of mountain trails and biked through Arizona deserts. I've canoed and biked through Upstate New York and Vermont, and polished off as much lobster as possible on the Maine Coast.

I've lived on a island in the British Columbia province of Canada, and now live on a magical cliffside in Mexico.

Have you figured out I'm kind of an outdoors gal? If it can be done outdoors, I love it! Hiking, biking, windsurfing, rock-climbing, roller-blading, snow-shoeing, skiing, rowing, canoeing, softball, tennis... the list could go on and on. I love to have fun and I love to stretch my body. This should give you a pretty good idea of what I do in my free time.

When I'm not writing or playing, I'm building Millions For Positive Change - a fabulous organization I founded in 2001 - along with 60 amazing people who poured their lives into creating resources to empower people to make a difference with their lives.

What else? I love to read, cook, sit for hours in solitude on my mountain, and also hang out with friends. I love barbeques and block parties. Basically - I just love LIFE!

I'm so glad you're part of my world! ~**Ginny**

Join my Email List so you can:

- Receive notice of all new books
- Be a part of my Launch Celebrations. I give away lots of Free gifts!
- Read my weekly BLOG while you're waiting for a new book.
- Be part of The Bregdan Chronicles Family!
- Learn about all the other books I write.

Just go to www.BregdanChronicles.net and fill out the form.

Made in the USA
Monee, IL
21 June 2024

60303578R00292